UPHONDO

ZANE SCHUMACHER

Crakatoa

To the three women, without whom this book would never have materialized:
** Robyn, who inspired me*
** Kirstin, who wrote along side me*
** Charlene, who believed in me*

It's the most important minute. You hold your breath
and your world is freeze-dried in the moment. A drum
in your ear thumps away the other sounds. The silence
between the beats judges you. You stand condemned for what
you are about to do.

You close one eye. The other dares not blink. Your world
is reduced to the crosshairs. An empty crucifix standing over
the barrel. You brace yourself and it comes into view.

You see the horn first. That is what you are here for.

Uphondo!

Then the face, with its twitching ears. It turns toward
you, sniffing the air. You avoid its eyes. It knows you are there
and throws a tantrum in the dirt. You focus through the dust.

*Stay away from the face! You don't want to damage that beau-
tiful nose. Aim for the heart, behind the front legs. Turn. Turn.
Broadside is best.* You have a few more seconds before your
lungs burst.

There's bile in your throat. With this type of killing, the
vomit always comes. You've swallowed it back fifty-seven

times. *You'll swallow it again.* But this time it feels worse. This is the last one in the park. *This is just plain wrong!*

It mock-charges you. Five futile angry steps before it stops in the grass, heaving. Its crowning glory sways from side to side like a phallic tombstone. It's daring you. A bizarre death grapple. Him or you in the next few seconds!

"What is wrong with you?" a voice whispers next to you. "Pull the trigger!"

You hesitate.

"Take that thing down. Now! OK? It's all we have."

He's right. The dumb-ass idiot next to you is right. It's all you have.

You swallow hard and take another deep breath.

God, forgive me.

You gently squeeze your finger. You've done this enough times before. Adrenalin drowns out the loud crack. Your right cheek is smacked and it stings. You hardly notice the kick into your padded shoulder.

When the smoke and dust settle, someone slaps you on the back. Your ears are still ringing. You feel sick. You hear a faint voice calling you. It's haunting and exigent.

Spitting on the ground, you walk away.

2

GENOA

Five years later he could still hear the voice. It was raining and a chilly wind fanned the hills above the City of Genoa. It was only there for a second, in the splattered orange haze. He thought it called his name.

"Benjamin Rodd," it seemed to yell. "You mangy old dog!"

But then he was not so certain. It might have been someone shouting from one of the nearby ships. Their grey hulls loomed around him as he stood alone in the queue. He shrugged his shoulders as he always did. He had dreamed long enough about this cruise holiday, even from his smelly cell. Now it was actually happening and to heck with the consequences. He deserved it. He'd paid his dues.

He glanced at the young couple standing behind him. She had on white earphones that dangled through her hair like popped bubble gum. She first glared at him and then ignored him. *Probably thinks I'm a weirdo or worse, traveling alone.* A huge ring dwarfed the middle finger she rudely rubbed on her temple. Her newlywed man scrolled incessantly in his own private world. *Off to a good start*, Benjamin thought to himself.

There was a family in front of him with a 'horde of kids'.

In his book, any number of children over one was a horde. The little girl was sniffling and her brother's shirt was already stained with food and snot. Benjamin took a step back from them and pulled a face at the boy. The parents hardly noticed. They looked tired and the cruise hadn't even started yet. Benjamin sized them up and hoped that they'd soon disappear into the game arcades of the ship and not re-emerge until at least Barcelona.

Rubbing his bloodshot eyes, he checked his watch for the hundredth time. It was only ten to ten. There hadn't been much time for sleep since he'd arrived in Genoa a few days earlier. No wonder he was nodding off and hearing voices. His head hurt. Irish flu! Drinking more water might have helped, but a crusty fist in his stomach kept punching it out.

Eventually, the queue moved and he finally heard them calling his name. A busty receptionist with too much makeup waved him over. A huge banner flapped above her head. It said, *'MSE. Living Your Dream'*. It was the largest cruise operator in the Mediterranean. Benjamin shoved the little boy with the snotty shirt out of his way and stepped forward. He took out his ticket and all the other tourist paraphernalia that he had been collecting. The receptionist snatched it from his hand without looking up. He glanced down her top.

"Is Mrs. Rodd with you?" the woman asked.

"No. She's not."

The receptionist typed into her computer, expecting him to elaborate. He looked at her blankly.

"Is Mrs. Rodd joining you later, then?"

"No, she's not."

"It says here that you're with a Mrs. Mary Rodd."

"Does it?" Benjamin said sarcastically. "Well, I'm not, as you can see."

"Are you alone?"

"Hopefully not for long."

"So, Mrs. Rodd is still coming?"

"Does it look like it?"

"There are no refunds, sir," the receptionist said. "The deadline for cancellation was 10 days ago."

"Am I asking for a refund?"

"You are alone then?"

"Have been for years!" Benjamin muttered

"I beg your pardon?"

"It's just me."

"For the full cruise?"

"Are you kidding me!" Benjamin snapped. "Yes, I'm alone. Mrs. Rodd is not joining me. Not now. Not Ever. Capiche?" The young man behind him finally looked up from his phone.

"What?" Benjamin shouted. The young man shook his head. "Yeah right," Benjamin said. "Enjoy your honeymoon, buddy. While it lasts." He turned back to the counter, regretting that he had ever thought Mary might be inclined to join him.

"Sign here," the receptionist demanded. He signed wherever she pointed to, without asking any questions.

"We need your passport, sir," she said. "We'll give it back when you disembark next week. Just a precaution, for your own safety, sir."

He had read that they would do that. "Safety my ass," he said under his breath. *More like leverage - bills needed to be honored.*

"I beg your pardon, sir?"

"Nothing. Nothing. Safety first. I agree," Benjamin mumbled back. The receptionist looked him up and down with disdain as she took his dark green passport. He opened his mouth to speak but then chose to rather keep quiet. It was too early to fight and he needed a drink. She handed him a room card and boarding pass.

Swinging his day-pack over his shoulder, he strutted away as fast as he could.

As he approached the gangplank, the people in front of him looked like sheep stepping over the slaughterhouse threshold. Out of the corner of his eye, he looked for his ghost again. Just in case. Then he dismissed his silliness and stepped aboard.

* * *

HIS CABIN WAS A DECENT ONE. NUMBER 749 ON THE starboard side of the ship. It had a nice sized balcony and was near the front, far away from the family suites, as he had requested. There was a double bed with starched white linen peeking over the covers from under the pillows. The stiff sheets reminded him of a hospital. He knew about hospitals. They normally only changed their sheets on Fridays. He wondered if he'd have better luck on the ship.

He ignored his bags, that had been placed at the foot of the bed, and headed straight for the mini-bar.

"Here's to you, Mary," he said, raising a miniature bottle of Bells Original at the mirror. "AWOL again, as usual." He downed the drink in one gulp and sat on the bed.

The ship was a massive floating resort with nine floors above the waterline. There were enough passengers to get lost in obscurity or find a companion. Benjamin was indifferent about it. Destiny could reveal itself to him in its own time. At least that's what his shrink had told him. He'd been seeing Dr. Miller every week since he had got out. She might have failed to get him and Mary back together but she had been useful in other ways.

He rubbed his thumb wondering what to do next. His fingers circled the scratched ring he was wearing. As though he had been waiting for this precise moment, he pulled it off and threw it onto the bedside table. He would no longer be needing it. He planned to bury it forever somewhere between Rome and Sicily.

The ship was only leaving at two. He kicked off his sneakers and laid back, sucking on another miniature bottle. Vodka this time. He closed his eyes. Africa, his home, was far away.

* * *

"DID YOU ENJOY THE BLACK RISOTTO LAST NIGHT?"

This time the voice was clear. Benjamin lifted his groggy head up from the pillow, not expecting to actually see anyone. A woman stood in a bright red dress at his cabin door, silhouetted by the passage lights behind her. Her hair was golden and long. He strained his blurry eyes, struggling to make out her face in the glare. Her chest was heaving as though she had just been making love in the room next door.

His dinner from the previous evening flashed across his mind. He'd ducked into a local Osteria and ordered the only thing on the menu he could understand. Black squid risotto and a bottle of wine. It might have been two bottles? It had been a dark night.

She stepped forward confidently.

"Do you mind if I come in?"

There was no need to answer, she was already in. She walked slowly across the cabin toward the couch. Her hips swayed provocatively. She looked about for a few seconds and then swung around. Moving a cushion to the side, she sat down and crossed her long legs. Benjamin couldn't believe his luck. He flexed his muscles and smiled. It'd been a while.

"You've been expecting me," she eventually said. "Here I am." Her voice had a velvet purr.

She sat there looking at him. Her lips moved slowly over each other, like a lioness considering her prey. She felt odiously familiar. Benjamin cleared his throat.

"It was the best risotto I've ever tasted."

"It reminded me of something," the woman said.

"What?"

"That sticky swarm of black rice," she said, "spilling off your fork onto the floor, making a mess? It was like an animal's coagulating blood, wasn't it?"

"Oh dear, here we go again," Benjamin replied, rolling his eyes. "Do I know you? What room are you looking for?"

"Oh, I'm in the right room," she said. "And while you might not know me, I know you. I've known you for quite some time now."

Benjamin's breathing quickened. The sides of the room blurred. He rubbed his eyes and opened his mouth to answer. No words came out.

"Speechless, are you?"

He was mesmerized but enjoyed the feeling, alive inside for the first time in ages.

Excitement and trepidation banged on his chest. He stretched his arm out across the bedside table, pretending to yawn. He scooped up the wedding band that was lying there, hoping she wouldn't notice. She did. She stood up and sighed. As she did so, Benjamin unbuttoned one of his shirt buttons.

He glanced at the door. It was still open. The passage light stared back at him. His spine tingled. The light grew brighter.

"How do you know me?" he demanded to know.

She just smiled.

"You don't know me at all, do you?" Benjamin said, fidgeting with his fingers. The ring dropped and bounced guiltily across the floor. They both watched it slowly spinning to a stop. A vein in his neck throbbed.

"You're right," she replied. "I don't know you. What was I thinking, Benjamin?" Her words seemed to scrape away the inside of his skull, as they bounced around in his head. It was the same voice he had heard outside in the queue.

"Wait," he called. "How do you know my name?" She reached out

to him with her slender arm. Her fingers now looked like claws. They hovered for a second or two and then she made a fist. Benjamin was intoxicated.

She then turned and left as quickly as she had come. Benjamin shouted after her before his head bounced up through the darkness. His heart was pounding. The room was losing its light.

HE SAT UP ABRUPTLY IN THE BED, KNOCKING THE EMPTY vodka bottle aside. His shirt was drenched with sweat. *Someone had shoved marbles behind his eyeballs.* Diesel motors whined and the sound of churning water percolated the air. The ship was finally moving. The cabin door swung on its hinges, as though someone had left in a hurry. He was alone in his room. *Why would he not be?* He rubbed the sleep out of his eyes. Other than a porter pulling some bags along at the far end of the passage, it was quiet.

He poured himself a stiff drink and walked to the upper level of the ship sipping his glass. Genoa was disappearing into the distant hills. The deck was full of passengers chattering and putting their worries on pause. Benjamin ignored them all and stood alone as the evening chill wafted around him. He was thinking of those claws with their manicured sheen. He'd sensed them before, but this time it felt real. He'd almost touched her. *Get a grip, Benjamin*, he said to himself, tasting a familiar sourness in his throat. A hand touched his shoulder.

IT WAS A WAITER WITH A TRAY OF APERITIFS. HE WORE A well-used white dinner jacket and had an apron tied around his waist. Benjamin replaced his glass with one of the elegant champagne flutes.

"Dinner will be at seven," the waiter announced to the

group who had gathered around the railing. "Will you be dining alone, sir?" he continued, "or will the lady be joining you?"

His accent was East European and he had shifty eyes. Benjamin shook his head, raising his forefinger.

"I'm solo," he said. "What lady?"

A few feet behind the waiter a woman shuffled, as though making a point. Benjamin noticed her spying him up and down out of the corner of her eye. He assumed she was also alone. The waiter had obviously thought that they might be together.

She was in her mid-thirties and wore a beige trench coat. She had buttoned up the studs to her chin, hiding whatever was underneath. Benjamin let his imagination do the math. *She'll definitely do,* he thought. *More or less.*

The travel agent back in South Africa had told him that there would be lots of single people on the cruise. He'd said it with a mischevious wink. "I'm married," Benjamin had snapped back. He booked the tickets anyway. Dr. Miller, who had never met Mary, had encouraged Benjamin. Not knowing about his financial dilemma, she had told him the cruise was a good idea. *You're a stud,* she had half-joked. *Mary doesn't know what she's missing and besides, she's moved on years ago. Go and make the most of it. Go pick up the pieces. Make it tangible.*

The woman in the trench coat smiled at him and threw back her hair. She blew a plume of smoke into the night. Benjamin grinned back but before he could do anything a group of Asian tourists bustled past between them. Annoyed, Benjamin elbowed one of them aside. He was met with a torrent of indecipherable jabbering and shaking fists. The clicking cameras killed the moment and the thought of ending up on a million little screens scared the breath out of him.

The woman in the coat giggled as Benjamin backtracked

from his show of bravado. Embarrassed, he rudely looked right through her, scanning the deck. He secretly hoped that the other woman, the one from his cabin, might also make an appearance up top. It was the alcohol thinking. He knew she was just a fantasy, but he could smell her. She had smelled like Bushveld jasmine after a storm.

The woman in the beige coat put her right leg forward. A flawless naked calf peeked through the slit. The rim of her glass rolled across her lips from side to side, as she sipped her champagne. She smiled again. Cutting a debonair silhouette in the dim light, Benjamin pretended not to notice. A loud foghorn sounded above them and his admirer burst into another ecstatic giggle, spilling her drink down her chin.

The *MSE Grande* had officially left the port jurisdiction. It was arcing slowly in a southwesterly direction. A translucent white water wake stretched back into the distance. Benjamin could trace it all the way back to the Genoa breakwater. He knew that they would be at Civitavecchia in the morning and buses would be waiting there to take them to Rome.

Benjamin stood staring into the distance. The women in the beige coat lingered longer than she should have. Benjamin could see her slowly getting agitated. He liked that and decided to play hard to get. He had all week after all to catch the right fish. She was clearly used to getting what she wanted and Benjamin's response seemed to be igniting something. The first ignition in a chemical chain reaction that inevitably would follow.

She eventually spun on her high heels and made for the swing doors, leading inside. Benjamin pretended not to notice until she was gone. Then he regretted his obnoxious behavior. He couldn't remember the last time he had gotten this type of attention, even if one of the women was a whispering dream.

Panicking, he realized he had let her go. He mumbled

angrily to himself as he headed back to his cabin. He needed to wash and get dressed for dinner. He decided that he would find the lady with the beige coat and make amends before some other man discovered her.

HE DIDN'T HAVE TO TRY VERY HARD BECAUSE SHE WAS seated right next to him at the dining table. They'd be eating together all week long now, together with the others about to be press-ganged together on their first night. The waiter winked at Benjamin as though he had done him a great favor. Which of course, as Benjamin soon realized, he had.

The woman had shed her coat and was sitting in an elegant dress. She had an air of expectation about her. Her long legs were crossed and her upper body projected over her waist. She didn't stand as Benjamin was ushered toward her.

Benjamin introduced himself and sat down.

"Pleased to make your acquaintance," she said, followed by a subdued, "Finally!"

Benjamin mumbled an apology for his earlier behavior. "It's the sea," he said. "Usually takes a few hours to find my legs."

"I recommend another drink then," she said, smiling.

He no longer had to speculate about what had been under her coat. Her silk dress accentuated her toned and well-proportioned body. Benjamin could tell she looked after herself. A pearl diamond brooch was pinned to her collar. Benjamin glanced at her breasts. "I Love your jewels," he said.

The woman straightened her brooch and nudged her chair a bit closer.

* * *

"I SEE YOU CHANGED INTO SOMETHING NICE," SHE SAID ambiguously, holding out her hand. "I'm Vanda."

The waiter sidled up and snapped open a stiff cloth serviette. He placed it on Benjamin's lap. Benjamin hated it when service staff did that. Getting in the way at precisely the wrong moment. He shuffled his chair closer to Vanda.

"A great pleasure," he said, keeping his eyes riveted on her brooch.

"Where might you be from, Mr.?"

"Rodd. But please, call me Benjamin," he said.

She leaned over, forcing him to look up. She had a delightful perfume on. He blushed ever so slightly as she stroked her brooch.

"Is it real?" he asked.

Vanda shifted back into her chair, tucking her dark hair behind her ear.

"Everything about me is real," she said. "Why would it not be?"

Benjamin signaled to the waiter to pour the wine. It offered a moment of slight reprieve. The waiter expertly picked out a bottle of French Chardonnay and started filling Vanda's glass. "I hope that's OK, ma'am?" the waiter asked. She nodded stroking her finger down the shaft of the glass.

"A red might have been nice if you'd bothered to ask."

Benjamin said it to annoy the overly confident Bulgarian waiter. He didn't really like Bulgarians, and their waiter sounded like he had just got off the plane from Bucharest. Bulgarian mobsters had caused half his problems in life. More or less. So he had convinced himself.

The waiter tottered, not quite sure what to do or say. Relishing the brief power he held over the waiter, Benjamin took out his buffalo skin wallet and slapped a five hundred euro note on the table. He neatly ripped it down the middle and shoved half in the direction of the baffled waiter.

"You'll get the other half at the end of the cruise, Mate," Benjamin said. "Just make sure you look after us now."

He caught Vanda excitingly spying out his wallet, where he tucked his half of the note safely away. The waiter muttered in Bulgarian as he popped open the bottle of red. They sat in silence until Benjamin's glass was full.

"Cheers. Here's to this cruise!" Vanda said. "To you, Ben and that ripped note in your pocket." She held up her glass seductively and then giggled. "That was crazy! Was it real?"

"Everything about me is real," Benjamin said slowly.

"Touche!"

They both smiled knowingly, sipping their glasses. *Holy Crap!* Benjamin thought to himself, *that was my last Bin Laden!*

"You don't mind if I call you Ben, do you?"

Benjamin lied and said that it was alright. *Benjamin? Ben? It made no difference. Benny? No, it made a difference.* He raised his glass, spilling on the tablecloth. Vanda swallowed hers in one gulp and pushed back her shoulders. It was clear what she wanted from the next seven days.

Benjamin smiled at her exuberance. He tapped his foot under the table and shifted his gaze back to her brooch. She pushed out her breasts and undid the silver clip of her brooch. The light from the candles reflected tiny rainbows of color. She motioned to the Bulgarian waiter for a refill.

"I bought it yesterday in St Marguerite," she said. "A little shop right opposite the statue of Columbus. I was just in time as well. While I was paying, some crazy women barged into the shop and insisted the poor shopkeeper sell it to her. But I got it first!" She took a large triumphant gulp of her wine. Benjamin's glass sat fully charged.

"Beautiful isn't it?"

She held out her hand. "Here, take a look."

Benjamin stared excitedly.

Vanda went on. "Ah, that crazy woman," she said. "Beautiful, but presumptuous, she was. Probably has dozens of young Italian men chasing after her."

Benjamin sat silent.

"She had one of those huge ugly Gothic tattoos on her arm. Right here."

Vanda stroked Ben's wrist, but he was leering at the brooch as though it was the magnetic center of the earth and his nose a steel stalactite.

"I got it, obviously," Vanda said, snatching the brooch back. "I have to give it to that crazy cow though. She was desperate. It got embarrassing. She started yelling at one point."

Benjamin watched her pin the brooch back onto her chest. She did it slowly giving Benjamin a peep of the lace of her bra.

"You're not much of a talker, are you? Are you with someone?"

Benjamin snapped out of his trance feeling stupid. He was still thinking about the five hundred euro note he had just torn up to show off. It was the last one. *Stupid!* He thought. *I hope it's worth it!* He could picture Dr. Miller telling him off again for being impulsive. *To hell with it! There was still the blackjack table.*

"I'm divorced," he said. "And I'm from Cape Town. You know, South Africa?"

"Ah, yes," Vanda immediately said. Her words were becoming slightly slurred. "I thought so, with your funny accent. That president of yours, Mandela? Doesn't he run around in skins? The best." She lifted her glass again, eyes shining.

"Armani suits are in fashion south of the equator right now," Benjamin joked. He raised his eyebrows and finally drew a long sip from his glass. *This is going to be a long interesting evening,* he thought to himself.

* * *

VANDA STRAIGHTENED HER TOP AND THEN DROPPED HER hand onto her lap, out of Benjamin's sight. His eyes kept straying to her chest. He couldn't help himself. She liked it and smiled.

"Tell me about Africa, Ben. Are there elephants?"

"On every corner," Benjamin teased. "Unless the bears chase them away. Or the drought. Not much rain out there in the desert."

His eyes were on her brooch. He was trying to somehow mentally wrestle it off her. Vanda uncrossed her legs and leaned into him.

"I've often wanted to go to Africa. Such a lovely country," she cooed. "Do you speak the language? You're obviously not, well African."

Benjamin squirmed uncomfortably in his seat. He hated being reminded of the contradictions between his skin color and his continent of birth. European Africans were usually an enigma, even after their viability was accepted. Reluctantly. Much like the Africans living in Europe, misunderstood and distrusted. Dr. Miller had once said that there might be some deeper issues in this area of Benjamin's life, but they had not had the time to explore it yet.

"Do I speak African? Not as well as I speak European," he answered sarcastically. "Which language are you referring to. The last time I checked there were a couple of hundred different languages."

"Then how do you talk to one another?" Vanda asked. "It must be terribly confusing with all those languages in the street."

"Sign language works sometimes."

"Like this?" Vanda said, making a sign with her fingers

that bordered on the obscene. "See, I know some African as well."

Her pearl and diamond brooch caught the candlelight. Benjamin's eyes followed it as she jiggled her chest with laughter. She shuddered and slapped him on his leg. "I'm kidding," she laughed. "I spent some time in Mozambique a few years ago. I know all about Africa."

"I thought you being serious," Benjamin said.

"Then the batteries on the remote ran flat," Vanda shrieked. "It was a good show. Discovery Channel, if I remember correctly?"

She subsided into giggles and hiccuped. "Here, pour me another."

Benjamin was at a loss for words. He wasn't sure what to make of her. *So much for him knowing how to read women?* At least he knew she was well on her way to inebriation. Vanda tilted her head to the side, showing off her dark hair. It was thick and beautiful and falling freely onto her shoulders.

"Where in America are you from?" he asked. Vanda moved confidently in her chair. Her fingers touched her lips, the diamond brooch constantly teasing him.

"You can tell, can you?"

Benjamin nodded.

"Down South," she continued. "Plaquemines is simply the best place in the world. Jazz clubs on all the corners. People from all over the world too. Just last week I met someone from Seattle."

"Never heard of it," Benjamin said. "Any animals on your side? Lions maybe?"

Vanda gazed at him as though he was from Mars. "Yes. Telephone lines all over," she said laughing. Benjamin wondered if she was acting dumb to make him interested? *Or was she thick?*

"The booze," she drawled. "The whiskey can't be beaten."

"I'm sure!"

"It's near New Orleans," she continued. "You know? Hurricane Katrina?" He nodded and she called the waiter over again. "Do you have any whiskey on board?" she demanded to know.

"No thanks," Benjamin said, waving his arms behind her at the waiter. "I'm sticking to the wine."

"Nonsense!" she insisted. "You will have whiskey with me tonight Mr. Benjamin. And then I'll let you have a closer look at my jewels."

Benjamin flushed.

"Madam," the waiter said stiffly. "We only have bourbon on the menu at meal time. Will that be in order?"

"Excellent," Vanda said, raising her voice. "I've never heard of that type, but please bring some anyway. In fact, bring a bottle."

Benjamin slumped back in his chair. He remembered what Dr. Miller had told him. *When opportunity knocks, make sure your door isn't locked.* He would wait and see what happened. He was starting to like this lively woman in front of him.

"Tell me more about the 'crazy woman'. You know, the one who wanted your brooch," he said, turning to her.

"She reminded me of one of those sad people, who life has disappointed."

"I know the type," Benjamin said.

"You know. The ones who start off in a safe happy place and then life wallops them. They have to leave town, or a sickness attacks them, or you're ambushed by a divorced. Or someone passes away."

"I get the picture."

"They adjust and lower their horizons to cope, and then it slowly creeps up on them."

"What?"

"The disillusionment!"

"At least we're here," Benjamin said, trying to change the conversation. "Free, on this beautiful ship."

"Yes, it's better than the other place."

"Plaquemines?"

"No, the other place."

"Enlighten me," Benjamin said, pouring a shot of bourbon into each of the shot glasses that had been laid out before him.

"Well, one day you are lying in the bath trying to sober up with a cigarette in your mouth and you realize that those bright old days are gone and you're in that other place.

"Stuck?"

"Yes, and then you drop into the filthy tepid muck around you until the water drowns out the noises."

"Like I said, I know the type."

Vanda threw back her drink. "It's a place you then spend the rest of your life desperately trying to escape from," she said.

"Are we still talking about the crazy lady who wanted your brooch? The one in St Marguerite?"

"Of course," Vanda said hesitantly. "Of Course!"

"Well, thanks for whiskey. And holidays," Benjamin said.

"Indeed," Vanda replied. "This trip is simply the best thing I could have wished for. A new start finally coming my way."

"As you were saying," Benjamin said, "Indeed."

They looked silently into each other's eyes, trying to bore out what lay beneath.

"Can I ask you something?" Benjamin eventually said.

"Anything."

"Our waiter? You arranged this, didn't you?"

"Are you against a little help?"

"It depends on what type."

"There's only one type of lubricant that works in these situations."

"You didn't! How much?"

"Fifty dollars," Vanda coyly admitted. "I think his boss might have confiscated it from him though. I saw the maître d' marching him off." She laughed. "The poor beak warned me not to pay him. He was going on about them watching."

"You're a good negotiator. I'd have paid double."

"Is that all you think I'm worth?"

"Much more," Benjamin laughed.

Vanda played with her brooch. "Tell me more about yourself, Ben. I suspect you might be more than just a dashing debonair traveler from Africa?"

Benjamin blushed, silently wishing he was at least that. *If only she knew?*

* * *

VANDA SLADE HAD A WAY WITH MEN. SHE TOLD BENJAMIN little of substance but dropped in enough tidbits to keep him begging for more. How Benjamin had started out, showing off with the banknote, aloof and playing hard to get, was nowhere close to where he found himself now. She reeled him in like a trout.

He learned that she was on the cruise because she had won a competition. Some online raffle while shopping for *'real'* lingerie. A fact that certainly caught his attention. She learned that he liked guns and collected watches. He conveniently left out the bit that he had not been able to pick up a gun for years or that the only watch that he had left in his collection was the old scratched Breitling on his wrist. *I'm going out in one last hedonistic blaze of glory*, he thought to himself. *Why spoil it with the truth?*

Despite his duplicity, Vanda expertly pulled him into her

ambit of craziness. It was where she took all her men. Naked, into no man's land. There they all ended up tottering, wanting to cross but hesitant about the potential minefield before them. It didn't take Benjamin long to decide that he wanted to run across that minefield. The 'crazy cow' from St Marguerite remained an enigma all night.

EVENTUALLY, THEY WERE INTERRUPTED BY ONE MR. Christopher Burlington and his eighteen-year-old companion. They were ushered to the table by a Malaysian waiter, who got two bank notes stuck into his pocket and a patronizing pat on the shoulder.

"Sorry I'm late," Christopher Burlington broadcast, so that the entire room could hear. "The door of our cabin got stuck." Benjamin noticed him gently squeezing the arm of the young girl at his side. *She was still a baby, dammit, and he looked ancient.* He reached out across the table and held out his other hand to introduce himself. It was fat and sweaty. Benjamin stood to receive it.

"Doctor," the man said. "Doctor Burlington."

They shook his hand and sat down. Benjamin covertly wiped his palm on the tablecloth. Burlington was overweight and spread his legs to allow his pot-belly to hang with ease as he sat. He flapped his linen serviette open and made a great affair of spreading it out over his lap.

"I can't wait for the oysters," he slobbered.

The young girl sat silent and miserable next to him. Benjamin thought she might have seasickness. Her evening gown was expensive, contrasting with the worn jersey she had thrown over her shoulders. Benjamin concluded that she wasn't wearing a bra. *And why the heck not*, he thought. *She didn't need one. She's virtually still a child!*

Doctor Burlington moved his jaw up and down, as though

warming up for the meal to come. As he did so, he sized Vanda out. A few pleasantries about the ship's departure were exchanged before the next two guests arrived.

Charles and Kevin O'Donnell chatted briefly to the waiter and then walked casually over.

"Good evening," Charles said, gently pulling out a chair. "How do you do?"

Kevin held out his hand to Vanda, smiling mischievously. Vanda flicked her hair back, reciprocating his twinkle. As they elegantly took their seats, Benjamin noticed their watches. They were matching pairs with massive round heads. Benjamin could swear that he could hear them ticking, they were so big. He caught Charles raising his eyebrow as Kevin chatted to Vanda. *Maybe they were disappointed with their table allocation,* Benjamin thought to himself. Their natural exuberance hid it well. When they mentioned their surname they shone with pride. As though it was unique. Which it was because the marriage laws had only recently been amended. *Mr. and Mr. O'Donnell,* that's what they wanted to be called. Forever!

Benjamin yawned and made a note in his mind not to come so early for dinner the next time. *No one else seemed bothered by the official times, so why should he? Except for Vanda. She had come on time. Good on her!* He noticed a crumb sticking to the corner of her lip as she chatted. Moving closer, he raised his serviette as if to remove it. She stuck out her hand and warded him off. As she confidently wiped it off herself, Kevin O'Donnell glanced at Benjamin. The corner of his mouth bent upward into a smirk. Benjamin felt like an idiot. *What was he thinking?* He was back in no man's land. He sat back indolently, folding his arms.

Kev and Charlie O'Donnell tried to engage in conversation with Dr. Burlington. He did his best to avoid their probes, but they were determined to succeed. It was as though they had bet each other over it. In desperation, Burlington turned to Vanda, who was sitting beside him.

"That brandy looks good," he said, out of the corner of his mouth, "I think I'll have some."

Vanda moved the bottle closer to herself. She had no intention of sharing her 'whiskey' with the sweaty old man. "We'll call the waiter for you," she said, signaling to Benjamin. He sat stiffly, not moving.

"Oh, common, don't worry," Vanda laughed, brushing some fluff off his collar. "It was just a crumb. There'll be more." Benjamin squirmed as she whispered in his ear. "My whiskey needs your help, Mr. Benjamin. Please?"

Dr. Burlington started to reach over for the bottle.

"It's for later, old chap," Benjamin said, firmly putting his hand on the bottle. "Why don't you order a good port instead?"

Burlington's face darkened.

"We're on honeymoon," Charlie suddenly announced to the table. He kissed his partner's cheek, instantly diffusing the whiskey tension, but creating another. Kevin sat back with folded arms, waiting to see if anyone would react negatively. Burlington grunted and turned away. His teenage girlfriend was busy ordering her entree.

Benjamin shuffled uncomfortably. He didn't mind that they were married but didn't know what they wanted him to do about it. *Kiss them on the cheek?* Vanda broke the ice, enthusiastically congratulating them. Benjamin thought she was overdoing it a bit. *Just like all women do around guys like that. It's just another flipping wedding!* The O'Donnells relaxed but kept a wary eye on the doctor. The other two seats at the table remained empty all evening.

THE DINING ROOM FILLED UP AND WAITERS STARTED

scurrying across the floor with puffed chests and silver trays. Benjamin looked around for a sommelier. *Maybe he should order some champagne for the honeymoon couple? Vanda would like that.*

The Bulgarian waiter was milling about nervously, a few meters away. He was twitching and sweating and nervously scanning the room.

"I didn't know it was such a hard job," Benjamin joked, pointing at him. The poor man pretended to fold some papers. Then he unfolded them again. The corners of his mouth turned downward. There was a fear in his face. Benjamin could have sworn he had just been roughed up. Looked like he was about to burst into tears. The man didn't notice that the entire table was looking at him.

"Oi!" Benjamin said loudly, clicking his fingers. The waiter immediately snapped out of his trance. He smiled like an undertaker jumping to attention, before scurrying over to the table. *Like a rat*, Benjamin thought.

He didn't notice the burly maître d' who was glaring into the back of the poor man. Vanda did. "I think he's in trouble with his ugly boss," she whispered to Benjamin. "Go easy."

"Monsieur?" the waiter asked in his thick accent. He had an unwavering blandness on his face but his body language was that of a hunted dog. The table went silent.

"Champagne!" Benjamin ordered. "Bring us a decent bottle and six glasses. We have a honeymoon to celebrate, so make it snappy!"

His eyes followed the waiter as he went to the bar counter on the other side of the dining room. So did the menacing gaze of the maître d'.

Vanda shifted closer to Benjamin and put her hand on his leg.

"Order an extra bottle for later," she suggested.

Benjamin decided at that moment that Dr. Miller was

right. His door should remain unlocked for the evening. It would be the first time in a while.

* * *

FOR VANDA, DINNER WAS EXACTLY WHAT IT HAD PROMISED to be. The guests were starry-eyed, checking out their fellow passengers. The food was novel and fresh and the chatter had not become dull yet. Their table thoroughly enjoyed it. Except for Dr. Burlington's girlfriend who didn't say a word. She kept checking her phone.

By the time dessert came, Vanda had Benjamin exactly where she wanted him. Although she had lost count of how much she had consumed, through the haze of her intoxication she was delighted that she still had what it took. The charms to attract a decent stranger. If she had been sober she would have realized that she had no way of knowing whether her 'stranger' was, in fact, decent or not. But that analysis could wait for morning.

Vanda had heard of Cape Town but had no clue where it really was. Somewhere in Africa. She realized that Benjamin was teasing her about the whole Africa thing but she had pretended to play along. It was more fun to do that and she enjoyed the flirting. She thought men liked a woman to act dumb sometimes. Even if they weren't. It made them feel in control. Even though they rarely were. All in all, Benjamin seemed like a good catch by her book.

AFTER DINNER, THEY STUMBLED BACK TO VANDA'S CABIN. Benjamin put his arms around her shoulders so that she could be steady. She felt her diamond brooch sticking into her skin. Benjamin was still fascinated with it, almost obsessed. In her inebriation, Vanda assumed that it had to do with his sophisticated tastes.

Vanda opened her handbag and started fumbling for her key card. They were at her corridor when she realized she had forgotten her bottle of Bourbon on the dining room table. It still had some booze in it. The image of the fat balding doctor swigging it for free flashed before her. He had been after it all evening.

"My Whiskey," she slurred out. She felt Benjamin tense.

"It was empty," he said. "Leave it."

"I'm not leaving one drop for someone else to drink," she said.

"You're being irrational," Benjamin answered. "No one wants to drink your left-overs. And I've got champagne here anyway."

She pulled her arm out from Benjamin's side.

"I'll be back in a second," she muttered. "Please wait. Over there at that bench. I'm going back." She pointed to a recess on the passage. Benjamin sighed and decided to oblige her.

As she stumbled away to recover her lost bottle, her thoughts were all over the place. So were her wobbly footsteps. She liked to keep her men in suspense. She glanced back as she got to the stairs. Benjamin was sitting in the cool breeze with his arms folded. She thought it a good sign that he was looking at her. She smiled and waved before staggering back up to the dining room.

When she got there the bottle was gone. So were Doctor Burlington and his teenage companion. The O'Donnell couple were drinking their coffee and didn't understand what she was going on about.

"Thieves," she mumbled, as she left the dining room empty handed.

IN THE PASSAGE OUTSIDE, SHE KNOCKED INTO THE Bulgarian waiter. He was rushing down the corridor and didn't notice her until he hit her. There was panic in his face. Life deals things like that. Little twists and turns when you least expect it. Trivial things that have huge consequences. Like a crossroad in the woods. For Vanda, this was one of those moments.

"They're after me!" he cried.

His mouth was a few centimeters from her ear. It was inappropriate and Vanda could smell his garlic breath as he rambled off in Bulgarian.

"You!" he snarled, realizing that it was Vanda, who he had just crashed into. "It's all your fault. That money you gave me. They wouldn't have searched me. I told you not to, you rich cow!"

"Watch it!" Vanda sloshed back. "You can get fired for this." The tipsiness in her system allowed it though.

She was slow to realize what he was going on about. His rotten breath blew through the strands of her hair. Little pock marks leaked up his cheek. Dark rings framed his dark eyes. He yelled at her in Bulgarian, as though she had done something terribly wrong.

"Bugger off, you creep!" Vanda yelled.

He was desperate and pathetic. Vanda pushed him away, stumbling as she did it. He responded by grabbing her and locking her hands in his weak grip. He was furious about something. She had drunk too much and it felt like stocks had been clamped around her.

What was he trying to do? Something about the tip she had given him? Vanda looked around for help. The corridor was deserted. *Should she scream?* None of this made any sense to her. *What waiter attacks one of the guests and thinks they can get away with it?* She decided to go with her Dutch courage and defend herself.

I might be slightly drunk but I'm also a tough Southern Girl, raised by a tough Texas Daddy, she said to herself. She had been in similar predicaments before, with all her bad men in and out of her life. She responded as she often did. Solo, messily and aggressively.

She yanked herself loose and spun around to face him. She swung, shoving the palm of her hand dead up his nose as hard as she could. It exploded red. He was not expecting it.

"You Americano whore!" he shouted, cupping his nose with his fingers. He shoved Vanda violently against the passage wall and raised his hand to hit her. She closed her eyes and held up her arm. Her enormous handbag dangled open as she tried to use it a buffer between herself and her attacker

Someone suddenly shouted from inside. "He's out here!"

The waiter froze for a second before panicking. He pulled at the open handbag. Vanda's eyes were still shut, waiting for the inevitable punch. The waiter joggled something out of the apron he was wearing and dumped it into the mouth of her bag. It smelled like a rotten corpse. Vanda didn't notice it falling in. She was winding up inside for the worst. The waiter jumped back, glancing nervously up and down the corridor, and then left sprinting toward the front of the ship. "I *finda* you later," he yelled. "You Americano cow!" He disappeared behind the kitchen doors, where Vanda could vaguely hear a commotion of yelling and bashing pots. No one had seen the incident.

Vanda's heart raced. She stood up shaking, trying to compose herself. Then she burped, half forgetting the whole thing. She was almost sick. She felt as though she was tied with ropes to the front of a tube train, disappearing into the darkness. She stumbled back to where Benjamin was waiting, but the bench where she had asked him to wait for her was empty.

* * *

"WHERE'S THE BRANDY?" A VOICE SAID, THROUGH the night.

Vanda was glad to hear that Benjamin had not abandoned her. He had just moved to the outer railings. Her arm hurt.

"Whiskey. It was whiskey," she replied. "Half a bottle is gone, even if it tasted like rubbish."

She decided not to tell him about what had just happened to her. *Why spoil the moment with Ben?* Her mind was like a pudding and she burst into tears.

"I've got Champers, don't worry," Benjamin said. "You OK?"

"Of course I am," Vanda answered. "Just a piece of dust?"

"Want to take a walk around deck before we..." Benjamin hesitated. He wasn't used to picking up American women and was trying to elegantly consummate the evening. "Before we...retire?" he mumbled.

"Why? you are charming," Vanda slurred, wiping her cheek. "I've never retired before. I'm looking forward to it."

She took his hand and they walked to the upper deck together. The night sky was clear, although most of the stars had been smeared away by the orange haze of city lights on the horizon. There was a chilly breeze and Vanda snuggled under Benjamin's arm. His blue sports jacket was comforting and warm. For the first time that evening she was not thinking about getting him into her bed. That box was practically ticked and now she wanted to just lie in the glow. Her head was starting to spin.

She wondered what the Bulgarian waiter's problem had been. *Is that how they are in Europe?* She'd never traveled outside America before. Her arm was aching where the man had grabbed her and a migraine was coming. She yawned.

"Which tour are you going on in the morning?" Benjamin

asked. "I see there were a few to choose from. Or are you staying on the ship?"

"The Colosseum. I've always wanted to see that," she slowly answered. She didn't mention that she had no choice. A day trip to the Colosseum was a part of her prize.

They reached the end of the deck landing. The engines thumped down below. It was still and only a few other passengers were about. Faint music and laughter wafted up from a bar a few floors beneath them. Benjamin stared into the night and fleetingly heard the voice of his dream again.

He kept trying to touch Vanda's brooch. He was still obsessed with it for some reason.

"I think that's enough now," Vanda said, pushing his hand away.

"You promised me a closer look!"

He lifted her arm and kissed her hand. She could feel his smooth cheek and liked the sensation. She turned her face toward his and moved closer. He bent to kiss her. She missed and her body convulsed.

* * *

"That's the problem with too much alcohol," Benjamin snapped, somewhat hypocritically. "It makes for an unpredictable ending. And with this rolling ship?" He shook his head angrily as he wiped vomit from his brand new jeans with a paper napkin. It was not a lot but enough to spoil the evening. *So much for the kiss,* he thought to himself. He looked around embarrassed. It felt as though the entire ship had come out to see him being messed on by a drunk girl.

None of the other passengers, however, noticed a thing. They were too preoccupied with own liaisons to care about Benjamin or Vanda.

"Let's get you to bed," Benjamin said as he firmly took her in his arms.

"Ouch," she cried. "That hurts, you brute!"

Benjamin was holding Vanda in the same spot where the waiter had manhandled her and it was still raw. She felt disorientated and started pulling away. She wiped her mouth, wanting to go to sleep.

Benjamin put her down apologizing. He placed his hands on her shoulders and walking behind her, steered her inside. He fumbled awkwardly through her handbag looking for her key card. She was starting to irritate him. And he hated handbags. One didn't know what one might find inside. And he hated being called a brute. It reminded him of his past.

As his fingers fumbled for the key-card they touched a round object that felt odiously familiar.

"Oh, good Lord," Benjamin muttered under his breath. "Do I dare even guess?" He took a peek.

It sat there at the bottom of her handbag taunting him with its putrid smell. He went white.

"Oh no!"

It was a nemesis from his past. It was pointing at him, both summoning him and giving him the middle-finger at the same time. It was 20cm long and black, with a beautiful sharp point. Electricity pulsed through his body.

He instinctively grabbed it as though to hide it or put it away. As he did so, Vanda pulled her handbag away from him and defiantly tucked it securely under her arm. The object fell and bounced onto the carpet of the passage.

Benjamin had it firmly back in his hand before Vanda noticed. He quickly stuffed it into his inner jacket pocket. It just fitted. *Nice replacement for the torn Bin Laden,* he thought. Vanda fumbled out her card and handed it to Benjamin. He squinted in the poor light. Number 514. It was around the corner.

He opened Vanda's door and went in with her. Any chance of a romantic liaison was gone. Vomit tended to have that effect. Vanda stumbled off to the bathroom.

Her cabin was tiny and Benjamin stepped out onto the balcony where it was less claustrophobic. He sat down at the little round outdoor table. It was loose and rattled from side to side. *Nice little escape route this is*, he thought to himself. He pictured himself, a cat burglar, hopping down from the balcony into the darkness below.

Benjamin fell back onto the couch. He thought he'd wait and see what happened and he wanted to use her towels to clean himself up properly. His jeans smelled terrible and he lifted his nose in disgust. He felt polluted and tired and his mind was racing. *Who was this woman Vanda? Why did she pick him? And why this thing now in his jacket pocket? It dredged up so much!*

She was taking way longer than he thought she would. His head dropped onto his chest and he dozed off.

* * *

"BENJAMIN RODD," A VOICE CALLED. "COME IN HERE PLEASE."

It sounded similar to earlier on. Benjamin thought it might be the booze. He hesitated. Perhaps I should leave whilst I can? The couch creaked loudly as he stood up. There was going to be no sneaking out quietly.

"Vanda?"

He reached for the bathroom door but before he got there, it opened wide from the other side.

The room was dark now with a purple periphery. The floor sparkled from beneath. It was crystal with reflections dancing off it from all angles.

She stepped deftly in front of him, her hair blond and haunting in the purple light.

"It is you!" Benjamin said. "How did you do this? I'm confused."
He tried to stay calm.

"You should have been nicer, Ben," the woman answered. "You
come in here with that awful cheap jacket and think you can have
me. I'm not who I used to be or what you think I am."

"You know my name!" Benjamin said. "How? I don't think I
know you."

She stepped forward, holding out her hand. Vanda's brooch was
clasped between her fingers. There were veins sticking out on top. It
wasn't Vanda though! She had thicker fingers. And these nails were
black. A Stunning black.

The woman didn't answer. She stood there gaping at him until he
could no longer look her in the eyes. Her mouth showed no emotion.
She had a silk shawl thrown over her with nothing on underneath.
She was floating on the floor. It's crystal colors misted up. A small
porthole window was open and the evening chill blew in. Blinds
knocked against the frame.

She then started talking. It felt as though she talked for ages.
Benjamin soaked it all up but then forgot it as each new sentence
started. A sponge under a running faucet.

"It's cold," he said, rubbing his arms. There was a mist coming
out of his mouth and it filled the room. Another dream!

"I'm hot," the woman replied. She lifted her shawl over her
shoulders and it dropped to the floor. She stood there motionless. The
curves down her side melted perfectly into her hips and framed her
breasts like a Renaissance masterpiece.

Benjamin was drawn in by the unfolding beauty before him.
Vanda and her vomit were gone. He didn't care where to.

The tattoo on her arm was a creeping rose vine, penciled by a
Grand Master. Michelangelo! It was growing up her arm in brown
tendrils that curved and settled into coils of magical perfection. Her
whole arm was a living art piece.

Without saying a word, she handed Vanda's brooch to
Benjamin.

"Let's do a trade," she said. "This trinket for you. You should be happy with that, don't you think?"

Benjamin took the brooch. It was warm. It felt light in his palm.

"Is that all I get?" he asked. She turned her back on him. Her curves had no beginning or end. They flowed like dunes in the desert.

"No," she replied. "You're going to get much more than you can imagine. It'll be a fair swap."

There was seduction in her voice and Benjamin grinned.

"I accept," he said, before stepping forward and reaching for her naked body. His arms swept through the misty air that elusively retreated to the porthole.

Outside, screaming purple chords of anger, the sky pulled at his ghost. She flowed back, blowing him a kiss. Her lips were the color of dark blood.

"Wait. I don't know your name. I don't know who you are. What about the swap?"

"I told you before Benjamin," she answered. "We're old friends. You'll get what's coming to you when the time is right."

And with that, she faded away as though being sucked out of Benjamin's head. Benjamin loved dreams like that. Lucid ones he could walk with and feel. Dr. Miller told him that dreams weren't real, but she was wrong. He was convinced of it.

"No! Wait!" Benjamin shouted. "Your name?" He no longer knew where to look for her. He heard a faint whisper in the night.

"Astraea," her vanishing voice said. "My name is Astraea."

He relaxed. She was gone. His head bounced up and he opened his eyes.

BENJAMIN WALKED SLOWLY AROUND VANDA'S CABIN. IT WAS pitch dark. He felt for her bed and sat down. Vanda had passed out. The voices and colors in his head were gone and a dark cloud was consuming him. All he could remember was the creeping vine on her arm and her name.

"Astraea," he said out loud so he won't forget it. "Astraea!"

He could feel the thorns on her tattoo stretching over to him and touching him. Scratching him and entwining him. He breathed deeply waiting for his heartbeat to slow.

There was a dark object in his jacket pocket, tugging at his very soul. He stroked his chest, feeling it's evil outline. He couldn't bring himself yet to take it out and have a decent look, but it might be just what he needed.

He pulled a blanket up over Vanda. After tucking her in, he stumbled back to his room on the seventh level. The air had turned heavy and no stars were twinkling through the night sky anymore.

$\maltese$ 3 $\maltese$

ROME

Benjamin woke an hour before breakfast. He lay in his bed looking at the ceiling. A pair of dirty jeans were strewn over the end of the bed. A silver chain curled through the thick hairs on his chest. The first thought on his mind was his dream. He remembered her name. Astraea. It no longer sounded powerful. It sounded rather childish, like a fairy tale character. Her voice, however, haunted him. He struggled to recall what she had said.

He pulled a cushion up behind his neck and sat up. He tried to hold onto the thoughts of her but eventually gave up. They were squashed out by the reality of the day. *It was just a dream!* He thought of Dr. Miller in her dull office. She had a disapproving look on her face. *Who cares?*

Putting on his reading spectacles, he examined one of the tour brochures lying on the table next to the bed. His blue eyes felt assaulted as he squinted through smudge marks on the lens. He made no attempt to clean them. *The Colosseum tour! That was the one!* He got up and opened the curtain. The bright sunlight stung.

A red lighthouse with peeling paint stared at him before

sliding into the left window frame. The Port of Civitavecchia had been up since dawn. Benjamin could see workers on the quay. The shadow from the MSE Grande engulfed them, like the shadow of death. He felt well qualified to know what that looked like. The workers stopped and watched as the ship silently crept past.

He checked his watch. *45 minutes to shower, eat and join the tour.* As the last few items from his suitcase were stuffed into the cupboard, an overpowering feeling of claustrophobia engulfed him. He couldn't wait to get into the City of Rome.

Vanda? What had happened to her? If she asked about the previous evening, he would blame the 'whiskey'. I'll probably see her on the tour, he said to himself as he fumbled for his toothbrush. His fingers curled around a sharp object on the basin edge. Little diamonds surrounding a pearl. *That brooch!* He couldn't remember everything about the previous evening. *Wine and Whiskey - not conducive to memory!* Examining the piece of jewelry again, he wondered how the heck he had ended up with it. *Who cares? He'd keep it. Maybe flog it in town for a few bucks?* Fifteen minutes later he was out the room, ready for the day ahead. The round object in his jacket pocket lay forgotten, hanging on his bathroom door.

* * *

THE BUS INTO ROME WAS PACKED. BENJAMIN SAT NEXT TO Dr. Burlington. He hadn't been able to find Vanda anywhere in the crowd of people. There was lots of excitement in the air as the seats filled up. Up front, some kids were shouting and jumping up and down on the seats. Benjamin was glad he chose to sit toward the back of the bus. He bit into an apple he had smuggled out of the dining room. Juice dripped off his chin, staining his white t-shirt. As he fidgeted with the pearl and diamond brooch, it turned wet and sticky.

A local tour guide stood up and tried to get the microphone working. She signaled to the children to sit still. They half-obliged, glancing nervously at their parents, who didn't give a toss what their kids were up to.

"Can you hear me at the back?" she asked in broken English.

A lone man at the front of the bus replied. She didn't care much about the lack of response and carried on talking, providing all the information on how the tour would work.

The group sitting behind Benjamin were confused and kept asking each other what was going on. Benjamin glanced back and recognized the young man who had been scrolling on his phone in the queue. His bride sat next to him, still looking bored. He was with a German party of tourists. He sneezed and Benjamin felt the blast on the back of his head. He wanted to clobber the man but restrained himself. He pulled his jersey up over his mouth and bent down with his head between his knees. He was furious. The young man sneezed again. Benjamin swore into his lap, wondering why it was taking so long to get going.

Outside in the parking lot, two men in uniform were running about amongst the snorting buses. They were ship security. One of them had a baton in his hand, the type riot police carry. They moved from bus to bus looking for someone. Rome, however, was waiting and the coaches started leaving one by one.

Benjamin's bus was already in second gear as it rolled past them. They scanned the rows of seats through the window, their heads bobbing up and down like the Pinocchio dolls being sold along the quayside. They didn't see Benjamin. His head was still buried down between his knees. As the last bus disappeared down the road, they returned to the ship.

Vanda, wearing dark sunglasses, was waiting for them at the gangplank. She had recovered from the previous evening's excesses. She wore jeans and a T-shirt and her pink scarf flapped in the wind. She had on yellow sandals, that she had bought in Portofino.

"We couldn't find him, ma'am," one of the men said. "He must be on the ship. Would you like to come and make a formal statement?" The men undressed her as they spoke.

"I already told reception," Vanda replied.

"They passed it onto us to handle, ma'am."

"Are you the police?"

"Ship security, ma'am," one of the men said. "Just as good."

Vanda looked them up and down. They were unconvincing. "Well, I'm sorry," she replied. "I'll do it later. I've got a private tour guide waiting for me. It's part of my prize."

The men tried to persuade her to go with them but eventually gave up, shrugging their shoulders.

"As you wish then," one of them said, and they disappeared back on board.

By the time they reached the ship's security office on the lower deck they had written off the pretty American's story. *A stolen brooch? By a man, she'd spent a drunken evening with? Impossible to prove*, they thought.

"I've got her in my sights now!" the one man kept saying. "She'll regret that she wasted my time!" They spoke loudly in Italian, whilst sharing a cigarette. They kept laughing over rude innuendoes.

Outside, a black Mercedes Benz pulled up and the driver got out asking for a Mrs. Slade. Vanda walked towards him as though she was a Princess on the Cannes Catwalk. They chatted for a minute and then she got into the car. It sped off toward Rome.

Ten minutes later it passed the bus that Benjamin was on. Vanda could see him arguing with the young man behind him. Dr. Burlington was dozing off. He had been up most of the night. His young girlfriend was not with him on the bus.

Vanda settled back into the leather seat of her executive taxi and paged mindlessly through some brochures. She didn't like thieves. She thought of Benjamin. *How could he have?* He was the only person who could have taken the brooch from her. *It might not be worth a fortune, but he's still a lying crook if he took it*, she thought to herself.

She failed to notice that another taxi was trailing her. Inside, the Bulgarian waiter, who had accosted her the previous evening, sat glaring. He was chain-smoking and agitated, holding onto the seat in front of him, constantly pointing. His eyes were watery. He had a black cap on his head and was wearing a white tracksuit. He had been given one day to recover the object he had slipped into Vanda's bag and return it to the people he had stolen it from. Or else, they had promised him that he'd be swimming home. Swimming along with his brother, who also worked on the ship. Neither of them could swim.

This is what happens when you get pissed, lady, he thought to himself as he glared at the car in front of him. *Dangerous things end up in your handbag!*

* * *

THE PACE OF ROME HAD NOT CHANGED SINCE ANCIENT times. No matter where you found yourself, you felt as though you were part of a big machine that was emitting little electric shocks of vibrant energy.

Sixteen hundred hours was the key time. That's when they had to be back on board the MSE Grande. It was leaving an hour later and would not be waiting for stragglers. The tour guide harassed the group from site to site as fast as she could. She carried a thin bamboo stick with a little yellow flag on it.

The German party was sticking to her as closely as the chewing gum on the Spanish Steps.

The rest of the tour group was struggling to keep up. There was barely enough time allowed for photos before she whisked them off to the next attraction. Ancient Roman columns and dirty facades started blurring, like a black and white silent movie.

Dr. Burlington had his sleeves rolled up and was fanning his sweaty face with his Panama hat.

"Slow down," he kept pleading. "We're meant to be on holiday, for Pete's sake." He gave up after an hour. "I'm catching a private cab back to the ship," he insisted.

"No! You are not!" the tour guide snapped back. "You signed the legal form and will remain with me. I have to get you back myself. No cabs allowed. I will go slower. OK?"

Burlington reluctantly nodded. The tour guide turned to the Germans. "Let's get a move on!" she loudly said. "Schneller!" Burlington failed to see her sadistic grin. He spent the rest of the tour moaning loudly.

Just before lunch, Benjamin spotted an ice cream shop up ahead. He knew that Rome was famous for its gelato and he intended to get one, with or without the tour guide's help. He ran on ahead to get it. He planned to have it in hand by the time the group caught up.

"Two scoops, please. *Duo bole*," he said in pidgin Italian. "*Chocolade and Vanilla, gratsi*." He felt stupid trying to speak a language he couldn't. The ice cream vendor took his time. He had no intention of rushing for a tourist who had mangled the Italian language.

Benjamin eventually stepped back out into the mid-day sun. The ice cream started to melt. He soon realized a cold beer might have been a better option. He looked up and down the road. The tour group was nowhere to be seen. He licked the vanilla topping, shrugged and headed off in an easterly direction. There were plenty of taxis around and nothing to worry about. Two blocks later he was well and truly lost in a thriving throng of people. There was a sign pointing to the Trevi Fountain and he knew that the tour group was headed there on their way to the Colosseum. It was so crowded that Benjamin started to sweat from the body heat around him. Wet patches appeared under his arms and he regretted that he had not put on shorts and slops. He half wished he were back on the ship.

At the fountain, Benjamin pushed past a Bangladeshi man selling plastic toys and stepped to the edge of the water. He threw in the change from the ice cream shop and made a wish. As he stood back he bumped into someone, stepping on their toes. The first thing he saw was yellow sandals. He gulped. Vanda looked beautiful.

"Vanda! I was looking for you this morning," he said awkwardly. "What a pleasant surprise."

"Hello, you thieving con!" she snapped back. "You didn't look very hard, did you?"

* * *

"What do you mean?" Benjamin said. "What are you doing here?"

"What do you think?" Vanda yelled. "Have you forgotten that I'm also on holiday? Now, my brooch. Give it back! I know you've got it."

Her pink scarf flapped in the breeze, framing her angry face. Her bright red lipstick smoldered like a burst plumb. Benjamin shook his head, looking down at her sandals.

"Aren't your feet sore?" he asked, trying to change the subject. Dipping his right hand into his pocket he felt for the brooch. It was still where he had shoved it, as he climbed off the bus. It felt toxic. The pin pricked him and he yanked his hand away.

"Got an itch in your pants, have you?" Vanda asked. "Wasn't last night enough? Let me see your hands. What have you got there?"

There were people around and Benjamin didn't want a scene. He hated domestic conflict. Running from embarrassment was a tactic that had saved him many times before. The couple next to them turned as Vanda's voice rose.

"Look, this is not what you think. Last night. The brandy, or rather your whiskey. Don't you remember? You gave it to me. The brooch. You gave it to me."

"So you do have it! I was right. You are a thieving con!"

"Stop calling me that. I'm no thief."

"How about a con then?"

"Vanda, you overindulged last night."

"I did not!"

"You were completely pissed!"

"So were you!"

"Can you remember anything?" Benjamin asked, smiling.

"Yes. I mean no. I don't know Ben. All I know is that last night all you were interested in, was my brooch. And this morning it was gone."

Vanda couldn't remember much from the end of the previous evening. She had woken up half-naked, without the brooch and her head pounding. Stumbling into her bathroom was the last thing she could vaguely remember of her night.

"Common, let's get out of here," Benjamin suggested.

"Let's not, Mr. Ben. Show me what's in your pocket first."

He slowly took his hand out of his pocket like a schoolboy who had been caught with cigarettes by his teacher. He looked at Vanda sheepishly. The diamonds on his palm caught the sun and twinkled. He swore his innocence.

The fountain gurgled in the background but its cool moisture couldn't stop the rising heat of the moment. Some children laughed as they tried to recover coins from the pond. Italian music played from a nearby shop. Benjamin held his left hand up away from his body. Ice-cream melted down his wrist and dripped onto the pavement. Vanda tried to grab his other hand, the one with the brooch in it.

Eventually, Benjamin gave up and shrugged. "Alright. Alright," he shouted. "Take you piece of junk back. Even though you gave it to me."

"It's not junk," Vanda said. "I bought it in St Margurite at a little..."

"Yeah, I know," Benjamin interrupted. "At a little jewelry shop inhabited by a strange woman who also liked junk. What did you call her? A crazy cow? I now understand what you went through."

Vanda hesitated. "Oh, c'mon Ben," she eventually said. "What do you expect me to think? I paid a grand for it because it reminded me of my grandma. And now you have it in your pocket. I am right, aren't I?"

"It reminded me of something as well. A stupid dream I've been having." Benjamin mumbled, holding out his palm. "And I liked it on your blouse. Made you look fabulous."

Benjamin took the last lick from his aborted ice-cream cone before it collapsed into a muddy pool on the steps. He scooped up some water from the fountain to rinse his hands. He playfully splashed a few drops on Vanda like a priest seeking absolution for his sins. He tried his puppy dog eyes and they worked.

"I'm innocent, Vanda," he said, "I didn't steal anything from you. You must have given it to me. When I got you into bed safely."

"That sounds bad!"

"It's not what I meant. I just helped you to your room. Your key card was in your..." Benjamin suddenly remembered what had fallen out of Vanda's bag. "Oh crap," he mumbled. "My jacket!" He looked her in the eyes, rubbing his nose. *Did she notice it missing? Who was this woman? It seemed incredible! Maybe this trip was not going to be his last after all. That could be a hundred grand hanging on his bathroom hook! Play it cool!*

"Did I mess on it?" Vanda asked.

"Uh?"

"Your jacket. I apologize if I messed on it." Vanda started to soften. She'd forgotten and forgiven much bigger things than this before.

"You are a fascinating woman," Benjamin replied.

"OK," she said. "I declare a truce."

Benjamin playfully splashed some more water on her.

"Stop it," Vanda said, wiping water drops from her cheek. "You'd look ridiculous wearing that thing anyway." She put her bag down next to her on the steps and placed her hand on Benjamin's chest.

"I never planned to ever wear it," Benjamin replied, somewhat ambiguously.

"I want it back before we get to Tunisia." She looked him dead in his blue eyes. "Agreed?"

Benjamin nodded.

"Don't do anything like that again," she insisted. "I don't like chasing cons halfway across Italy."

They both laughed. Benjamin a little too much.

"Deal!" he said. "Now do you feel like a drink? I saw a nice little cafe down that road."

Vanda didn't get a chance to answer. She jumped up flapping her arms.

"My bag. Where's my handbag?" She yelled. "Benjamin someone has stolen my bag. I put it there right next to you. My purse, my money!"

Jumping to attention, Benjamin scanned the crowd. He hadn't fully realized how crowded the Piazza was. All types of heads bobbed up and down. Mostly tourists and Bangladeshis selling stuff. He spotted a man dressed in a white tracksuit pushing suspiciously through the crowd. He had a black cap on. Benjamin squinted in the sun. A handbag strap was dangling from a scrunched up packet the man was clutching.

"I've got him!" Benjamin shouted. He knew more or less what to do. He was once trained for situations like this. He could picture Dr. Miller shaking her head at him. She was shouting at him. *Don't do it, Benjamin!*

But it was his chance to fix things with Vanda. He needed her to trust him, so he could get to the bottom of what was stuffed in his jacket pocket, back in his cabin. He gave chase, slipping into a fast jog. The thief had at least a thirty-meter head start in the crowded square. Benjamin couldn't see his face yet but his walk was familiar. And the stooped shoulders. He kept his eyes on the white tracksuit as he pushed past the masses of tourists. *What idiot pickpocket wears a white tracksuit in Rome*, he thought to himself?

The thief headed toward a narrow lane off the main Square. Benjamin increased his pace to a run. His fingers curled into a tight ball. Inside he was completely calm. He knew what to do. He knew how to bring down a man. And bring this thief down, he fully intended to do.

As the man turned the corner, Benjamin caught up with him. He grabbed him roughly, squeezing hard above the elbow. The arm was soft and bony. The startled thief instinctively swung his arms, trying to get away. His sunglasses fell onto the cobbles as Benjamin pulled his cap down over his face. *Easier to fight a man who can't see much,* Benjamin reckoned. Swearing profusely, the thief jumped around as though Benjamin was attacking him. Which he was, more or less.

Benjamin partly recognized him, but in the moment couldn't place when or where. The man clung desperately to the handbag he had stolen. Instead of trying to help, the people around them scattered away. A muted scream cut through the clatter of running feet. The thief's attempts at escape were pathetic. Benjamin thought that a child would have put up a better fight.

"Where is it?" the thief shouted, as he struggled. He twisted out of Benjamin's grip and flung the contents of the handbag onto the pavement. He was more interested in the bag than Benjamin.

"It's not here," he screamed.

He kicked Vanda's purse away in anger. A lipstick rolled into the gutter. Then he kicked wildly in Benjamin's direction and attempted a weak swing with his left hand. Benjamin sidestepped, and then expertly socked him square on the jaw with one solid punch. The man's face contorted and he fell to the ground like a shot pigeon.

Whistles and shouts came bellowing through the crowd. Benjamin knelt and scraped Vanda's things together, stuffing them back into her bag. He didn't want an incident with the local police. He wanted to stay off their radar. By that stage, Vanda had caught up. He grabbed her hand firmly.

"We're leaving now!" he insisted.

They were around the corner and back in the jostling crowd just in time. Two Carabinieri came running from the opposite end of the street and spotted the thief, who was groaning in the gutter holding his cheek.

"Shouldn't we report this?" Vanda asked.

"No! Let's get out of here," Benjamin answered. "I got your bag back and that's all that matters. And they'll have us tied up all day at the police station. We'll miss the boat."

Vanda didn't argue and put her hand on his. They walked off briskly. The crowd was already forgetting what had just happened. Ten minutes later they were far enough away to feel safe and they stopped to get their bearings.

"You were amazing," Vanda said, checking the content of her handbag. "Are you alright?"

She'd forgotten about the diamond brooch and was glad they were back together. She held onto him tightly. Benjamin said he was fine. He said it with a touch of pride, knowing that she was starting to trust him again.

"Look. There's the Colosseum," he said. It was down the road, between two old buildings. Benjamin spotted a little yellow flag waving over the thousands of heads.

"We're saved."

"Where have you been?" Dr. Burlington asked Benjamin as soon as they caught up with their tour group. "You missed a fight. The police got one of them. He was in bad shape." Spit flew from the doctor's mouth as he embellished the story. As he wiped it away, he noticed Vanda. "Oh, hello," he said, undressing her. "Nice of you to finally join us." Vanda rolled her eyes and ignored him.

"We got there as the fight finished," Burlington continued. "The other chap got away. We didn't see him but you should have seen the mess he left."

Benjamin held his bloodied knuckles behind his back. "I don't like violence," he said. He felt drained and dizzy. His face went white.

Vanda put her arm around his shoulder to support him and whispered, "I agree with you. Let's not mention what happened to anyone. OK?"

Benjamin nodded, keeping an eye on Burlington.

Someone next to them cleared his throat as though he had something important to say. It was the young German man who had been sneezing in the bus. He still had his phone in his hand and snapped a quick picture as if to make a point.

"I saw what you did, mister," he said in broken German. "You say you don't like violence? Nice one... buddy!"

Benjamin wished it had been him who he had punched.

* * *

THE BUS DOORS CLOSED SHUT WITH A HISS AT PRECISELY three o'clock. The Italian guide packed her yellow flag away and made a quick exit. She was not going to be working one minute overtime if she could help it. Vanda stayed with Benjamin and went back on the bus. They had been ejected from Rome like a pip that got stuck in someone's throat. Coughed away in a phlegmatic mess.

She took a seat next to Benjamin, holding his hand. There was a shake in her grip. The mugging incident had bonded them together. The young German man couldn't keep his mouth shut and gushed about what he had seen. He sneezed on each of his hapless victims as he gleefully embellished how Benjamin had knocked the mugger unconscious. Benjamin neither confirmed it or denied it.

"What do you think he wanted?" Benjamin whispered.

"My money," Vanda replied. "I read that pickpockets are prolific in Rome. It was my fault. I shouldn't have put my bag down. I'm sorry."

"Mmm," Ben said. "He seemed to be looking for something specific. The way he emptied your bag and kicked through your things. He didn't touch your cash. It was right on top."

"He squashed my lipstick, and that is unforgivable. Besides, you took him out rather quickly, remember. He didn't get a chance to take the money."

Vanda turned towards Benjamin noticing for the first time how thick his eyelashes were. They were long and dark. He was much stronger than what she had initially thought and she especially appreciated a man who could look after himself in a fight.

"I know that thieving bugger from somewhere but I can't place him," Benjamin said. "I didn't see his face properly. His hat was in the way and it happened so fast."

"You remind me of my father," Vanda said. "The way you handled yourself back there."

"He's a good fighter as well?"

"Was a good fighter."

"I'm sorry."

"It was a long time ago. Happier days."

"I'm not actually a fighter," Benjamin said, trying to change tack. "More of a hunter, I like to think."

"Surely not Benjamin?"

"It was also a long time ago."

"Happier days as well?"

"At one point. Been out of it for years now."

"Why did you stop?"

"Let's say I had no choice and leave it there," Benjamin said. "Part of my past."

"Is that why you're here? On this trip. Running from your hunting past?"

"Hardly," Benjamin replied. "More like hunting for my future."

"Well, you just had some good practice on my mugger. Thanks again for helping me."

Her touch on his arm was warm and soft. It felt sexy and comforting and Benjamin liked it. He sat back, thinking about their day.

The bus edged its way out of Rome through the afternoon traffic. The harbor was fifty kilometers away and they would make it back just in time. The tour group was exhausted. Their route march through the major attractions of inner City Rome had been a blur. Dr. Burlington moaned about his sore legs. The bus eventually went still, as though everyone had stopped talking at the wave of an invisible conductor's baton. Only the throaty roar of the bus's engine could be heard. The light outside was bright. It was being sliced up by the street poles and the shadows were hypnotically flying across the bus windows. To Benjamin, it felt as though it was an early ceasefire. Vanda closed her eyes to try and sleep. Benjamin stared outside allowing the shadows to seduce him into a trance.

A FAMILIAR FACE STARED AT HIM THROUGH THE GLASS. HIS ghost. His voice. Astraea! She neither threatened nor comforted. She looked blankly at him. A drop of blood oozed out the side of her mouth.

"Are you going to tell her?" she said softly, over and over.

Benjamin looked around. He was alone. Astraea pulled him toward the open window. She had his arm, but Benjamin resisted, feeling his adrenaline rise again. His heart pounded the panicked rhythm of a battle retreat.

"Leave me alone," he said. "Why are you here, anyway?"

Astraea's stone-walling smile cracked her dry lips.

"Try being honest this time," she said.

"To her?"

"And to yourself!"

"I don't know if I can do that," Benjamin said.

She let him go and Benjamin fell back into his seat. "We'll finish this chat later then," she said. "In the meantime, why don't you ask your waiter, Benjamin?"

She faded away, waving. Soon she was gone.

"OH, GOODNESS," BENJAMIN QUIETLY BLURTED AS HIS HEAD snapped up from his chest. He tried to get Vanda interested.

"Our waiter from dinner last night," he whispered. "You know? The Bulgarian chap with the scowl. He was the man in the white tracksuit. Your mugger. Of course. That's where I recognized him from. I'm sure of it."

Vanda murmured not paying attention. She was dozing in the idyllic late afternoon heat, like most of the other passengers.

Benjamin couldn't wait to get back to the ship. His jacket was hanging on the bathroom door and in its pocket lay the thing their waiter must surely have been after - the small juvenile rhino horn that had fallen out of Vanda's bag.

Benjamin knew exactly what it meant. In fact, he knew rather a lot about rhino horns. *Uphondo*, they called it in Zulu. He'd try not make the same mistakes as last time. He wouldn't be able to survive jail again. *Talk about luck,* he wondered. *Maybe this Astraea is my lucky charm?* He could smell the money. And the freedom.

I wonder if Vanda knows I've got it? Can I even trust her? He glanced at her. She was sleeping like an angel.

* * *

THE BUS ARRIVED JUST AS THE BULLHORN OF THE SHIP FIRED across the water. Thousands of seagulls jived and twisted in uncoordinated chaos. They had already released most the hoisting and only two last remaining ropes kept the ship at bay.

Some crew were milling around making sure no one was left behind. A serious looking man in a dark coat was amongst them. He was the same officer who had been inspecting the buses earlier that day. Salvatore Bollini was the Principal Security Officer on the ship. He puffed aggressively on a cigarette watching the guests file past. He wore an arrogant condescending expression, knowing that as soon as the ship embarked, he would be the law.

He looked Vanda up and down as she passed him shaking his head in disgust as he saw who she was holding onto.

"This morning her thief. This afternoon her lover," he said in Italian, under his breath. He had not forgotten how Vanda wasted his precious time earlier in the day over her so-called 'stolen' brooch.

Up until that point, he had not decided yet whose holiday he was going to make miserable. Bollini normally picked one poor tourist on each cruise. Someone who had been rude to the crew, or who had gotten too drunk or who had leered inappropriately at the girls in the public Jacuzzi. Someone who he felt deserved it. He would make his victim's life hell, scaring the crap out them with random room searches or lengthy interrogations about a conjured up security threat. No one ever questioned his approach, even the Captain of the ship often boasted that Salvatore Bollini was the most vigilant security officer in the MSE fleet.

Bollini noticed the woman's brooch on Benjamin's collar. He'd pinned it on as a joke, back at the Colosseum. Bollini stretched his neck to see if it had diamonds and pearls. That's when he noticed Benjamin's knuckles. The blood had congealed and his hand looked a mess.

He gave Benjamin an uncomfortable, blink-free eyeballing that all decent security officers know how to pull off. Benjamin tried his best to ignore it.

He's hiding something, Bollini thought to himself. Years of experience had trained him to spot such things. *The man looks guilty. I don't like him! Ms. Slade neither.*

He turned to his side-kick who was standing next to him.

"I'll have them both shitting by midnight," he said.

* * *

THE MSE GRANDE WAS A CRUISE SHIP WORTHY OF HER name. She was by far the largest ship in the port of Civitavecchia that day. There were three swimming pools and a water theme park on board. Wherever one looked there were elevators, grand lobbies, eateries, shops and entertainment attractions. The main sun tanning deck could be cleared for a private match of expensive tennis or, as was done each afternoon, for communal games like volleyball, basketball or softball.

Wherever one looked, there was crew scurrying about. They were mostly Eastern European and Malaysian. The officers in charge were Italian or Greek. Dressed in black trousers and white golf shirts, they looked overworked and underpaid. All the major languages of the world were spoken somewhere on the ship. At any point in time, there were over a thousand merry holidaymakers on board. All of them were trying to find some unique magic in the paradise that had been sold to them on the internet or by a travel agent earning a fat commission. Most of them would be back at the numbness of their dull lives within a week. If one wanted any sort of privacy or quiet on board, one needed to know where to go.

Benjamin walked with Vanda to a little Tuscan themed bar on the second floor. It was tucked out of the way and he liked that. He planned to finally drill her about the rhino horn he had found in her bag. A waitress calmly placed a menu in front of them before walking off to another table.

"Bunch of trained circus poodles, these ones are," Benjamin said. "Plastic personalities, false smiles, no spontaneity and no individualism."

"You're a 'glass half empty' type of guy, aren't you?" Vanda replied.

* * *

BENJAMIN PRETENDED HE NEVER HEARD AND WENT UP TO the bar to order drinks. A beer shandy for himself and a Long Island iced tea for Vanda. The barman said he'd bring them over and then turned to join the commotion going on behind the bar counter. Crew members and waitresses were huddled together nervously, whispering and glancing about.

"Something's wrong," Benjamin said, as he sauntered back to Vanda. "I can smell some sort of fear back there?"

Dr. Miller had told him once that fear had no smell and that it was just a feeling. Benjamin knew she was wrong. He'd smelt fear before. Many times before. From things, you'd never dream of.

"Are you planning to report your mugging here on the ship?" he asked Vanda, keeping one eye on the bar.

Vanda had already decided what she would do. She had cried wolf once already that day and judging by how Salvatore Bollini had looked at her when she came back aboard, she didn't think he'd believe anything she had to say now.

"No, what's the point," she said. "I didn't lose anything in the end. My money, cards, the jersey. It's all still there." She patting the leather bag at her side. "Thanks to you, my hero. Just my lipstick wrecked. I've got some others anyway."

"He wasn't after your lipstick, Vanda. Or your money. But you know that, don't you? Is there anything you want to tell me?" *He wanted to hear her say it!*

"What do you mean? You make out that I'm hiding something."

"Let me put it this way. Is there anything else that could have been in your bag?" Benjamin asked. "Other than the normal rubbish."

Say it! He wanted her to admit that she had that illegal horn in her bag. Then he could figure out why and see if he could benefit somehow. Vanda raised her eyebrows.

"The normal rubbish?" she said, questioningly. Her body

language went cold.

Benjamin realized that upsetting the person he needed answers from, was not the way to go about it. His mouth had been faster than his brain. He re-calibrated.

"OK," he said, "sorry, I didn't mean it that way. Vanda, your things aren't rubbish. I meant, maybe he thought something else of value was in your bag."

"Other than my money?" she answered. "What else do I have that a little scab like that could possibly want?" She folded her arms. "He was trying his luck."

"He wasn't a pickpocket," Benjamin said. "I was trying to tell you on the bus. Remember our waiter from last night? The one from sun-downers and supper?"

She squirmed and rubbed her forearm. It was slightly bruised where the waiter had grabbed her. She remembered all right.

"You really think so?" she said, "They all look the same to me."

Benjamin thought her surprise unconvincing. "It was him! I looked him in the face as I hit him. And he had that same crooked walk."

Vanda said nothing. She sat rubbing her arm as though it were a victim of a serious mozzie attack. She honestly had no clue what anyone, especially their waiter, would want with her. She felt a hollowness in her stomach and stretched her mind to remember her drunken escapades of the evening. It was a bit hazy. Whiskey has that effect. Slowly, the memory of what happened in the passage outside the dining room, came crawling out of the recesses of her mind. She sat still as she tried to remember.

"Do you think he got back to the ship?" she quietly asked. "Probably," Benjamin said. "Unless they arrested him in Rome. We didn't get a chance to see."

"Burlington said they took him away."

"To get a cooldrink around the corner, no doubt."

"A cooldrink?"

"A bribe," Benjamin explained. "The tourist police in Rome can be incentivized to do anything with the right flavor."

In reality, Benjamin had no idea what could have happened once the police arrived. For all he knew, the police might have thought he was the mugger, and they might be looking for him. He hoped he was wrong. He wanted Vanda to admit the truth. *Why was she carrying around a baby rhino horn in her handbag?*

"What could he have wanted from your bag, I wonder?" Benjamin said, somewhat sarcastically.

"I'm going to my room now. You can have my drink if you want. We'll talk at dinner. I need to shower and think about this."

"You didn't answer my question," Benjamin said.

Vanda got up and walked out without saying another word. She smiled awkwardly back at Benjamin as she disappeared through the doors. She was putting the drunken pieces together about what had happened to her.

Benjamin was buzzing inside but decided to let her be. Besides he couldn't follow her. Their drinks hadn't even arrived yet and he still had to sign for them. He stood up as she walked away. *There are still five days to get to the bottom of this,* he thought. *And I have the horn, so I can make her talk.*

"I'll see you at dinner, then," he shouted.

Eventually, the waitress returned with two Coronas on a silver tray. Benjamin took the drinks even though they were wrong. He didn't want to make a scene.

"What's going on," he asked, twitching his eyes towards the bar where the other waiters were huddled together in nervous conversation. The waitress pretended not to understand English.

Benjamin put five euros on the table.

"Please tell me?" he asked. He was worried that it somehow had something to do with him and the mugger. Or the horn.

The waitress bent over and started wiping the table. The note disappeared. She whispered as she spoke.

"There has been a terrorist attack, sir," she said. "In Tunisia, at the Carpathian ruins. One of our sister ships is involved. The one I worked on last month. They will inform the guests later tonight how this impacts on us, sir."

"Good grief!" Benjamin exclaimed. Inside he was happy that it was that and nothing which involved him.

As the waitress walked away, her left hand shook. Her right hand clutched the banknote. Ben was completely calm. Sitting back in his chair, he sipped his Corona. The lemon stuck in its glass throat. *What a day it's been*, he thought to himself. *Now, what else could go wrong? I doubt that we'll go to Tunisia now.*

As he drank, he mind wondered to Astraea, his mysterious voice. He wondered why she was always there when he closed his eyes. It was weird. *Who the heck was she, anyway?* Then he threw back his Corona and reached for Vanda's.

* * *

THAT NIGHT IT WAS GALA EVENING ON BOARD THE MSE Grande. The ladies dressed in their most elegant evening wear and the dining room was awash with haute couture fragrances from Paris and New York. The men mostly wore Tropical Black Tie, but a few odd traditional tuxedos frolicked like black sheep in the white fields.

Vanda wore her hair in an upstyle with fake Swarovski earrings. A low-back halter neck dress swept the marble tiles as she walked toward the banquet room doors. Her silver stilettos exhibited perfectly toned calves and turned the heads they passed. An usher opened for her. It was everything she had dreamed of. A string quartet played Tchaikovsky as sparkling flutes of champagne were ferried across the room over the shoulders of waiters. The guests stood around in little groups and an exciting undercurrent of energy and excitement filled the air.

The talk of the evening was the bomb attack in Tunisia. It was excitedly discussed with both astonishment and scandalous outrage.

"It'll never happen to us!" Vanda heard a hoity-toity old lady say as she walked past. "This is, after all, an upmarket cruise."

Pompous ass, Vanda thought to herself. *Bad things only happen to other people, don't they?*

She looked around for Benjamin. He hadn't arrived yet. She stood for a few minutes milling around the flower arrangement. An Officer in a white jacket with gold braiding approached her.

"Good evening ma'am," he said stiffly, trying not to look down her cleavage. "The captain requests that you join him at his table for dinner this evening."

Vanda instantly accepted. She had a weakness for uniforms and sailors. She'd catch up with Benjamin later. In any case, she was getting tired of playing twenty questions with him.

The Head of Security, Salvatore Bollini, watched her from behind the bandstand. He shook his head as though deprived of a victory he'd been waiting for. He wisely chose to leave Vanda alone for the time being. Most single women invited to the Captain's table ended up having their digestif's in his cabin and this meant that Vanda had to come off his 'hit list'. Benjamin Rodd, however, was an entirely different matter.

"I'll get her boyfriend by himself," he said to his sidekick. "Capitano would want him out the way. What was his name?"

MEANWHILE, BENJAMIN WAS IN HIS ROOM GETTING READY to leave. His jacket was exactly where he had left it the previous evening, hanging on the hook of the bathroom door. It's stuffed pocket had lain undisturbed all day. It didn't take him long to confirm and check exactly what had been in Vanda's bag. It was after all, very close to home. Too close in fact. He struggled to believe it was just a coincidence. His heart pounded as he examined the small rhino horn for the umpteenth time. Above him, the darkness hovered. It was as though he was in the tunnel about to run out onto a soccer pitch, with antagonistic crowds baying for blood. And his dream kept haunting him. *Was that voice a coincidence as well? I could fetch a small fortune for this trophy*, he kept thinking. *Or another prison sentence*, the voice seemed to say!

He eventually decided he couldn't look at it anymore and locked it up in his cabin safe. He hoped to get some answers from Vanda over dinner, even if he had to feed her drinks in order to get them. As he left his cabin for dinner, images of Astraea haunted him and he wished they'd go away.

* * *

BENJAMIN ENTERED THE LOUNGE CONFIDENTLY AND spotted Vanda straight away. She was in a huddle giggling with the Captain of the ship. He walked calmly up to her.

"We need to talk," he said, tugging on her elbow. She had been enjoying the Captain's good company for half an hour. The entrees were about to be brought out and many of the guests had already sat down at their tables. An empty magnum of champagne lay on the table near Vanda and the

Captain. Another was being poured by an overly enthusiastic waitress.

Salvatore Bollini watched Benjamin enter the room and trailed him across the floor. He spied the captain out of the corner of his eye, like a puppy who was worried that the big dog would snap at him. Impressing the Captain was Bollini's highest priority in life. His father had taught him the importance of keeping important men feeling important. He strolled a few meters behind Benjamin in his starched white safari suit.

"Benjamin," Vanda said enthusiastically. "I've been looking all over for you." She was loud. "Have you heard the news? About the bombing in Tunisia! Here, Javier will tell you." She pulled the Captain over.

Captain Javier Pizarro looked as though he spent more time on the tanning deck than the control deck. His brilliant white teeth shone past his middle-aged wrinkles. He formally put out his hand. Benjamin shook it unenthusiastically.

"I see you're enjoying the wine again," he said to Vanda. "With... Javier!"

* * *

"IS THIS THE MAN YOU WERE TELLING ME ABOUT?" CAPTAIN Pizarro asked Vanda. He had a Spanish accent with the charm of an Anatolian matador. Suave and dashing, he exuded testosterone. Especially when a beautiful woman crossed his path. He puffed his chest out like Lord Nelson commanding his fleet.

"Benjamin was a great help for me today in the City," Vanda said. "He's from Africa."

"Couldn't keep your mouth shut, could you?" Benjamin whispered into her ear.

"Blame the Dom Perignon if you want, but Javier said he

could help."

Captain Pizarro looked Benjamin up and down, less than thrilled that a rival had arrived on the scene. None had beaten him yet though. He silently decided that Vanda would be his at any cost. He would feign friendship with Benjamin and then launch a flank attack against this usurper from the African bush. He shook Benjamin's hand firmly as they introduced themselves to each other.

"I am a man of absolute discretion," he said pulling Benjamin toward him, refusing to let go of his hand. "It's not the first time one of our guests have been mugged. My man will know exactly what to do." Benjamin eventually managed to wrestle his crushed hand free. He glared at Vanda.

"Aha, there he is," Captain Pizarro continued, clicking his fingers. "Senor Bollini. Come here please."

Salvatore Bollini had been slowly inching across the room toward them. He now lunged forward like a schoolboy who had finally been chosen for the sports team.

"Mr. Rodd," Captain Pizarro said. "I'd like you to meet our head of security, Mister Bollini."

Bollini puffed out his chest and clicked his heels together. "Mr. Bollini runs the best cruise security in the entire Mediterranean," Captain Pizarro boasted.

Bollini glanced at Vanda. It was unclear who was more uncomfortable. Vanda had been hoping not to bump into him again. Not after her false alarm of the morning and the dirty stares he had given her when she returned from Rome. Captain Pizarro now changed that in an instant.

Bollini held out his hand to Benjamin, ignoring Vanda. His grip felt like a stiff piece of cardboard. *Man, they all have hands like vices,* Benjamin thought.

"Salvatore," Captain Pizarro said to his head of security. "My friends here today had a nasty incident in the City. A mugging in broad daylight. He's a hero this one."

He slapped Benjamin hard on the back. A bit too hard. Benjamin didn't want to be the center of attention. He had come across to try and pry Vanda away. *She still had some explaining to do.* The Captain clinked his glass. He strutted about like a peacock before his hens as Bollini beamed next to him.

These were the last two people Benjamin needed in his life at that moment. He blushed at the attention being publicly showered on him. The Captain took him by the arm and turned him around for the room to see. He felt like a trophy. Like one of his horrible stuffed animals.

"Salvatore. I need you to help our hero here," Captain Pizarro instructed. "He needs to make a statement. A full statement for the record." Benjamin's heart sank as the Captain carried on. "We cannot allow our guests to be attacked in broad daylight."

The captain winked at his security officer who had been around long enough to know the modus operandi of his boss. Bollini glanced at Vanda who was at Captain Pizarro's side. *I hope you enjoy your Spanish bull*, Bollini thought. *Most of the women do.* He smiled sadistically. He had been about to trump up a conjured reason to get Benjamin into his interrogation room, and now the Captain had delivered him directly into his clutches. Legitimately! He knew he'd have to careful though. The captain was bound to ask Benjamin the next day how the security procedures had gone. Bollini clicked his heels.

"Of course," he said, taking Benjamin's hand again. "What was your name again? Mr?" Benjamin hesitated before answering.

"Rodd. My name is Rodd," he said, pulling his hand away. "It's not necessary, really! I don't want to make a statement."

He felt a tinge of panic in his gut. It was a feeling he usually got when he was around law enforcement. Dr. Miller had told him once, that policeman were the good guys and that he should learn to trust them again. But, he wasn't ready for that yet.

"You fought the mugger?" Bollini asked, as though he was Sherlock Holmes. Benjamin nodded. He had no intention of supplying any more detail.

"Then you have no choice. It's the law," Bollini said, "A statement is required."

"When?"

"After dinner!" Bollini was enjoying the power he had. "I'll be in the security office at around 10 o'clock tonight. Second floor down below deck. It shouldn't take long."

Salvatore Bollini snapped his heels yet again, turned and walked away. As he left, he caught the approving eye of Captain Pizarro, who would now have Vanda to himself for the night.

Vanda shrugged her shoulders and told Benjamin she would catch up with him later. They stood awkwardly for a few moments and then Benjamin said goodbye and walked furiously across to the far side of the room where his table was already seated, waiting for their starter to arrive.

* * *

BENJAMIN FELT DISTRAUGHT AS HE SAT DOWN NEXT TO Vanda's now empty seat. The previous 24 hour hours had been a roller coaster ride of adrenaline, surprise, intrigue, and disappointment. And his dreamy visitor, Astraea, who came back whenever he fell asleep, taunted him. He had been expecting a lazy leisure cruise, relaxed and without any problems. Not some crazy mixed up mission into the Mediterranean.

He had developed an instant dislike for both Salvatore Bollini and Captain Pizarro. He had known men like them in his life and he knew what they were about. *Always trying to bring down the better man, they were. It's what kept them going in their miserable lives of arbitrary smallness.* Dr. Miller had once told him as much.

He planned to keep his official statement about the mugging, short and simple. Something along the lines of, *'I helped Mrs. Slade when her bag got stolen. It happened very quickly and the details are fuzzy. I hit someone to defend her. I can't remember much else. Sorry old chap'*.

Benjamin decided that Bollini was a man to avoid. He didn't think he could trust him. There was a callousness in the man's eyes, and it was disturbing. It was almost as though Bollini knew he was hiding something. Those eyes drilled into Benjamin's nasty past and made him feel like he was back home in the African bush, with a wild animal snorting behind him. Only this time it wasn't a live animal - just a horn. A horn that Benjamin had no intention of allowing Bollini to discover. It was worth too much. *At least a hundred grand! His golden goose was back! Unless Bollini cooked it?*

Dr. Burlington had the entire table on edge with the tales of the day's trip to Rome. He went on and on about his sore legs. Kevin and Charlie O'Donnell, disapproved with how Benjamin had fought with the mugger. Benjamin tried to kill the conversation, but Burlington embellished the tale to the heights of an Olympian street brawl. The O'Donnell's said they were pacifists who hated the sight of blood.

"I agree on that with you, wholeheartedly," Benjamin said, with a look of feigned disgust as though he didn't want to see blood again in his life.

The two vacant seats from the previous evening had now been filled. Benjamin introduced himself.

"Please to meet you," Benjamin said, holding out his hand.

"Yes, yes. Us too!" came the reply. "I am Mr. Ng. Tram Ng. This is my wife, Lesley Ng."

They both wore expensive designer outfits. It looked as though they had walked down the Champs Elysees in one afternoon and picked up whatever they could get their hands on. They exhibited it proudly like a post-Maoist consumer badge of achievement.

They said they were from Manila and on the cruise celebrating an anniversary. When they spoke quietly to each other, however, Benjamin realized that they were actually Vietnamese; he knew the street culture and language well. He'd had no choice with that.

"Thực phẩm tốt," Benjamin casually said, smiling.

Their eyes almost popped out and they stayed with broken English the rest of the evening. Benjamin pretended that was all the Asian he knew. *She must be his secretary or something*, he thought to himself. *Typical!*

Dr. Miller had told Benjamin once that his image of the Vietnamese was biased. He disagreed. *Dr. Miller had not been to Hanoi. She'd not rotted in a Vietnamese jail and she had no clue what she was talking about.* As Benjamin thought about Vietnam, the rhino horn in his safe flashed before him. *That's what had landed him in that mess over there. Another co-incident?*

Dr. Burlington's girlfriend was dressed modestly and wore, even more, makeup than the previous evening. She remained elusive again, smiling when she had to and resisting most attempts at conversation. There were new waiters serving their table. Benjamin called one over.

"Where's our waiter from last night," he asked. "The Bulgarian chap."

The new waiter hesitated, nervously. His eyes glanced over the table.

"I'll call my manager," he said before darting off. Benjamin watched him briefing the maître d' on duty. The maître d' scowled, looking like a pit manager from Las Vegas who had just spotted a card counter. He made a call, keeping his eyes on their table. Benjamin assumed it was to Bollini and grimaced.

The maître d' finished his call and then walked up to the table. "Mister?" he asked, expecting Benjamin to fill in the blanks. Benjamin ignored him. The maître d' continued, "How may I help, sir?"

"You can't!" Benjamin answered. "I just asked where our old waiter from last night was. It was a simple question. No need to involve management." Benjamin was dreading yet another incident.

"I am management sir," the maître d' said, "You knew this man? Why do you want to know?" He loomed over the table with his back to the Ng's.

"Forget it," Benjamin said, angrily, "No! Never mind. I didn't know him, he was a good waiter for goodness sake and I was only asking a friendly question."

"Mister sir," the maître d' said in his accented English. "The old waiter you ask about is not on duty tonight. He is sick. Can I please ask again, why do you ask?"

Sick my ass, Benjamin thought. *Since when was a black eye considered a sickness?*

"The Bordeaux," Benjamin said, lying. "I wanted him to tell me about the Bordeaux. I was considering a medium Red and he knew his wines."

Benjamin could feel his pulse rising. He wanted the big ugly man in front of him to leave. He'd had enough of security officers, captains, waiters and cruise managers. *Dr. Miller! Help*, he thought. The maître d' relaxed and snapped his fingers at a sommelier standing idle at another table.

"This one will help you, sir," he stiffly said, before walking briskly away. He kept Benjamin in his sights for the rest of the evening.

Benjamin ordered the first bottle of Red he spotted on the wine list. He hated feeling pressed in and under pressure.

It made him want to explode. He offered the wine to the table when it arrived. He missed Vanda and felt alone. She was over on the other side of the room. Benjamin glanced across to see how she was doing. She fluttered like a young butterfly around Captain Pizarro. Benjamin groaned inside. She caught his gaze and waved. The Captain immediately noticed and whispered into her ear. She giggled and looked back to Benjamin over the Captain's shoulder. The evening was not turning out as Benjamin had hoped.

* * *

BENJAMIN INTENTIONALLY DRANK MORE THAN USUAL. HE had to deal with Salvatore Bollini later and needed some Dutch courage. Besides, it eased the pain of having to watch Vanda cavort all night with the captain across the room.

The food was excellent. There had been five courses, starting with a light seafood broth and ending with a Danish chocolate-infused cream pastry with a ball of ice cream on the side.

Benjamin warmed to Charlie and Kevin O'Donnell. They were one of those idealistic couples who lived in a bubble of rainbow optimism, thinking that all the world around them did too. They expected society to be progressive, prejudice was a relic from the previous century and anything with a beautiful form was worshiped with sacred adoration. Benjamin wished he saw life like them.

The Ng's spun out conflicting energies and stories all night. When coffee was over and the guests were retiring to the jazz lounges and discos, they still remained an enigma to Benjamin.

Dr. Burlington, it turned out, was not a medical doctor at all. At least not by any traditional academic standards. He had graduated with a diploma in homeopathy from a quack college when he was thirty-three. Over the years his homeopathic skills had morphed into 'energy healing'. He promised wellness with a few mystic waves of his hand - if you had faith. He was, however, the worst possible advert for what he did. There was nothing holistic or healthy about him, whatsoever. He was overweight, drank like a thirsty camel and went through meat as though he had descended from a cannibal. *Snake oil salesman*, Benjamin kept thinking.

As for the young girl with him, the only possible explanation Benjamin could think of was that the good 'doctor' had picked her up on a website somewhere. *A Russian bride site or something.*

Benjamin was the last one left at the table. He waited to see what happened between Vanda and the Captain. He was not in a rush to see Bollini, either.

Vanda delayed leaving as well. She had eaten slowly and kept ordering more drinks. With each new gulp thrown back, Captain Pizarro had wound himself up to a new height of erotic anticipation. He now wanted to move on. Cigars and cognac followed by a short slow dance in the piano lounge was how he normally transitioned from Captain to lover. He had yet to meet an American woman who didn't fall for it.

Vanda glanced over to Benjamin with a look of panic on her face. Benjamin wondered how she could be so naive about Pizarro's intentions. There was nothing he could do about it though. It was just after ten and Officer Bollini was waiting for him. He'd come back after giving his statement and save Vanda from her Iberian bullfighter.

He got up and made his way down to the security offices. A crew member escorted him to a little room. It had no windows and a single light bulb dangled from the roof above the table. It reminded Benjamin of a place he had once been in before. In Hanoi. In jail.

"You can wait here," the crewman said, in poor English. "I'll let the Commando know you are here."

Benjamin heard a lock turn as the door closed. He thought it strange that he was locked in but it was too late for him to do anything about it. He sat down on one of the chairs. It was made of aging wood, like an old school bench.

The light bulb above him swayed gently from side to side. Benjamin studied its hypnotic motion, wondering what sort of sadistic would-be policeman needed an interrogation room on a tourist cruise ship. He breathed deeply and closed his eyes. He planned in his head what to say. His eyes were sleepy.

Salvatore Bollini sat at his desk in the office next door, playing with some keys. The crewman announced that Mr. Rodd was ready. Bollini waved him away saying he'd only be a few more hours.

* * *

THE DOOR TO THE INTERROGATION ROOM CLOSED AS FAST AS IT had opened. Before Benjamin could stand up, the chair opposite him had been turned around and occupied.

"You!" he exclaimed. "What are you doing here?"

The hairs on his back were like acupuncture pins.

Astraea straddled the chair and folded her tattooed arms over the back of it. As she leaned forward, Benjamin noticed the contours of her body diving down under her loose cameo top.

"Alone again, Benjamin Rodd," she said, "Alone again."

Her deep dimples were idyllic caverns of perfection each time she smiled. Her hair was the color of an old picture frame with golden streaks catching the light. Old world patina and ageless perfection merged into beauty.

Benjamin noticed her legs pressed against the inside of the chair. The slatted wooden backrest stood between them like impenetrable burglar bars. She was a contradiction of light and dark, good and evil, the past and the future. Foreign yet familiar, hostile yet friendly. Part of Benjamin wanted her, but it also raged against his common sense which told him to run away as fast as he could.

"I'm just dreaming," he said calmly.

"Are you?" was her instant reply. "How do you know?"

Benjamin pinched the soft skin on the inside of his wrist, squeezing as hard as he could.

"That won't wake you up," she said. "It's a pleasure zone. No pain nerves there. I can assure you of that."

"So, I am dreaming!"

Benjamin's self-inflicted pinch morphed into a circular massage of the loose skin. The pain did indeed feel nice. He felt moved from within.

"Dreaming? What is a dream?" Astraea asked. "The fragmented images of a troubled mind? Your eternal spirit out for a stroll while your body sleeps?"

She gazed at him with piercing introspection.

"How about nothing," Benjamin quipped. "You're not real. You'll be gone in a few seconds."

"I hardly think so. We have some work to do, don't we?"

Benjamin tried to imagine her away. She looked back at him and her shoulders went dark. There was a blackness about her now. She wasn't leaving, irrespective of what Benjamin might want.

"How come you are here all the time?" he asked. "Whenever I go to sleep you come to me. What do you want?"

"You!"

Astraea plunged her hand down into her loose top and pulled out a little package. It was black and round and looked like an extension of her hand. Benjamin recognized it straight away. Uphondo!

"How did you get that?" Benjamin asked. "It was locked in my room." Astraea ignored him and rolled the object over her open palm.

The paper fell to the floor. The rhino horn moved in her hand like molten licorice. It dripped through her fingers in large drops of slow-

moving sludge. As each globule hit the floor it splattered into bloody red patterns. The ground turned dark crimson. Benjamin tried to take a step but his shoes were tacky and warm with the coagulating goo.

"I'm finished with that life!" he shouted.

"But that life is not done with you," Astraea shot back. "You can't just walk away. Not after you stole this from Vanda's bag." The last of the rhino horn melted through her fingers onto the floor.

"I never stole it. It fell out."

"Did it?"

"I was protecting her, dammit!"

"Were you?"

"I don't need this in my life!" Benjamin jumped up and tried to open the door. Locked. He banged on it, shouting for help.

"Do you think you can get absolution without earning it?" Astraea calmly asked. "Life doesn't work that way."

She stood over him, whispering into his neck. She felt toxic.

"This is not life. It's not life," Benjamin whimpered. "This is a dream, you crazy thing. Now leave me alone."

"You crossed over here yourself, Benjamin," she said, pointing to the door. "None of that means anything. It is here where you live or die. With me. And we'll start with this."

She thrust another rhino horn toward him. He made no attempt to stop it and his chest swallowed it up as it hit him. He could feel it rattling inside and its warm death filling his veins. It felt as though death had enveloped him.

"There are fifty-eight of those," Astraea said.

"They're all mine," he mumbled to himself, crumpling to the floor. "Hell, I feel bad!"

"Do you?"

"Yes!" he yelled. "You crazy ghost. I'm sorry! Sorry for all those poor rhinos!"

"Well, that's a good place to start, Benjamin Rodd," Astraea said. "Down there in a heap on the floor, saying sorry. That's a good place."

She moved to the door and opened it. "But it's not nearly enough!"

"It's all I've got!" Benjamin shouted as he snapped awake.

SALVATORE BOLLINI WALKED IN LIKE A TRIUMPHANT general. Benjamin rubbed both his eyes. He'd been in the room for hours. Bollini tapped his clipboard with his pen and looked down. Benjamin was curled up in a ball on the ground. Bollini had him exactly where he wanted him, groveling like a frightened child.

"Sorry about the wait, Mr. Rodd," Bollini casually said. "This shouldn't take too long." He picked up one of the wooden chairs that were lying upside down.

"What's the time?" Benjamin demanded to know.

"A quarter to one," Bollini said with indifference.

"This is ridiculous," Benjamin shouted. "I've been here for hours. You had me locked in!"

Bollini was dismissive. "Would you like to lodge a complaint?" he asked. "How about directly to the Captain?" He paused for maximum effect as though he was interrogating the world's most wanted criminal.

"No, I thought not," he continued. "Now let's start with the little issue of a pearl and diamond brooch. It was reported stolen this morning."

Benjamin wasn't expecting that tack, but he knew how to deflect it. Stonewalling officers of the law was a skill he had mastered.

He looked at Bollini and then at the closed door. He wondered if Astraea was listening outside. He didn't know who could be worse, crazy Bollini or his haunting Astraea. He thought of Vanda. He hadn't been able to rescue her from the clutches of Captain Pizarro. *What if she didn't want to be rescued?* He wished he was in her arms and cursed Captain Pizarro under his breath.

"Let's get this over with," he curtly said.

4

PALERMO

By the time Benjamin woke up it was almost lunchtime. He'd had, way too little sleep. Bollini had kept him up most of the night, drilling him about his life. It felt at times that Bollini knew all about his past, even the rhino horns. He tried to pry information out, but Benjamin kept him going round in circles and Bollini discovered nothing of substance. It was exhausting.

The diesel engines of the ship were quiet. Benjamin got up and stumbled across the floor to open his curtains. He was expecting sunlight but outside it was raining and miserable. *So much for a sunny cruise on the Med*, he thought to himself.

The MSE Grande was berthed in the center of Palermo harbor. The quayside was still, with the odd umbrella twirling through the mist. There was little sign of life outside. Benjamin's cabin was eerily quiet. He gazed out, enjoying the moment of peace. Heaven knows he needed it, after his interrogation through the early hours of the morning. The packaged excursions ashore had already left.

Downtown Palermo stared back at him through the swirling haze. Miserable and bland, it's dirty grime was washed away fleck by fleck in the rain. The streets were brown and the terracotta roofs blurred into one another as the buildings crept inland as far as one could see.

Benjamin showered and got dressed. As he brushed his hair there was a knock on his door. Vanda stood there, hands on her hips.

"Finished with the Captain, are you?" Benjamin asked, inviting her in.

"A very good morning to you too," Vanda replied, as she sat down. "I hardly got started with the Captain to be honest."

"I'm sorry I didn't get to save you," Benjamin said. "That blasted security officer, Bollini is his name, had me locked up until four in the morning. I could have killed him."

"Just as well you didn't," Vanda replied. "One death a day is quite enough."

"What do you mean?" Benjamin asked, kicking the door shut.

"The bomb in Tunisia. It killed a crewman from another MSE ship," Vanda explained.

"I know," Benjamin said.

"They were two days ahead of us. He was found blown to pieces in the rubble. That's why the waiters last night were so jittery. He was one of their friends."

"I know," Benjamin said again.

Benjamin sat down on his bed as Vanda continued.

"The Captain swore me to secrecy about the details," she said. "He had to rush off after dinner because of it. Something about diverting to Malta and scrapping Tunisia." She rubbed her hands together and shivered.

"Malta sounds like a nice alternative. I've always wanted to go there." Benjamin opened the tiny cupboard under the TV set. "I'll put some coffee on. Tell me more about your Captain boyfriend."

* * *

"I WAS NEVER GOING TO SLEEP WITH HIM IF THAT'S WHAT you mean," Vanda said. She knew it been bothering Benjamin ever since Captain Pizarro appeared on the scene. "It was just a few drinks and some giggles."

"I suppose it was the uniform too," Benjamin said. "I saw your hand on his leg during pudding. Was it wood? Most of these sailors have a wooden leg somewhere, don't they?"

Vanda blushed. "Is that a streak of jealousy I detect?"

Benjamin poured some milk into the coffee cups.

"Sugar?"

Vanda topped up with a miniature bottle of Kahlua. As Benjamin handed her a napkin, he noticed that she was radiant. Pulling his hair back behind his ears where it belonged and straightening his trousers, he tried to hide his own exhausted state.

"Vanda, is there anything else you need to tell me?"

"About last night? I told you. Nothing happened," she said. "Captain Pizarro ditched me."

"No, not him. About what was in your bag!"

Vanda ignored him and licked some coffee off her finger. As she did so her jersey slipped up her arm.

"What on earth happened to your arm?" exclaimed Benjamin.

"Oh, nothing at all," Vanda replied, pulling her sleeve back down.

"Like hell!" Benjamin exploded. "It's bruised! Did Pizarro do that? I'll kill him!"

"Calm down, Ben. Javier is nothing but a gentleman. It was..."

Vanda sipped her coffee before continuing. "It was the waiter."

"I knew it! Our mugger! You and he are acquainted,

aren't you?"

"He served us dinner."

"And?"

"I don't know what you are implying Benjamin, but he attacked me. On the first night. When I went back to fetch my whiskey."

"What?" Benjamin put his hand on Vanda's shoulder. "What did he do?"

"He yelled incoherently about something and then he grabbed me. Tried to throttle me for some reason. He was all over me Ben. Look."

Vanda pulled her top down to expose her right shoulder and upper arm. There were bruises where the waiter had manhandled her. A tear welled up in her eye.

Benjamin hardly noticed the bruises. His eyes were drawn to her turquoise bra strap. It had sexy lace stitched along the edging. He flushed guiltily and roped his eyes back in.

"Why didn't you tell me yesterday?" he demanded to know.

"It had nothing to do with you, Ben."

"Did you report it to security?" Benjamin asked.

"I was going to, but the brooch, Benjamin. The one you took, I was so mad about it that I never told them about the waiter."

"You reported me to Bollini over the brooch?" Benjamin said, shaking his head in disbelief. "That makes sense. No wonder he targeted me last night. Why did you do that Vanda?"

"Maybe because you took it, Ben," Vanda snapped back. "Your ridiculous insinuations are starting to wear me out. Remember, I was accosted! I was mugged! My brooch was taken from me! And you keep implying I've done something wrong. If you hadn't had saved me yesterday, I probably wouldn't even be in here now."

Benjamin walked to the window and stared at the rain running down the glass. "You're right," He said. "I'm sorry."

"I understand you are under stress," Vanda softly replied. "Let's forget about Javier. Nothing will ever happen there. I promise."

"Did you have your bag with you?" Benjamin asked. "When our waiter 'friend' assaulted you."

"Of course."

"The bag he tried to steal in Rome? Was it the same bag, Vanda?"

"It's not left my side all holiday."

The bag still hung off her hip like an AK47 on a Cuban Guerrilla. She opened it. She couldn't understand where Benjamin was going with his line of questioning.

"There's nothing in here," she explained. "Just my usual stuff. Look. My diary, a raincoat, some makeup and my purse." She snapped the bag closed.

"There was something else in your bag," Benjamin said. "He must have slipped it in. Gosh, that now makes sense."

Vanda looked at Benjamin as though he were mad.

"You're saying he slipped something into my bag the other night and then he tried to take it back again in Rome? Common Ben. That's a bit far-fetched. Why would anyone do that? What was it anyway?" She laughed nervously.

"You have no idea what it could be then?" Benjamin asked. He surveyed her body language looking for any signs of lying. Vanda curled her legs up under her and leaned in toward him.

"No," she said with a straight face. "I have no clue what you are going on about."

Benjamin stood up flexing his shoulders. "Well, I've got it. It's right here in my safe."

"Did you take it together with my brooch?" Vanda asked sarcastically.

"It fell out of your bag when you were, you know?" Benjamin smiled at her. "I'm sorry," he continued, "I'm just tired and trying to get to the bottom of this."

"I wasn't totally drunk."

"I picked it up off the floor when you, when you... fell over then. When you fumbled for your keys and retired for the night."

"Yes, I did retire. I like that word. Retired."

Benjamin went to his cupboard, shaking his head. The safe was tucked away on the fourth shelf behind some t-shirts. He started jiggling the combination. "I've got it right here," he said. "This is what he was after and it's going to shock you."

"Your plane tickets?"

Vanda had followed him and was peering over his shoulder. Her chin playfully touched him. The safe was empty except for a blue folder and some cash. Nothing else. Benjamin stood there flummoxed, before exploding.

"It's gone! I can't believe it's gone," he yelled. "It was worth something too. I should know."

He slammed the safe door shut. It bounced back open with a ricochet and the blue folder lay motionless, as though it were mocking him. His mind swirled all over the place. He was sure he had not imagined that horn. *Wretched horn!* How he hated it. It plunged him back into his past. That dreadful past. Dr. Miller told him once it would catch up with him. Now he knew what she meant.

He felt violated. No one knew his safe combination. He had used his special code.

"Someone must have come in here while I was locked up last night," he eventually said.

"Who could that have been?" Vanda asked. "And who would want to anyway?"

"Bollini, the snoop! He's got all master codes! That

explains the questions he was asking me. He's taken it."

Benjamin sank back into the chair rubbing his hair. One of the things he couldn't tolerate was people messing with his personal stuff. Dr. Miller had told him once that he was a hypocrite because of what he had taken from others, but he didn't see it that way. No one had got hurt, he had said. Mary did, she had responded.

Vanda put her hand on his back, rubbing it.

"The mugger was after my money," she said. "There was nothing else. Look your safe is empty. Maybe you're imagining this, Ben?"

Benjamin crinkled away from her. His eyes narrowed as his potential windfall faded away in his mind. That rhino horn would have been like a five-card-Charlie in a game of blackjack. Heaven knows he needed it. *And Bollini was now onto it! That crooked La Madama might try and blackmail me. Or worse?* He breathed out slowly, reminding himself that it wasn't Vanda's fault.

"I can't believe you reported me to Bollini," was all he could say.

He finished his coffee in silence, slowly calming down. Stress often made him highly focused. It was a mental state that he hadn't planned to be in on day two of his cruise.

Vanda held his gaze. She seemed genuinely puzzled. Benjamin realized that she was telling the truth. She knew nothing about what had been in his safe or in her handbag. He thought that she must be very confused. First her trinket and now this. Dr. Miller would know how to handle the girl. He wished she was there. He was dead tired. He rubbed his red swollen eyes again and went outside onto the balcony.

Vanda remained inside. She heard him talking to someone on his cell phone. He eventually came back inside with a spring in his step.

"We need to get off this ship before Bollini does anything

stupid," he said.

"Are you mad?"

"He could arrest us!"

"What have we possibly done wrong?"

"The stuff that was in my safe, Vanda! The stuff I found in your bag. It's illegal you know."

"What stuff?" Vanda asked. "The 'stuff' that wasn't in your safe."

"It was worth a fortune," Benjamin answered, ignoring her sarcasm.

"Thank goodness," Vanda said, throwing up her arms. "We're going to be rich."

"Listen, Vanda. There's this place called Mondello, just outside the City. It's a quick ride from here. I've got a friend there. He can help."

"Is that who you were talking to just now?"

"I knew him from long ago. We used to do business together. He said he could help."

"Will we be back before four?" Vanda asked.

"I'll get you back if you want. Just come and hear him out. He knows about all this stuff. He'll tell us what to do."

"You know I don't believe anything you're saying," Vanda said.

"I fully understand, but we will end up in trouble if we stay here."

"I guess it is rather exciting and I always love an adventure."

"We'll be back before the ship leaves," Benjamin assured her. Inside he was already planning how they'd 'conveniently' be late and miss the departure. *I have to leave all my clothes here, or else she'll suspect*, he thought. He grabbed the blue folder and the cash from his safe and stuffed it into his pants.

Vanda threw Benjamin his hat. "I'm coming along only because I want to see some of the island. Can't stand to be cooped up in here anymore. Maybe we can grab a drink some-where." As the door closed, she continued. "I have no frig-ging idea what you're talking about though."

* * *

THE TAXI CURLED ITS WAY EASTWARD THROUGH A MISTY Palermo. "What's this Mondello place like?" Vanda asked.

"On a normal day, it's the best of Sicilian bliss," Benjamin said. "Silky beaches stretching out like golden sickles. Tourist shops. The rocky mountains in the North West."

"You've spent some time there, I assume?"

"I loved it! The sea looks like God himself painted a splat-tered blue masterpiece. You'll see. Loungers and sun tanning chairs everywhere. Little Tavernas selling the best wine between here and France. Young couples lying in their bathing suits, soaking up the sun."

"Was that you? When you were younger?" Vanda asked.

"I was like a dark Italian Demigod," Benjamin proudly joked. "Toned, a thick black mop on my head. I'd spend days patrolling up and down, searching for the Venus of my dreams."

"Did you ever find her?"

"No! Life got in the way."

"It looks like the weather might be doing that today," Vanda observed.

It was no normal afternoon in Mondello. There was a major storm warning for later on and it had already started to pour with rain. No one was outside and the loungers had been fastened down with ropes and stakes. The tourist shops were closing early and the blue palettes that normally graced the coast were morphing into angry shades of sepia.

Benjamin and Vanda arrived as the last restaurant on the strip banged closed its door. The wind had picked up and the pressure was dropping. Some old plastic bags were two-stepping around the fountain in front of the local Hotel as the wind courted them with combinations of hostility and grace. Benjamin sensed it was going to be a big one.

Their taxi driver asked if he should wait. Vanda told him not to, as she paid him. They'd catch another taxi back if they needed to. The driver was thankful and drove off with a skid.

Benjamin pulled his collar up around his neck. Vanda noticed, for the first time, that he had a jagged scar extruding up from his wrist. It hadn't been stitched up well. Benjamin covered it when he realized she had noticed. He didn't like people to see his bush scars. It resulted in questions being asked and he didn't want to have to explain to anyone. Except to Dr. Miller. She kind of understood.

"It's about three roads back from here," Benjamin said pointing into the heart of the old town. "Chatunga's place was up there somewhere."

He glanced at Vanda for the hundredth time. She looked vibrant and sexy in the drizzling wind and he couldn't keep his tired eyes off her. He, on the other hand, looked as though he had gone through a rugby scrum.

They scrambled up the cobbled lanes avoiding puddles and overhangs. Old broken copper gutters aimed their water pistols at their luckless victims passing beneath and baptized Benjamin and Vanda as they ran past. By the time they reached an old dilapidated archway off one of the side roads they were both drenched.

Benjamin knocked confidently on the oak door of a building that looked as though it hadn't been maintained since General Patton rolled past in 1943. The stone walls were two feet thick. Benjamin banged three times before he heard someone scuffling on the other side. Still, no one opened and then the scuffling stopped. There was complete silence except for the water dripping. It was a bad silence.

"That's odd," Benjamin said. "Chatunga should be around here somewhere. I confirmed with him that we were coming."

Benjamin tried the door handle to see if it was locked. It wasn't.

"Don't ever do this yourself," he warned Vanda. "At least not in Sicily. You'll get your ass shot right off. Sicilians hate strangers opening their doors."

"Thanks for the advice Mr big-shot,' she replied. "This Chatunga fellow? Is he also from Africa? Maybe he's napping?" She still thought that their afternoon sojourn was nothing more than a fun crazy adventure, with the man she was starting to really like.

"Zimbabwean," Benjamin replied, slowly prying the door open.

"I hope the Zimbabweans aren't as bad as the Sicilians and your ass stays in one piece," Vanda innocently said.

Benjamin didn't have a chance to say anything else. A pick handle came flying through the gap he had opened. He should have listened to his own advice. It hit him dead on the head. Fortunately, it also snagged on a security chain attached to the door frame, deflecting the full impact. He was very lucky for that chain.

He stumbled back onto one knee, holding his head. Vanda froze. The door swung open and a burly man dressed in a dark raincoat rushed out, pushing Vanda aside. She fell back into the mud outside. Neither of them saw his face and before they could gather themselves, he had disappeared around the corner.

"Whoah!" Vanda yelled. "I thought you were joking about the Sicilians." She stumbled to her feet. "Are you alright?"

She could hear watery footsteps running away in the distance. She lifted her head, walked up the two steps and looked through the open door of the house. Inside the dim room, she could see someone. She assumed it was Benjamin's friend, this Chatunga fellow whom Benjamin had been harping on about all afternoon. He looked dark enough. He was splayed across a couch lying on his back. His face looked an overripe peach after a bunch of thugs had played soccer with it. Beneath him, a pool of blood was edging its way forward, centimeter by sticky centimeter. Benjamin groaned behind her.

"Get inside! Quick!" he said.

Vanda felt her gut dropping through the threshold.

* * *

She remained surprisingly calm though. It felt like slow motion. She propped Benjamin up as he stumbled into the room and kicked the door shut behind them. He was dazed and had a gash on the side of his head. He over-reacted as he usually did and started muttering nonsense about Astraea.

Vanda thought him either loopy or concussed. She didn't pay much attention to what he was saying. She looked around the room again. They were in a dirty lounge that had a bar running down the one wall. It stank of stale cigarettes and was an eclectic mess from hell.

She scrunched up her nose. She had been in plenty of places similar to this, but could never get used to them. Benjamin's friend groaned and then dropped back into unconsciousness.

"Ben!" Vanda shouted, "He moved. Here, help me."

Benjamin ignored his own sore head and rushed over.

"Who exactly is this man?" Vanda demanded to know.

Benjamin did his best to explain as he tried to wake his old friend up. Vanda grabbed a half empty bottle of cheap whiskey from the bar counter and took a swig as she listened.

* * *

"CHATUNGA MPOFU IS HIS REAL NAME," BENJAMIN explained.

"Funny name?"

"He prefers Chatunga Lazarov though."

"That sounds familiar? Lazarov? I know it from somewhere?" Vanda said.

"Who hasn't?" Benjamin replied. "The Lazarov name is all over the news. Old Basil Lazarov owns half the Med. A football club in the UK too."

"Is he the one they are charging for bribery? The eighty-year-old guy?"

"Bribery is the least of his problems."

"The papers said he was Russian mafia or something?" Vanda said.

"Bulgarian," Benjamin replied. "He's a frigging Bulgarian."

"I read about him on the plane over here." Vanda gasped. "Benjamin, this isn't him is it?"

"Hell no," Benjamin replied. "This is Chatunga, not Basil. Basil Lazarov is the crook everyone knows. This is just his boy!"

"That's not good!" Vanda exclaimed. Benjamin grinned as he wiped Chatunga's head.

"Relax Vanda. They haven't spoken to each other in decades. Basil ditched him in Africa when he was 14. Lost interest in his poor Zimbabwean mother. Apparently ran off and married a red-headed heiress from Moscow. He left Chat's Mum to die in misery after he tired of her."

"What was Basil Lazarov doing in Africa?" Vanda asked. "He's one of those old oil magnates, isn't he?"

"He wasn't always," Benjamin explained. "He was just a young officer back then. You know? The Rhodesian liberation wars in the 70's. The Soviets sent him out as an adviser. Probably a punishment for the trouble-causer he was. He made the most of it though, sowing his oats everywhere."

"Chatunga?"

"Yip, my friend here was the result of scandal and love in the deep African bush. Old man Lazarov ditched him with a handful of rubles and a kick up the ass. Told him he never wanted to hear from him again. Ever."

"But he's a billionaire?" Vanda exclaimed.

"A bent billionaire. Trust me, he never made his fortune from oil."

CHATUNGA LAZAROV SUDDENLY WHEEZED IN BENJAMIN'S arms. "Hand me that bottle," Benjamin said. Vanda had her last swig and handed it over. Benjamin poured it over the gash in Chatunga's head.

"You care for him?" Vanda said.

"He saved my butt a few times," Benjamin replied.

"What's he doing here in Mondello?"

Benjamin explained that Chatunga had been in Sicily for over a decade. He'd smuggled himself over on some cock and bull story of being a refugee. Which in fact, he was, because he had had to flee from Zimbabwe when it got too hot on the ground. He'd been smuggling cigarettes, diamonds, and endangered animals ever since his father ditched him; and the President of Zimbabwe was cleaning out the crooks who weren't buying him 'cooldrinks'. Chatunga had fled with the shirt on his back and a suitcase full of US dollars.

"Is that how you met him?" Vanda asked. "Smuggling?"

"I bought a gun from him. In the Zambezi Valley. I did mention that I was a hunter once, didn't I?"

"Maybe you should stop talking, Benjamin?"

"He's a friend," Benjamin said. "I trust him."

"I don't!" Vanda exclaimed. "Just look at him! Look at this

place! It's vile. These walls look like a million caterpillars have been smeared over them. Benjamin, I'm scared."

* * *

CHATUNGA COUGHED AGAIN. BENJAMIN PROPPED UP HIS old friend's neck with a dirty cushion. His own head throbbed and he could feel the blood starting to congeal down the back of his ear.

"Chat, my old friend! This is becoming a bad habit." Benjamin half-joked. "Isn't this just how I left you last time?"

"Roddy?" Chatunga replied softly. "Is that you?" He wiped his head with the cushion. "You were late again, mate!"

His eyes turned wild as his senses returned. They jumped around the room like the silver ball in a pinball machine. He stopped on Vanda.

"*Eish!*" he spluttered with saliva and blood spraying from his lips. He coughed again, which made it worse. His eyes darted from Vanda to Benjamin and back again. He tried to mouth the words, *'does she know?'*. Benjamin flicked his head negatively, hoping Vanda wouldn't notice.

"He's delusional," Vanda said. "Ben, why are we here? And what the heck has he got to do with anything? I don't like this." As her words tumbled out, she held a dirty rag to Chatunga's mouth, wiping away the mess, but also part smothering his speech.

"He can help us. We worked together," Benjamin said. "Long ago. It's a long story."

"You should tell me," insisted Vanda.

"Later," Benjamin replied. He sat back, looking at a shard from his past. Chatunga dropped his bruised chin onto his chest, utterly exhausted. He was barefoot and had a stained vest on. He desperately grabbed Benjamin's shirt.

"Gotta get me out of here," he gasped. "... big...red haired Lazar..." He dropped back babbling incoherently.

"You're going to be fine, my friend," Benjamin replied. "We've stopped the bleeding."

"Bugger my bleeding, Roddy! You, you gotta get out of here. With her."

Chatunga pointed at Vanda. His voice was barely audible. "They'll be back if they recognized you," he added. "You were after all pretty famous once upon a time."

He unsuccessfully reached toward Vanda and then shook Benjamin by his shirt. He started to moan again about the big red-haired man, but he stopped as Vanda gently pushed him back onto the couch. Something bounced on the tiled floor and he fell back in a semi-conscious heap.

"Give him a few more minutes," Benjamin said. "He'll wake up properly soon enough."

"What type of name is 'Chatunga'?" Vanda blurted. "Is it code or something?" She peeked out the curtain, checking the rainy lane outside. It looked as quiet as Mars.

"It's a Shona name," Benjamin explained. "His mother gave it to him. It means 'fighter'. His father hated it."

"You said he uses his father's name, the Lazarov name? Why?"

"Only in public, he does. It's leverage in our world."

"Our world?"

"Your world as well now," Benjamin said. Vanda turned pale.

"Chatunga hates his East European family," Benjamin explained. "But the Lazarov name is famous. It opens doors."

"Infamous, you mean," Vanda said quietly.

"I remember when we used to work together," Benjamin said. "Me and Chatunga here. He used to always boast, *'Baz Laz is my Father!'* He would boast about it in his Bulgarian

African accent. *'Do you know who you're talking to? Do you know the boss? Do you know who I am, you mother?'* he would say."

"This is not impressing me, Ben," Vanda replied.

"Hardly anyone took him seriously," Benjamin continued. "He only survived because no one was prepared to touch the son of a notorious Bulgarian mobster. The fact that he had been disowned and was the laughing stock of the entire Mediterranean underworld, did not mean that his blood wasn't Lazarov."

"Can we trust him?"

"I trust him, Vanda. And I need you to trust me."

"Shhh," Vanda said, "He's coming around again."

Chatunga started moaning again. This time he was calmer.

"We don't have much time," he whispered after a few minutes. "They had my line bugged. They heard everything you told me, Roddy."

"But why this?" Benjamin asked. "Over a simple phone call? One little stick of the stuff? It doesn't make sense. You said you would help us."

"It wasn't just one simple phone call they listened to, mate."

"Don't tell me you told someone?" Benjamin growled. "You thought you could broker a stupid deal? Didn't you?"

Chatunga lips curled into a grin.

"You and your stupid hair-brained schemes!" Benjamin shouted. "You haven't changed at all, have you?"

"But I did save your life once, didn't I?" Chatunga replied.

"Can someone tell me what is going on!" Vanda interjected. The men ignored her.

"Listen, Roddy," Chatunga said, suddenly getting dead serious. "I made some calls to the Italians. They want in. It's just like the old days. I'm not 100% sure of all the facts but I know it's on your ship. A whole stack of it. A fortune!"

He pulled Benjamin down to within inches of his face and gasped. "...Uphondo!" he said. "Lots of Uphondo!"

"Since when did the Italians get involved with this business?" Benjamin anxiously asked.

"You have been gone for way too long, my friend," Chatunga said. "They're always involved once the stakes get high. They own this part of the world. Just reclaiming what's rightfully theirs"

"A fortune you say?"

Chatunga nodded and smiled.

"Vanda's little piece was just part of it?"

"Just a sample! Probably nicked by one of the dicks involved."

"I don't know, Chat?" Benjamin said. "One little sample I thought I could handle. A whole shipload? It's too risky! I can't go back! And I think the ship's security know anyway. That's why I'm here. Getting away from their head of Security, Bollini."

"You promised that you'd get me back to the ship, Benjamin." Vanda angrily interrupted. "I'm not running away from anything!" The men ignored her again.

"You need to go back," Chatunga said. "I'm told that this Bollini fellow is just a blackmailing opportunist. This is your big chance, my friend. Your big chance to pick off where you left. In the big league. Go and seize the day. You always were a good broker. Go figure out what is going down and then let us know."

"Us?"

"Me! I meant me," Chatunga said. He sank back into the couch again. "They have been tapping my calls for weeks now. I don't know why? When you called and told me about what you had found, they were here within twenty minutes. Beat the crap out of me, they did. Thank goodness you arrived when you did."

Benjamin's past bumped into him like a bus and his heart sank. It had been a long time. *'Uphondo'* he hated the word. It meant horn in Zulu. It punched him in the gut. He had suspected that something bigger was going on, ever since finding the rhino horn in Vanda's bag. Chatunga now confirmed it.

"Who?" Benjamin asked. "Who is *'they'*?"

"Who do you think?" his friend answered.

Benjamin went white. "Your father?"

"The one and only Bulgarian bum," Chatunga said. "It's him all right! Can't you feel it? Just like old times, hey?"

Benjamin swallowed back vomit. His head pounded. *Basil Lazarov? He was a dangerous man, notwithstanding the fact that Chatunga was his bastard son. Those Bulgarians had got him locked up. They'd spilled the beans to the Vietnamese police, and then stolen his life away. He hated them!*

"Your father often had a hand this racket," he said calmly. He caressed his old friend's bloodied head for a second before embarrassment stopped him. "But, I thought we had retired from this game?"

"Speak for yourself," Chatunga replied, coughing up phlegm. "What are you doing here anyway?"

"Holiday," Ben answered honestly. "That is all. A holiday. One last innocent nice holiday!"

"I'm sure it is," Chatunga chuckled.

Vanda cried out from the window, "there's someone out there!"

The men finally seemed to notice that Vanda was in the room with them. She had overheard everything they had said to each other. "You are now as much part of this as we are," Chatunga said pointing at her. "Now, my *sawdy*. Get me my *sawdy*, Ben." He glanced to a wardrobe behind the bar counter.

Benjamin walked over to the cupboard as though he had

been there the day before. He rubbed his hand down the side and fiddled with a wooden latch. A panel fell away revealing a gap big enough to hide a hockey stick. Or a gun. Inside lay an aging double-bore shotgun. Its barrel had been expertly sawed off at the one-third mark.

"You remembered," Chatunga said, trying to grin.

"Benjamin!" Vanda cried. Her face changed color to a bright red. "Who the hell are you?" She took a step toward them.

"I'll explain later," Benjamin calmly said.

He placed the shotgun in his old friend's hands. "Right now we have to get out of here in one piece. If we want to live. Chatunga can you sit up?"

His friend nodded his head. "I'll be ready next time," he said, cradling the shotgun as though it were a baby in swaddling clothes. "I'm feeling better already with this here on my lap."

Benjamin could tell his friend was going to be OK. He just needed a doctor to patch him up. Zimbabweans were tough ones.

He went to the door, pulling Vanda's arm as he pushed past.

"Vanda, I promise you," he said. "I don't know what is going down here yet, but I will soon."

His voice was calming, as though he knew exactly what to do. Vanda, surprisingly, felt safe in the moment. She held onto his grip and went with him.

As they opened the door, Benjamin hesitated for a second, looking back at Chatunga. He looked like a dog that had lost a fight and was being abandoned on the street to his fate. He stood up and swayed unstably. The shotgun dropped out of his hands and Benjamin grimaced, hoping it wouldn't go off. It fell dead on the floor.

"Let's get him to a hospital," Benjamin said. "I can't leave him. Not again. Not like that."

He picked up the shotgun and handed it to Vanda. "Here. See that bag over there," he said pointing to an old canvas duffel bag that was on top of the cupboard. "Put the shotgun in it."

Vanda did what she was told. She picked it up as though it were a dead roach.

"No, it's not loaded," Benjamin said. "Best you get some ammo though. Over there." He pointed to a pile of birdshot rounds at the bottom of the cupboard. Vanda nervously scooped them up in her spare hand.

"Put them in the bag," Benjamin instructed. "We might need them later. I'll get Chatunga to his car."

"What's the combo lock number on this zip?" Vanda asked.

"Four zero's," Chatunga answered. "But best you keep it unlocked. Just in case."

Vanda was glad that they were not leaving Chatunga behind. *He might die left alone*, she thought.

"Why aren't we going to the police," she asked. "Surely they could sort this whole mess out?"

"You are in the middle of this, I'm afraid," Benjamin said. "Those thugs think you've got some of their little illicit cargo and they'll be coming to get it back. Guaranteed! We report this, we all go down. Your bag remember? It was in your bag. The police will put the pieces together quickly and the mob will want to get rid of the loose ends. We cannot win if we go the cops. Best we sort this ourselves."

"Good Heavens, Benjamin," Vanda exclaimed. "What have I got you into?"

"It's not your fault," Benjamin said, glad that she wasn't blaming him. "You can stay here if you want and have no further part of this."

"No way!" Vanda snapped. "Look what they did to your friend. My papers are all on the ship!" She paused and gained her composure. "Benjamin," she said slowly. "I know how to look after myself. I'm going back with you."

Sure you do? Benjamin sniggered to himself. He picked up his old friend and they moved outside into the rain.

"His van," Benjamin said. "It's in that shed, over there. He usually leaves the keys in the ignition." They climbed in, securing Chatunga into the front passenger seat. Vanda sat in the back. Benjamin started up the engine.

As he floored the accelerator, a shot burst through the windscreen. Vanda screamed. "Go!" she yelled. "Drive!"

No one was hit. The bullet had made a hole but the glass didn't shatter. The sound of it hitting the van, echoed around the cabin. It was surreal, like the movies. Except for the adrenalin. That was real. They couldn't tell where the shot had come from. No one said anything as Benjamin's foot pumped the controls and the van sped off toward Palermo.

THE WORLD LOOKED ALL WHITE TO BENJAMIN. HE HEARD THE roar of a stampede. He could see Astraea and she was coming toward him riding an animal. She looked like the Beast of the Apocalypse. He was in a tunnel, and at the far end was a bright hole. The edges of his sight were jagged. He drove as fast as he could, without noticing where he was going. Astraea was left behind. She stood in the road, breathing in the fear.

BENJAMIN'S ILLUSIONARY PANIC DROPPED AWAY AS SOME loud blasts roared through the air.

Vanda was firing off the shotgun! Two short bangs. It looked as though she knew exactly what to do. It looked as though letting rip with a sawn-off shotgun was what she did every day. She no longer held it like a dead roach but gripped it like a pro. Someone yelled in the distance.

The van buzzed around the corner and it went quiet again. "They were on foot," Vanda calmly said. "It's clear."

The main Palermo road was about two kilometers away. Earlier on in the day, Benjamin had seen a sign with a red cross on it close to the harbor. It was a clinic and that's where he was heading.

Once they reached the main road, Benjamin was confident that they would make it back in one piece. He was back in the present again. Alert and thinking. He made up his mind to dump the van outside the hospital. They'd find Chatunga easily enough and then he and Vanda would slip back onto the ship in one piece. There was no way he was staying in Sicily. He checked his watch and wiped away the blood on his cheek as he steered.

He turned to look at Vanda. She was sitting with the smoking shotgun on her lap. She was calm, looking straight ahead like a Hindu Goddess! Peaceful, pure, and noble. Her skin looked flawless and her posture was perfect. It elongated her slender neck. She was tapping her finger on the gun barrel as though it were an old friend. A tiny bead of sweat trickled down her nose. A swell rose in her chest, accentuating her breasts. Benjamin noticed her nipples straining through her top. In the moment he thought she was the best thing he had ever seen in his life and he wanted her more than anything.

"Where did you learn to shoot like that?" he asked.

"What exactly is Uphondo?" she replied. "You may as well tell me because back on the ship, everything I want to know is just a click away."

They both sat in silent awkwardness. Chatunga had blacked out again in his seat. The rain pelted the window and it ran in through the bullet hole.

"OK, I'll tell you," Benjamin eventually said. "Just try not to judge, OK?" He took a deep breath. "Rhino horn. It's Rhino horn. The most valuable thing God made between here and Beijing."

"How could you?" Vanda gasped. "That's not frigging hunting. It's poaching! It's wrong!"

"It's complicated."

"No, it's not!" They sat in silence as they sped on.

* * *

AN HOUR LATER BENJAMIN AND VANDA STOOD IN THE LINE to get back on board the MSE Grande. The tension between them had eased. After winding around in circles for 20 twenty minutes to ensure they weren't being followed, they had parked in front of the dockside clinic, leaving Chatunga propped up on the front seat. The last thing they heard him mumble was that he'd be in touch. Benjamin had dropped an anonymous call to tell the nurses that there was an injured man outside who needed their attention.

"He'll be fine," Benjamin said. "He just needs some painkillers and a strong Sicilian nurse."

"What's the difference?" joked Vanda.

It was chaotic on the dockside. Most of the guests had arrived back at the last minute. The storm was starting to reveal its angry side. The rain spat in at 60 degrees and even umbrellas that were strong enough to withstand the gusts were useless at keeping their owners dry. Most of the guests were horsing around laughing, trying to avoid getting completely drenched. Some kids were kicking around in the puddles. Benjamin pushed past them, hoping that in the rainy chaos, they could slip on board inconspicuously. Their next stop was Malta, an expeditious change of plan from Tunisia.

Benjamin looked up. "It's going to be a turbulent tonight," he said, "with the storm closing in."

Vanda pulled his hat down over his ears. Most of the blood from his earlier smack on the head had been diluted in the rain, but Vanda wanted to make sure that no-one noticed. *They might think he had been out fighting again.* Benjamin insisted it was just a scratch.

Vanda was relaxed. Shooting the shotgun off had strangely dissipated her nerves. She was elevated onto a hypnotic plain the moment she had pulled the trigger, and she had not yet come back down. She stood aloof, highly attuned to her surroundings.

Benjamin was seeing less and less of a ditsy whiskey loving working girl in her. *I think she's going to be wonderful sober,* he joked to himself. It was wishful thinking.

They eventually got onto the gangplank leading up to a door on the side of the ship. Dwarfed by the magnificence of the massive cruise ship, they felt like bugs climbing into Noah's Ark. Benjamin looked around for Salvatore Bollini. He wanted to look him in the eye again. This time to decipher if he had indeed been snooping in his safe. He was nowhere to be seen. *The coward is hiding,* Benjamin thought.

"There's no security around," Benjamin said quietly to Vanda.

"That's good."

She said it too soon. As they stepped through the steel door they saw a counter up ahead. It was manned by a full security detail. The passengers, who were crammed in like sardines, were passing through one at a time.

"Oh, crap," Vanda said. "A metal detector!"

"Keep calm, we'll be OK."

"Like hell, we will," she gasped, "I've still got the bag with me, Benjamin. Remember?" Benjamin had forgotten about the canvas duffel bag. The one they had taken for the shotgun.

"Please don't tell me that you have that darn thing in there?" Benjamin said. "Oh, no!"

"What the heck do you think is in the bag? Bottles of plum jam?"

"What were you thinking?" he snapped. "We're trapped here like hogs in the slaughterhouse."

He instantly regretted his obnoxious behavior. He could picture Dr. Miller shaking her head at him in disgust.

There were about twenty people in front of them and they only had a few minutes to make a plan. The line was slowly ticking forward. It felt like a time bomb counting down to explode.

"I'll dump it," Vanda said.

"No. They'll see and think it's something bad. Besides they have cameras. Here, give it to me."

"It's not my fault!" she said under her breath. "There were no metal detectors or security checks on the first two days of the cruise. How was I meant to know?"

They could hear one of the crew members explaining why the extra precautions had been put in place. She said because of the bomb in Tunisia, they had stepped up their security. Captain's orders. Vanda was relieved to know that they had not brought out the metal detectors because of them. She initially had thought that maybe someone had seen her blasting away with the shotgun, and reported it. It had after all been a public street. She thanked heaven for the rain and the wind. Everyone had been indoors. Her adrenalin suddenly faded and she felt weak. *I don't even know who I shot at,* she thought to herself.

They were still trapped like lab rats. The queue edged slowly forward. Vanda had a trickle of sweat down her nose again but it blended into the raindrops that had pelted her outside.

"Give me the bag." Benjamin insisted. "I'll take the heat

on this. I'll say I bought it in town. At one of those old junk shops."

His mind meandered all over the place as he inched closer and closer to the security checkpoint. "I'll say I didn't know it was real or live, or whatever. I'll say I bought it as an ornament. I can't even speak Sicilian anyway." His voice squeaked.

"Keep it down," Vanda said. "People are going to notice!"

Her eyes scanned for escape routes in the tiny space. She couldn't find any.

"How will we explain the cartridges?" she asked, "There must be fifty of them in here. Are those also ornaments, Ben?"

"Dammit. Did you bring those too?"

Benjamin was starting to recede back into a state of nervous oblivion. He balked at a fleeting thought of Astraea. She was starting to make an appearance whenever he zoned out. He wasn't good in confined spaces. He had never been. He wished he was 400 meters away behind a telescopic lens. Then he could do his thing. Dr. Miller glared at him again.

"Give me the bag anyway," he demanded, tugging at the strap on her shoulder. "I'll take the heat."

The security crew was looking straight at them now. They had been trained to spot suspicious behavior and Benjamin was losing it with his sudden panic attack.

"Give it to me now," Benjamin grunted under his breath.
"No!"

Vanda pulled out of the queue and gestured to the crewman that she was going back out.

"I left something on the quay," she said calmly. She retraced her steps back, past the people behind her. Space was tight. She was back at the metal external door and about to escape when a loud voice boomed out. Head of Security, Salvatore Bollini had finally appeared on the scene from nowhere.

"Madam. Stop!"

Vanda's heart seized. She kept smiling though and pretended nothing was wrong.

"I left a package down there," she said, pointing towards the taxi rank. "My shopping bags. I'll be five minutes max." Benjamin had stepped aside, breathing heavily against the passage wall. He was trembling. He hated authority. He hated the police.

"Madam!" Bollini shouted, sternly. "You will stop and bring me that canvas bag. Now please?" There was a tear in his coat and mud on his shoes. Benjamin thought he looked very different from the pristine sadist he had been the previous night.

"Why?" Vanda asked impertinently. "I don't understand? Have I done something wrong?"

Bollini was angry and agitated. And soaked. He signaled for them to stop letting new passengers in and quickly ushered the few bewildered faces around them through without even looking at the x-ray screen. Vanda dared not move. Eventually, only Benjamin and Vanda were left in the entrance to the hold. They were trapped. Salvatore Bollini stood to attention and shouted in his excited Italian voice. "If you don't bring me that canvas bag now, I will be compelled to take it by force. And that my dear madam will not be pleasant."

Bollini pulled a gun out from his holster. It was an electric Taser gun.

"Now just one minute," Benjamin said, holding out his arm toward Bollini. "No need for that."

"Stand aside!" Bollini ordered.

"I will do no such thing," Benjamin said, his courage swiftly returning at the site of a weapon. "This is harassment!"

As he said it, he made the fatal mistake of touching Bollini's shoulder. *Rule number in jail: don't ever touch the jailer.* It was too late to remember. Without any warning, ten thousand volts jarred into his body and he fell in a contorted and shaking mess onto the steel floor. The last thing he heard before blacking out and nearly peeing himself was Vanda's shout.

Bollini stepped forward like John Wayne and stood proudly over the comatose man at his feet. Benjamin lay in a fetal position. Bollini gestured with his finger for Vanda to approach him with her bag. He had every intention of tasering her too if she did the slightest thing wrong. Vanda felt powerless. She walked slowly toward him without arguing. Her hands were shaking.

At that moment another large form filled the steel door and the room went silent.

"Stop! What is going on here?" The voice was familiar to Vanda. Captain Pizarro had walked in to inspect their new security measures. He immediately noticed Vanda's tears.

"Bollini!" he shouted. "What have you done?" He looked long and hard at Benjamin, almost dead on the floor, and then glared at Bollini. Vanda sniffed.

Bollini instantly turned pale. He had not been expecting the Captain, who should have been up on the bridge by then. He had overstepped the mark and he knew it.

"He attacked me, sir," Bollini stammered.

"You've had it in for him since last night," Vanda replied.

"You told me he was a thief," Bollini said.

"We're together now, Mr. Bollini," Vanda shouted. "You shot him and there is no excuse for that. Should we get the camera footage reviewed?"

Bollini had no idea how he was going to explain away his heavy-handedness. It wasn't even Benjamin who had been holding the canvas bag. Vanda had it.

"But he touched me," Bollini whimpered.

Captain Pizarro loomed huge, six foot six with an overpowering presence in the confined space. He immediately took control of his officers. His face puffed red with anger, as Bollini retreated backward.

Vanda saw her gap and took it like a pro. The situation needed rapid cooling. *Maybe she could even win Bollini over?* She put her amateur acting classes from college into practice - the distraught maiden was her specialty.

"Oh, Captain," she said stepping in front of Bollini. "I'm so glad you are here to help us. I was looking for you this morning. I'm very scared. It might have been a mistake."

She pointed to Benjamin lying on the floor. "I think he did actually touch Mr. Bollini's Tasergun. Maybe Mr. Bollini wasn't at fault. Maybe?"

She glanced at Bollini who had turned white. She knew that sometimes one has to pet a growling dog so that it doesn't bite you. Bollini was as good a dog as any! She hoped he enjoyed his ear scratch.

"But sir," Bollini said. "I...?"

At first, he was unsure what to do but then quickly decided to go along with Vanda to save his sorry ass. He incoherently tried to explain how it was all just an accident.

"Good Lord. Bollini!" the Captain said. "Get this man to the medical center now. Common. Move it, man!"

Captain Pizarro knew a potential lawsuit when he saw one.

"Captain, I'm so scared," Vanda said, still acting. She held her hand up to her head. "This is so tragic. Oh, Javier."

"Hold onto me, Vanda," Pizarro instructed. Vanda was glad to see that he remembered her name from the previous evening. "Here give me your bag to carry," he suggested.

Bingo! Thought Vanda.

Vanda handed him the duffel bag with its shotgun and cartridges tucked snugly inside. The captain threw it casually over his shoulder and walked Vanda to the metal detector. He stepped around it as any officer would and Vanda stumbled through it. There was no alarm. Benjamin was being carried by Bollini and two other crew down the corridor. He was still unconscious.

"Bollini!" Captain Pizarro yelled after him. The security head stopped and looked back like a child caught with his hand in the cookie jar. "I'm watching you. Now give that man the best possible medical treatment. We'll talk later. You do a report. Go. Go."

He tapped his nose. Vanda noticed their obtuse signaling to each other but pretended she didn't. She just wanted to get away from the problem of the gun in the duffel bag. Bollini nodded his head like jello pudding.

Captain Pizarro turned to Vanda as Bollini disappeared down the corridor with Benjamin.

"Vanda," he said, "I'm sorry for what happened. On behalf of MSE Grande, we will offer you and your friend the best possible compensation for this terrible mistake. Imagine. Firing off a Taser by mistake?"

The Captain, sized Vanda up to see if there might be a bigger problem. He didn't think they were insured for Tasering guests by mistake.

"I think I'll go with Mr. Rodd," she said. "He'll hopefully wake up soon. I'll help him to his room. Is that alright, Captain?"

Pizarro reluctantly nodded. It was difficult for him to argue against Vanda's sweet southern drawl, it was the sexiest voice he had heard on that trip.

"I'll personally get this sent to your room then," Pizarro said. He tapped the canvas bag on his shoulder. "What's in this, by the way? It feels heavy."

"A sword," Vanda said calmly, looking him deadpan in the eye. "A medieval sword."

"Oh, Excellent," Pizarro replied. "Can I see?" He started to unzip the bag.

"It's just a fake," Vanda shouted. "Nothing really. I bought it at the market in town. Completely blunt of course. It's for my mantelpiece back home."

"Let me see," Pizarro said, "Maybe I can tell you what type it is."

"It's wrapped up!" Vanda said firmly. "In bubble-wrap and paper. There's nothing to see and I don't want the packaging messed. Please, Javier?"

She took Pizarro's hand out of the bag and whispered seductively in his ear, "I love swords, My Captain. All kinds."

"Duo excellento," Pizarro replied, beaming. "Perhaps you can join me for dinner again sometime?"

"Not tonight My Captain," Vanda said. "There is a storm remember? I might get seasick."

She paused with her soft hand on the Captains elbow. It moved gently to the duffel bag slung over his shoulder and she zipped it up again. She clicked closed the small combination lock that was hanging on the slider.

"You can tell them to drop this bag off in room number 514 please," she said.

Then she turned and confidently walked into the ship, grinning to herself.

* * *

BENJAMIN WAS TAKEN STRAIGHT TO THE SHIP'S MEDICAL facility. He had yet to stir from the tasering that had jolted through his system. Bollini dumped him on a bed and scampered away as fast he could. As he rushed off, he pulled out his phone and called for a nurse to come down.

Vanda arrived at the same time as the nurse.

"This looks more like a torture chamber than a hospital,"

she said, on seeing the huge hooks hanging from the ceiling.

"They're for drips," the nurse said curtly.

"Hopefully there are no depressed loners around," Vanda half-joked.

"We take our medical care very seriously here, ma'am," the nurse replied, casting an evil eye toward Vanda.

"Of course you do."

Vanda spied out the two beds that looked like they had never been used. The room was cold and sterile. There were no windows or portholes and fluorescent lights cast shadows around the space.

The nurse checked Benjamin's pulse, then swatted his cheeks and splashed some water on his face. She started babbling in a language Vanda didn't recognize. She checked his head. The gash above his ear was nothing to worry about, more of a graze. She pulled his hair down over it and tapped him on the crown, as though he were a Golden Retriever. As he stirred, she forced a pill down his throat. He gagged and she shoved a tumbler of water to his lips.

"He'll be fine," she said, turning to Vanda. "No problem." Then she started packing up her medical kit, preparing to leave. She was clearly annoyed that she had been disturbed.

"Excuse me," Vanda exclaimed. "Where do you think you are going? This man is still unconscious."

"No, he is just sleepy," the nurse said in broken English. "No problem."

"Do you even know what that term means?" Vanda asked.

"No problem," came the stoic answer again. The nurse turned and rushed out of the room as though another emergency was waiting for her. *Where the heck could she be going,* Vanda wondered? *To help with open heart surgery?*

She was left alone with Benjamin. His eyes fluttered as though he was dreaming. He looked tormented.

Benjamin looked up at the ceiling through the grogginess. He was floating on an electric charge of 10 000 volts. He couldn't feel any pain whatsoever. Yet! The air was static and he turned slowly as though he were the second hand on an old grandfather clock. He felt something touching him and reached out to grab it. A hand, as cold as an undertakers handshake, took his. He felt veins and ridges on the skin. They were moving, expanding and contracting and magnetic. He felt his way up to the soft elbow. The entire arm felt alive, as though there was a mythical Gorgon under the skin with hundreds of little snakes twisting and spitting, trying to get out. Letting go, he tried to sit up but couldn't move properly. He couldn't feel his body. Only his eyes moved.

"Hello, Benjamin Rodd." It was the same old voice.

"How does it feel Benjamin?" she asked. "How does it feel being badly hurt?"

"What do you want with me?" Benjamin snarled.

"You used to think it was nice hurting things, didn't you?"

"That was different!"

"Was it?" Astraea said, "Come and dance with me." She held out her hand.

She flowed across the floor. Her silk dress caressed the vacuum between herself and the crystal floor.

"Come."

Benjamin couldn't feel his body. It lay motionless on the hospital bed. There was white all around him. Then he felt himself sit up. It was calming and peaceful. He folded himself off the bed and holding onto Astraea, he looked back at himself. His body lay there inert. His skin glowed as he floated away with his ghost.

"Where are we going?" he asked.

They danced through the air brushing past ribbons of light and pools of darkness. They danced down into the black. The night was thick around them. He could sense the silver cord of his life through the air around him. He felt it in his soul. It was weak and asthmatic.

Then they were flying over the African Savannah. It was rushing by like white-water rapids splashing over the rocks. There were thorn trees dotted around and the ground was rumbling. The beige grass shook and a low pitched sound wailed from the horizon. It was the sound of death.

The ground turned black and there were rhinos everywhere. Snorting, wailing, crying and running for their lives. Panic spread through their ranks like the angel of death running amok. Someone was crying.

"Uphondo! Uphondo!"

They fell one by one and the brown grass turned crimson until fresh blood filled the furrows. It splashed on the earth and fell down the folds of the horizon.

Astraea finally stopped. Her bloodied lips whispered in Benjamin's ear. Her face was pale. She was death itself.

Benjamin was cold. He felt nothing inside. An emptiness sucked at his chest.

"Do you remember?" Astraea demanded to know.

"It was only a handful," Benjamin explained. "It was nothing in the big scheme of things."

A black shadow ran past and something bit him. Benjamin cursed.

"And what do you know about the big scheme of things?" Astraea asked. "Tell me, Benjamin," she said.

"Only that I'm in the middle of them!" Benjamin replied.

"They were right?"

"About what?"

"You are a fool! A vain fool."

"Oh, piss off," Benjamin yelled. "You make out there is nothing good in me."

"Enjoy your agony!"

It hit his chest like a jackhammer. Benjamin dropped to his knees. He felt himself falling. Falling. He reconnected to his body with a bang. It was over. His dream was over. He had intense pain. His back was burning. His heart raced. He was crying out loud as he sat up.

* * *

"Ben. Ben! It's me."

Vanda took his hand, shouting to the nurse for help. She was long gone, *back to her open heart surgery*. Benjamin arched and rubbed his back where the Taser had hit him. The pain slowly receded away. He couldn't say much yet but he knew his tango with Astraea was over. It receded into the dreamy sponge of his murky memory. His normal feeling returned.

"Vanda. It's you," he said. "Where's that idiot Bollini? He actually shot me!"

"He's gone," Vanda said. "It's over Ben. We're safe."

"Get me out of here. Please," he said, heaving his feet off the bed. They felt like lead. The crew who had helped carry Benjamin down were nowhere to be seen. Vanda took Benjamin's arm and they stumbled out of the medical room holding onto each other.

"What happened to the canvas bag?" Benjamin asked as they reach the main atrium of the ship. Vanda smiled.

"I convinced the Captain to put it in my room himself," she said proudly. "We made it, Benjamin."

He looked at her with new respect. She was definitely more than your average American tourist. He smiled for the first time since his tasering.

"I guess I owe you thanks," Vanda said.

"What for?"

"You were willing to take the rap for the shotgun."

"But you never let me, Vanda."

"That's because I never needed to," she replied. "I told you I knew how to look after myself."

Benjamin grimaced.

As they walked through the busy hall, Benjamin felt as though they were the center of attention, but no one noticed them at all. They were just another couple meandering through the lobby. The crew was scuttling about and most people were immersed in their own worlds. The O'Donnells waved from the other side of the lounge. They were sipping colorful cocktails. There was a grand piano in the middle of the floor, painted in glossy cream. No one noticed Liberace as he belted out Annie's song for the hundredth time.

Benjamin scanned the room for Bollini. He was nowhere to be seen.

The ship rolled gently. The storm had arrived with its promised intensity but most guests were safely cocooned in a bubble of tinsel and caviar, oblivious to the rising swell outside.

"Vanda," Benjamin said. "You said just now that we were safe."

"Yes?"

"Well, we're not! I don't trust Bollini or anyone else for that matter. And I'm so messed up right now. How about letting me camp in your room tonight? I'll sleep on the couch."

Vanda responded immediately as though she had been waiting for this ever since she boarded in Genoa.

"Yes, you can," she replied. "And no, you won't."

* * *

A HUNDRED METERS AWAY, TAKIS EVANGELIS, THE SHIPS Culinary Quartermaster, paused outside a utility door tucked away at the back of a corridor leading to his stores. It had a no entry sign on it and may as well have been a hundred miles away. He wiped his dirty hands down his stained apron and dropped the padlock key back into the pocket of the puff jacket he always wore. He looked back to make sure that none of his staff were hovering around. The fruit and vegetable fridge across the way was deserted. The kitchen staff all knew better than to poke their noses into the private affairs of their cantankerous and violent Quarter Master.

There were no brooms or shelves on the other side of the door as one would expect, rather a spiral staircase hugged the welded ribs of the ship down into a small room. Takis Evangelis had hijacked it like a knight laying claim to a medieval dungeon, the minute he had seen it. Access to the food storage areas was strictly under his control and down there in the gut of the ship he called the shots. The room at the bottom of the staircase had initially been earmarked as a spill-over supply room, but it had never been officially used. Designed as an afterthought, to fill an empty space, it had been forgotten by the outside world.

"Everyone has one," the quartermaster mumbled to himself, as the smell from the room hit him. "It doesn't matter who you are or what you are, deep down somewhere there is decay and rot. It sits there stinking, waiting to pass through."

He liked to think of himself as a philosopher. His mother told him it was his Greek heritage oozing out - Aristotle. Everyone else saw him more as a Robespierre. "We're all like ships," he sang to himself. "When the wallpaper of culture and the coatings of pedigree are stripped away, we are all the same inside. Like ships. Rotting inside, on our way to the grave, like old haggard women."

The secret room was indeed the rotting innards of the MSE Grande. Anything that ever been in it was bad and stank, waiting to pass through. Its current illicit cargo was the most abominable it had ever swallowed. It was even viler than the two poor Filipino girls that Takis had smuggled into Istanbul six months earlier.

Small wooden crates lined the walls. They had been loaded two week's earlier in the port of Dar Es Salaam. Planned destination - Tunis.

"Hello my babies," Takis said, as he ran his fingers along them. "Let's wait for the others, shall we?"

* * *

TAKIS PULLED THE SLEEVES OF HIS JACKET UP TO HIS ELBOWS as though he meant business and silently went about inspecting his fiefdom as the room filled up. He sagely rubbed his long greasy hair and rubbed the silver streaks in his three-day chin stubble.

A single light bulb lit the room. It dangled down from a loose wire and swayed from side to side as the ship heaved its way through the rough seas and swell. Shadows moved with the storm, casting haunting illuminations with each roll of the ship. It was cold and dank, the last stop downward to Davies Locker. A Nazi U-boat captain would have felt at home.

A filthy foam mattress was propped up against one of the walls. A pile of linen was stashed at its base and empty water bottles and trash were strewn around next to the filthy sheets. A few plastic chairs filled the rest of the space. One of the small wooden crates had been opened. Ripped plastic was hanging out over the top. Takis peered inside and swore.

"Where's our little thief?" he snarled. He sat back on a chair, rocking it and picked at his nails with a six-inch chef's knife. He glanced through his well-tanned face at the man sitting next to him.

"Hello Panayotis," he said.

The restaurant maître d', Panayotis Pappas, smiled calmly through his rugged but handsome features. Six foot tall and built like a bouncer, his clipped hair and immaculate black service tux seemed out of place. He blew smoke from his thin lips and leaned over to the shivering man on the other side of him.

"Don't take offense," Panayotis said. "There's nothing wrong with you embezzling wankers."

"Except that you keep stealing, of course," Takis said.

The desperate man in front of them driveled off, half in poor English and half in his native language.

"I have no idea where my brother is!" he stammered.

"But the two of you quarter together."

"So? I haven't seen him around."

The man on the floor wore a waiter's outfit like his twin brother had. It looked as though he was half starved. His cheeks were gaunt and he had a thousand yard stare. The type you see in concentration camps, cold and emotionless. He tapped his foot up and down nervously. There were red streaks up his naked arm. They were screaming for more. *'Gimme more!'*, they yelled. He turned to the fourth man in the room and pleaded.

"Mr. Big, please you have to believe me."

A well-dressed skinny gentleman with short red hair sat in the shadows with his legs crossed. He looked as though he had just stepped out of a private Gentleman's Club. Thin framed and dapper, he wore an expensive suit with the panache of a Swiss banker. It was clear that he was the 'senior partner' in the room.

"Takis," he said, with his nose lifted. "You are my best friend." He often made a point of saying this as though his sense of self-worth depended on it.

"Tell me what we are going to do now. The boys were expecting our cargo tomorrow in Tunisia. And it looks like we'll be eating ice cream in Malta? Do you know what this means?"

"The Italians?" Takis ventured.

"Precisely. We're now right on their turf."

"It's not our fault," Pappas said.

"But it's our problem. We had a deal with the Italians.

They keep the Western Med and we stay in the South and East. If they find out that this haul is floating right past them, they'll be onto it. And us."

"We'll fight back," Takis said.

"My father said no fighting the Italians. They're too powerful. The diversion to Malta is a potential screw up. We're going to have to wait till this ship docks somewhere that we control before we even think about offloading."

"That's only one of our problems, George," Takis replied. "This Bulgarian idiot here and his thieving twin brother never managed to retrieve the horn they pilfered. It's still missing." He pointed to the open crate.

"We have to get it back," the maître d' said. "Remember the last time we shortchanged the delivery?"

The red-haired man smiled gleefully. "Yes, I remember it very well. Wasn't that how you lost your finger?"

Pappas folded his arms, tucking his fingers away. His face went dark. "We'll find it, Boss George. I promise you."

"This wanker's twin brother has run away with it. Isn't that so?" Takis lurched forward and grabbed the waiter by his throat.

"Isn't that so?" he shouted again. His chef's knife flashed in his hand.

"I told you not to involve these two Bulgarian idiots," the thin man in the expensive suit shouted. "Just because they had the same passport as me, didn't mean we could trust them!"

"Not me, Mr. Big!" the Bulgarian man blurted out in broken English. "Not me. This woman. She was with the Captain yesterday. The American girl. Missus Slade is her name. She got it. My brother put it in her handbag. When you were chasing him."

Takis slapped him as hard as he could. "So you do know about the missing horn!" he yelled. "You're all liars?"

He pushed his chef's knife against the man's throbbing Adam's apple. "I don't care," he continued. "Phone your brother. I know you're hiding him somewhere. I want that horn back in my hands before we get to Malta or else you're going into the next batch of pork goulash!"

Takis pulled the back of his knife slowly across the man's throat. It scraped a thin red line. The man pulled violently away and screamed. "No, please! I'll get him to get it back from her." He fell to the floor in a pathetic heap.

"OK. You've given him the stick," the red-haired man said. "Now give him a carrot."

"You need an incentive also?" Takis taunted. He pulled out a tiny plastic bag with some white powder in it and swung it in front of the Bulgarian waiter's red face. His wild eyes followed it in hypnotic seduction.

"Want some of this?" Takis asked. "Then go and do what you say. Go get your son-of-a-bitch twin brother to fetch me my missing rhino horn back. You moron Malaka!"

Takis emptied the white powder onto the floor and stomped on it with his thick heavy soled rubber boots. The groveling man at his feet tried to scrape some of it up.

"Get him out of my sight!" the red-haired man snarled. "He makes me sick."

The maître d' frog-marched the waiter away. The door at the top of the spiral staircase slammed shut.

"Now about the Tunisia debacle," George said, "What's the new plan?"

* * *

BENJAMIN LAY ON THE BED IN VANDA'S ROOM. HE WAS overtired. A splitting headache screamed from behind his bloodshot eyes. His mind couldn't stop racing and hypertension rose in his chest.

"I won't be long," Vanda shouted from her tiny bathroom. "Just having a quick shower."

"Take your time," he said. "I'm still recovering here, anyway."

He tried to scratch the mark where the Taser dart had penetrated his skin. It was behind his shoulder in an impossible spot to get to. The welt stung like a wasp. He had never been Tasered before and felt as though he had been thrown into a concrete mixer and rolled around for an hour.

Vanda turned on the shower tap and the sound of trickling water filled the room. Her room was smaller than Benjamin's. Benjamin closed his eyes and lay back, enjoying the watery sounds of the shower and the rain outside.

"I'm ready," he called out. "You may as well come out now." The bed gently rocked from side to side as the ship rode the swells.

"Astraea? I'm here."

Every time he had slept since the cruise started he'd had his recurring dream of Astraea. *I may as well get it over with, so I could get some real shut-eye,* he thought.

"Astraea?" he shouted. "What's wrong? Can't you take the competition?"

The only sounds coming back were from the shower next door and the rain. The two tangoed together in the night. Benjamin squeezed his eyes shut trying to conjure up his dream fantasy. "You are a dream?" he said, "Aren't you?"

Nothing.

Benjamin synced his rolling eyes with the swaying of the ship. He realized that there must be a huge storm outside to rock such a big ship. He could picture Astraea fading away with her lovely evil smile.

She's not coming tonight, he thought. She had been so real. Now there was nothing but emptiness. He thought of Dr. Miller with her tortoiseshell specs and stiff dresses. She had often been there when he needed her. She would have known how to conjure up Astraea from the dead.

She's not real, he moaned to himself. Turning over, he buried himself in the sheets. *She's not real!*

"BENJAMIN!"

He sat up abruptly up in bed. He knew that voice. Drifting in his pain it was impossible to sleep.

"I'M GOING MAD."

The running water in the bathroom stopped. Outside, Benjamin could hear the roaring sea and the storm. The swishing and sloshing of water rattled the balcony door. He got up and walked to the curtain. As he opened it, a lightning flash illuminated the room. White horses bounced over the huge swells and the wind raged. There were flashes of light off to the side of the ship, low in the clouds. Each time the air was lit, Benjamin could see the rain pouring down outside. The ship rocked and lurched.

Benjamin felt worse looking out the window. The ship groaned as though it might snap in two at any second. A spray of seawater shot past the balcony. He felt a hand on his shoulder.

"It's beautiful, isn't it?" Vanda said softly. She had a fluffy gown wrapped around her. Her hair was loose and wet and curling towards the ends. She tucked her hip into the curve of Benjamin's side and stood quietly with him, looking into the dark outside.

"Look at the size of these waves?" Benjamin said. "They're splashing up here on the fifth floor. It must be a monstrous swell we're going through."

"Who were you talking to?" Vanda asked.

Benjamin turned to her, embarrassed. "No one."

A bright flash followed by a drum of thunder interrupted them. It reminded Benjamin of the movies he had seen of the First World War, where the flashes of bombs exploding lit the night amongst death and darkness.

"Let's stand and watch for a while," he said, putting his arm around Vanda.

The ship rocked steeply and the little round table outside on the balcony fell over with a loud bang. It started rolling backward and forward, bashing between the glass door and the railing.

"It wasn't secured down. It'll break the glass," Benjamin said. "I'll get it." He reached down, unlocking the sliding door. As he slid it open the rain came spitting through, hitting him in the face. He brushed the water aside and stepped outside. Something suddenly moved in the shadows.

"Stop Ben!" Vanda cried. "Stop!"

It was too late. Somebody was there, outside on the balcony, crouching in the shadows. He'd climbed up from down below. Benjamin could see him silhouetted against the dark background as a lightning bolt expelled a terrifying electric blast. He shielded his face from the spitting rain. A boot stuck into the door frame. Benjamin looked up into a pair of desperate bloodshot eyes, dripping water.

"You!" he shouted. A hand lurched for his throat.

* * *

THE BULGARIAN WAITER REARED HIMSELF UP THROUGH THE dark as another lightning flash burst. He had a massive black eye from where Benjamin had punched him in Rome. In the semi-dark light of the storm, his purple bruising created the face of a hideous Frankenstein. Vanda instinctively screamed but the wind outside stole her cries like a thieving gypsy.

The intruder yanked the sliding door open as a massive wave crashed past behind him. Salty sea spray ricocheted into the room and Benjamin could feel ice cold water hitting his cheeks. He froze in the moment, like a stupid marble statue.

"My package!" the Bulgarian screamed. "Where is my horn?" His eyes were wild and his nostrils flared like a beaten racehorse after Ascot.

He kicked Benjamin in the thigh and blindly lashed out with a huge knife. As the blade flew clumsily past Benjamin's face, his lethargy snapped and his momentary frozen state evaporated. Benjamin saw himself suspended beyond his predicament, as though he were a giant looking down on it. His world slowed down. He planned his next few moves in a micro-second. He had fought off much worse before. In the bush. In Hanoi. It was imprinted on him. It had been there, even before he had sunk into his own bog of money and greed.

He instinctively dropped his center of gravity. He drew a long slow breath through his mouth, remaining completely calm.

The blade of the knife moved in slow motion toward him again. He could see reflective sparks on it as another lightning bolt flashed outside. He grabbed the Bulgarian waiter's hand and pulled the blade past him into the room. He swiveled on his hips, drawing his attacker's body toward him, crunching his wrist. The waiter swore in pain and dropped the knife. The two men grappled together inside the room. Benjamin could feel fingers scratching for his eyes. He swung with his left hand into the thin air. He could see the man's head. It was moving toward him like a bowling ball hurtling toward the skittles. There were pockmarks, ugly craters. It hit him in the face and felt like a concrete beam. Benjamin's nose cracked and he stumbled back. An arm twisted around his neck and he gasped for breath as it tightened its grip. He still had a few seconds before potentially blacking out. He tried to stay calm and braced for one last move. He was much bigger than his attacker but was in a lock-grip. *The jerk knew how to do that right!* Benjamin took another breath and lunged upwards with all his strength lifting his attacker clean off the floor.

They both tumbled toward the sliding door. The ship rocked on the swell and they tripped back outside onto the balcony. Benjamin finally ripped himself free from the man's grip. He jabbed with his right fist and hit flesh. He followed with a powerful left like he had done in Rome. The Bulgarian waiter took the punch and fell backward toward the outer railing. He bounced off it and for a moment his upper body was perilously suspended out into the dark void beyond. Another flash of lightning lit the sea. A loud bang erupted! A roar and blast of sound followed. *Thunder?* It sounded like thunder. *More like a thundershot*!

Benjamin's ears rang as though someone had slapped him. Speckles of white danced in front of his eyes. The rusted barrel of Chatunga's sawn-off shotgun pushed him aside.

His attacker froze in terror and then exploded in red blood. He bulged out as though someone was squeezing him like a toothpaste tube and flew upward off his feet. The shotgun blast flung him out into the dark night space, right over the railing.

A gigantic wave curved up, unstoppable and grabbed his birdshot body. Nature then finished him off like a monstrous windscreen wiper cleaning a bug off the window. Up he rose into the void, flung away into the black. Benjamin saw him spitting blood. Like a piece of drifting seaweed, he was tossed away, five floors above the watermark.

The wave receded and it was suddenly still again for a few moments. Benjamin panted, holding on tightly to the railing and then he stumbled back into the room gasping.

Vanda stood there with that same look on her face that she had had in the van. There was smoke around her. A red shotgun cartridge was rolling about on the floor. Benjamin's knuckles were bleeding again. He slammed the sliding door closed and turned to her. The thunder was muzzled as the edge of the door sealed.

Dipping the warm shotgun toward the floor, Vanda rushed over to him. He held her closely, feeling her body under the gown. They both breathed fast in unison, their chests pounding, overloaded with adrenalin. It was a cruel erotic moment that lasted only a few seconds and then it drained away. They both felt sick to their stomachs.

"I think we just killed someone," Benjamin slowly said.

He could picture Dr. Miller laughing. *I told you so*, she was saying, mocking him. *People like you don't change.*

They stood there forever, holding each other.

Eventually, Vanda released her grasp and went to fetch a towel to clean up the blood on Benjamin's face and hands. As she wiped the open grazes on his knuckles, she looked him in the eye. "This rhino horn nonsense! It's actually true, isn't it? You say it was in my bag?"

"For the hundredth time, I'm not making this up. It was in your bag." Benjamin replied. "But it's long gone now. These thugs just don't know it yet."

"I heard what you and your friend were saying in Mondello," Vanda said.

Benjamin stood still for a few more seconds. He was calming down from what had just happened.

"It's not what you think," he said, trying to convince her.

"We're both stuck in the middle of a scary mess," Vanda said, curling away from him. "I'm scared."

"Let's wait till morning to figure this out," Benjamin said. "I can't think straight after this."

"We'll be in Malta by then."

"That might be a good thing."

"Why?"

"The ship was meant to be in Tunisia tomorrow. That's a classic transit hub for rhino horn. Diverting to Malta might throw them. It'll give us time to figure this out."

"Let's go to the police," Vanda sniffed.

"Out of the question!" Benjamin shot back. "I'm not going back to..."

"Who? Bollini?"

Benjamin shook his head. "Your best chance is to stay with me, Vanda. I know this world." He gently pried the warm shotgun out of her hands. "I can handle Bollini, now that I know he's as crooked as a dog's hind leg."

"I hope you're right."

"We'd better go spend the night in my room," Benjamin suggested. "They might come back here tonight."

"You think there are more of them?"

"I'm convinced there are," Benjamin said. "Smuggling is not a solo act. There'll be a couple of them in the ring, here on the ship."

"A whole smuggling ring? Oh, good heavens! This is real!" Vanda banged her fists on Benjamin's chest. Tears welled up in her eyes.

"It's going to be OK," Benjamin stammered. "Now get dressed, we need to move. And where's the duffel bag? I need to bring this along. We might need it again."

As they scurried through the empty corridors up to Benjamin's cabin on the seventh floor, he turned to her.

"Are you now going to tell me where you learned to shoot that thing or not?"

VALETTA

To Benjamin and Vanda, Malta didn't look like a fortress that had withstood pirates and Turk attacks for hundreds of years. It looked like freedom from the floating prison they were sailing on. The immensity of her cliffs and causeways dwarfed the MSE Grand as she came into harbor.

They had spent the night in each other's arms, falling in and out of troubled sleep. Benjamin had locked the front door to his cabin, propping the couch up against his balcony door, just in case. They had felt trapped, against an unknown adversary.

"I've got another idea," Vanda suggested, as they watched the sun creep up out of the eastern sea. "I can go to Captain Pizarro? He'll help us, I'm sure of it."

"Ah, yes, but you'll have to scratch his back before he scratches yours," Benjamin said, sarcastically.

Vanda rolled her eyes. "You're jealous, aren't you?"

"Do you really think he wants any scandal on his ship? He'll bury this and we'll disappear." Benjamin said, changing the topic. "I've known lots of men like the Captain. They can't be trusted."

"You mean you can't trust him," Vanda replied, rolling over. Benjamin never answered. He was thinking of the fortune hiding somewhere beneath him. *Millions,* Chatunga had said!

They lay watching the limestone cliffs of the harbor. The cool air had a reflective calm that had washed the space after the storm. Only scattered clouds were left in the early morning sky.

"Can I ask you something?" Vanda asked. "Who is this Astraea? I heard you mumbling about her last night and it wasn't the first time either. Is she part of this rhino horn nonsense?"

"Have you ever felt as though you are going mad?" Benjamin asked.

"Like last night? Yes, that was completely mad."

"No, I mean inside. Inside your head?"

"Astraea is a figment of your imagination then?"

"I wish she was," Benjamin said. "At least she'd then leave me alone. She's there whenever I close my eyes. It's a nightmare, Vanda. And now this situation we've somehow fallen into. It's all linked! I just don't know how. But I know that she's right there in the middle of it all."

"Where? In your head?" Vanda asked, looking at him weirdly. "I don't understand."

"Do you know what a Mexican wave is?" Benjamin asked. "They do them in the soccer stadiums?"

Vanda nodded. "Of course." The morning sun caught her eyes and she squinted.

"Have you ever noticed that you can only appreciate them from the other side of the stadium?"

Vanda smiled.

"What are you trying to say? That we go watch some soccer?"

"I'm saying, let's get out of here. Off this horrid ship. We need to look at this from the other side of our stadium. We need to step back a bit. Formulate a plan."

Benjamin checked his watch, that was lying on the table next to the bed.

"There's a tour leaving in an hour. Let's join it and then get lost on the island somewhere. Away from this pressure. We'll figure out what to do, somewhere in those stone walls and alleyways."

He pointed at the steep stone fortifications that the ship was busy docking next to.

"It should be OK to go back to your room now," he continued. "Lots of people about. You should go put on some clean clothes?"

Vanda agreed. It was a good idea. It was their only reasonable sounding option at that point. She had however already been back to her room. At five in the morning, whilst Benjamin was fast asleep tussling with his nightmares, she had gone back. She went back to pick up the used shotgun cartridge, that had been rolling across the floor all night. And to double check that there was no blood trail anywhere. To her horror, the room had already been cleaned up by someone. She had slipped back into bed at Benjamin's side, without him even realizing it. She decided to not mention it to Benjamin.

"I'll see you outside then," Benjamin said. "In an hour?"

She left in his gown, walking barefoot to her cabin on the other side of the ship and just missing the early risers going for breakfast.

* * *

EXACTLY 60 MINUTES LATER, VANDA WAVED AT BENJAMIN through the crowd. She pointed to a public bus on the far side of the street and they both made for it. Climbing aboard, Benjamin noticed the flowery summer dress and brown leather sandals she was wearing.

It was already hot, as the morning sun streamed through the glass windows, and she fanned her face with a map of Malta. Her handbag was slung over her shoulder, as usual. She'd put on makeup, and it made her look younger. Benjamin noticed her necklace flowing down her chest against the gentle contours and curves. There was an ivory talisman on the end that Benjamin couldn't recognize. She was also wearing her brooch and the diamonds caught the light and shimmered. Benjamin was about to comment on the brooch, but let it go. He had bigger things to worry about than a stupid trinket. It had caused enough trouble.

A lot of people were getting off the ship to explore Malta. The young family Benjamin had seen on his first day in the queue marched past their bus window. Benjamin grimaced. The parents were arguing whilst the children stood wide-eyed, mesmerized by the towering walls and ramparts. The little boy pulled his mother's sleeve and pointed upward. His sister was lost in the moment. Benjamin and Vanda watched them being ignored by their parents until the packed bus left with a snort.

"Do you have children?" Vanda asked. Benjamin shuffled uncomfortably on his chair.

"No. What's the point?"

"I've often wondered what it would be like," Vanda said.

"I stopped thinking like that years ago," Benjamin replied. "Had no choice."

It was Vanda's turn to now shuffle uncomfortably. She put her hand on his leg and squeezed gently.

"I'm sorry."

"You don't have to be," Benjamin said. "It was no one's fault. If you can't have them, you can't have them."

He could see Dr. Miller in his mind. She was applauding. She was saying, *at last Benjamin, at last. You said it.*

"Is that why you got divorced?" Vanda continued. "I hope you don't mind me asking?"

"Oh, good lord, no!" Benjamin replied. "That was something else entirely." He paused. "That was my fault."

Bravo, Dr. Miller said again. *You're finally moving on.*

"I know what that's like," Vanda said, lowering her voice. "I know what it's like to bugger things up."

"I don't really want to get into it," Benjamin replied.

"Benjamin, if you ever want to talk about it, I'm here."

Benjamin turned and cut her off. "You sound like my shrink, you do!" Then he checked himself. He liked Vanda and didn't want to drive her away. "I'm sorry," he explained. "It's a painful part of my life. Long ago."

They watched the empty fields quizzing past.

"Have you phoned Chatunga," Vanda asked, changing the subject. "To see if he's OK?"

Benjamin patted his jacket. "I couldn't find my phone this morning," he explained. "I think it might have gone overboard with our friend last night. My pocket, where I put it last night, was half ripped off." He rummaged through all his pockets again.

"So we're uncontactable then?" Vanda asked. "Stuck on our own?"

Benjamin sheepishly nodded.

"So much for your Chatunga plan, then!" Vanda said angrily before sitting back and folding her arms.

Maybe I can do this on my own, Benjamin suddenly thought to himself. *Millions could become even more. Maybe ten!*

Turning to Vanda, who was pouting sulkily, he snidely

asked, "I thought you said you understood about buggering things up."

"That's not what I meant!"

"Look, we'll figure it out. But we can't talk here," Benjamin said. "Not on the bus, there are too many ears."

"Where is this bus going anyway?"

Behind them, a skinny man cleared his throat. He had climbed on the bus right after Benjamin and Vanda, but they hadn't noticed him. He had on dark sunglasses and a Panama straw hat, that hid the red hair on his head.

"It's going to Mdina," he interrupted. Benjamin and Vanda swung around.

"Sorry, I couldn't help but overhear your conversation," he said. "Mdina. It's a marvelous place. Here, take my map."

He shoved a crumpled tourist brochure onto Vanda's lap.

"I recommend you visit the Vilhena Palace," he continued. "See, I circled it."

Benjamin grabbed the brochure off Vanda's lap and said a muffled thanks. They both sat back trying not to talk anymore. Benjamin properly noticed his immediate surroundings for the first time. The bus was packed with other tourists heading inland for the day. Most people were dressed for the early summer weather that had been forecast and the previous evening's storm had been already forgotten.

The skinny man behind them smiled chillingly while sending a message on his phone.

* * *

THE BUS DEPOSITED THEM ONTO THE PAVEMENT OUTSIDE the walls of medieval Mdina. As they meandered through old stone streets worn down by Romans, Templar Knights and RAF Aces, Vanda felt they were about to play out another chapter in the exciting history of Malta. The foreboding nostalgia was daunting and frightening.

She thought about the man she had shot. Her heart sank. *What if they find the body? What if there were cameras on the side of the ship?* She shivered and held onto Benjamin's arm, trying to force the negative thoughts out of her mind.

A light breeze blew and the blue sky was clean and pure after the storm. A few leaves and old pieces of paper whipped up in front of them. They twirled around in a dance of graceful pirouettes. Vanda eventually found a spring in her step, as her summer dress joined the dance and fanned around her knees. *I had no choice! It was him or Ben!*

Vanda liked the way Benjamin kept glancing at her. It was a combination of attraction and hesitancy, that perfect yin-yang that interesting relationships should have. She normally loved balmy days like this, they reminded her of her childhood in Louisiana. It was a pity about her present circumstances.

Mdina was enchanting. It was exactly what she needed, the perfect distraction for someone who had just put a blast of birdshot into a man who was trying to attack them. She thought again about their Bulgarian waiter and his last seconds. She could see his belly opening up like gut fish, just before he was swept away.

She kept trying to justify it to herself. What she had done.

Her 'trigger happy' finger had done it. The snake was trying to kill Benjamin. He stole from me. He was a no-good thug.

Deep inside though, she knew it had been her survival instinct. An anger had welled up in her and she had grabbed the shotgun out of its bag, put it 6 inches from the waiter's body, and just pulled the trigger, without thinking. Exactly like her late father had taught her. Just like he had trained her. She had expertly aimed and silently squeezed. *Benjamin was struggling with the man! He was being throttled. It had just kicked in.* Up until then, she didn't know that she had the killer instinct.

She wondered where the waiter had ended up. Benjamin had said that he'd sunk to the bottom of the ocean. The blast must have knocked out his air, he had said like a knowledge-able expert. *Good riddance to him*! She was happy with the thought of him buried under a kilometer of water. She had removed the threat and no one would be able to pinpoint anything on them or back to them. *I hope so*, she thought. *I hope there were no cameras and that he was alone!* The thought that he might have been part of a broader smuggling ring, made her feel queasy.

She took Benjamin's hand, holding it tight. He had not said much since they arrived in the charming town. He was distracted, lost in a million thoughts. Vanda liked him but she was struggling to fully get him. He clearly had a dark past. She'd figured that out, at least. *A shady background, as some sort of ex-rhino horn dealer. Animal skins. More or less.* He had admitted as much.

That's why she felt attracted to him. She felt a synergy and a kindred spirit. She wondered if his background could possibly be worse than her own.

* * *

BENJAMIN POINTED TO AN OLD BUILDING DOWN THE street. "That's the place the man on the bus told us about," he said. "Let's check it out. It looks like an ancient lodge or something."

Vanda pulled out the crumpled tourist brochure. "The Vilhena Palace," she said. "Home to the ancient Grand Master of the Knights of Malta, Manoel de Vilhena." Benjamin leaned over and read over her shoulder. "He was slaughtered by a Turk," he said. "Good omen, don't you think?"

His thoughts about shotguns and being locked up by Salvatore Bollini changed to heads being sliced off by scimitars. He pictured his own head, replacing that of the Grand Master. *I'd deserve it if it happened.* He'd been unable to come up with a plan yet. *Vanda must think I'm a complete moron.*

As they walked over a giant Maltese cross embossed in white stone on the road, the towering old building pressed in around them. It was claustrophobic and Benjamin snapped. He liked to be able to see the horizon. To know that he could run in any direction if he needed to. He needed to feel free, even if he knew it was unlikely.

The arched doorway to the palace was in a shadow. It was quiet and eerie and no one else was in the courtyard. Their footsteps amplified on the cobblestones. A curtain twitched in a window. Benjamin yanked Vanda's sleeve.

"I've got to get out of here," he said. "I'm not going in there. Let's not go in. It's such a beautiful day and I don't feel like dark Palaces where heads were cut off. Let's keep walking in the open. The fresh air, the birds, it's good for us. What do you say, Vanda? Let's spend the day walking around."

She squeezed his hand, bringing it to her lips. "I agree," she answered.

They turned and headed back into the narrow stone lanes of Mdina.

"Please tell me about Astraea," Vanda said. "You promised."

As Benjamin spoke, the sky was blue with strings of white cirrus wafting off the horizon.

* * *

"Had you ever been haunted by your past?"

Benjamin's hands were in his pockets and Vanda clung onto his arm. She nodded.

"I often have this feeling," she said. "I'm stuck in a swimming pool, trying to get to the sides. I feel this great hope but I never make it out. I'm tied down with a huge elastic band that pulls me back under the water." She giggled. "Stupid isn't it?"

"I'm talking about being haunted," Benjamin said, ignoring what she had just said. "Stalked and hunted, not swimming" He gazed wistfully up the road in front of them.

"She talks to me," he continued. "Astraea talks to me. When I close my eyes, she's there, in my face. She's enchanting and beautiful and horrible all at the same time. And she's chatting to me. A real conversation. And I talk back."

"Astraea is a beautiful woman, then?" Vanda felt a pang of jealousy. She pushed it away. It was ridiculous.

"I think she's beautiful and hideous," Benjamin said. "The thing, however, is that she feels real. Have you ever had a dream where it felt real? As though you could touch it? Feel it? Smell it? Screw it?"

"Of course," Vanda replied. "Especially when I'm falling out of a tree or something, or if I'm reliving some old scene from my past."

"No, I'm not talking about that. I've had lucid dreams. This is different. It's real. I mean, she is real. She's actually real. And it doesn't stop. She's there whenever I fall asleep. She continues on exactly where she left off each time. And she gives me stuff. Real stuff."

"Like my brooch?" Vanda laughed. She couldn't help herself. "Benjamin. Have ever spoken to someone about this?"

"I'm talking to you, aren't I?"

"No, I mean to someone who can help you. It sounds so bizarre."

"You think I'm loopy?"

"No. It's just that... that this is not normal. None of this is normal. We shot someone! Common! And you are thinking this crap about a woman who doesn't even exist. We should be focusing. I'm scared, Ben. What have we landed ourselves in?"

Benjamin stared silently up ahead. A green valley peeked up from the end of the road with the colors of an impressionist masterpiece.

"Beautiful, isn't it?" he said.

Vanda took his hand again. She could feel it shaking.

"We all have our demons," she said.

"Do yours talk back to you?" he snapped. "Do they give you things? Actual physical things?" He hesitated in frustration. How could he explain what made no sense? The pitch in his voice rose as he got angry. "What do your demons do, Vanda? Make you fire off shotguns, I suppose?"

"Ouch! I didn't take you for an asshole." Vanda let go of his hand. "It was with your gun, Benjamin!"

"I'm sorry," Benjamin said, calming down. "That was a bit harsh."

"I wasn't always a waitress in Plaquemines," she said, with a stiffness in her voice. Benjamin drew out a long breath.

"I suspected that," he said. "What was it then? The military? CIA? Clay pigeon shooting club?"

"It's a bit simpler than that. A lot simpler in fact." She turned and smiled. "I had a wonderful father once, who believed in preparing me for life." Her answer made Benjamin feel awful.

"Don't say anything else," he said.

"You can give but can't take it, isn't that so?" Vanda laughed.

"Like I said," Benjamin replied. "Have you ever felt you were going crazy?"

Vanda rolled her eyes and took his hand again. She squeezed it. "You already asked me that."

"You didn't answer."

"I guess I am now," she replied. "Going crazy that is."

They walked in silence. Eventually, Vanda pointed to a cafe on the corner ahead of them. "How about a truce?" she asked. "And a good glass of Maltese wine?"

"The stronger the better."

They joined the tiny queue in front of the counter. As they waited, they silently soaked up the antiquated ambiance around them. Everyone was eating el fresco in the delightful square they had landed themselves in.

They paid when their order arrived and turned around to look for an empty table. As they did so, wine glasses in hand, the same man who had briefly spoken to them on the bus appeared as if from nowhere. He stepped forward with his Panama hat half over his skinny face and knocked Vanda's glass. Vanda cried out as wine hit her skin and the rest of the glass evaporated into the dirt.

The man profusely apologized and immediately offered to buy her some more. He insisted on doing so in his half Russian, half English accent. Benjamin said an emphatic, no, but the man was as persistent as a mosquito. Before they knew it, the man had convinced them to sit with him at a table perched on top of the medieval town walls.

He ordered a new bottle of wine and some cucumber sandwiches before he sat down and crossed his thin legs. He apologized again and again until the fresh order arrived. Then he sipped his wine slowly, analyzing Benjamin and Vanda over the rim of the glass.

"Tell me about you two lovebirds," he said, with a wry

smile. "Wait! Don't tell me. Honeymoon? Right? From down under, I reckon?"

Benjamin raised his eyebrows toward Vanda. "Mr? What was your name again?" He asked.

"Sorry, most rude of me," the man answered, held out his scrawny hand. "I'm George. Good to meet you both."

Benjamin cautiously introduced himself and Vanda. George hesitated slightly when he heard Benjamin's name but then acted as though they were new best friends. As he spoke, he slowly got under Benjamin's skin. He started off with how wonderful Malta was and ended up interrogating them about why they were there. He was an expert manipulator. And he didn't stop talking.

Vanda didn't trust him one bit. Her instinct again. She sat silently, while Benjamin and the man chatted.

"Mr. Rodd," George suddenly said after the small talk was over. "I take it you are a hunter, being from South Africa? Ever shot something interesting? Or traded it?"

It was such a loaded, brazen question, that it caught Benjamin off guard. Vanda couldn't take it anymore. She'd had enough of the charade and interrupted them rudely.

"Don't tell me," she said. "The MSE Grande. You're on it. Aren't you?" She drawled her words in the best southern drawl she could muster. She found that doing this usually unnerved her opponents.

Benjamin glanced at her inquisitively. Her rudeness with the red-headed man was out of character, but he realized that she was right. *What was he doing chattering to a complete stranger in the circumstances?* Vanda was like Dr. Miller in that respect. Picking up things before he did. *How could they trust anyone right now? And they certainly should be cautious of accidentally bumping into friendly strangers.*

He retreated in his mind and emptied his wine quickly

down his throat. George avoided answering the question. He pretended he didn't know what Vanda was on about.

"George, it was nice to meet you, but we need to get going," Benjamin firmly said. They stood up and thanked their obtrusive host for the sandwiches. The final apology from George was his most insincere. He watched them closely as they walked away. As they got to the corner, Vanda glanced back. George was on his phone, talking intensely to someone. She watched him glaring at them. Switching to a platonic smile, he waved one last time when he realized she was onto him.

"He's part of it," she blurted, as soon as they were out of sight. "I'm convinced of it. His beady little eyes. I know evil, Ben. He planned to bump into me and spill my wine. There was no crowd pushing him." Benjamin knew inside she was right.

As he walked along, he forced himself to think back and started to stitch some things together. Old images, he long thought had died, flicked through his brain. Like when the Bulgarian mob had handed him over to the Vietnamese to be thrown in jail. When there'd been talk of a man. A man who sat back in the shadows, pulling all the strings. A son-of-a-bitch who could have saved him, but didn't. A red-headed man! They used to call him 'Big' - 'Big George'. *It had to be!* Chatunga had tried to warn him. *Maybe Chat wasn't as delusional as I thought?*

Benjamin remembered how his Zimbabwean friend had always hated this 'Big George' with an unbalanced venom. Benjamin never took him seriously though. Thought it was just another one of his friend's hair-brained obsessions. Besides, no one back then knew exactly who this George fellow really was. He was a legend. A fable. The phantom hand pulling all the dirty tricks up and down the eastern Med. They called him 'Big' but the only thing big about him was that he epitomized the saying, *'there is no honor amongst thieves'*.

Benjamin's imagination went wild. Drugs, trafficking, weapons, animals, diamonds, cigarettes, ivory, rhino horn. *Rhino horn! The trade was growing exponentially every month! The game had changed while he'd been locked up in Hanoi.* Any mobster financier lurking in the shadows was bound to have stepped forward at some stage waving their bulging moneybags around. *And their skinny red-haired arms*, Benjamin grunted to himself. *How could I have been so blind?*

He couldn't think straight. *Heck*, he thought, *there must be hundreds of 'gingers' wearing straw hats in Malta. No! It had to be him. Too much coincidence with what had happened. And Chat? He'd tried to warn us.*

Benjamin snapped out of his introspection as a group of Chinese tourists walked past them clicking their cameras. Vanda was still right beside him.

"Where have you been, Ben?" she asked. "We're almost at the end of the town."

"This is bigger than I thought," he said. "And it's about to get a heck of a lot more dangerous as well."

"What Benjamin? What is bigger?"

"This smuggling racket we've gotten mixed up in," he replied.

"This could be really huge if that man is who I think he is. Hundreds of millions of dollars worth. And he knows that we know. He's onto us."

"Benjamin, tell me you're not having another little episode. Another dream?"

"The redhead! I know of him," Benjamin said. "They call him 'Big George.' He's after us."

"Why would he be after us?" Vanda asked.

"For starters, one of his valuable rhino horns ended up in your handbag. He'd want to recover it. And he'll figure that we know the rest."

"Know what?"

"That's he's smuggling. Rhino horn! Lots of it. Trust me, he wouldn't be here if there wasn't huge money involved. And if he just thinks we're onto him, it's as good as we are."

"And what would that mean?" Vanda asked.

Benjamin put his arm around her shoulder.

"I'll explain," he said. "But not here. Mdina is too claustrophobic, he'll be watching our every step. Let's go back to the City."

Vanda played along. She felt she had no other viable options at that stage. She said nothing as they hurried away, making sure they weren't being followed. They walked briskly back to the bus terminus and caught the first red bus back to the bustling capital city of Valetta. The sun was high above them and the air clean.

As they approached the high walls of the city, Vanda felt as though she was an ancient marauder. She turned to Benjamin and said, "I know nothing about this rhino horn stuff. How evil is it, actually? What do they use it for? Drugs?"

Ben closed his eyes and whispered in her ear above the noise of the bus engine. Although it wasn't him talking. She was talking. *Astraea was explaining.*

* * *

"Tell me, Vanda. What happens when the president of a country goes on TV and claims that he found a cure for his cancer? Or when some billionaire boasts about a sacred powder that keeps him going for hours in bed? Or when boozers start swearing that they have found the perfect cure for a hangover? You know what

happens? I'll tell you what happens! Everyone wants it, that's what happens!

Just one problem though. This miracle powder, this natural gift to weak men, it can't be farmed or mined or built or made in a lab.

No, no! It needs to be hunted. It needs to be shot. It has to be hacked off the bloodied carcass of an animal. An animal who has stared down the barrel of some rusty AK47 in the crude hands of another animal.

'Diceros bicornis'. That's what it's officially called. Sounds like some Latin Demigod doesn't it. Diceros bicornis, the majestic Rhinoceros.

Some people say that rhinos are just dumb beasts. The real beast, however, has a rifle swinging at his side. Do you know that a trigger is squeezed every hour?

Gram for gram, Rhino horn is more valuable than gold or diamonds or oil. There's no other higher valued natural product on the planet. Forget drugs, cocaine, heroin, LSD? Oh, they have nothing on Rhino horn.

Tell me, Vanda, what do you think happens when demand increases and the supply decreases? That's right! The price shoots through the roof. So what does a good rhino horn sell for? $300 000? $400 000? It only goes up. Up, up up! It can only go up as this beautiful and graceful animal heads toward the cliff face of extinction.

Twenty years. That's all. A window of opportunity for the worst of us to make vast fortunes. Twenty years and then the game is over. Because in twenty years' time, some bastard is going to lock'n load and blast the life out of our planet's last Diceros bicornis.

There's a race to that last horn. Only God knows who will get there first or what price it will go for? A million bucks. A billion? What price can be put on extinction?

A symbol of status. Consumed by the Asian black market. Cherished in the underbelly of Vietnam. It's a race, Vanda.

Seven billion humans verse 25 000 Rhino.

And we've got the guns."

A tear rolled down Vanda's cheek as the bus hissed to a stop in the middle of Valletta.

* * *

It was a perfect afternoon in Malta. Young craftsmen, lined the limestone streets leading to the Cathedral, selling their filigrees and silk doilies. Some of the older ones had already packed up and retreated into the siestas of a bygone era. Thousands of people bobbed to a colorful hypnotic pulse as the ancient stones under them heated up in the sun. It was the first sunny day of the season and it felt as though the world had come to town, to bid farewell to winter's shackles.

Wrinkled Phoenicians worked their way among the throngs of tourists as families licked ice cream together and laughed. Young lovers dangled onto each other as they strolled blissfully past temples, lodges, and palaces. A red balloon floated above the hats and selfie sticks, straining against its cotton cord like Icarus being pulled up to the sun. As it popped, someone laughed nervously. The sidewalk cafes and restaurants were full. Tables spilled out onto the pavement outside the Grand Masters Palace, opposite St Georges Cathedral.

Vanda sat under a large umbrella embossed with a beer logo. She was waiting for Benjamin who had popped into a local Internet cafe. He was trying to get hold of Chatunga to see if he had recovered. Judging by the decrepit computers in the window it must have been the last internet café left on the island. Vanda suspected that it was about more than just that. She was concerned about the glint in Benjamin's eye every time he mentioned the rhino horn. *It's as though he's happy about it, she thought to herself.*

She ordered one of the craft beers on the menu. As she gulped it down, she sat back in the sun, closing her eyes. She felt calmer as the beer washed away the reality of her predicament. She raised her hand and ordered another. As she did so, she examined her pearl and diamond brooch. It had been the start of her troubles and was still there right in the middle of the madness.

She lazily blinked her eyes, alternating them so that the empty beer bottle on the table jumped from left to right and back again. With each flick, she gained confidence and strength. She didn't see Big George silently coming up behind her.

"We can do this the hard way or the easy way," he menacingly said. Vanda spun around and stared into the thin face of the man who had spilled wine on her earlier that day. His Panama hat made him look like a Columbian drug lord. His red sideburns glowed in the bright sun.

"You!" she exclaimed.

"Yes, it's me. We can dispense with the niceties."

"How did you find us? Are you following us?" Vanda asked.

"Let's stop pretending Ms. Slade," he snapped. "You know what this is about, don't you? I saw it in your eyes."

"I don't know what you are talking about," Vanda said nervously, scouting the street for Benjamin. He was taking forever in the darned internet cafe.

"Let's make this is simple," Big George said. "I haven't got time for games. You've got a little horn that doesn't belong to you. It belongs to me and I want it back. It's as simple as that. You give me what is rightfully mine and I will leave you alone and let you finish your cruise."

He wiped his sweaty face with a paper serviette as he

spoke. Vanda found him repulsive but remained calm. *After last night, it's going to take more than this to rattle me,* she thought to herself. She expected him to show up at some point again. She wasn't afraid at all. It could have been the craft beer. Beer always had a calming effect on her. Whatever it was, she hardly flinched as she stared him in the face.

"Are you going to spill another drink on me?" she defiantly asked. "What's with the straw hat? A two-year-old could have thought up a better disguise"

"You watch yourself, lady," he snarled. "I'm trying to be nice to you. Give you a chance here."

"I don't have it anymore," Vanda continued. "Maybe I should go and tell the police that it got stolen from me?"

"Oh, I don't think you are going to do that, my Sweetie," he said. "They might check your room on the ship and they might find something incriminating there. Or out on your balcony?"

"What are you talking about?" Vanda said.

"Do you really think that we weren't watching you last night. You know, your midnight skeet shoot! And sneaking back to your room at five in the morning? Ms. Slade my dear, we've got the evidence of what you did."

"I don't know what you are going on about!" Vanda said.

"Malta has the death penalty, you know," Big George said. "Or is it life? Same thing here on the island. Death or life? No one ever survives long after being locked up."

Strangely, Vanda didn't feel any fear from George's threat. "Life?" she continued. "Don't you think that's a bit ironic? Threatening me with life."

She looked him up and down in disgust. His thin ginger hair reminded her of an alley cat that had been on the street too long. She noticed his hands. They were tiny and swollen, like unhealthy potatoes. She doubted they had ever picked up a hammer or shoveled dirt or done a day's hard work.

"I know," she continued. "I know what you've got on the Grande. Mr? What did you say your full name was? George someone? 'Big'?"

As she said the word 'Big', his eyes narrowed and his lips turned thin. He now needed to be dealt with this threat as soon as possible. *That Zimbabwean blabbermouth in Mondello,* he thought. *We should have finished him off with the pick handle when we had the chance. He's been blabbing about me to his old friend Benny Rodd.*

"And I'm talking about way more than just one animals blood." Vanda continued. "It's a bucket load. Isn't it? Or is that a whole container of animal blood I smell?"

She sat back in her chair, pleased that she had stood up for herself. She noticed that Big George had turned the color of ash. His miniature hands were curled into little balls and his knuckles cracked. She had completely rattled him, and she felt great about it.

"Where is Benny?" Big George demanded to know. "I assume he has not abandoned you, yet?"

"You mean Benjamin," Vanda corrected.

"You don't know much about him, do you?" George said. He coughed without putting his hand in front of his mouth. Vanda ignored his question. After what Benjamin had told her on the bus she despised the man in front her. She egged him on some more.

"So, you are 'Enormous George'?" she said, sarcastically. "Aren't you? Yes. Although I can't see why?"

It hit a raw nerve with him. *She knew, for sure.* She had just crossed his line.

"It looks like it's the hard way then," he said, softly.

"Look around you," Vanda replied. "There are police all over the place. I'll scream. I swear to God, I'll scream so loud, that they'll have you locked up in interrogation till Christmas.

Attempted assault is a big crime on the Island. Just like murder!"

Big George smiled. He pulled out his wallet and counted off some notes.

"How much?" he asked, waving the bank notes in Vanda's face. He put his face right up to Vanda's nose. She could smell his breath and tried to pull away.

"Last chance for you, missus. No one can say I'm not fair. I always give a carrot. A little cash incentive for you perhaps," he said.

Vanda sat back and folded her arms. "Do you think I'm Bugs Bunny?"

"Fine. You prefer the stick. I'll give you 12 hours. Go and get my missing horn back from wherever the hell you are hiding it."

"Bollini took it from us," Vanda tried to explain.

"Don't think you can conjure up some cock and bull story now," George snarled. He reached up and pushed his piggish fingers into Vanda's cheeks.

"If you don't bring it back to me, I'll be swapping the pointed nose you stole for your own cute little schnozzle." He grabbed her nose violently and squeezed it. Vanda pulled away in pain.

"As for Benny Rodd. Tell him, I'll be sending him back to where I put him the last time. No carrots for him. He'll be pissing in diapers when I'm done with him."

Spit flew into Vanda's face. He let go and slapped the money down on the table. It was less than a hundred dollars.

"Tomorrow! You deliver by tomorrow, or else." He turned and marched away.

Vanda watched the back of him disappear down the street. Her heart was racing and she shook like a smoothie maker.

A few minutes later, Benjamin arrived back. He was smiling, oblivious to what had just happened.

"I couldn't get hold of Chat," he said.

"Really?" Vanda shouted. "Is that all you are worried about right now? Your idiot Zambian friend?"

"Zimbabwean!" Benjamin corrected. "You look terrible Vanda. Like you've been in my nightmare with my ghost. You know my ghost? Astraea?" He laughed and then felt stupid as he saw the look on Vanda's face.

"Is everything OK?"

Vanda welled up, a tear dripping down her cheek.

"The redhead," she said. "That pig. Big George. He was here. He threatened me. Ben, we're in a huge mess here."

"Where did he go?"

Vanda pointed down the road. Benjamin turned and ran in pursuit. *This needs to be ended,* he thought as he ran. He didn't hear Vanda shouting to him to be careful, as he scuttled down the road after George. He wanted it sorted. *Man to Man.* That's how they did it in Africa. Man to Man! He needed to cull the threat. *Hit first and hit hard!* It had often been his motto and had saved his hide more than once. Besides, there was a potential fortune to muscle in on. Dr. Miller once told him that only bully's and bastards thought like that. He had laughed at her, knowing he was neither.

Vanda downed her beer and scrambled together some change to pay as Benjamin disappeared into the distance. She decided she'd better go along as well. *Maybe she could help?*

Benjamin caught sight of Big George going into an old stone building. He recognized the Panama hat and the skinny legs. He ran to the building. It was a church of some sort. An old worn sign on the door mantle said, 'St Paul of the Shipwreck'. *I'm not shipwrecking my life. Not again,* Benjamin thought to himself as he went in. He confidently jumped over the threshold.

The grandeur inside was staggering compared to the staid facade outside. Big George's high pitched voice greeted him immediately.

* * *

BENJAMIN SQUINTED, ADJUSTING HIS EYES FROM THE SUNNY brightness outside. He looked around to see where the voice was coming from.

The crusader chapel was ancient. It was named after St Paul who was shipwrecked on the island thousands of years before. Filled with all manner of rusty old relics from desperate Islanders, it gave Benjamin the shivers. *They must have dumped all this junk in here whilst praying and weeping to Mary,* he briefly thought to himself. *While the Moslems battered the walls outside.*

There were no windows and the only light came from old wizened candles and oil lanterns. A coat of silver armor from the Grand Master of the Lodge hung on the wall, looking down with solemn austerity.

Benjamin followed Big George's voice into the bowels of the vestry. He didn't see the ambush coming! He should have known better. Gangsters always work in teams. Big George wasn't alone. Takis Evangelis was with him and snuck up silently behind Benjamin.

His hairy arm shot around Benjamin's neck, locking its hold like a pro wrestler. He squeezed like a boa constrictor eating its dinner. Benjamin gasped for air trying to pull loose from the stranglehold, but it was the grip of someone who knew exactly how to immobilize a man.

The energy started sucking away from him. After two failed attempts, it seemed as though his adversaries were learning their lessons. They did not intend to give Benjamin a chance to fight back. They wanted him laid up in the Malta hospital, off the ship for good. Then they could deal with Vanda alone and easily retrieve their missing horn. Besides George had insisted that 'old Benny Rodd' was a threat to the entire operation.

The last thing Benjamin remembered hearing was a shout from an old monk who was hovering around some red candles at the baptismal altar. The light faded from his eyes and he flopped down onto his knees. He stumbled blindly into a bench, holding onto an old stone pillar. He scanned the church to see what other surprises might be waiting for him.

"THEY'RE GONE, IF YOU WERE WONDERING," A VOICE OFF TO HIS side said. Astraea was there!

She was hiding behind a statue of the Madonna. Silver buckles and badges smothered the statue, so one could hardly tell what it was made from. Each decoration was from some long-dead warrior or King or Knight. The Madonna was dressed in a nun's habit and her weeping eyes looked upward. She had one hand on her heart and the other reached out to Benjamin, through a string of pearls. Pearls were all over Mary, running through her fingers and over her shoulders. Her fingers caught them as they slid toward the floor. Each little dusty pearl left a luminescent sheen on the fingers that sought to restrain them.

As her fingers soaked up the pearls, a rainbow-tinged gloss flowed up her arm and she became covered in fluorescent light. Madonna's moroseness disappeared and Astraea stepped through her and stood in front of Benjamin. She was beaming.

Benjamin had promised himself that the next time his Astraea dream appeared, he'd face her, hear what she had to say and then get her to leave him alone forever. He was sick of her madness.

"It's not what you do that makes you mad," Astraea said, as though reading his mind. "It's who you are."

Benjamin could picture Dr. Miller looking down at him over her rimless spectacles, her eyebrows slightly raised. She was nodding in agreement.

Benjamin knew exactly what Astraea was talking about. He stood silently in the dock. He expected her to change. To change like she did all the other times. To become dark. Evil. Bring him to his knees.

But she didn't. Not that time.

She morphed into the exact opposite. A warm light lit up around her. Her face was youthful and radiant. Her lips and mouth were no longer bloodied and ravaged by death but rich with life and beautiful energy. She came straight to him and held out her hand. Benjamin took it. He couldn't help himself. She felt warm.

"Why are you going back?" she asked.

Benjamin felt a sickness in his gut. His past had not let go of him one bit. He'd been lying to himself. He had been trying to get a release for years but there were still fishing hooks in his soul. He was falling and sinking into his own hole. His own wretched dark hole.

"Think about why you're going back to the ship," Astraea said.

She let go of his hand and withdrew back into Mary's bosom.

"Healing is more than just saying sorry," she called. "Saying sorry, simply won't cut it. There's a thing called atonement and it's complex."

And she was gone.

BENJAMIN CAME ROUND WITH VANDA SHAKING HIM. A FEW monks had gathered round to help. One of them held up a bright torch and shone it into Benjamin's face

"Benjamin. Ben. Wake up. Please?" Vanda pleaded. "You passed out! Oh, dear! What are we going to do?"

Benjamin regained his senses quickly. "Our future is on that ship," he said defiantly. "We're going back!"

"We have to," Vanda whispered into his ear. "They want their stolen horn back and they're got evidence from last night if we don't give it back. He said they'd hurt you and hand us over to the police."

"Then let's go get it," Benjamin replied. "My head hurts!"

* * *

TAKIS EVANGELIS SUCKED HARD ON THE CIGARETTE STUMP he was squeezing between his forefinger and thumb. Each desperate draw seemed to build up his anger and frustration. The smoke he blew into his friends face, filled the room with reflections of retribution and hatred.

"Are they back on the ship yet?" he demanded to know. Panayotis Pappas waved the smoke in his face away.

"No, not yet," he answered. "I thought you and Big said you would sort out this today?"

"Benjamin Rodd would be wrapped in plaster in a hospital bed right now if it hadn't been for that blasted priest."

"He was a monk, not a priest."

"Monk, priest, father? They're all the same," Takis said. He took a final drag of his cigarette and threw the butt onto the floor, obliterating it with his boot. He coughed the last bit of smoke out of his lungs and spat into the pile of rubbish next to him.

"We think they know," he said. "The girl said as much. She told Big that they know about this." He waved at the boxes behind him.

"We've got two days before we get to Barcelona to clean this up," Pappas said. "Room 749, did you say?"

"Yes, 749 is Rodd's room," Takis said. "I checked this morning with reception. That old poacher must now be properly dealt with by morning. And the Girl. She's got the horn they stole hidden somewhere. We'll deal with her once we have it back."

"She said Bollini now had it."

"She's talking rubbish!" Takis snapped. "How could he possibly be involved."

"We know where her room is."

"Send the second Bulgarian twin to get rid of Rodd," Takis said. "He'll be more successful than his brother. I don't want any of us exposed here anymore. No more loose ends please."

"Rodd will be sorted, cleanly and quietly," Pappas assured. "He won't be the first depressed man to overdose from loneliness on a cruise, will he?"

They both grinned.

"What about Bollini?"

"He'll be busy sucking up to the Captain and picking on innocent guests. I'm in real control on this ship!" Takis shouted. "Everyone knows it. Even Captain Pizarro."

Pappas shook his head and said nothing.

"Any sign of the other twin? The thieving son-of-a-bitch?"

"No, he's completely disappeared. He didn't come back last night."

"Rodd and the girl?"

"Must be. We checked her room last night, found some interesting things rolling about on her floor."

"But not the horn!" Takis said.

"Talk about being in the wrong place at the wrong time," Pappas laughed. He stood up and swung his big frame up the steel steps.

"We have to recover it, Panayotis," Takis shouted after him. "Or it's coming off our paychecks and Big will be done with us."

Pappas disappeared and Takis stood alone in the steel room under his food stores. He walked over to the wooden boxes and lovingly stroked the side of one. *Unless I'm done with Big George first*, he said to himself. He lifted a huge Rhino horn from the open box.

"Ah," he said out loud. "My retirement plan in Ibiza."

* * *

BENJAMIN RETURNED TO THE SHIP FOR THE THIRD DAY IN A row with an injury he'd just incurred. *It's becoming a habit*, he kept saying. He pretended nothing was sore as he hobbled along. His mind was a fruit salad.

"Listen, Vanda," he moaned. "This is not only about those crooks and their blasted smuggling. It's about, you know." He struggled to find the right words.

"Tell me, Ben," Vanda said, getting irritated by his constant whining.

"Fine then! Astraea! Astraea," he said. "There. I said it. It's about her. She was there again. In the church. She was the Madonna."

"Ben," Vanda said slowly. "I think you should go and lie down. You have been through the mill over the past few days. I understand, but this Astraea is in your head. Your imagination. You have bigger things to worry about. Big Jim, whatsisname? George! He just tried to throttle you and you're now going on about dreams."

She took him by the arm to steady him.

"Big George is his name," Benjamin replied.

"We need to go to the authorities," Vanda insisted.

"Are you crazy?" He pulled loose from her. "We've been through this! Which cops do you suggest? The Maltese ones? Or should we wait for the Spanish police now? How about Bollini? Maybe he can taser me again to get my statement? They'll throw us in the brig, and then we'll never get to the bottom of this. Just what George wants."

"You're the one acting crazy, Benjamin," Vanda said. "All the time, you're acting crazy. And this Astraea woman, for goodness sake!"

"I told you about Astraea as a friend. Because I trusted you," Benjamin whispered, as though it was taboo to even question her existence.

When they got back to the harbor, the queue onto the ship crawled along slowly. Benjamin looked around for Bollini. He was nowhere to be seen. It was still hot and Benjamin wiped his face with his sleeve.

"I thought you understood last night when I tried to tell you," he said. "Anyway, do you think they'll believe you? Last night? The gun? Your shot? Have you forgotten what you did?"

A female cruise concierge interrupted them.

"Mr. Rodd?" she asked. "Ms. Slade? Will you please both come with me? We've been trying to contact you all day. The Captain needs to see you urgently."

"Ben," Vanda whispered, as the concierge turned her back. "What do you think this is about? Is he part of it? The Captain?"

"Let's go along with it. I'd rather face him than Bollini or Big George's chaps," Benjamin said. They pushed through to the front of the crowd and into the empty first class Yacht Club queue.

"The Captain. He is right here."

The concierge pulled open the door to a room off the entrance. It had one-way glass and Captain Pizarro had been watching them approach. He was vivacious and friendly as they walked in.

"Ah, Vanda," he said, taking her hand and kissing the back of it like a randy Casanova. "It is so nice to see you. Did you have a wonderful day?"

He completely ignored Benjamin as though he was not in the room.

"I promised you something special last night," he said,

with a romantic machismo. "For the inconvenience of your friend, here."

He looked over to Benjamin for the first time. "How are you today, sir?" he casually asked, not caring what the answer might be. "You know? Your little accident with Senor Bollini."

"Ah yes. My tasering," Benjamin replied. He was glad it was about that and had nothing to do with the real mess they had found themselves in. The Captain waved his hand in agreement.

"We would like to compensate you for your... your little accident," Pizarro said. "For the inconvenience." He was again only talking to Vanda, despite who had been tasered.

"Vanda," he said. "We are very, very sorry." He took her hand and tried to kiss again. She pulled it away but played long.

"Javier, it was terrible, most terrible," she sniffed, raising her palm to her brow. "What can you do? My poor Benjamin here. His body is still in pain. And we're together now, you know." She pulled a funny face at Benjamin behind Pizarro's back.

"The presidential suite!" The Captain insisted, clicking his fingers. "Nothing less than the presidential suite."

He was enjoying himself, throwing around rooms that cost ten grand a night, as though they were small change. "It's our finest room," he continued. "Hardly ever used. It's too expensive. Sarkozy booked it last year for two weeks."

Sarkozy's mistress was his best story. It made women weak at the knees, he said. "We offer this to you, free. For you little accident of last night. We hope it makes you happy?"

He turned to Benjamin as though a business negotiation was about to start.

"Two small things," he said, "Firstly, are you sure you are happy sharing a room together? I know you each came on this trip alone but regrettably, we only have one Presidential suite."

Vanda quickly replied. "Of course, Captain. Mr. Rodd and I would love to share the suite, wouldn't we Ben?" Benjamin didn't respond. He didn't trust Pizarro.

"Wouldn't we Benjamin?" Vanda said again, a bit more forcefully. She raised her eyebrows to him. Finally, Benjamin got it. It was a potential safe haven from Big and his goons.

"Oh, yes, no problem, no problem," he said, pensively. He could picture what Vanda was thinking. *Clever*, he thought to himself.

Vanda turned to Pizarro and asked, "Can we please also ask a favor of you?"

"Anything, anything," the Captain said saluting. His chest puffed out and his colorful epaulets shone in the light.

"We want to go to this suite completely incognito," Vanda said. "No one is to know. Only you and us? It's such a horrible thing to boast about to other passengers. They might think you have shown favoritism. They might get jealous seeing us upgraded and all."

"Not just upgraded," Benjamin interjected. "We're going to Sarkozy's suite."

"Yes, Sarkozy's suite," Captain Pizarro said. "We do the same for him. Off the radar. Yes, incognito of course. We'll only tell the housekeeper that someone has moved in there."

"No," Vanda said, firmly. "No one is to know. Just the three of us. No other crew. We don't want a housekeeper, a butler or anyone!"

"Why?" the Captain asked. "You surely need a maid or a butler? Don't you want to be spoiled?"

"Like when you tasered me illegally in the back," Benjamin said, now finally playing along. "For no reason, I might add."

"Captain, it has to be our way," Vanda explained. "We

don't want Mr. Rodd here to continue the conversation he's started with his lawyers back in London, do we? We want it this way and no more questions!"

The captain reluctantly nodded in agreement.

"What was your other request?" Benjamin asked.

"You sign this piece of paper." Captain Pizarro pulled out a document already typed and prepared. "It's just a little disclaimer," he explained. "It says that you have been fully and finally compensated for your little accident, sir."

Benjamin and Vanda both realized that this was not just goodwill from the captain. It was a well-planned corrective business decision to avoid a lawsuit.

"I'll sign it after you keep your side of the agreement," Benjamin said. "No one must know where we are staying. Not even the cockroaches! Got it?"

The captain nodded his head again. He had not got exactly what he wanted but at least they'd accepted the compensation. He knew it would cost the MSE Shipping Co virtually nothing if the Presidential suite was occupied for a few days. It was always empty. He folded the disclaimer up and put it back into his pocket.

"Don't cross me, Mr. Rodd," he warned. "We will release your passports only after you sign."

"Agreed," Benjamin said. "The same trust from us to you. Absolute secrecy about our room change."

"Let's go and pack our bags then," Vanda suggested.

Pizarro handed them their new cabin key cards. He turned and disappeared out the door. His business was done.

For once, things were going their way. They took extra care that no one followed them as they headed into the ship.

* * *

"Wow!" Vanda exclaimed as they opened the door to their new quarters. "So this is how presidents do it?"

Benjamin dumped all the bags he had been heaving along inside and closed the door. The canvas bag with the shotgun fell with a thud onto the marble.

They began exploring. There were two full separate bedrooms in the suite, each with its own massive luxuriant en-suite bathroom. The cherry wood doors clicked shut like a Maybach.

"My cupboard is bigger than my entire old room," Vanda shouted. The balcony ran the full length of the stern of the ship.

"It's like being on our own private luxury yacht," Benjamin said.

"The whole Yacht Club section is like that," Vanda explained. "I read about it. It is virtually impossible to know that hundreds of other people are on the same ship."

"You mean hundreds of Yobbo's," Benjamin joked. "I can understand now why no one hardly ever stays here. It must cost a bomb."

He jumped on one of the beds and stretched out, star-spangled. The wooden ceiling with its inlays of mahogany and oak stared down at him like an old sea captain. The linen was the finest Egyptian thread and embossed on the edges with gold thread and the letters PS.

"Which room do you want?" he asked.

"We're hardly strangers," Vanda replied over her shoulder, as she stepped into her bathroom. "Which room should *we* use?"

Slipping off her dress, she climbed into her shower. Benjamin caught a glimpse of her through the open door. His pulse rose and an old hibernating thump in his chest struck. He felt guilty.

"You're amazing," he shouted, before turning toward his own bathroom on the other side.

He was hot and sweaty and rubbed his neck. It was red where he had nearly been strangled. His neck pain merged with his welted back and bruised head. *My whole body aches,* he muttered as he dropped into his hot bath.

As the grime of Malta washed off his body, he thought of Vanda in the other bathroom. She was the only woman he had known who was not easily scared off by his crazy antics. She had gumption and grace. And she knew how to handle a gun.

I'm so glad she hasn't run away yet, he thought to himself, before guiltily sliding into the bubbles. *I need her for bait!*

* * *

Dinner on the MSE Grande was a posh affair that evening. It was meant to be the gala highlight of the entire cruise. Benjamin convinced Vanda that it was better for them to be seen in public places than to just suddenly disappear. It was their new cabin location he wanted to keep secret, not the fact that they were on the ship. Vanda had reluctantly agreed.

"I suppose if Bollini doesn't see us mingling, he'll get highly suspicious," she sighed.

"And if Big George sees us dining, as usual, he won't suspect that they have changed rooms, which means at least we'll be safe here."

"I'm worried about Bollini,' Vanda said. "If he took the rhino horn from your safe, then why doesn't he just confront you? He's a loose cannon."

"He's a jerk!" Benjamin said, straightening his bow tie. "And probably a corrupt crook."

Vanda had kept her best clothes aside for this evening. As

she entered the antechamber of the dining room, heads turned. Elegant couples, sipping champagne and telling each other tales of how Malta had entranced them, were brought to silence as she walked past. Captain Pizarro, who was surrounded by long-legged ladies and their worried partners, nearly choked on his gin and tonic. He recovered his decorum though and turned away. *He's either jealous or angry. Probably both*, Vanda thought, giggling to herself.

Her simple green dress brushed the marble floor. Matching earrings peeked through her hair, that had been swept up into an elegant bun held together with two wooden pins. She strutted as though she was on the Milanese runway at Fashion Week.

Benjamin felt a thump in his throat as he looked at her from the bar where he had picked up two Martinis. She was chatting to Kevin O'Donnell but constantly scanned the room over his shoulder. Her neck was taught and long and tanned. A jazz quartet played Miles Davis in the background. The clarinet jammed out an improv and its irregular rhythms intoxicated and enchanted the evening air.

Doctor Burlington came up like a fat python and jostled Benjamin who was meandering back to Vanda. His young girl-friend was at his side. She was more relaxed than she had been on the previous evenings. Miming a little dance to the jazz rhythms, she punched out her shoulders in slow motion jabs.

"Two days at sea, Old Chap," the doctor said, clanging his champagne glass against Benjamin's full hands. Drops messed onto the floor. Benjamin felt his temperature rise, despite the jovial energy of the night.

"Do you think you'll survive, Old Chap?" The doctor continued, tipping his beady eyes in Vanda's direction. He flicked his eyebrows, with a dirty smirk.

It may have been just evening banter, but for Benjamin, it

was a loaded question. *Would he survive? Would they make it? What could he have to do to get in and out of the game again, without hurting himself? And Vanda? Poor Vanda, what about her?* She was becoming more and more compelling and he could feel deep flames starting to light up from within him. Like strings, they slowly tightened and pulled him closer. And he liked it. He was terrified. *Was he ready? Was she the one?* All this passed through Benjamin's mind as he tried to civilly engage the hideous fat doctor blocking his way.

He balanced the martini glasses up in the air where they couldn't be knocked again. He had dressed in a simple tux. He had packed it only because Dr. Miller had said he should. *You can never be overdressed*, she had said. And this was meant to be the high point in a week of high dining.

"Love is four letter word," Benjamin said. "Isn't it Christopher?"

Burlington smacked the butt of his young girlfriend. "Who's talking about love?"

Benjamin felt ill inside but smiled as politely as he could. "Vanda's waiting," he said, before walking away.

The guests started moving toward the dining area to take their seats. Vanda worked their table like a society expert. She had the table wrapped up in giggles all night.

Benjamin, on the other hand, spent most of his evening trying to rev up the Ng's in his broken Vietnamese. Lesley Ng made the fateful mistake, early in the evening, of telling Benjamin that she found Captain Pizarro attractive. She'd meant it as a casual pass away remark, but it gave Benjamin a nice gap to ruin their evening. *She might just be trying to make her husband a wee bit jealous, but I'll turn that jealousy into a raging inferno by the time I'm finished,* he decided in his head. He had no time for the Vietnamese. Not after what they did to him in prison!

Whilst he wound them up over the Captain, he dumped

extra salt into Tram's chicken curry when he wasn't looking and then tried to ply Lesley with cheap wine. He embarrassed them with rude renditions of Vietnamese jokes whenever he could. Surprisingly, they put up with it all.

He turned to Vanda to see if she noticed. She hadn't. *How could she?* She only spoke English.

By the time dessert came around, the Ng's were having a huge argument with each other. Something about Tram losing money at the tables. Benjamin kept stoking it. Lesley eventually stormed off in a huff to Captain Pizarro's table. Benjamin caught the Captain, pulling out a chair for her and kissing her hand.

Tram stormed out the dining room. "Enjoy the crap tables," Benjamin shouted after him in Vietnamese. He chuckled to himself. *Couldn't have happened to a nicer couple.* He took a sip of his drink and then felt terrible.

Vanda thoroughly enjoyed the wine and spirits. Again! She couldn't help herself once she got going. With each swallow, she forgot their nasty day and rose with optimistic Pyrrhic jubilation. Benjamin hoped she kept sober enough to keep quiet about the pickle they were in. He needn't have worried. Vanda became more and more adept at deceit as she got intoxicated. No one observing her meander vivaciously around the table would have thought that in the last 24 hours, she had shot a man and had her life threatened. Not to mention, getting mixed up in some illicit rhino horn racket or having Captain Pizarro eating out of her hand like a French bulldog.

Benjamin knew he was falling for her despite his aching body telling him to back off and retreat. As he watched her with growing affection, he also kept an eye open for Big George and Salvatore Bollini. With the attention they had grabbed with their flashy entrance and Vanda's growing loudness, he was convinced that they would come snooping around sooner or later. It was what he wanted to happen, draw them out. They'd be snooping about after Vanda to find their missing horn, then he could try and follow them and find out where the real stash was.

He felt he could handle them, but he was worried for Vanda, despite the fact that she kept saying that she could handle herself, with or without his help. Benjamin half believed her. *She shot a man for goodness sake, without blinking! There's something more to her? Or she's got as screwed up a-past as me!* She had been full of surprises since the day he met her.

As the evening wore on, Benjamin noticed the maître d' who had given him a hard time on the second night when he asked about their thieving waiter. He was doing his job a bit too well, hovering incessantly around their table, but with no real purpose. He eavesdropped under the guise of opening bottles and picking up dropped serviettes. Benjamin suspected that he was watching their every move. He checked out the name tag the burly man was wearing. It said, 'Panayotis Pappas', in big bold capital letters.

Benjamin watched him closely. There he was again, sizing Vanda up and straining his ear to listen to her. He eventually realized that Benjamin was onto him, and waddled off to the square pit in the middle of the restaurant. He had a clear line of sight onto their table though and continued his amateur surveillance.

Overall, the evening was a jovial mixture of intoxicated tale-telling and small talk. Cruises tend to have that effect on guests. By the time coffee was finished and Doctor Burlington was staggering back to his room, it was after midnight. Benjamin took Vanda's hand and after bidding the remaining table guests a good night they left. Vanda wobbled, holding onto Benjamin.

"That maître d' in charge!" Vanda said, as soon as they

stepped outside. "Papay...? I can never pronounce Greek names properly. Did you notice him too, Ben?"

"Panayotis Pappas. Yes. He was watching us like a hawk all night." It was good to know that it had not been his wild imagination. "Watch over there," Benjamin predicted. "One, two, three. There we go."

The door behind them opened and Pappas, in his smart maître d' attire, stepped outside, opening a box of cigarettes. As he lit up, his eyes scanned the area, briefly stopping on them.

He thinks he's a pro, Benjamin thought to himself. The *idiot couldn't trail a blind elephant.*

"He's following us," he whispered to Vanda, pretending to kiss her ear. "He must be part of it. No sign of the others. Bollini or Big George."

Vanda responded by turning her head and kissing him. "Don't let him know we're onto him," she said. "We'll lose him in the dance lounge."

Benjamin put his arm around her, pretending to ignore the man sucking on his cigarette a few meters behind them. They turned, walking off in the direction of the late-night club. There were lots of people about. Everyone knew that they could sleep in the next day, it was going to be a full day at sea. As they walked they whispered to each other, planning how they would split up and then slip away secretly back to the presidential suite.

Benjamin pulled away at the doors to the club.

"Oi, waiter!" he shouted to Pappas, catching him by surprise. Pappas looked up pretending to just be an innocent crewman walking by. Benjamin sized him up.

"We need a bottle of scotch. And a packet of crisps." Benjamin said, handing him his old room card. "Here, take my card. Room 749. Bring it with ice, please."

Pappas took the card and turned around grumbling.

There were people around and he couldn't afford to make a scene.

"Make it snappy, man!" Benjamin shouted. He and Vanda turned into the club. "That'll give us a bit of time," he whispered.

Their plan worked. Vanda left Benjamin to 'slip out' to the bathroom and Benjamin disappeared three minutes later when the strobe lights on the dance floor turned on. When they rendezvoused with each outside the spa, the maître d' was still barging his way through drunk gamblers and dancers, trying to figure out where they went. He swore constantly in Greek.

Benjamin and Vanda were confident that no one had followed them as they opened the door to the presidential suite. Vanda collapsed on one of the enormous beds. "I could do with about a week of sleep," she said.

She flicked off her high heels. Benjamin agreed. He hadn't slept one decent night since Genoa. *Astraea! All her fault.* He locked the door and propped a chair up against it, just in case someone visited them again. He fell on the bed next to Vanda and looked up at the ceiling.

"So, we now know that the maître d', this Panayotis Pappas fellow, is part of their racket," he said. "We'll keep an eye open for him now."

"We're stuck on this ship for two days now," Vanda said. "We get to Barcelona on Friday. We should hole up here for the whole time, just to be safe?"

"We have to get that horn back from Bollini," Benjamin said. "We can take control of this if we're clever." Inside, he was thinking of using the horn as a magnet to get him close to the rest of it.

"I hope you friend Astraea stays away tonight. We both need some good shut-eye," Vanda casually said.

Benjamin wondered what Astraea might do next to

torment him. The last thing she had mentioned was something about atonement. *Atonement?* He fell back into the soft duvet and closed his weary eyes. That word rang in his ears as he quickly drifted off to sleep.

Vanda lay frustrated, propped up next to him on a cushion. She wondered what was wrong with him.

* * *

BENJAMIN SLOWLY DROPPED INTO A DARK TUNNEL. THE WALLS had ingrained lines twisting toward to an orb of light at the end. They were white twirls of contrast on a dark lollipop of tubular metal. He stopped at the end. He stood full height in the tunnel, looking toward the glare at the other end. Squinting, he tried to see where he was. Two steel bars dissected the tunnel. One was horizontal and one vertical. They met in the dead center of the space, splitting it into four perfectly equal quarters. The glare at the far end faded and Benjamin could see a picture in the round space beyond. It was a familiar scene, a viewing lens into his past. Green fields and thorny bushes swayed gently in the African breeze and the sun was high in the sky.

The distant cry of a Fish Eagle wailed through the dry air. And there were animals. Lots of them. Herds of antelope, elephant families, zebra, giraffe, and wildebeest. Benjamin followed them one by one through the tunnel. Each was highlighted as the cross of the steel bars floated over them. He imagined his finger squeezing. Everything was through that dirty lens. He stopped moving as the sights settled on a pile of white bones on the dusty ground. The bones moved. Someone was under them! Someone was struggling to get through. They pushed, trying to get out.

Astraea! She was gaunt and pale. She called to Benjamin to come closer. The bones enclosed her like prison bars. As he walked towards her, encircled by the barrel tomb around him, he realized that he was the one behind the bars.

He wasn't surprised to see her. She had pursued him whenever he had closed his eyes and he no longer fought it. All men need to face their demons at some point and it's never the right time. But he knew it was just a dream. He had nothing to lose.

"Your soul, Ben," Astraea said. "That's where the death wells up from. That's where you swirl in your muck. It's more than touching and doing. It's being! Down there in your soul. That's what matters. And that darkness of yours never goes away, does it?"

Astraea moved behind the bones as she spoke. Benjamin felt as though he was floating. She was grounded. He could see the world through the crosshairs of the telescopic lens he was stuck in. It was as though whatever he encountered could be blown away with a simple squeeze of the finger. Just like the old days.

"It can be blown away," Astraea said, reading his thoughts. "It needn't be though. You know that."

"What do you mean by atonement," he asked. The word was lodged somewhere in his conscience. It was dangling tiny sparks of hope in front of him whenever he thought about it.

"I can't help you," Astraea said. "You are stuck there behind that gun barrel and I am here, stuck behind these old bones. Do you recognize this one?"

She picked up the closest bone to her. It was a huge femur, white and aged like a weather-worn piece of marble in the cemetery. "No one remembers who has been buried. No one cares."

"Maybe I do care," Benjamin heard himself saying.

"Are you going to bury Vanda?" Astraea asked.

"It's complicated," he answered. He looked at Astraea through the crosshairs. He had the sights focused on her forehead and wanted to blast her to smithereens.

"Go ahead," she taunted him. "Pull the trigger. Pull it! Do you want to stay there forever tormented by the demons of your rotten past? Then go right ahead."

She stopped moving to give him a clean shot.

"We all have to survive," Benjamin said. "It's a crappy world out there!"

"But you like it?" Astraea replied. "The hunt, the blood, the death!"

"If I don't do it, someone else will."

"What gives you the right?" Astraea asked.

"I paid my dues."

"And now you think Vanda must pay hers?"

Benjamin looked at her sheepishly. "I can explain, Astraea. I think I can explain," was all he could hear himself saying.

BENJAMIN SAT DOWN IN THE DIRT. IT FELT AS THOUGH THE world was listening as talked to her.

* * *

"EVER SINCE I CAN REMEMBER," BENJAMIN SAID, "THE SMELL has been there. The dry acrid smoke tattooing my nostrils with the stench of death. I'm addicted to that smell.

I remember the first time I shot an Impala. My father lay next to me in the high grass encouraging me to leave my innocence behind. 'Only after you kill, can you become a real man,' he had said.

I can remember the guffawing and boasting as we walked that long fifty meters to the scene of death I had created. I remember the eyes of that buck. They were black and shining with heightened fear. As we knelt down, they froze in an immortal glower, embedded into the back of my brain. Those eyes held my hand as I shot my way to manhood. The smell of that kill excites me. And it haunts me.

You see, when you kill, a piece of shrapnel always finds its way back to your soul. It falls with a clunk into a tin bucket and it rattles around there forever. And as you kill again, as your skills grow and you kill more and more, the little pieces of lead keep falling. Until that bucket starts filling up!

One day it becomes so full that the rattling stops. It's just dead weight.

I'm a hunter!

I'm hunted!

It's all I know.

I wasted too much time around roaring campfires, drinking brandy and coke, listening to tales from American billionaires who had shot a caged lion or bagged a buffalo at two hundred meters with a telescopic lens. There was no glory for them, just the bravado of weak cowards who came to Africa looking for a sick adventure to fill their shallow voids.

I wanted the real glory! I wanted to be the story.

To hell with it all. The jaded line was gone. I'd shoot anything. Hunting? Poaching? What's the difference? A license?

Did I mention the money? It was sweet! It was easy!

Mary? She wasn't.

My conscience lies squashed at the bottom of my tin bucket"

ASTRAEA PUT HER HAND ON BENJAMIN'S SHOULDER. IT FELT *warm and understanding.*

"It's going to be OK," she said. She smiled and then she was gone.

❧   6   ❧

AT SEA

Benjamin woke up late with a pounding headache. He had spent all night grappling with his demons. It was Thursday morning and there was a full day and night ahead of them on board the ship before it arrived in Barcelona.

Vanda greeted him, stretching and yawning. She looked beautiful in the morning. Benjamin studied her as she propped herself up on the pillow. Her auburn hair glowed in the morning sun. The room had lost its dark wood-paneled dankness of the night and was alive with energy. Eclectic blends of expensive decor were lavishly thrown about.

Benjamin got up and walked to the kitchenette. He popped a coffee pod into the espresso machine.

"I hope you woke up with some good ideas," Vanda said. "We need to fix this and get off this ship!"

"We're going to get our darned little horn back after breakfast," Benjamin boldly said. He had not figured out how to get into Bollini's office undetected.

"I wonder whether Bollini even took it in the first place?

Why would he risk his job and go rummaging through the guest's safes?"

"I was a suspect remember?" Benjamin reminded her. "Your so-called stolen brooch? He was probably just fishing around for something to nail me with."

"I'm sorry about that, Ben. I really am. It's what got us into all this trouble."

Vanda got out of bed and walked over to Benjamin in her white tank top. She put a comforting hand on his chest before continuing. "Or he thinks he's detective Colombo trying to get famous."

"That horn was definitely worth a few fair dollars and George's crew won't take us out while they think we have it."

"So, we should pretend that we have got it?" Vanda said, stirring her cup.

Benjamin nodded.

"What happens if they find out we don't have it?"

"They won't believe us. And if they did, we'd then be nothing more but a few loose ends to get rid of."

"So that's why our best option is for us to get it back and just give them what they want."

Benjamin hesitated before choosing his words carefully. "We don't have to give them anything," he slowly said, watching for Vanda's reaction.

"What are you saying"

"Think what we could do with a few hundred grand?"

"Forget it!" Vanda instantly replied. "Not from that! Not ever!" Benjamin went silent and finished his coffee. *Was she right? Maybe there were better ways to get back on top in life?*

"It was just a thought."

"What about your friend, Chatunga?" Vanda asked.

"I can't get hold of him. His number was on my phone and that's lying at the bottom of the ocean right now."

"I think that's a good thing," Vanda said. "Let's keep him out of this. I didn't like anything he said back in Modello."

Benjamin looked Vanda up and down. *Who's in charge here,* he wondered?

"There's another evacuation drill scheduled for later. They do them every three days," Vanda said. "Bollini will be up on deck with a whistle and life jacket. That will give us a gap."

I love this woman, Benjamin thought.

"Excellent idea," he replied. *At least I have a plan now.*

Vanda sat down on the sofa. "One more thing," she continued. "I'm not going anywhere or doing anything until you tell me exactly why you know so much about this wretched business. What's it really got to do with you, Ben? Do you know that I saw on TV once that the rhinos are almost extinct?"

She patted the seat next to her and sipped confidently on her coffee.

* * *

THE EVACUATION DRILL WAS USUALLY A HIGHLIGHT FOR Salvatore Bollini. While the drill was taking place, he had complete control over the ship's passengers. Even Captain Pizarro was meant to listen to him during the drill, although he rarely did.

Bollini had been up early. He'd put on his orange life jacket an hour early, to show the crew how important it was and that he was the one running the show. There was an over-sized white label on his life jacket that read, 'Officer In Charge - Emergency and Evacuation.' He puffed out his chest so that everyone could see the label clearly.

He scrambled around with a walkie-talkie in one hand and a clipboard in the other as the siren blew three short blasts. All staff and guests were required to immediately congregate at their designated meeting points. There they'd be reminded about the evacuation procedures. It was a compulsory drill for all, crew, and guests. Bollini insisted it be religiously done every three days.

The fake evacuation alarm went off at precisely 11 o'clock, as the daily schedule said it would. Within minutes, the ship resembled an ant nest that had been kicked open, as hundreds of people scurried to their rendezvous points. For most guests, it was part of the fun and experience of being on a ship, a jovial communal affair. There was no real concern or worry from anyone. The orange life jackets reduced the guests to an egalitarian equality and laughter, joking and shouting filled the air. They all knew it was just a practice drill.

In the babel of fun noise, Bollini almost bumped into Benjamin and Vanda as they swum upstream to the flow of people. Vanda saw him first. He was just in front of them strutting about telling the crew what they already knew. She grabbed Benjamin and they spun around so that Bollini wouldn't see their faces.

"Keep walking," she whispered. "He didn't see us."

"At least this confirms what we thought. The one place he won't be in the next hour is in his own office."

A pile of orange life jackets lay on the floor of a lounge they passed through.

"Here, put this on," Benjamin said, handing Vanda a jacket. "We'll blend in better with it."

They had both dressed to try and look like crew. Dark trousers, white shirts, and black shoes. They also put on the wide brimmed straw hats, that the pool staff wore so that cameras wouldn't pick up their faces.

"I reckon we have about ten minutes," Vanda said. "After that everyone will be at their meeting points going through the drills. What floor did you say we need to go to?"

"Second floor below deck," Benjamin answered. "That's where he took me the other night. I remember walking past his office."

They stepped through a service door at the end of the passage that had a large no entry sign on it.

"If we get caught we'll say we got lost in the confusion."

"We're not going to get caught," Benjamin replied. "I need to do this. I want to fix it. All of it!"

His mind briefly wandered to his dreams of Astraea and the previous evening. *Maybe he should do the right thing?*

The staff elevator door opened and they casually stepped inside. Vanda hit the buttons. As the door closed, Benjamin thought of the rhino horn he had found in Vanda's bag. It had stank like a rotten corpse. He could picture the poor animal behind his telescopic lens, having its brain shattered to pieces. The elevator ride felt like a drop into purgatory. A hell full of old memories. And rhino horns!

Vanda stood quietly watching the elevator lights change on the panel. What Benjamin had told her about himself, earlier that morning had left her chilled, despite his insistence that he's left that life. She kept reminding herself that it had happened a long time ago and that he had been a different man back then. *So she hoped.* She decided to be supportive and non-judgmental.

What else could she do? Dump Ben and try to get a new relationship going? No! She had no choice. Her destiny was tied to his.

She had plunged into his world, the moment she had pointed that shotgun and there was going back now. The bell for their floor snapped them both back into the present. As the door slid slowly open, someone charged into the elevator, pushing Vanda aside.

"You!" a familiar voice rang out.

* * *

LESLEY NG LOOKED VERY DIFFERENT TO HOW SHE HAD looked when dressed for dinner the previous evening. The Gucci dress and Italian leathers were gone. She was dressed in black gym tights and a black tank top. Her hair was tightly tied back and she hid behind dark sunglasses. She was out of breath and flustered. They caught her by complete surprise.

Benjamin had been rehearsing in his mind what to say if they got stopped by someone. He didn't think, however, that it would be by one of Ng's. He had expected Bollini or Captain Pizarro or a low-rank sentry.

"Emergency evacuation," he tried to casually explain, as they stepped out. "The sign on our door told us to come here. The 2nd floor?"

Lesley Ng deftly ushered them fully out of the elevator. She hit the button to the lobby floor a few times, glaring at Benjamin.

"Wrong second floor," she said in broken English. The elevator began closing and Lesley Ng smirked at Vanda, as though she had just won a hand of poker.

"Javier says hi!" Lesley said in Vietnamese. Benjamin immediately understood. *The randy Spanish Captain has been at it again,* he thought.

"Wait!" Vanda instinctively cried, blocking the closing door with her hand. "Why are you down here?" Their eyes meet like two fighting cats about to pounce on each other.

Lesley Ng pushed the elevator button again as though it would override the hand blocking her escape. She hammered it over and over. "Emergency! Evacuation!" she stuttered in broken English.

I'm sure it was, chuckled Benjamin to himself.

Lesley Ng suddenly regained her composure. She grabbed Vanda's hand that was blocking the elevator and twisted it with the fluidity of a Kung-Fu master. It was a firm warning, that said, *'back off or be broken'*. Vanda grimaced and yanked back her hand.

"Ouch!" she exclaimed. "You need to relax girl. I was only asking you a simple question."

"I go now. I go now," Lesley Ng shouted. The door slid shut and she disappeared as the lift moved up to the lobby. It became eerily quiet in the windowless corridor.

"Are you OK?" Benjamin asked.

"What the heck?" Vanda moaned. "What was that all about! I don't trust her a bit, Ben. She was up to no good down here."

"Maybe," Benjamin said.

Vanda rubbed her sore hand.

"You'll be OK. She knew what she was doing. She wasn't trying to hurt you," Benjamin replied.

"Thanks for the sympathy," Vanda said sarcastically. "So, do you think she was after the same thing we are? This can't be a mere coincidence."

"No, she wasn't" Benjamin confidently answered.

"They joined the cruise late," Vanda said. "I think they only got on in Rome. It's suspicious! Especially after what you told me about the Vietnamese."

"They're not all bad,' Benjamin said. "Common, let's get what we came here for. We're running out of time. You can raise it with Javier at dinner."

"What's he got to do with it?"

"Everything," Benjamin chuckled.

They headed down the staff corridor. It felt exactly the same as it had at midnight, artificially lit by lights that cast odious shadows all over the place.

"Here!" Benjamin pointed to a door next to the room where he had been locked up, two nights earlier. A gold sign on the door said, 'S. Bollini. Head of Security. Private.'

"It's locked."

Benjamin scanned the ceiling as though a key might drop out of the sky. He rubbed his nose wondering what to do next.

"I'll kick it in."

He took a step back and got ready to swing with his leg. It was a typical response from someone who was used to bashing their way out of trouble.

"No need for a broken foot," Vanda said. She stepped up to the door and ran her room card down the side edge. The door swung open and she smiled at Benjamin.

"My Father had some locksmith skills," she whispered with a sly smile. "Always prepared, I am, for lost keys. He taught me that."

Benjamin didn't believe one word of her story, but again, she had pleasantly surprised him. The more he got to know her, the more of an enigma she was. She was a weird combination of transparency and secrecy. He suspected that there was way more to her than what she made out.

"They didn't have that badge when I was in the boy scouts."

"Never had locks back then either," Vanda teased. She peered into Bollini' s office, turning on the light switch as she did so.

"We have a problem!"

The room had been ransacked. The floor was strewn with papers and the drawers of Bollini's desk had been flung out onto the floor. One of them had been smashed on the side. A picture frame from his desk had been flattened and the safe in the corner, behind his chair, was lying open. The contents were still intact. A pack of unused cigarettes had been emptied into the mess.

"They'll think we did this if they catch us."

Benjamin stepped inside the office. His plan had been to quietly slip in, find the rhino horn and then get out without anyone realizing it. *Now, this disaster!* He checked for surveillance, before scanning the room for some sign of the rhino horn. A camera had been pulled from its mount in the corner and was dangling loosely on its wiring.

"Don't know if that's good or bad," he said, pointing.

"There's no rhino horn here," Vanda said.

"Wait!" Benjamin replied. He walked over to Bollini's desk. It had been roughly cleared onto the floor but right in the middle of it, someone had intentionally put something wrapped in a blood-splattered hand towel.

Benjamin felt his gut drop as he opened it up. "We need to get out of here," he said. "We're playing into someone's hand!"

"Who? Bollini?" Vanda asked as she bent over the towel. Then she went white and swallowed.

Benjamin's old room key card was lying on the bloodied towel. On top of it, carefully balanced, was a red shotgun cartridge. It was burnt on the open edge and had been recently fired. Bird-shot! They both instantly recognized it. Vanda instinctively grabbed it and shoved it into her pocket.

"Oh my," she cried. "Someone found it! Bollini is onto us."

Benjamin scanned the room.

"Don't touch anything," he said. "It's not Bollini. Someone put this here to spill the beans on us! Frame us! Double crossing cowards!"

"Someone is coming!" Vanda cried.

Benjamin went to the door and carefully peered out through the thin split into the corridor. Captain Pizarro was casually walking past, straightening his buckle. He was whistling to himself. "I wondered when he'd emerge?" Benjamin said under his breath. "They probably used the sickbay."

Pizarro disappeared to the tune of, 'to all the girls I've loved before'.

"Let's go," whispered Benjamin. "Bring that towel as well."

"So much for your big plan," Vanda said as they shut the door. "We're still empty handed and now in an even bigger pile of trouble."

"We're not empty handed!" Benjamin muttered. "We got the shell back and it's got your prints on. Don't blame me for the rest!"

"Your blood is on this towel," Vanda angrily shot back. "We're in this together!"

"Indeed we are," Benjamin said, double checking that the corridor was empty.

They ran to the elevator and emerged a minute later into the lobby. It was an entirely different world to one they had just come from. They blended effortlessly into the laughing crowds as the door closed behind them. The drill was over and people were heading for the swimming pools, lounges and to wherever they planned to spend the day.

"Bollini is going to hit the roof when he sees his office," Vanda said.

"Serves him right," Benjamin replied.

* * *

"YOU IDIOT!" TAKIS EVANGELIS SHOUTED AS HE THUMPED the chair in front of him. The gaunt silent faces of Big George and Panayotis Pappas stared through the smoky confines of the room beneath the kitchen storeroom. A skinny waiter lay in a heap on the floor in front of them.

Takis pulled his jacket sleeves up to his elbows. The sweat on his face made it look as though he had embalmed his skin in green olive oil. A vein popped in his temple, syncing with the dull beat of the diesel engines thudding through the steel hull. "You got the wrong person," he yelled. "You got the wrong blinking person!"

He held a .45 revolver in his right hand and shoved its barrel up against the lip of the frightened Bulgarian waiter trembling under him.

"You're as stupid as your piss-willy twin," Takis continued. "Wherever he is."

"They kill him," the waiter whimpered in broken English. "The Rodd man. He kills my brother during the storm. My brother, he is gone!"

"Gone with our expensive merchandise, no doubt?" Big George threw in from the shadows. He folded his arms, sucking on his Cuban cigar. "That is convenient, isn't it? Do you know what my father would have gone to a weasel like you?"

"I'm sorry Mr. Big," the man pleaded. "But it's my brother!"

"Abandoned ship in Malta, did he?" George mumbled.

"Forget about his brother," Pappas said. "We have another complication now. One dead tourist thanks to this idiot Bulgarian. Unconnected to anything and found in Rodd's bed in room 749. Bollini is going to have a field day."

"Bollini's a mouse," George said. "And I've already taken care of it. I left enough evidence on Bollini's desk to keep him and Rodd tied up in circles for days."

"And besides, it will need an autopsy to figure out that there might have been foul play," Takis chirped in.

"Where is Rodd, if he wasn't in his room last night?"

"Maybe he skipped in Malta too?"

"No, I saw him at dinner last night," Pappas said. "He's onboard the ship somewhere with the woman."

"So if he was in her room last night, who was in his room? Who did our moron here, bump off? 'Cos unless Rodd shrank and dyed his hair black last night, it sure as Sherlock wasn't him under that blanket!"

"Vanda Slade's room is also unoccupied. He wasn't there."

"Neither was she. I checked."

Takis grabbed the hair of the waiter in his left hand and pulled his face backward. The revolver played with his cracked lips. The man shook like a Pentecostalist.

"He's pissed himself," Big George said. "Takis you're getting nowhere. He knows nothing."

"Wrong," Takis said angrily. "He doesn't know nothing. He knows about us. About this." He waved his gun around the room pointing to the stack of wooden boxes piled along the wall. Pappas ducked as he did so.

"I tell no one, I swear," the waiter pleaded, in his yellow puddle. There were tears staining his grubby cheeks. Big George sighed. "You look like an albino cheetah," he mocked. The others laughed at their victim shivering in front of them.

"OK," Takis said. "We have three days to take care of Rodd and his girl, or we could do it in Barcelona, away from the ship. Too much has now happened on board."

"Let's find them first," Pappas said. "They've both disappeared somewhere."

"Rodd will find us," Big George said. "I know men like him. I know exactly who this Rodd is. The old *Dilletante*. He's a player with a grudge and we need to be careful. He's old mates with our friend, Chatunga from Palermo."

"I thought we taught him a lesson? Scared him away from trying to muscle in on our routes?"

"Great lessons you boys gave in Mondello," George said. "Like how to miss an easy shot when your target is running away in a van."

"I only had one shot," Pappas said.

"Yes, one shot and you missed!" Big George replied. "As for Rodd! He was one of the first players in this game. A brilliant dealer but what really made him famous was that the man actually shot all the animals himself. Can you believe it? Made a fortune before I sorted him out. Dispatched him to our friends in Hanoi, I did. There's no space for small players. I'm surprised he survived and had the gall to creep back."

"Yeah, and just as we get our biggest shipment ever," Takis said. "Talk about coincidence."

"I'm sure he'll come to us unless Bollini gets to him first," George continued. "He can't help it. The smell of money will be irresistible. And the stench of death. Besides, we'll use the girl to flush him out. Get her and we have him. Get rid of him and we have no threat."

Big George stood up and threw his smoldering cigar onto the floor. As it ground out under his leather shoe, he nodded to Takis. "But no more mistakes," he instructed. "Clean up the loose ends!"

The Bulgarian waiter bounced his eyeballs from Takis to Big George and back again. They went wide. He knew exactly what was coming.

"No!" he cried. It was the last thing he ever said. Panayotis Pappas came up behind him and thrust a syringe deep into his neck. He did it with precision and finesse. The waiter's dark pupils dilated and instantly went blank. Takis grinned, lighting up another smoke. The waiter's eyes glazed over as his breathing stopped.

"That's for pissing on our floor," Takis said, with contempt in his voice.

"Take care of the rest," Big George said. "Be careful this time, Pappas! Find the Slade woman and get her down here." He looked around the room. "I hate this place. Next time we meet upstairs in my room. At least there's light and fresh air up there." He hesitated at the stairwell and looked back at the anxious eyes watching him.

"Actually, with all this heat," he said. "It's best we don't meet again on this trip. We all know what we have to do. Keep a low profile from now and don't try to contact me. I'll contact you when I need to in the usual way."

He then left the room. Big George couldn't stomach the aftermath of violence.

* * *

They sped past the bar toward the door opening opposite it.

"Did you hear the news?" Dr. Burlington suddenly boomed as they headed across the room. He expertly intercepted them, coming out of the crowd wearing an over-sized pair of Bermuda shorts. He had a sun hat on and was heading up to the pool deck for the day. A newspaper was tucked under one arm as he struggled to balance three different bottles of suntan lotion with his other hand.

"Looks like you need a bag?" Benjamin said, trying to appear normal.

"I had one, but she did a sly one on me this morning and sneaked off somewhere," the doctor said.

Vanda grimaced.

"I wonder why?" she said under her breath.

"What news?" Benjamin asked, still trying to behave as though nothing was wrong.

"They've cordoned off some of the 7th floor," Burlington explained. "I saw the ships doctors running about and Jessica said she saw them carrying someone off on a stretcher." Burlington dribbled out of the corner of his mouth as he spoke.

"Oh, so her proper name is Jessica then," Vanda replied. "I wondered when we'd find that out. She was so shy at dinner. I didn't realize she spoke English."

"She's Russian," Burlington said.

"Of course she is," Vanda sarcastically replied.

Dr. Burlington's eyes bulged as he sized her up. Benjamin interrupted before they could say anything further. "The stretcher was probably for seas sickness or something," he said. "It happens all the time."

"Yeah, right," Burlington said, sounding annoyed. "It must have been pretty severe seasickness for them to throw a blanket over the face of the sick person. What do you think Miss Vanda? Do you like having blankets over your face?"

The tension from what they had just done down in Bollini's office, finally exploded. Vanda stepped forward angrily and leaned right up to the doctor. She was two inches from his chubby nose and could smell his stale beer from the previous evening.

"If the blanket is frigging 70 years old and the face is a teenager, then no, it's not nice," she yelled. "Not ever, under any circumstance! Don't you get it?"

Benjamin touched her elbow to calm her down. "What are we talking about here?" he asked, nervously.

"You know exactly what," Vanda said. "Do you think this is OK?"

"You should sit down," Benjamin suggested.

"No, I'll see you upstairs," she said, before glaring at Burlington and turning on her heels for the exit. Burlington went dark in his face.

Benjamin tried to get more information from him but the doctor was too upset from Vanda's impertinence. Benjamin couldn't figure out if it was embarrassment or anger. *A bit of both,* he thought. *And Vanda was right. This so-called doctor puffing in front of them had been bombastic and disgraceful from the start. As for his poor teenage escort, it was brazen exploitation.*

Dr. Miller had often said that some things needed to be done for their own sake. *Vanda was right and good on her!*

"You need to control that woman of yours," Dr.

Burlington said. He pointed with his puffy finger to where Vanda had disappeared.

"What? Like you control your Jessica?"

"Yes! My Jessica likes to be controlled if you must know. And by the way, you can take off your ridiculous life jacket now."

He turned and marched off in the opposite direction to Vanda. Shaking his head in disappointment, Benjamin left to go and walk past his old room. He wanted to confirm his suspicions about what Burlington had just told them.

The elevator wouldn't work for the seventh floor. As Benjamin kept trying, one of the crewmen next to him casually remarked that part of the 7th floor was out of bounds.

"Which part?" Benjamin asked.

"Just a tiny section up on the left side at the front. It shouldn't inconvenience you too much, sir," the crewman said, as he pushed for floor eight. "It'll be open again before you know it."

"What happened?" Benjamin asked

"That I cannot say, I'm afraid," the crewman replied. "It's off limits to guests. Our Security Head ordered it so."

He shrugged his shoulders as if he didn't care. Benjamin, on the other hand, did care. He cared very much because his old room had been up on the front left side of the seventh floor. Big George wouldn't have known that he had moved or that someone else had maybe occupied his old cabin. *And he gave the maître d' his old room card! Now someone was up there was covered in a blanket! It was meant to have been him!*

Benjamin's pulse raced and his peripheral vision narrowed. His world pressed in through those telescopic lenses again. He hurried to catch up with Vanda, making sure no one was following him.

* * *

"Why should I help you?" the receptionist asked the burly maître d' who was standing in front of her. "You know that we are not allowed to share information on guests."

Panayotis Pappas stepped forward toward the counter. He wasn't in the mood for rules and he needed to be back at his station in the dining room in five minutes.

"How long have you been working here?" he asked.

"Three weeks," the young lady said.

"Let me tell you how this pans out, my love," Pappas said. "What you do in the next ten seconds will determine if your three weeks becomes four. Or you get thrown off this ship tomorrow morning for harassing one of the guests."

"I haven't harassed anyone, sir. I don't know what you are talking about."

"He says you did," Pappas said, pointing to the doorway. "He said that you accosted him in the lift last night. What was the word he used? Molested! Not accosted. He says you grabbed his privates. Yes, that's what he said. He wants to go to Bollini, he does."

She glanced at the doorway. Big George stood there with a smug look on his face. He put one hand over his crotch and pulled, nodding his head.

"You see," Pappas explained, "they'll believe him. He's a close friend of the captain, I believe."

The receptionist sat quietly glancing between her two bullies and the screen in front of her.

"And there'll be a little reward for you if do this for us. He believes in carrots," Pappas said pointing to George.

He slapped some rumpled notes onto the table. The receptionist hesitated for a second and then made up her mind. Her hand closed over the notes.

"What was the name again?" she asked.

"Rodd. Benjamin Rodd."

"Let's see," she said, scrolling the screen in front of her,

"Richardson, Reece, Rindel, Ryan, Saad... There's no Rodd here sir."

"What? That's impossible," Pappas said. "Try Slade. Vanda Slade."

"No. No sir. No Slade either."

"Let me see that." Pappas stretched over the woman and swung the screen around so he that he could fully see it. He bit his bottom lip as his eyes scrolled the lists in front of him. "Are you sure this is all the guests?"

"Yes, sir. It's the full list of all normal guests. This is the master program."

Pappas swore.

"Of course there's also the VIP list," the receptionist said, "but I don't have access to it."

She checked again to make doubly sure. "We definitely have no Benjamin Rodd or Vanda Slade on this list. I can assure you they would be on this list if we did. And I doubt that they are on the celeb list. No Sarkozy's on this trip, I'm afraid. Look! Each room is listed with the guest's name next to it. Nothing like you ask."

She kept tapping her screen, pointing at one line. Pappas squinted his eyes and then smiled. "VIP's did you say?"

The receptionist pulled her screen back to face her.

"You need to go now, sir. Please," she said. She put her head down and started typing as though nothing happened. Pappas joined Big George and they both left whispering to each other. Big threw his hands up in the air and didn't notice the receptionist cursing him.

"What did he want?" the receptionist's colleague asked from the other end of the counter.

"Nothing," she said. "He just wanted to send a bottle of wine to some guest on the fifth floor."

"Be careful. That Pappas is bad news. My boyfriend got

mixed in with him and his friends and I haven't seen him for two days. I'm getting a bit worried."

"They've probably got him scrubbing the floor somewhere down below."

* * *

BENJAMIN AND VANDA LAY LOOKING UP AT THE CLOUDS IN the tranquil haven of the private Yacht club spa. It was as good a place as any, for them to lie low until they figured out what to do next.

A few other privileged guests lounged in the sun alongside the swimming pool. A marble statue of Aphrodite stood in the shallow end. Soft lounge music played in the background and butlers, in white and blue uniforms, walked effortlessly back and forth pampering to the beckoning waves of manicured hands. Benjamin and Vanda had found some sunbeds at the far side of the pool which were discreetly hidden behind some trellised pot planters, tempting those who wished to suntan more naturally.

"You should have stayed in Malta," Benjamin said. "You were right."

Vanda turned in the sun, handing Benjamin some sun-tan lotion.

"Here, make yourself useful," she said. "I wouldn't have stayed there alone. I said I'm with you Ben, and I mean it."

As Benjamin rubbed some suntan lotion onto her he checked out her tattoo. It was a tiny flying dragon breathing a plume of fire in the center of her toned back.

"Except that poor sod in my room might not have been dispatched if we had acted differently," he said, moving his hand around her lower back.

Vanda turned over. Her bikini top just covered her breasts. "That was not our fault," she said. "They would have got to whoever was in that room irrespective of whether we stayed on Malta or not. And we should be thankful for Bollini and his taser gun. If you think about it, he saved your life by tasering you. That's the only reason Pizarro upgraded us."

"I owe Bollini nothing," Benjamin said. "It might have been him who, you know, stiffed the poor man in my old room."

"I doubt it."

"Look, we know that our waiter was involved," Benjamin said. "The one who started this. And our maître d', for sure. He had my old room card, the one we found planted in Bollini's place. Heaven knows who else? Big George, for certain."

Benjamin gazed up at some seagulls who were diving into the water like aquatic Stuka dive bombers.

"Let's confront Bollini," Vanda suggested. "Let's just be honest, tell him what we know and ask for his help. Ben, I can't stand just lying here, doing nothing."

"Too risky," Benjamin replied. "We're sitting ducks if we go to him. Do you really think he'll do anything to help us after his humiliation yesterday with the Captain? You yourself said he was livid with us. And now his office morning!"

"Thank heavens we were in his office. At least that incriminating shotgun cartridge is now gone. And the towel, I threw them overboard like you asked."

"Backstabbing liars," Benjamin said. "We still don't have our missing horn though, which means Big ugly George will be coming for us."

Benjamin bit his lip and turned his eyes away. That is what he actually wanted. He wanted George to emerge from the shadows so that he could somehow track him back to the real haul on board. He wanted in. He wanted his life back even if it meant one more crooked deal. *I feel terrible about this,* he thought.

"How about 'accidentally' bumping into Bollini then. See

what his reaction is. We don't have to say anything. Common Ben, we need to move forward, or else we're going to be back in this same pickle tomorrow. And the next day."

"OK," Benjamin conceded, after considering what Vanda had said. "No point in hiding from him. After lunch though. Let's let him discover his office surprise first."

Benjamin glanced at Vanda's barely concealed body. She seemed to be entirely at home with or without clothes.

He smiled awkwardly. *I hope she doesn't get hurt in all this,* he thought.

Vanda stretched. "I'm going to the steam room. It'll clear my mind. See you at lunch," she said. Benjamin watched her leave. The sun was lazy in the sky. White jet contrails cut the blue expanse above him like knife scars on the face of a street fighter. He counted them and then focused on one that was moving. He was warm and tired. As he closed his eyes, Benjamin felt himself slipping away to a familiar place. He didn't fight it. He couldn't wait to get there. He knew Astraea would be waiting for him there. He'd ask her what to do.

* * *

THE WOODEN DECK WAS STILL. BENJAMIN TURNED HIS HEAD sidewards and there she was. Her blond hair was loose over her shoulders and she faced straight ahead, looking into the distance. Her skin was luminescent and she radiated the sun rays that seemed to be photosynthesized into her body. Her bright eyes absorbed the empty sky above her.

It was as though the cupboard door, into which Benjamin had thrown his dark past, finally creaked and bulged. He stood with his back to it, half-naked and spread-eagled, not sure if he was trying to keep Astraea from opening it from the outside or holding back the pressure from the inside. The weight bore down on him, as his back bent and his knees strained. He felt as though it was going to fall right on top of him and squash him flat.

"Help," he whimpered. "Common Astraea? Please?"

He fell to his knees, his back about snap. Astraea didn't answer at first. She floated around him like a ballet dancer stalking her lead. The tattoos on her arm started to move, the little vines twisting as though worms had taken over her arteries.

"Why are you running?" she eventually asked.

"What do you mean?"

"You're running somewhere, aren't you?"

"Is that a bad thing?" Benjamin asked.

"It depends, Benjamin," Astraea said. "It depends on where to?"

"What are my choices?"

Astraea's veins thumped and her tattoo crawled up her neck and swirled around her face. She signaled with fingers in each hand, one at a time. "Decency. or Indecency. It's as simple as that. Two places. Two types of people. And two types of choices."

"I already know who I am!" Benjamin snapped. "It is what it is."

"Vanda doesn't think so."

"That's why I like her."

"It's going to be complicated, painful and costly."

Benjamin swallowed. Complicated and painful, he felt he could handle. "How much?" he asked. What's the cost?"

Benjamin felt her reach out and grab him. Rambling rose branches with huge thorns morphing from tattoo to life wrapped around him. He was on his knees. The weight on his shoulders had him buckled completely.

He could see it! Vanda! She would be the cost!

He cried and a tear fell onto the floor, disappearing like a raindrop into a stormwater grate. The ground washed with his tears. He saw green fields and fresh grass blowing gently in the breeze. Astraea walked around in them. Her skin was pure, the ghastly vines and twists of thorns had returned to the buds that birthed them. She held *up a mirror and Benjamin looked into it. His father was there, yelling at him to be a man. Then he withdrew and all Benjamin could see was his own sad face. He punched the glass, smashing it into a million pieces.*

"Stop blaming other people. Stop blaming your father. It's your life." Astraea gently said.

Benjamin's head reeled.

AS HE WOKE UP FROM HIS NAP, BENJAMIN COULD FEEL sweat dripping off his jawline and his skin burning in the sun. A lone seagull cried before it retreated away for its afternoon siesta. Benjamin was alone in the heat at the poolside. He looked at his watch.

"It's half past two," he said out loud. "Vanda?"

She wasn't there. Her book was lying open, crumpled in the sun and her towel had been thrown down at the foot of her lounger. Benjamin scrambled up their things and hurried out of the baking heat.

He went up to one of the spa assistants and asked her if she knew where Vanda was. "She went to the steam room," the thin lady said, pointing down one of the corridors. "I don't know if she's still there. I've been doing a treatment." Benjamin rushed off to find her. *I can't let her get hurt!* He kept saying to himself.

The steam felt strangely refreshing compared to the bare dry sun outside. Drops falling from the ceiling played marimba music on the wet floor. It took Benjamin a few seconds to realize that the steam room was empty. A white towel had been perfectly stretched out on the bench. He was about to rush out and go back their cabin to see if Vanda was there when a piece of paper lying in the middle of the towel caught his attention. Benjamin tentatively opened it.

It read, 'You might have found the spent cartridge, but we found your girl. 19h00. Tangerine Bar.'

His heart sank.

* * *

VANDA OPENED HER EYES TO A COLD AND DIMLY LIT ROOM. Her head was sore and spun. The last thing she remembered was drinking lemon-flavored water and climbing into the steam room. She felt for her clothes. She had been half naked in the steam room, breathing in the warm moist air and feeling her body sweat, but now someone had put clothes back on her. A dress that was too big and a dirty wool jersey. She shuddered as she thought of who it might have been who changed her. A sense of failure kicked her in the gut. She had not seen anything coming and had thought that of all places, the steam room would be safe. She thought of the lemon flavored drink. It had tasted a bit off.

A steel staircase twisted upward on the one side of the room she was in. Boxes were piled high around her with yellow stencil stamps. On the wall opposite her lay an old mattress with a pile of rubbish at its base. She could hardly see it in the poor light. Vanda held her nose. The room stank. It stank like a butchers fridge that had never been cleaned. She felt as though she had been swallowed up by Jonah's whale, and now lay helpless inside its belly.

She was angry with herself and that kept the fear at bay and enabled her to focus. She pulled the jersey up around her, and smelt it. It was filthy. *The man who had worn it hadn't washed.* She could practically taste the tobacco and fish. She got up and tried to open the door at the top of the staircase. It was Locked. *I'm dead!* She thought. *They're going to kill me! Why else lock me down here?*

She had left Benjamin sleeping outside in the sun. *Where is Benjamin? Did they get him too?* She wondered.

Placing a hand against one of the steel walls, she slowly dropped onto her haunches. As she breathed, the condensation formed balls of misty candy floss in front of her mouth. She stared into nothing, thinking back. The emotions pulsing through her felt strangely familiar.

She remembered back to another time when she had been locked up. Confined like a rat and taunted through colors of psychedelic drugs and hazed emotions. She could feel the pain rising up inside her, suffocating her. She had promised herself that she would not go back to that place. She thought of the disparity, the gulf. Two nights earlier, dining like royalty with Captain Pizarro on French champagne and caviar, and now this. Squatting in the dregs of what looked like a hell hole.

Making a fist with her hands, she could feel her knuckles pulling hard against the tight skin. She walked over to one of the boxes and rummaged through it. She reeled back as she realized what was there. "It's true!" she gasped out loud. The acidic taste of vomit crept up her throat. She forced herself to swallow it back.

Rhino horns were packed tightly in the wooden container with dirty plastic twisting between them. There were different shades of gray and black and it all stank like old dog bones. Different sizes also. *Some must have come from babies*, she thought. She lifted one up in the dim light and examined it. It weighed four or five kilograms and there was dry blood on the stump where it had been crudely hacked off. It was nicely balanced in her hand. As she touched its sharp point, she felt repulsed and dropped it back into the crate.

Benjamin was right, she said to herself. There was a lot of it on the ship. Crates of it! She held her breath and scavenged around the open box looking for a suitable weapon. She found the perfect size horn in the second layer and felt its tip. It was sharp and hard.

"I'm fighting my way out of here," she muttered to herself. "Even if I only have this!" She tucked the small horn neatly into her side and moved back to the steel staircase, crouching down beneath it.

"Whatever comes down those stairs is going to wish they stayed at home," she said out loud.

Her eyes had by now fully adjusted to the semi-dark in the room. As she sat and waited, she started properly inspecting the space around her. An odiously familiar shape was sticking out from under the mattress. It was opposite the boxes of rhino horn. Vanda squinted her eyes to make out what it was.

It looked like a human foot and it wasn't moving. It lay there inert, with its heels twisted inward. She then noticed the smell of pungent ammonia and almost threw up. Her throat went dry and the claustrophobic steel walls crashed in around her. She sat in a huddle and prayed that Benjamin would somehow come and find her.

* * *

THE TANGERINE BAR WAS AMIDSHIP ON THE STARBOARD side. Cocktails were its specialty with Pina Colada's, Daiquiri's and Mojito's the order of the day. It was a warm humid evening, the sun had recently set directly in the path of where the cruise was headed. Barcelona, the city of ancient Catalan secrets and hipster modernity, lay ahead. Benjamin swung himself onto one of the empty counter stools lining the glass and neon bar counter.

"Give me a Jack," he ordered. "Neat."

He checked the bar out as he sipped it back, secretly hoping that Vanda might walk in and say it was all a joke. But Benjamin knew it wasn't a joke. *These people will do anything to protect themselves,* he thought to himself. *We're just collateral damage waiting to happen.* He nervously tapped his foot wondering if going to Bollini might be a better option after all.

Most of the sundowner crowd had finished their drinks and had left to get ready for dinner. A few German tourists hung about at the bar, guffawing, and sniffing. Benjamin noticed the young man who had sneezed on him in the bus on its way to Rome. He was drinking a pint of the ship's finest. Benjamin turned his shoulder away.

The barman wiped down some high balls and put them on the rack above his head. He keenly watched Benjamin and the others. *If they left, he'd be able to take a quick smoke break.* His hopefulness dissipated as Benjamin gestured him over.

"Another, please. On ice this time."

Big George was as stealthy as a B-2 Bomber as he quietly filled the chair next to Benjamin. "I'll try not to spill a drink this time," he blandly said. Benjamin spun around to face the man who had taken Vanda.

"Where is she?" Benjamin demanded to know, the words angrily tumbling out. Before George could answer, the telephone on the bar counter rang loudly. The barman picked it up and started whispering as he got Benjamin's drink. He placed the glass on the counter, threw his cloth over his shoulder and disappeared through the swing doors behind the bar. Benjamin and Big George were left alone at their end of the bar. The drunken Germans were too far away to hear them.

"What the heck have you done with her?" Benjamin growled, his hand shaking.

He didn't give a tinkers cuss if he was talking to a notorious gangster, he wanted Vanda. He wanted her back safe and in one piece. He was sick of everyone around him getting hurt. *Vanda stuck by me and now, I'm going to do the same for her, no matter what. I really like her!*

He eye-balled Big George, without flinching. *The man wasn't that 'big', sitting there with his white shirt hanging on him as though he had just come out of a refugee camp.* Benjamin reckoned he could take him down on any day of the week in a fair fight.

"Life is interesting isn't it?" Big George said slowly. His lips were thin and dry on the edges. "You run away from home. From your past. You come to this beautiful place. Book a cruise. And now you are back in it again? Aren't you? You and your Sicilian refugee."

"Oh, no, you don't!" Benjamin angrily replied. "I've got nothing to do with any of this. Nothing!"

"I don't know where you've been for the past few years," Big said, with a sneer. "It's amazing how your past catches up with you, isn't it? Like a fly on dog shit."

George picked up Benjamin's whiskey glass and waved it in front of his face. "I know who you are Mr. Rodd," he said.

"If you drink that you'll regret it," Benjamin threatened.

Big George sniffed at the drink and held the glass under his chin.

"I came on this ship as a tourist, nothing else," Benjamin continued.

"Of course you did," Big George said. "Of course you did. So did I. And what a coincidence. The poacher returns to claim his kill! I suppose that this is just a confusing mistake?"

He wiped his forehead with a paper towel and paused before continuing. "I don't believe in coincidence, Mr. Rodd, not me," he said. "Now about our little game? We are not messing around with this anymore."

"I'm not playing," Benjamin said. "I stopped years ago. I swear. Ask around."

Big looked him up and down. "You don't get out. You

know that. The moment you squeezed that trigger, you were in for life."

"I don't hunt anymore."

"You may as well have shot yourself now, Mr. Rodd," Big George said. "There is no 'get out of jail free' card. No atonement."

"Don't tell me that word!" Benjamin said.

"Look, Mr. Rodd," Big continued. "It's really simple. You have a little rhino horn that is mine and I now have a young lady that is yours. I can't afford to lose what is mine and I'm sure you want your girl back before she..." He paused for maximum effect. "...before she is, let's say, aesthetically compromised. You know how messy this business can get, don't you Mr. Rodd?"

"I don't like threats!" Benjamin replied.

"Why not?" George casually said. "Scared you might go back to prison?"

The words hit a raw nerve. He wanted to climb into the skinny man sitting next to him and teach him a real lesson, once and for all. The thought of Vanda stopped him. A few years earlier he might have abandoned her, leaving her to her unfortunate fate, but he couldn't this time. He was falling for her and she was the only person who filled the weird void between his dreams and reality. He sensed that Astraea was somewhere close, hovering above them, but he couldn't see her.

"I don't have it anymore," he tried to explain.

Big George laughed. "Nice try, Rodd. Do you think I'm stupid?"

Benjamin realized that he would have to play to George's perception. The reality was irrelevant. He needed to play for time.

"What guarantees do I have? How do I know you'll let Vanda go?"

Big George smiled. It was the smile of a psychopath about to squash a bug.

"I guarantee I won't hand you over to Salvatore Bollini."

"You already tried to do that? Yes, I'm not stupid either."

"Your girlfriend was though, wasn't she? Shooting Paolo like he was an animal!"

Benjamin breathed out slowly like he used to do before taking down an animal. He wondered if there was anyway Big George could prove if he or Vanda had done anything wrong.

"Vanda has nothing to do with this. Leave her out of it."

"I just want my missing horn back," Big demanded. "One little horn. What do you Africans call it? Uphondo? Bring me my uphondo, keep your nose out of my business and you won't have to see us again."

Benjamin tried again to explain what had happened but was unconvincing.

"I'm not an amateur, Mr. Rodd. What do you take me for? Don't try and con me. I've dealt with plenty of piss boys like you before. You're a small time cat burglar who owns an elephant rifle. You and your girlfriend have my missing rhino horn. Paolo put it in her bag. If you lost it, then go and find it. No excuses. I just want it back. It's that simple."

Big George stood up and hovered over Benjamin like a vulture circling the prey it was about to tear apart. "I swear on my mother's life," he then continued, his cheeks growing red. "I will rip out your liver and feed it to this Vanda woman in a stew if you don't bring it back. Do you understand?"

He slammed his hand on the counter and threw back Benjamin's whiskey. He swirled it in his mouth a few inches from Benjamin's face and then swallowed hard. "Aah," he said, wiping his mouth. He grinned with vindictive self-satisfaction, his worn teeth glimmering through his thin lips. "Understand?"

Benjamin recovered quickly, and an unusual energy filled

him. In his mind Astraea swirled around him, warming him and empowering him. He could feel her energy in his heart filling him with courage and strength. He had nothing to lose. He took a step back out of the space that Big George had invaded,

"I told you not to drink that!"

Big George sniggered and opened his mouth to respond. Benjamin, however, didn't allow him a chance to speak.

"Are you prepared to jeopardize an entire shipment over one little horn? I want Vanda back first," he confidently countered. "Then you get your horn back. I can go to Bollini. Or Captain Pizarro. He likes the girl you know. Think what he's going to do when he hears you've kidnapped her. Your whole shipment will be at risk."

The whole shipment! Benjamin secretly thought. *I'm going for it all. I deserve it. Vanda too!*

The smirk on Big George's face slowly dissipated. "Keep your voice down," he said, glancing at the German party on the other side of the room. "If you do that. You will die. I guarantee it!"

"I don't care," Benjamin answered.

Big George said nothing. Benjamin grabbed the empty whiskey glass from his hand and smashed it down on the countertop. "I'll get you your wretched horn but the ball is in your court. Get me, Vanda, first!"

"You'll get a piece of her finger, you cheeky little prick," Big George said. "That should kick you into action. And maybe you'll get the rest of her after I get the horn back. Don't think I've never played poker before, you idiot. I can see a bluff when I see one. Dumb-ass!"

The German group had gone silent when Benjamin smashed the glass. They stared at Big George as he sauntered past them tipping his cap.

"Guten Abend, lads," he said as though it was another

mellow evening aboard paradise. He turned and walked away muttering to himself. "The poor idiot doesn't know who I am."

* * *

BENJAMIN LOOKED AT HIS WATCH AGAIN. HE THOUGHT about Vanda for the millionth time. He had a sinking feeling in his gut. She was gone. *They wouldn't hurt her.* His mind raced. *Vanda was just leverage. No-one knew where that rhino horn was now.*

He wondered how his cruise might have turned out if he had not met Vanda. He sipped his lukewarm drink. It tasted like putrid dishwater as it went down.

Grabbing his suitcase from the top of the cupboard, Benjamin starting to stuff it with his clothes. He threw his shoes in and his scrunched up dirty washing. Sitting on the bag he forced its bulging zip closed. Then he remembered all the clothes still on hangers inside the left door of his cupboard. "Darn clothes!" He shouted. "How did you fit in here in the first place." Throwing his suitcase down in a tantrum he jumped on it as though it was a spider to be squashed. The edge split and a pair of dirty socks spilled out onto the carpet. "Damn you!" he yelled, throwing the suitcase back on top of the cupboard. He wished he could chat to someone. *Astraea? Dr. Miller?*

Dr. Miller, she was always smacking the inside of his head! She was never far from his thoughts. It had been weeks since he had sat in her office. He missed her dry humor and acrid directives. He could picture her sitting in her usual white turtleneck. Her tortoise-shell rimmed glasses on the end of her nose, bouncing her pen on the blank page in front of her, hesitant to write anything. She'd then look up at Benjamin. He'd know what she was thinking. He had sat through so many of her long counseling sessions that he could read her mind. *Why did he even bother?* He knew exactly what crap she was going to tell him. She once told him that it was better to live a true life and be punished for it than to live a false life in security.

That's why this mess happened, he thought? *Because I messed up with Mary. I need to find the true path again. I need to step out from the shadows!*

Benjamin put the glass down and looked into the mirror as though he was expecting Astraea to appear in solidarity.

"I need to atone for this mess," he said out loud to the mirror. "Don't I?"

There was no answer, just a dull stare back. He stood for a minute or two looking at his own face. He needed to shave. Grey stubble had covered his droopy facial skin like lichen on a winter rock.

"You look terrible," he said out loud again. "Where did your life go?"

Indeed *where? Shot away in the bush, one Rhino at a time.* He smiled in defeat. He had gone mad. He was convinced of it.

The ship's horn blasted loudly and grounded Benjamin back into a semblance of reality. He stepped into the bathroom to clean himself up. He had to go and face his demons.

As he paced up and down his suite, he could have sworn that he saw both Dr. Muller and Astraea high-fiving each other across the room. He then collapsed on the couch in mental exhaustion and darkness overcame him.

* * *

BENJAMIN SLOWLY TURNED OVER A HORN IN HIS HAND. IT FELT familiar - from an adolescent black rhino. He could tell by the color and the curvature. He peered into the dull patina, like a fortune teller gazing into her crystal ball, wondering what stories might lie in the shadows. *What fortunes could be made? What jeopardies screamed their warnings?*

It weighed about two kilograms. It was his ticket back to the big time. He reckoned it was worth about two hundred grand in Ho Chi Ming City. Two fifty in Hanoi, if you could survive the dangers of the sale. He'd survived a few. The Vietnamese used to call him "The Dilettante." A jack of all trades, going solo from the actual killing to toasting Veuve Clicquot with the high-rolling end buyers. Then that fateful night, when they stabbed him in the back and his world crashed down around him.

"Tempting isn't it?" The voice of Astraea whispered, warm and near. She was in the smoky reflections of the horn, somersaulting around as though a miniature trapeze has been set up inside the constricting circumference. Colors followed her, jumping around, trying to swallow up her white dress in her dancing wake. Benjamin peered closer, caressing his hand over the densified dead hair. His hand washed the scene and cleaned away the colors until it was clear like the sky in the early African morning.

"You know there's more of the stuff," Astraea says. "Tons more, right beneath you." She swooned in his imagination as the blue sky chased her. Her loose hair and flowing white fabrics graced her body like the alluring tautness of a Rodin sculpture. Benjamin didn't answer at first. He was enjoying it, watching her. With each twirl, she moved closer and the horn in his hand grew bigger and bigger. She was growing and Benjamin was fading away.

"Stop," he eventually said. "Can't you keep still for one second?"

She touched his face. Her hands were cold, as though she had dipped them in ice water. Benjamin could feel the freezing moisture brushing his cheeks. He wiped his face with the back of his hand.

"You need to let her go," Astraea said.

"I can't. I dragged her into this and now she's in their clutches. How can I let her go?"

"I'm talking about Mary! Not Vanda."

He felt a knot in his stomach. "She left years ago. When I was I jail. There's nothing to let go of."

"But you bought her a ticket. For this cruise?"

"It was wishful thinking. Mary's long gone!"

"And Vanda?"

"Gone too, it seems"

"There's a huge difference, Benjamin," Astraea said.

Benjamin's chest constricted. A numbness assaulted him inside and he shrank back, dropping his head. "I lose everyone I love," he moaned.

"Vanda's not gone. You haven't lost her," Astraea said. "Wait for the right opportunity."

Benjamin nodded, and then his body hit the floor and a black cloud closed in over him. He lay there for ages.

Eventually, he groaned and opened his eyes. No one was there. He shook his head thinking he'd gone completely mad.

7

BARCELONA

The breakfast lounge opened at seven but Benjamin had come down ten minutes early. His night had been rocked by dreams and he'd been tormented in his gut every time he thought of Vanda. He had shaved and put on some clean jeans and a t-shirt, that he had bought somewhere in Genoa.

He picked up a coffee and threw some fruit and a crois-sant onto his plate. *I'm sick of this food*, he thought to himself as he sat in the morning shadows with his back to the wall, so that he could clearly see the door. He didn't want to draw attention to himself. He needed to get quietly into the City and try call Chatunga back in Palermo. Maybe he could help save Vanda. Benjamin felt he had no other options.

Some English tourists, dressed in various combinations of golf shirts, Bermuda shorts, and leather loafers were the first to arrive for breakfast. They seemed eager to get going early, even though the Catalan culture waiting for them on shore, was unlikely to cooperate with such idealistic thinking.

Other families start arriving soon after. Some children took the table next to Benjamin. He recognized the same little boy from the queue of the first day. The boy seemed to gravitate towards Benjamin for some reason. He still had snot on his shirt. He'd joined forces with some new friends and they noisily stuffed their plates with doughnuts, pancakes and any other sugary treats they could lay their juvenile hands on. This time, the boy pulled a face at Benjamin. As Benjamin watched them misbehave, he didn't feel the same aversion he had felt earlier. He wished he was free like them. He smiled back.

At around nine o'clock, the doors flew open. The late crowd arrived all at once as if coordinated. They were the party junkies who had stayed up most of the night dancing, gambling and picking each other up. A quick snack was all they needed before hitting the lunchtime bars of Barcelona. Benjamin picked out Doctor Burlington from the crowd. He was the only one over 40. He was exhausted and looked like he was losing weight. *That's what going with a girl half one's age does*, Benjamin thought to himself. His Jessica was nowhere to be seen. Dr. Burlington spotted Benjamin and sauntered over like a brown hyena. Benjamin groaned. He wasn't in the mood for casual chit-chat, especially with Burlington.

"Morning ol' Chap," Burlington said, gruffly. "We missed you two last night."

He plonked his large butt on the chair next to Benjamin. "You don't mind, do you?" he asked. "Our maître d' was asking for you at dinner rather fervently."

Burlington shoveled a pancake into his mouth and carried on talking. "What is that about, ol' Chap?"

"Nothing," Benjamin said, offering Burlington the syrup. "He probably had me confused with the Ng's?"

"Who are the Ng's?"

"You know, that Asian couple, Lesley, and Tram?"

"Ah, of course, the Chinese," Burlington slobbered. "They

were also asking about you at dinner. Everyone seemed to have a fixation about where you two might be."

He put a pathetic juvenile smile on his old fat face and nudged Benjamin with his elbow. "I told them you and Vanda... you know..." He simulated some obscene shaking with his waistline.

Benjamin bit his lip. The man was nauseating. "They're from Vietnam," he corrected.

"No, from China," Burlington insisted. "They told me so. Shanghai or Peking? They were talking about the Wall."

"If you say so," Benjamin said under his breath. He noticed that the doctor was sweating already. He tended to sweat a lot. His armpits had wet patches and he kept mopping his brow with his dirty hankie. Benjamin sipped on his coffee as Burlington started pontificating about the architecture of Barcelona. Eventually, he wiped his mouth and left. Benjamin sat alone again.

Five minutes later Tram and Lesley Ng waltzed in, wearing broad-brimmed hats and enormous sunglasses. The short safari suit pants and leather shoes with white socks that Tram had on, looked ridiculous. They both had cameras hanging around their necks. They headed straight for a table in the middle of the room and sat down, signaling to the closest waiter that they wanted to be served immediately. Neither of them smiled. It was as if they were in the middle of a cold war with each other.

Benjamin spied them from where he was sitting, wondering why they might have been asking questions about him. He was sick of it all. He just wanted Vanda. And he wanted to get off the ship. He decided to walk right past them and see how they reacted. *Maybe they knew something? Maybe they saw what happened to Vanda?*

The Ng's were too busy throwing passive aggressive darts at each other and didn't see Benjamin walking over. He stopped at their table and greeted them in Vietnamese, with an unsuccessful Saigonese urban drawl. They seemed astonished that he had come to them and didn't say a word back at first. They looked at him through their dark glasses. Deep in thought, Tram slowly finished his croissant and then sat back, folding his arms.

"I believe you were asking for me last night," Benjamin said.

"I sure was... *Mr. Dilletante*," Tram Ng replied in perfect English. "Maybe you should take a seat."

* * *

"How do you know that name?" Benjamin blurted as he sat down.

"I'm from South East Asia," Tram said. "The *Dilletante* is pretty well known over there." He opened up another croissant and started smearing butter over it. He shoved it in his mouth before a butter blob, dangling loose off the side, fell loose. The butter drooled down his chin. He ignored it and took another bite.

Benjamin stiffened. They were both speaking in Vietnamese now. The changeover from English had felt natural. *That's what comes from spending three years in a Hanoi jail cell with 25 other half crazy convicts who couldn't speak English.*

"You can relax," Tram said, with a smile. "I'm not what you think. I assume they've got Vanda?" Crumbs shot from his lips like grapeshot.

Benjamin folded his arms. "So you know about her, do you?"

"I knew she'd get into trouble the moment I first met her," Tram replied. "The drunk ones usually do."

"She is just here on holiday," Benjamin said. "Like me."

"Sure she is," Tram said, selecting a piece of pineapple from his plate.

He refused to look Benjamin in the eye. He seemed desperate to shovel as much food into his mouth as he could. A piece of fruit hit Benjamin on the cheek. He grimaced as diplomatically as he could. Lesley Ng sat demurely at Tram's side. She looked like a cat about to pounce on a mouse.

"We recognized you the moment we saw your picture," she said, slurping her tea.

"I don't understand," Benjamin replied.

"Face recognition apps," Tram explained. "It's a very connected world today, Mr. Rodd. Check-in photos in Genoa can end up at the Hilton a few seconds later, with a flashing red light."

"The Hilton?"

"You know, the one in Hanoi? They say your old room is ready for you again."

Lesley sniggered under her breath.

Oh, my word! They're police! Benjamin screamed inside. *Freaking undercover police! No wonder they only came on board on the second night. They're onto this whole mess and think I'm involved!*

Benjamin rubbed his hand over his mouth, recalling the details of his 'old room'. It always hurt. His stint in Xom Ap Lo Prison was not too far back in his past. It had been three years of cockroach infested hell. They might have called it the 'New' Hanoi Hilton but it was just as bad as the old one from the American Vietnam war. And it was the polar opposite of the real Hilton Hotel, that lay a few miles away on a high street in downtown Hanoi.

Benjamin had been hauled out of his room at five in the morning and roughly deposited in his new 'suite' by six. It felt like only yesterday to him. Every single day of that three years felt like yesterday! The cargo he had been delivering conveniently disappeared along with his life.

His case was eventually thrown out for lack of evidence and all he got was a ticket back home to South Africa. He had chosen to keep his head down and not complain. Diplomatic squabbles tend to become public and the last thing he wanted was questions being asked about why he was in Vietnam in the first place. He'd not shot a rifle since. The demons, however, kept their grappling hooks embedded deep in his soul.

"What are you implying?" Benjamin snapped.

Tram reached over and gently pulled Benjamin's t-shirt down over his right shoulder. The tiny inked number was there, squawking like a parrot who wouldn't shut up.

"Ah yes," Tram said. "They all get those. And your accent. You know, it's got a gutter twang to it. Like that scum from Ho Chi Ming would have taught you."

"I wasn't found to have done anything wrong," Benjamin said, lowering his voice. "Like now. I'm on holiday."

"A coincidence, Mr. Rodd?"

"I don't care what you believe in. I paid my dues."

"I let you go, back in Vietnam," Tram said, sitting back. His shoulders shuddered under his oversized flower shirt.

"You were there when I got released?"

Tram grinned like the Cheshire cat and nodded with glee.

"Then you must have been involved with it all! When they locked me up! When I got double-crossed?" Benjamin's fists tightened in a white ball on his lap.

"Let's let the past be the past," Tram casually said. "It's today that counts."

"I'm on holiday!"

"Yes, we know that now, but think how it looks? Interpol hears that a huge shipment of Rhino is heading for Tunisia. We just don't know how."

"Then the old *Dilletante* himself lights up on our radar," Lesley interrupted.

Tram waved her aside and continued himself. "You're boarding a ship in Genoa which is heading for Tunisia. We think, brilliant plan! A public cruise ship with a thousand tourists sitting right on top of it. What a perfect cover."

"And you're on the next flight to Rome," Benjamin said, shaking his head in disbelief.

"The Med is always appealing," Lesley butted in.

"You must know by now that I have nothing to do with this!" Benjamin said.

"There is the problem of the little horn Senor Bollini found in your room, is there not?" Tram replied.

"You're working with Bollini?" Benjamin replied in exasperation.

"He thought it was a horn from a bull," Lesley laughed. "A Matador's trophy."

"I've got it safe now!" Tram said.

"I'm sure you do!" Benjamin mocked. The Ng's smiled evilly.

"They planted that in Vanda's bag," Benjamin explained. "A red-headed guy called George and his crew. It belonged to them. It wasn't ours!"

"But you still tried to steal it back," Lesley said. "I saw you that day of the drill, going down there to Bollini's office."

"Thought you could make a quick buck, didn't you, Mr. *Dilletante*?" Tram said, chewing on some bacon. "We've been watching out for you."

"You were the bastard responsible for locking me up in Vietnam? For stealing my life away?" Benjamin snapped.

"Responsible?" Tram replied. "No. I was just doing my job. Was I responsible for what happened to you? No, you have that honor to yourself!"

"You're here to break up this new syndicate?"

"The only thing you should be concerned about is that I've got your balls in a vice now," Tram said. "Whether you like it or not, you are involved now."

"And you've confirmed that there is rhino horn on this ship!" Lesley interrupted again. Tram glared at her to keep quiet.

"You can help us," Tram said. "And then we'll help you."

"Why don't you just search the darn ship and confiscate it yourself?" Benjamin asked. "Arrest them all?"

"Captain Pizarro doesn't believe it. He wants no scandal on his watch. He says unless we have proof, no-one is to scare the passengers."

"And you couldn't persuade him, could you, Lesley?" Benjamin said, grinning at Lesley. "Even with your best charms, the other morning?"

Tram glared at Lesley and she dropped her gaze into her lap.

"You are going to assist us, Mr. Rodd," Tram snarled.

"Can you save Vanda?"

"I have no idea where your girlfriend is."

"They took her. They think she's got their horn and they are squeezing me to get it back to them."

"And that is exactly why you are going to cooperate with us! So Vanda doesn't get hurt."

"For Pete's sake, I'm not involved in this," Benjamin exploded. "Neither is Vanda. We don't know anything. We're on holiday!" He spelled the word out.

"I believe that's what you said the last time," Lesley sniped. "Back in Vietnam! Would you like to go back to your old room at the Hilton? You were in the South Wing. Am I right? The one where those sickos were?"

Benjamin slumped into his chair.

"Mr. Knight, your pretty partner will go to the Hilton with you this time. And we're not talking only three years.

Rhino horn has become a high priority crime in South East Asia."

"Why won't you listen?" Benjamin shouted.

He knew that he was trapped. They were about to become patsies. He was damned if he did and damned if he didn't. *These were the same people who had screwed him before and he had no doubt they would do it again.*

"What do you want me to do?" he asked.

Tram pulled him down and whispered in his ear. Lesley Ng watched them with a look of amusement on her face.

"You're going to rat them out," Tram said smiling. "You're going to find out exactly where on this ship they have their merchandise and once you've done that, we can talk about helping Vanda."

"Why don't you find it yourself?"

Tram sat back and folded his arms. "A wise man once said, a man who commits a mistake and doesn't correct it is just committing another mistake. I'm giving you a chance to fix your old mistakes!"

"Sounds more like you are scared of getting your fingers dirty," Benjamin said. "Did you know that Confucius also said that before you embark on a journey of revenge, you should dig two graves?"

"One for you and one for Vanda!" Lesley interjected.

"Fine!" Benjamin sighed. "How do you suggest I do this?"

"I've got just what you need to ferret them out," Tram replied. He took out a piece of paper and wrote down an address in Barcelona. He folded it carefully and stuck it down the front of Benjamin's shirt, with a patronizing pat.

"Have you ever heard about a Pouch Rat?" Tram asked.

"Don't they sniff out landmines? Sure I've read about them."

"They can sniff out anything, with the right training," Lesley proudly said.

"Don't tell me," Benjamin said. "Rhino horn!"

"It took us nine months and a lot of patience. Who would have thought?"

"Why don't you do it yourself?" Benjamin asked.

"I hate rodents almost as much as ex-cons," Tram said. "Now, go fetch your rat at this address."

* * *

As Benjamin climbed the Las Ramblas into old Barcelona, he couldn't believe the so-called 'deal' he had been forced into with Tram Ng. It sucked him deep into a quagmire of danger but it also gave him a chance to get out. Cooperating with the authorities had never been his thing. He'd never been a snitch in the past but this was different. He had to do it for Vanda. The Ng's wanted him to locate the rhino horn shipment for them. Go in as some unofficial undercover agent. *Or was the right word traitor?* Turning on his own kind and breaking the unwritten codes. It was tearing him apart inside. *What type of rat can be trained to sniff this stuff out,* Benjamin wondered to himself? They were setting him up somehow! His gut told him to cut and run. His heart pulled toward Vanda.

He thought of her as he walked. He wondered where she was and whether she was OK. He wanted to save her at all costs. He felt trapped. *Could he trust the Ng's?* This was the primary thought clouding his brain as he walked. *He knew he couldn't. What the heck was he doing then?* Everything in him said the answer was no. *Niet, nein, nada!* It would not the first time the Vietnamese cops had swept in at the last minute and screwed him. Benjamin knew that, first hand.

He hardly noticed the colorful tiled buildings he was walking past. Some bright yellow mosaics, that had been laid by the Master himself, shimmered in the mid-morning sun and eventually caught Benjamin's eye. They called to him. No one got past them without noticing! They called it 'Gaudi's spell'. It felt as though Astraea was walking alongside him after that. Benjamin talked to her. *Why not*, he thought, *I've got nothing to lose?*

"Astraea, I'm walking into a firestorm," he said quietly, under his breath.

"Yes, you are."

Her voice was so clear in his head that Benjamin looked around to check that it wasn't real. He'd gotten used to her elusiveness, but she now stepped out the shadows and move beyond his mere dreams. She was in his head and not going away.

"Fire purifies things, Ben," she said.

He could picture her. Her explosive eyes and her hellish tattoo growing up her arm. He wished he was dreaming. At least in the dreams, he could see her. Now he only heard her and her voice was so sharp that Benjamin knew he was losing it. He had to be.

"It also destroys things," he said. There was a pause while he walked up some stairs. "Astraea? You there?" he asked, "or are you taunting me again?"

"A tree sometimes needs to be pruned before new life can appear."

"What does that mean?"

"Well, what do you think life is?"

Benjamin waited a few minutes before answering. "This!" He waved his hand around. He no longer talked softly. Their ethereal conversation had moved to normal decibels, but no one around him noticed or cared. The tourists were taking pictures or gawking at the buildings. The locals seemed accustomed to people talking to themselves.

"This is life, Astraea," he said, lifting his head and taking in a deep breath. "The fresh Spanish air, the good and bad of people and the crap on the ground. This is it!"

"So you're happy then?" she asked. "With the crap?"

They turned right, up to a cobbled street, lined with shops and restaurants. And then she was gone again.

BENJAMIN FELT A VACUUM SUCK AT HIS BRAINS. A LITTLE ball was rolling around making a rattling noise as it crashed against the sides of his skull. It was the start of a headache. He was looking for number 49 Carra De Texeira. It was the address where Tram Ng had told him to go to. He double checked the piece of paper he had been given, to make sure he was on the right road. Tram said that they would be waiting for him there. To tell him exactly what to do. He had no idea who they were but it seemed it was his only hope. *They're the same scum who double-crossed me the last time*, he thought.

The sounds of Barcelona droned in Benjamin's ears. He knew the City had always stood at the crossroads of competing cultures, like an old Catalan bullring where fresh Matador's tangoed with snorting beasts in death rituals. He counted off the house numbers, confused and angry.

Number 49 was a modern apartment block covered in glass. Benjamin was met by a thick set man with a bushy mustache. He said little but made sure Benjamin saw the nine tucked into his belt. *Glock Gen 2*, Benjamin said to himself. The man didn't look at all like he worked for the police. Benjamin felt an odious flush down his back.

He was ushered into the lift and taken to the top floor. A modern apartment with full-length glass windows looked out over the old town. Gothic church spires waved in the distance. There was only one other person in the white-walled room. He looked like some crazy middle-aged professor. His eyes were withdrawn and his matted gray hair hadn't been brushed for days. He answered none of Benjamin's questions as he studiously explained what Benjamin had to do.

"He's got an RTLS tracker chip in his collar," the man said. "You just have to let him loose without being seen. He'll lead us right to it."

"You've got to be kidding me!" Benjamin exclaimed as the man whipped a towel off a small box on the table.

"It's my special baby," the man said, rubbing his hands lovingly over the gauze lid. "I've been training him for months."

"It's enormous!" Benjamin said.

"Beautiful isn't it?"

"A rat!"

"A Giant African Pouch rat."

"Looks like plain vermin to me."

"He eats, sleeps and thinks animal horn!" the man said smiling, as though he had just unlocked the secrets of quantum physics. "It's all he instinctively thinks. He'll smell it out from miles away."

Ingenious, Benjamin quietly thought to himself. He'd read about this type of stuff. Small animals specially trained to hunt down drugs and things. *But giant rats? And rhino horn? Why the heck not?*

"Where's the tracker receiver?" Benjamin asked.

The man laughed. "Definitely not in your hands," he said. "You're just the rat handler! Your job is to get him aboard and let him loose. Like this."

As he demonstrated how to open the box, two black eyes and some long whiskers popped up over the rim of the lid. Benjamin stepped back. The rat was light gray and the size of a small cat. His instructor lovingly picked it up and kissed it on the head. "Look after my baby," he sniffed. "And please get him back after Marseilles. He's worth a small fortune."

The man handed Benjamin an electronic clicker. "See, if

you click this button, he'll come running for food, so you can get him back when he's finished his work. He's very tame and friendly. He only lives for two things. Tracking dead bones and horn or chasing this clicker to get his food."

"How does the transponder work?" Benjamin asked.

"Turn on this here," the man said, showing Benjamin a tiny switch on the collar. "Then let my baby loose into an air duct. The police will then be able to track her, as she sniffs her way through the hold."

"The police?"

"Interpol. But it's top secret. Mr. Ng, their head, said so himself."

"Did he?" Benjamin sarcastically said. "When must I do it?" Benjamin asked.

"Early tomorrow morning, about two hours before the ship gets to Marseilles. Not before."

Benjamin's throat was dry. He hated rats as well.

As he hurried away from the apartment block with the rat box tucked inside a small backpack, Benjamin planned in his head what he'd say if security caught him with it. He knew that small transistors got past most metal detectors, but what if they did a bag search? He was now convinced that Tram Ng was setting him up as some sort of fall guy. There was no logical reason why he had to offload this tracker rat. *Anyone could have done it. The police needed more than just the rhino horn. They need to arrest someone! Some patsy. El Dilletante! I'm being set up somehow! Again! Run!*

He headed north, away from the harbor, but Vanda tugged at his conscience.

I'm sorry! Benjamin said himself. *I can't go back to jail! I just can't. Vanda, please forgive me for abandoning you.*

He was torn apart. Each step away from the boat became

slower and slower. Eventually, his body could no longer move. He was stuck in orbit. Should he disappear off forever into space and be lost in the galaxies of regret, or should he fall back to earth, where somewhere, amongst the dirt and grime he might make it right again? And find Vanda! She'd become his symbolic icon of atonement for all the bad things he had done in his life. The buildings swirled around him and his head throbbed with pain.

Then, almost from nowhere, a hand touched his shoulder. Benjamin jumped as high as a crack addict. Spinning around, he expected the worst.

"Holy Moses!" he gasped, as he saw who it was. "What are you doing here?"

Chatunga Lazarov stood smiling in front of him. His face had a two-day shadow and was still slightly swollen from Sicily. Other than that, he looked fine. His long hair was tied back into a bun and he wore neat clothes. Chatunga gave him a manly hug and whispered in his ear, "I've got your back, my old friend."

"Good to see you!" Benjamin exclaimed. "I lost my phone and had no way of contacting you. I thought you were still in hospital?"

"I'm a quick recoverer," Chatunga replied. "It only took me a few hours before that place was history." He had a familiar twinkle in his eye. "Besides the nurse had a syringe, this big." He exaggerated like a trout fisherman.

"I've been waiting for you here in Barcelona since yesterday. Caught one of those little private planes over. I saw you get off the ship this morning. Do you know that someone is following you?"

Benjamin hardly heard the last part about him being followed and glanced nervously down the road. He then dipped his shoulder and hugged his old friend again. *Tram Ng and his snitch plan could be 're-aligned' now.*

As they walked off, Benjamin started to unpack every-thing that had happened since they had left Sicily.

"Where's Vanda?" Chatunga asked. "The wild one. She nicked my sawdy you know."

"It's now minus a good cartridge or two, thanks to her," Benjamin said. "It's 'Big George', Chat. You know him? He's in the middle of all this and he's kidnapped Vanda. And my balls are being squeezed by my old cop friends. They all think I'm here for the rhino racket - setting me up again."

"That's why I came," Chatunga replied, showing no further concern for Vanda. "We've been tracking the old man for weeks and it's time for revenge."

"Who's we?"

"I'll explain soon," Chatunga said. "First we need to be absolutely sure that they're using the MSE Grande."

"Trust me on that," Benjamin replied.

"And you need to know, I'm not working alone anymore," Chatunga explained. He looked around as though he expected someone might hear him. "Not here though. We're going somewhere safe. And there's someone I need you to meet. Common let's get going! I'm your best hope now, Ben."

Benjamin knew it was true. At least his old friend could be trusted. Then and there, he finally made a firm decision. *To hell with them all! He was going to save Vanda at all costs. And if he could make a buck or two along the way with Chatunga Lazarov, so be it! And if he could screw Bollini, George, the slimy Ng's and the randy Captain along the way, all the better!*

He could sense Astraea pulling him. She was on both sides, pulling on both arms. And he could see Dr. Miller with a look of anticipation on her face, waiting for him to make the move. He knew it was a big one to make, a tipping point moment.

Yes! Benjamin said to himself. He fell into a rhythm beside Chatunga Lazarov as they walked down the road together.

A hundred meters behind them, a man in a knee-length coat bent over pretending to use his phone. Salvatore Bollini had been tailing Benjamin all morning. For his so-called skills, however, Bollini failed to notice that he was also being followed. Panayotis Pappas was also playing hide and seek.

They all headed in the direction of the de la Sagrada Familia, Gaudi's famous Cathedral that dominated the Barcelona skyline with its dark esoteric presence. The Gothic towers called them like Torquemada from the Inquisition, but none of them noticed any danger. The gargoyles on the rain ramparts yelped in anticipation as Benjamin and Chatunga stepped over the cathedral threshold. They were in the innards of one of Europe's greatest pieces of stone masonry. The gargoyles were positively laughing by the time Bollini and Panayotis Pappas stepped inside.

* * *

THE CATHEDRAL WAS FULL OF PEOPLE, BUT NONE OF THEM were worshiping. The flow of tourists moved in an anti-clockwise direction around the Alter, stopping at alcoves where yesterday's heroes lay eternally prostrate before their own mortality.

Vanda should be here, was Benjamin's first thought. *She's as brave a saint as anyone.* But there were no female tombstones anywhere in the Church. No beatified nuns, or noble women, who might have saved the city or done great things in its violent past. Their grand memories remained silent among the echoes and clicking cameras. *You women deserve better, Vanda*, Benjamin thought.

Chatunga Lazarov walked over to a table where some candles were burning. He popped a five euro coin into a wooden box and picked out a new candle. As he lit it, he turned to Benjamin.

"Take one," he said. "We're going to need all the help we can get."

Benjamin hesitated. Burning church candles was not his thing. He wasn't religious, let alone Catholic. He didn't even know if he believed in God.

"For luck," Chatunga said, noticing his hesitation. "Light a candle, Ben. Here, I'll put in the coin for you." A coin rattled in the box like a gun being cocked.

Benjamin reluctantly picked up one of the thin wax tubes. As it lit up, the orange flame blinded out the sunlight squeezing into the dark vacuous spaces through the enormous stained glass windows. He silently hoped to see Astraea in the mystic halo around the flame. She might feel at home in the Gothic energy and symbolism.

"Let's go," Chatunga said. "This way."

They walked against the flow of crowds, toward the left tower annex. As they left, Benjamin jabbed his candle into the tray of sand. He didn't say a prayer.

They headed for an oak door partly hidden from view by a huge stone sarcophagus. There were no ushers or guards and a sign above the door said, "Congregants Only." Chatunga opened it confidently, as though he'd been there before, and stepped into the room beyond. Benjamin followed cautiously.

A short passage led to a stone chapel, away from the main Cathedral. It was empty, except for a few bowed heads. It was a peaceful contrast to the main Cathedral. Beautiful Gothic columns rose down the center and the Alter glistened with yellow gold. Some gargoyles had sneaked in from the outside and were hanging upside down from the cornices like black bats.

Simple wooden benches were set out on each side of the aisle. It was contemplative and calm and candles burned from old candelabras. Benjamin reckoned that the room could manage about 200 people. As the oak door shut behind them, the noise from the main cathedral muffled itself to a distant hum. Benjamin felt uncomfortable.

"Why bring me here of all places?" he asked. "I hope it's not to pray for help."

"You should try it sometime," Chatunga chuckled, as he scanned the room. They walked down the aisle together. Halfway down, Benjamin grabbed his friend's shoulder.

"Stop, dammit!" he said. "Chatunga, let's talk. Now! I don't have time for this cloak and dagger rubbish. I have to get to Vanda."

Chatunga brushed him aside, walking confidently toward the front pew, where an old man sat with his head bowed. It looked as though he was deep in prayer, or worse.

Chatunga slipped into the bench behind the man and kneeling forward, brought his mouth to a handsbreadth from his head. As Chatunga whispered, the old man was relatively unresponsive. Eventually, he slowly lifted his head, set his sights on the crucifix behind the Alter, and shuffled his old frame around on the bench. Sizing Benjamin up, his gaze was cold and piercing.

Benjamin didn't recognize him. *This old codger must be close to eighty years old.* There were deep lines in the man's tanned leather face. He looked as though he had survived more than his fair share of fights over his life. His large nose was crooked. His thick hair was as white as the snow on the hills above the city. Despite his bent back, his clothes were tailored and expensive. His Italian shoes were boned and shone in the reflections of the candles. They were not what one would expect from an old crock praying in Church.

Excreting out, through his ancient body, were the dying embers from a fire that had once raged brightly. One could see it in the eyes, flickers of power and invincibility.

"Benjamin. Come over here," Chatunga instructed,

waving him over. "I want you to meet someone." The man stayed sitting as Benjamin approached.

"Don Valente," Chatunga respectfully said. "This is the friend I was telling you about, Mr. Benjamin *'Dilletante'* Rodd."

Benjamin held out his hand.

"Ben, meet Mr. Luigi Valente. You might have heard of him?" Valente didn't take Benjamin's hand but rather held out his own with the palm facing the floor. *What is this?* Benjamin thought. *The Sopranos?*

There was an awkward moment as the two hands stood off against each other. Benjamin glanced over at Chatunga who pointed with his eyes at Valente. With his pulse racing, he took the frail hand with its popping purple veins and lifted it to his lips. He felt stupid now.

Luigi Valente pulled his hand away at the last minute. Benjamin flushed red, trying to connect the dots in his head. *Chatunga was a Lazarov for goodness sake, not Italian Mob. The Lazarov's were at perpetual war with the Italians! What was he doing here with this man, who clearly was more than what he initially appeared to be? His friend had been in Palermo for way too long!*

Benjamin looked into a pair of eyes that were dark and piercing. *He wondered how many souls Valente might have bumped off in his time? Was it more than his own fifty-eight? At least his were animals and not humans.* Benjamin stepped back saying nothing.

He knew it was no trivial thing to be introduced to the man sitting before him. *There must be a vast pyramid of bad stuff behind this man,* he thought. *Covered by a thin veneer of respectability.* Benjamin was getting nervous. It was the first real Italian Mafioso he had ever encountered.

"So you know where the uphondo is?" Luigi Valente bluntly said, with an air of complete authority. The voice did not betray the age of the man behind it. It was high pitched and youthful, crisp and clear. If Benjamin's eyes had been closed, he could have been listening to young Italian Casanova in the prime of his life. Chatunga nodded vociferously behind the man's back.

Benjamin realized he had better show some respect. He'd heard of men like this. 'Great white sharks', they were called, coming up from the depths to devour their meals. He had never known if they really existed, until then. Until he found himself standing right in front of one, trying unsuccessfully to kiss the wizened hand, as though it was the Pope or something. At least they were in a church, it sort of felt appropriate.

Benjamin noticed that Chatunga was beaming with pride. He wondered how his simple friend, a nobody from the fringes of the underworld, could possibly be so close to Luigi Valente. *People didn't ever get close to these old Godfathers. Godfathers? Yes, that was the right word.*

Chatunga sensed what was going on in Benjamin's head. "Don Valente and I both hate the same person," he explained. "It's funny how common enemies bring people together and Mister Don Valente here has now welcomed me into his family. Our interests, how shall I say it? They merge."

Basil Lazarov! Benjamin saw it straight away. Basil Lazarov had often bumped heads with the Palermo families, trying to dominate the Mediterranean trade routes. *And what was Chatunga's over-arching obsession in life? Not money, or power, or women. Not even his reputation. It was his birthright! It was to get back at the man who had abandoned his mother and dumped them in Zimbabwe.* Chatunga wanted revenge. He wanted to reverse the humiliation he had suffered at his cruel father's hand. 'Justice', was the word he had so often used. It now made sense why Chatunga was teamed up with this Italian mobster. He had a few wrongs to make right.

Benjamin tipped his head to Luigi Valente and dropped his eyes in respect.

"Have you seen this man on the ship?" Chatunga asked. He handed Benjamin his phone. Big George smiled back at him, slightly younger but just as thin and with a mop of red hair.

"Big George! He's the one who kidnapped Vanda and is smuggling the horn on the ship."

"We know," Chatunga replied. He hesitated for a moment before dropping his bombshell. "He's my brother. Or my half-brother bastard to be more precise. I only recently found out."

The words rolled casually off his lips, but it was the last thing Benjamin expected to hear. Was Big George a Lazarov? *The* Lazarov? That would make him the official heir to Basil Lazarov's empire! And Chatunga's worst nemesis.

Benjamin slumped onto the bench beside his old friend and rubbed his temples with both hands. His skin was warm and clammy. "You are after some justice," he said, peeking through his fingers.

"No," Valente interrupted. "We are after much more than justice. The whole eastern Med! That's what we want! It belongs to this man, Chatunga, the rightful firstborn son of that Bulgarian thief."

He paused and turned to Chatunga with a warmth in his old eyes. "Chatunga, my adopted son," he exclaimed. "My only son who is still alive." He patted Chatunga on the arm with paternal pride before turning back to Benjamin.

"Now about this rhino horn?" he snarled. "My rhino horn! Do you know how much it's worth?" The warmth left the conversation as quickly as it had arrived and Benjamin realized that it was pure business again.

Chatunga flushed and looked away.

He's using me, Benjamin realized! *Another hair brained scheme from my friend! Are they blackmailing him?* He wondered how gullible someone had to be before they lost everything. *Could Chatunga not see how he was being used as a pawn in a much bigger game of power and control?* It was no use arguing the point. Benjamin had no alternative but to co-operate. He'd ditched Tram Ng and thrown his lot in with Chat. He knew that if he didn't play ball now, he wouldn't make it back to the ship in one piece.

"Of course I know what it's worth," Benjamin bluffed. "It's on the Grande. Completely hidden away. They were meant to offload it in Tunisia. Until that attack happened and the ship went off to Malta instead. It's well hidden. Out of sight and smell from snoopers. Including Bollini. I know where it is and I know who the henchmen are. Do you?"

Benjamin felt empowered by what he'd said. It was pure gyp though. He had no idea where on the ship the horn was, but he knew it was there somewhere. He instinctively pulled his bag, with the rat in it, close to his side.

"We know exactly who they are," Luigi Valente said.

"Big George Lazarov is fronting for our father," Chatunga said. Valente glanced at him. "But I'm not his son, anymore," he weakly concluded.

"Can you get us to it?" Valente asked. "Tell us where it is hidden on board?"

"I'll need some guarantees?" Benjamin said. "Firstly, you have to help me find Vanda and guarantee our safety."

"I promise not to put concrete shoes on you," the old man replied. "For the sake of my boy here." He patted Chatunga's hand as though he were the family cocker spaniel. "If you find it, that is."

Benjamin's nerve finally fell apart. In that split second he could see Dr. Miller confirming what he knew to be true. The past comes to haunt you.

"I might need your help," Benjamin nervously said.

Chatunga rolled his eyes. Benjamin glanced angrily at him. *How could you get me into this crap hole?* He thought.

"Of course."

Valente waved Benjamin closer as though he was in the confessional booth. Their voices dropped to whispers as Benjamin explained to them what he would need. He made most of it up as he went along, but Valente didn't think it was a bad plan.

He also told them about how Tram and Lesley Ng were sniffing around trying to make a bust. Valente laughed it away.

"Vietnamese cops are as crooked as a bag of Asian snakes," he said. "Especially when it comes to rhino horn. They're insignificant. Trust me, no one knows they're on the ship except themselves. We'll sort them out if they interfere."

Benjamin didn't know whether to feel relieved or worried. He hated the fact that the slimy Italian mob was planning to sweep in and take the rhino horn for themselves. *Typical wise guys.* But he had no choice and whatever stupid plans Chatunga conjured up, he was still infinitely more trustworthy than the Ng's or the Lazarov mob. It was Vanda's best chance!

"I'll get the exact location to you," Benjamin said. "As soon as Vanda is back safe with me."

"No!" Valente said firmly. "This Vanda is not my concern. I don't want to hear about her again. And I want to pick up the merchandise directly from your room. We are not going to mess around on that huge ship looking for it. That's your job. That's what saves your skin." His eyes were like lasers.

"Why my room?" Benjamin asked. "Surely you want it somewhere else that's easier to access?"

"The presidential suite is the most secure spot on the ship," Chatunga explained. "Hardly anyone is allowed up there, and the head porter can be convinced to do anything with the right gravy. He'll easily get it out disguised as luggage or something."

"You've been doing your homework, I see. I thought our presence in the presidential room was a secret?"

"Javier is on my speed dial," Valente said, smiling.

Benjamin shook his head in disappointment. He was not surprised by Captain Pizarro's duplicity. *So much for our 'deal'*, he thought.

"If I do this, do we both then walk away then?" Benjamin asked. "Out of the picture completely, with no further involvement?"

Valente nodded slowly. "Si," he muttered. "No debt. You have my word, but only if you get all the horn to your room. My boy here will take it from there."

Benjamin tried not think how many people he was double-crossing or walking up the garden path at that precise moment. *I'll figure it out*, he thought. *Maybe this rat will come in useful after all!*

There was a sudden shuffling in the back of the chapel. Salvatore Bollini had quietly slipped into the little chapel and had been standing in the shadows for a few minutes straining to listen to the three men up front. As he stood there, Bollini went white and almost pissed in his pants. He knew exactly who Benjamin and his friend were talking to. Any Italian or Sicilian worth his salt knew Valente's old face.

His face was covered by a low-brimmed hat, and he tip-toed out before anyone spotted him. He'd met his match. If Benjamin knew Don Luigi Valente, then Benjamin was a man to befriend, not someone to get on the wrong side of. Bollini half wretched as he slipped away. Panayotis Pappas kept on his trail, thinking that they were still following Benjamin.

Benjamin eventually exited the Cathedral alone and hailed a cab back to the ship. No-one stopped him at the security checkpoint or picked up that he was bringing an animal aboard in his bag. As he made his way through the ship, being extra careful that he wasn't being followed, he looked around in vain for Vanda.

* * *

A CRACK OF LIGHT PIERCED THE DIM SHADOWS UNDER THE steel staircase. Vanda kept absolutely still. *Someone was there!*

It had felt like ages since she had woken up in that vile place with her head spinning. She had the rhino horn in her hand and caressed its sharp point. The thick end gripped perfectly into her palm like any good Yemeni warrior would have wanted it to. She had been over her plan a hundred times in her head.

"Step out," Takis Evangelis snarled. "Don't think I can't see you under there."

He was edging slowly down the steel stairs. His dirty boots were inches from Vanda's face as she stood silently under the open treads. The smell of fish guts from his soles made Vanda pull her nose up. Together with the stench of dried urine and stale nicotine slob, it was too much. She felt like vomiting but resisted it. She put her right hand behind her back and clutched her makeshift dagger as tight as she could. Takis jumped around the balustrade.

"Hello there lovely," he said, through his crooked ivory teeth. "Are you gonna give Takis a good morning peck on the cheek?"

"Keep dreaming," Vanda said, stepping back against the wall. She lowered her center of gravity and waited for him to get closer, within striking distance. He stood back however and lit a cigarette, laughing at her prudish attempts to swear.

"I see you've still got my jersey on," he said, blowing smoke at her.

"I thought this was a non-smoking ship?"

"Then, my lovely, why are you on it?" Takis asked. He had a cocksure arrogant manner about him. She felt like retching on the repulsive man in front of her.

"Where do you fit into this?" she asked. "Bartender? Masseuse? Another Waiter?"

It hit a raw nerve. Takis liked to think of himself as someone a bit more important than that.

"Higher," he said arrogantly, with a smirk on his face.

"Receptionist? No, I know, you're a cook," Vanda said. "Or is that cook-boy assistant? The redhead man's secret boy perhaps?"

Takis' face turned dark, and Vanda wondered if she hadn't pushed his buttons too much. A drop of sweat broke out on her forehead.

"Enough of the twenty questions," Takis snarled. He threw down his cigarette and put his hand into his jacket pocket and pulled out his six-inch chef's knife.

"Definitely cook-boy assistant then," Vanda said instinctively.

Takis lurched forward and pinned Vanda's left hand against the staircase. He swiped the air with his knife.

"The redhead man wants a piece of your finger," he said. "To give to your boyfriend." He swung the knife down toward Vanda's hand. She tried to yank it away but his grip was overpowering. The razor sharp knife caught Vanda above the fingernail on her little finger. A piece of skin sliced off.

Vanda saw the blood before she felt the pain. It flowed down her hand and dripped onto the floor. Stunned at first, she shook her hand free spraying some blood toward Takis. He finally slackened and let her go.

"You pig!" she cried.

Takis dropped his eyes to the floor, looking for the piece of skin he had just sliced off. It was the moment Vanda had been waiting for. She knew it would be an important second and she'd not get another chance. It was now or never. She swung her right arm around from behind her back.

The roof of the filthy hideout room was the last thing Takis' left eye ever saw. The rhino horn impaled him square in the retina. Vanda hit him so hard that she could almost feel his eyeball explode.

He let out an instant scream and dropped the knife on the floor. He knocked away the rhino horn and his eye fell apart in a bloodied jelly trifle that dripped through his fingers in a gooey mess. He wailed and swore in Greek.

"Bitch Americano," he shouted, hopping around the room in bewilderment.

Then he sank to the floor looking in vain for his popped eyeball. There was a hollow and empty hole where his eye had been five seconds earlier.

Vanda made a run to the top of the spiral staircase. She had one last glance back as she pulled the door open. Takis Evangelis was bumping into one of the crates screaming for his Mother.

"I'm no one's bitch," she said calmly, before slamming the door closed and clamping on the padlock lying open on the latch.

She put the key into her pocket and walked out as calmly as she could, holding her bleeding hand. The kitchen storage area was empty.

She headed unsteadily toward the exit, hiding her bleeding hand and the rhino horn in the dirty jersey she was wearing. *Blimey, it hurt!* She wanted to get to Benjamin and safety. Some voices babbled from the corridor outside. The chefs were filing in. Vanda had no idea who might be working with the man she had just impaled, and the thought of being caught and sent back into that hell hole terrified her. She ducked into a cupboard that was piled high with tomato puree cans.

By the time she was able to slip out unseen and make her way back to the presidential suite, the sun was lying low in the afternoon sky. Benjamin was not back from the City yet. She hoped he had not run out on her.

Wrapping her cut finger in tissue paper, she curled up for half an hour in a ball on the floor. Then she ran a bath and waited for Benjamin to return.

* * *

THE ROOM OF THE PRESIDENTIAL SUITE WAS HALF DARK AS Benjamin stepped into it. He thought it strange because he had opened the curtains that morning himself and no-one was meant to be servicing the room. The TV was playing in one of the bedrooms, and Benjamin's heart raced as he peeked around the corner.

Vanda sat cross-legged on the bed with a blanket wrapped around her. She jumped up as soon as she saw Benjamin and raced over to him. They fell into each other's arms without saying a word. She clung tightly and he comforted her as best he could.

"I was worried to hell and back," he said.

"I've been waiting here for ages for you," Vanda said. "Where have you been all day?"

Benjamin dropped the bag with the rat box in it and kicked it aside.

"I've been all over Barcelona trying to get help for you," Benjamin answered. "I've made some deals with the devil to try and get you to safety."

"I took care of myself," Vanda said. "I told you I could."

"Are you alright?"

Vanda shook and sniffed. The harsh reality of what she had been through was still sinking in. She remembered Takis' eye vividly. Her lunge toward his ugly face replayed over and over in slow motion in her mind.

She slowly disengaged herself from Benjamin and picked up an oversized woolen jersey from the chair. It still stank of stale blood and cigarettes. She slowly unwrapped the rhino horn she'd used to stab Takis and held it out to Benjamin.

"I got this for us," she said.

Benjamin looked at it with a combination of excitement and trepidation. It had part of a rapidly drying eyeball hanging off it. He grimaced and could only guess what Vanda had done with it.

He remembered the words of Astraea, his recurring dream angel. *'You can't avoid destiny'*, she had said. Dr. Miller had once said the same thing. *Life follows you wherever you go, and all your old garbage, it doesn't go away.*

As Vanda handed it to him, he noticed her still bloodied finger.

"Sweet Zulu, Vanda. What happened?"

Vanda squeezed the end of her sliced finger. It oozed blood. She wretched and dropped to the floor.

"The cook guy," she sobbed. "He did this. Before I got him."

"Hang on," Benjamin said, "I know what to do."

He gently put the horn on the bedside table and attended to Vanda's finger as best he could. The tip had been sliced but it was not as bad as it initially looked. A few mill's of skin had been removed. The challenge was to stop the blood oozing out.

"At least you never left fingerprints," Benjamin unsuccessfully joked, as he dressed it with some band-aids. He gave her a pain-killer and poured her a large shot of whiskey.

It was not her first of the day, but she eagerly took the glass. As she sipped it down, she told him about the room she had been held in and how it was packed full of rhino horns.

When she described what Takis had done to her, Benjamin's face went dark. He was ecstatic though, to hear about the rhino horns.

"How much was there?" was the first thing he asked.

"At least twenty crates," Vanda replied. "They were all full." Benjamin whistled.

"Do you realize that this could set us up for life?" Benjamin said, half seriously.

"I don't give a rats ass about those horns," Vanda said. "That thug who cut me, however, is another thing. After what he did, I'd kill if I got the chance!"

"Sounds like you already did!" Benjamin said reaching for the rhino horn she had brought back with her.

"That's only part of him. The rest of him is still jumping around in pain."

"Bastard!"

Vanda started to relax. She was absorbing the pain in her finger deep down somewhere.

"At least you got away," Benjamin said, as he packed his first aid kit away.

"You can pour me another drink," Vanda said. "But I need to shower again. I can't get the smell of that place out of me."

She dropped her top from her body. It fell to the floor like a dead phantom. Benjamin jerked his head away, feeling guilty. She trailed her good hand over him as she walked semi-naked to the bathroom holding her bandaged hand up in the air. The pills were making her float.

"There's no going back now," she said, before closing the door and turning on the faucet.

Benjamin examined the Rhino horn she had brought in with its sticky mess. It was a nice one. He knew exactly where it was from. How it had been hacked off with an ax. And he knew exactly where it was being shipped to. He'd been in both places. He thought about its worth. *Hell is full of fortunes*, he thought to himself.

The rat in the bag on the floor squeaked and hissed as it grew intoxicated by the smell of the rhino horn. Benjamin moved the bag to the second bedroom and closed the door. The Ng's were not expecting him to let the rat loose until the next morning. *They're probably partying and gambling up a storm tonight,* Benjamin thought to himself. *Before things get serious in Marseilles.*

Marseilles! The next port. It seemed as if everything was going to come to a crux there. For once Benjamin felt ahead of the game. He had Vanda back and she knew where the stash was. The leverage that both the Ng's and George Lazarov had had over him earlier in the day, melted away.

He sat on the sofa waiting for Vanda. He couldn't believe his luck. Vanda had been taken exactly to the location that everyone was looking for. He just needed her to now unpack things again, exactly where it was where the rhino horn was being hidden.

They'd be safe in the Presidential Suite for the night. Access to the Yacht Club suites was restricted, and as far as he knew, Captain Pizarro was still the only one on the ship who knew their exact location. He propped a chair up against the door just in case though. Then he looked wistfully around.

Astraea was nowhere. He wanted her. He missed her. The night was young and she was missing in action. There was plain nothing. The air was the color of brandy and the sound of water from the shower next door was a percussion cymbal playing with the distant thumps of diesel engines.

* * *

VANDA JOINED BENJAMIN ON THE BALCONY AND AT SIX

o'clock the quayside illuminated orange in the evening sunset. It sparkled in the soft light.

"Don't you love how a sunset always fills one with a nostalgic vitality?" she said. "It's as though you trick your own body and thrown a towel over the clock that is ticking away inside."

They pretended for a few moments that they were rich and free and longtime lovers. It could never last though. The reality of their situation was bound to eventually snatch away the few good thoughts and spit them out again with the hand they had been dealt.

Benjamin was exhausted deep inside. But for now, as the sunset looked for a worthy friend to expend its energy, he felt strangely alive. He was glad though, to be leaving Barcelona.

As the MSE Grande slowly pull away from her berth, they both looked forward to a decent night's sleep. The next day they would be in Marseilles. They watched the La Sagrada Familia waving goodbye in the distance, burnished in Gothic glory.

The bedside phone in the suite suddenly rang. Benjamin ran to answer it.

"Yes?"

He held the receiver with his cupped hand, as he spoke to Chatunga. Vanda vaguely heard him whispering, "I've found it!"

Vanda noticed the puffy bags that were starting to form under his eyes. She ran her fingers over her own cheeks to convince herself that she wasn't in as bad a condition as Benjamin. The bandage snagged on her skin and she pulled her cut finger swiftly away. She had put on loose jeans and a pair of slippers. She smiled as she thought about what her friends had said to her before the cruise. *You'll put on ten pounds*, they had said. She must have lost as much.

Vanda couldn't make out what Benjamin was saying or

who he was talking to. He finished off his conversation and gave her an affirming smile.

"Would you be able to explain to me how to get back to that secret room?" he asked.

"Of course, it's pretty straightforward, once you get down into the kitchen storage areas."

"Are there lots of staff down there?"

"No. I hardly saw anyone," Vanda said confidently. "Some cooks walked by, but they weren't working down there in that corridor. I think it's where they keep bulk stores for the longer cruises. But Ben, I don't think you should even try it. It was a hellish place and the other end of that eyeball is still down there."

"I'm no longer worried about Big George," Benjamin said. "I had to choose a side and I chose the Italians. There is, however, one thing you have to do for me, Vanda."

Vanda shrugged her shoulders. "What now?"

"I want you to get the heck off this ship as soon as it arrives in France and not come back. It's way too dangerous for you. I want to finish this alone."

"I'm not leaving you again," Vanda insisted. "We're in this together, remember?" She twisted his shirt cuff. "You don't have to be a dick, you know," she said. "Besides, after all I've been through, I deserve to get half of what you sell this horn for." She picked up the rhino horn again. "You are planning on flogging it for yourself, aren't you?"

Benjamin never answered her. He was torn apart inside. Money always seemed to complicate his life.

"It got rather hectic in Barcelona after they took you," he explained. "It's not so simple. You... we are not going to do anything stupid with this horn! It's now about getting out of this situation in one piece."

Vanda opened the curtain up more to view Barcelona's

night lights trailing off to the right. "The cash would be nice," she said.

"I need to update you properly on what happened with the Ng's and Chatunga," Benjamin said. "But first, you'd better have another scotch."

As they both sipped their glasses and he unpacked what had happened to him whilst Vanda had been locked up, Benjamin sensed that he was not alone in his quest to put things right. Vanda wanted it too. And he finally felt Astraea again as he spoke. She was empowering him from within.

Vanda slumped into her chair and covered her face with her long hair as Benjamin explained how Chatunga had brought the Italian mafia onto the scene.

"The bottom line is that we had two bad options open to us. Tram Ng or Luigi Valente! Both of them said they'd destroy us if we don't get them to the stash of rhino horn."

"What about Big George and his thugs?" Vanda asked. "And that pig who chopped up my finger? And Bollini? Goodness Benjamin, where do we turn? Maybe we *should* both run?"

"Vanda, I'm the one at fault here. I'm the killer. I shot so many of those poor animals."

"And hacked off their poor noses?" Vanda snapped.

"I did," Benjamin said sadly. "You're right. You got stuck in this mess through no fault of your own. I chose what I did. I'm really sorry. You should leave tomorrow. I have to stay though. I just have to. I want to clean this all up or die trying. Everything. Everything I ever did. Or else I'll be running forever."

They stood silent for a few minutes. The events of the previous few days seemed to weld them together. Vanda then stood up angrily and marched to her cupboard, swearing under her breath. She roughly gathered her things together, throwing them into her suitcase. Then she took them out again.

"Why did I have to meet you?" she mumbled to herself. "Why do I like you so much?"

She checked the duffel bag as she sobbed. The sawn-off shotgun was still there.

"OK!" she finally said. "I'm staying too. We need each other to get through this."

"You're amazing," Benjamin said.

Vanda's lips quivered. "So, how do we get off the ship in one piece?" she asked. "And how do we get that rhino horn to the right person? What's your plan, Ben?"

"We have to get it all up here, into this room. It was our part of the deal. Chatunga will get it off the ship from here."

"You've got to be kidding me," Vanda exploded. "How do you intend to get that done?"

"Distraction!" Benjamin replied. "And some good acting. We'll move it in the chaos. From what you described to me, we could get it up here in luggage trolleys in three trips."

"Chaos?"

Benjamin nodded.

"Ben. Don't hurt anyone."

"Of course not!" Benjamin said, smiling. "I'm going to turn Tram Ng's little secret weapon against him."

"What's that?"

"I'll show you in the morning, or else you'll never sleep. You'll never believe it," Benjamin laughed.

"What if Ng brings in the police to search the ship when he realizes you aren't helping him anymore?" Vanda asked.

"I'm banking that he won't," Benjamin replied. "Valente said he was crooked and I know he is. Screwed me back in Vietnam. And besides, your friend Captain Pizarro, won't want any negative publicity. Especially after the Tunisian attack. Our challenge will be ensuring that none of this is ever linked back to us."

"I want to get rid of the shotgun," Vanda said. "It implicates me. What if they come in here with sniffer dogs and find it."

"They won't. Aren't you listening?" Benjamin said. "If it makes you happier though, we can toss it overboard right now."

Vanda walked over to fetch the duffel bag. She thought about Takis Evangelis, how he had screamed as she had taken out his eye. It made her feel sick.

"Don't toss it yet," she said. "You never know, we might need it with your dumb plan." She pulled the curtains closed.

"I wonder what Big George will do to him?"

"Who?" Benjamin asked.

"The man who cut my finger. I took out his eye, you know. I left him locked up in his own hole. And here's the key." She threw the padlock key to Benjamin.

As she packed away the duffel bag, she turned toward him. "Ben, I don't think the police will ever find that room where they put me. It was pretty well hidden and with those smells of food down there. The dogs will never pick it up."

"I told you there won't be any sniffer dogs," Benjamin said. "Rats maybe, but not dogs!"

"That makes no sense." Vanda went into the bathroom to brush her teeth. "I think we both need some shut-eye," she said.

* * *

IT WAS MIDNIGHT AND THEY COULDN'T SLEEP. BENJAMIN paced up and down the room while Vanda had stared blankly at the television. It was playing a looped documentary of the ship's entertainment.

"It's going to work, it's going to work," Benjamin kept saying out loud. He was wearing a white gown and hadn't brushed his hair. Vanda thought he looked like a mad professor. She lay there quietly, wondering how she had got into the mess they were in. The painkiller had worn off and her hand throbbed. From her perspective, it was her fault and her mess. *She had shot that waiter into the ocean. She had taken out an eye with the crudest weapon imaginable. She was one who had the stolen Rhino horn in her handbag in the first place. It was her fault!* She felt terrible lying there watching Benjamin trying to now fix it.

She thought about his name. Rodd. He certainly was acting like a lightning rod, helping her with all the trouble she had caused. *And yet he was the one who probably shot that rhino in the first place.* She closed her eyes as the rhino horn raised itself like a huge monumental middle finger in front of her. In her wildest dreams, she never thought that she'd end up in a room with a poacher from Africa. But there was a side to Benjamin that was endearing and authentic and lovable.

"I'm sick of these bar snacks," she moaned. "We should have ordered proper room service. And we've run out of drinks."

She knew they had no choice. There was no way they could have safely ordered room service. Bizarrely, Captain Pizarro had kept his side of the deal. No-one had come to their room to clean it or check its supplies or even drop off a newspaper. *The staff must all think it's still empty.* Big George Lazarov and his goons, would have been watching the room service orders. And they would have come. Out of the darkness like the other night on the balcony, or in the steam room.

The sawn-off shotgun lay next to Vanda like a benevolent dog protecting its master. Both barrels were loaded. It made her feel safe. She wished she could use it and bring it all to an abrupt end. A real end. Not a cock and bull ending like Benjamin was thinking.

Benjamin walked up and down. "It's going to work," he said for the millionth time.

"What?" she snapped. "What are we going to do? Please tell me."

As the words tumbled out she immediately regretted them. *This man had helped her. He was on her side.* She liked him. But part of her wanted to punch him right in the face. *Why did she have to pick the complicated men? The tragic ones. The dark horses.*

She sucked her glass trying to get the last drop of whiskey to dribble down her throat.

"You still don't trust me, do you?" Benjamin said, getting slightly annoyed. "I told you, we're going to take this fight right back to them."

"You said that," Vanda said, finally calming down. "The best form of defense is attack, isn't it?"

"Kind of. Except we're not going to attack straight on," Benjamin said. "We're going to snipe at their flanks, Vanda. We're going to snipe them so hard that they'll wish for your shotgun. I'm going to make you proud, Vanda, and we'll be toasting to our health before you know it."

Vanda sat quietly. Just as Benjamin was starting to annoy her, he bounced back right into her soft spot. She got up and put her hand on his side.

"I'm in. Tell me what to do."

"You can start by getting me my reserve bottle of hooch from my suitcase," he said, smiling.

"Man!" Vanda cried, throwing a pillow at him. "How could you keep me waiting so long?"

They drank while Benjamin unpacked the details. They giggled like tipsy teenagers until it was almost dawn.

❧ 8 ❧

MARSEILLES

By the time the sun rose, Benjamin and Vanda were dressed and ready to go. They had put on clothes as similar as they could find to make them look as though they were part of the crew. White golf shirts and black trousers.

"What time are we arriving in Marseilles?" Vanda asked.

"Eleven," Benjamin replied. "That gives us plenty of time to do what we have to do." He pulled Vanda over into the second bedroom.

"Promise me you won't scream," he said, with a crafty smile on his face. He slowly unzipped the backpack and pulled out the box with the rodent. He braced himself as a furry nose peeked out. Vanda bent over the box, inquisitively.

"He's gorgeous!" she exclaimed. "I love hamsters."

"It's actually a Giant African Pouch Rat. A she."

"Give her to me," Vanda affectionately said. She scooped the rodent up by its tiny collar and rubbed it on her cheek. It smelt Vanda's neck. Benjamin took a step backward. The rat sniffed the air with its stiff whiskers and scratched loose from Vanda's grip. Benjamin jumped onto the bed. Vanda chased it through the lounge. It headed straight for the drawer next to the bed, where Benjamin had thrown the rhino horn. After scratching the drawer handle, the rat squealed and started running in little circles.

"Look at her," Vanda gushed. "She's so cute. Who trained her to do that?"

"The Ng's have some crazy animal trainer in their employ," Benjamin shouted from the bed. He had no intention of stepping down until Vanda had the rat back in its cage.

"I see she has a love for rhino horn," Vanda said, trying to catch him.

"Took months to train it, Benjamin shouted. "Clever, isn't it? Apparently, it can track horns from a kilometer away."

"We don't need it for that anymore. I know now where Big George has put the rhino."

"I've got some other plans in mind for it," smiled Benjamin.

"How do we get her back in the bag?" Vanda asked. "It's like trying to catch a furry eel."

Benjamin scratched in his pocket and pulled out the electronic clicker that he had been given. He pushed the button and the rat immediately came charging back into his room and stood on its hind legs scratching the side of the bed. The electronic clicker worked like a silent dog whistle, at a pitch they couldn't detect. Vanda laughed as Benjamin almost climbed up the wall.

"I'm calling her Missy," Vanda said, as she scooped it up. "She's starving, Ben. Go get a banana from the fruit bowl, please. And a saucer of water."

"How can you touch it?"

"How can you not?"

Benjamin washed his hands, as Vanda fed and played with her new friend.

"She's as tame as a Burmese kitten," Vanda said. "Look, she even has a tartan collar."

"It's got a tracking device on it," Benjamin yelled. "I'm supposed to turn it on when I let her loose. Tram Ng is waiting for the signal to kick in this morning."

"I'm taking the collar off," Vanda said. "Just in case he's already tracking her."

"Tell your Missy we still need her skills later," Benjamin said, opening up the box again. "Put her back in here for now. Common, we've got some work to do."

Benjamin slipped the tiny tartan rat collar into his pocket as Vanda gently placed the box back into its backpack.

"I'm going to go down and get us some more food," Benjamin said, throwing the backpack over his shoulder.

"You'd better stay put here. We don't want anyone to see you. George probably still thinks you're locked up."

"Look after Missy," Vanda said.

"I've got a nice surprise waiting for our old maître d'," Benjamin gleefully replied.

"Your diversion plan?"

Benjamin grinned.

"I hope it's not a stupid one," Vanda shouted as he headed down the corridor toward the breakfast area.

"I just need some chaos. A tiny bit really," Benjamin answered. "It's going to be hilarious."

He reckoned they needed a one-hour distraction. One hour to raid the secret room and get the horn up into their cabin as fast as they could. After that, they would leave the ship and be somewhere in downtown Marseilles by the time Chatunga Lazarov arrived to collect it. How Chatunga did that probably had something to do with the fact that Captain Pizarro owed Luigi Valente a favor, but Benjamin didn't really care. They'd be safe and free and he might even get a small share for helping Chatunga out.

* * *

Benjamin's plan had two parts and both involved the rat. As he entered the dining room, he smiled at the irony of using Tram Ng's own ingenuity against them all. Panayotis Pappas saw him straight away and almost choked on the croissant he was surreptitiously eating from behind the service counter. Benjamin walked straight up to him, ignoring the other staff who milled around.

"Where's George?"

Pappas stumbled over his response. "Who?" he answered unconvincingly. "I don't know what you are talking about?"

"Look," Benjamin said. "I know you work for Big George Lazarov. I've got a message for him."

Pappas looked nervously around the room as Benjamin mentioned the Lazarov name. He knew George liked to keep his real identity secret. His bulky frame loomed over Benjamin as he looked him up and down.

"I'm the maître d'," Pappas said, stepping around his counter. "I can keep messages for anyone on this ship." He held out his hand, pretending to the other staff around him as though nothing was untoward. Benjamin took his hand and pulled him forward. *The man is built like a brick shit-house,* Benjamin thought to himself.

"Tell Big George, *El Dilletante* needs a few more hours," he said. "He'll have it tonight. One Uphondo returned, as ordered."

Pappas pretended to not understand. "I'm not quite sure what you mean, sir?" he said.

"Of course you do," Benjamin sneered. He pulled Pappas toward him and as he whispered into his ear he dropped the rat collar into Pappas's side jacket pocket. It's tracking transmitter flashed a tiny green light.

"Watch out for Interpol," he said, before letting go. "And no tip for you!"

Tram Ng will be all over him like a rash when that lights up on his receiver, Benjamin laughed to himself, as he walked off to the other side of the dining room. Panayotis kept his professional demeanor as Benjamin walked away. Inside he was boiling.

Benjamin looked around for the next stooge to use. He spotted the young boy with the snotty shirt, who he had been pulling faces with all week. He was at the cereal bar, filling his bowl with colorful puffs and chocolate crisps. He had brushed his hair for once and was all alone. Benjamin sidled up to him and smiled. The boy recognized Benjamin and hesitated.

"How are the chocolate puffs?" Benjamin asked.

"I'm not allowed to talk to strangers," The boy answered.

"Oh, I'm not a stranger," Benjamin replied, smiling. "I met you on the first day of the cruise, remember? And I've been here all along."

The boy said nothing, looking suspiciously at the man in front of him who was suddenly being nice.

"Do you like animals?" Benjamin asked. The boy nodded.

"Well I've lost a little friend of mine and I was wondering if you could help me find him," Benjamin said.

"Is it a dog?"

"Oh no!" Benjamin said. "Dogs aren't allowed on the ship. Do you have a dog?" The boy nodded.

"What's his name?"

"Rocky," the boy answered.

"I'm sure Rocky would help me if he was here," Benjamin said. He leaned over close to the boy. "Do you like secrets?"

"Yes," the boy confidently answered.

"Well, my secret is that my pet mouse is missing and I need some help to find him. Can you and your friends help me?"

"Is he tame?"

"Very," Benjamin answered, "and he's the biggest mouse you ever saw. I'll buy you an ice-cream if you find him for me. Can you help me find him?"

"Yes!" the boy said, starting to get excited.

"I've got a magic buzzer here that will help you," Benjamin said, taking the electronic clicker out of his pocket. "Here's what you need to do."

The boy's eyes lit up, as Benjamin showed him what to do.

"Push this magic button three times," he explained. "Keep pushing it and eventually my mouse will come to you. It's like magic!"

"And then?"

"Then you need to catch it and keep it for me," Benjamin said. "OK?"

"And my ice-cream?"

"Let's find my mouse first," Benjamin explained.

"I want a triple scoop," the boy insisted, "with chocolate sprinkles."

Little shit, Benjamin muttered to himself, as he handed over the electronic clicker. The boy snatched it out of his hands and hurtled away as though he had just been given the best digital wonder ever invented.

"Remember it's a secret," Benjamin shouted as the boy disappeared.

Back outside, Benjamin stopped near a pot plant in the corridor. Checking that no-one was coming, he carefully unzipped his backpack and tilted the lid of the rat box open. The rat slithered into the ferns.

"Good luck Missy," Benjamin said. "Go cause some havoc."

THE FIRST SCREAM RANG OUT TEN MINUTES LATER. SOME OF the guests were still lying in bed looking at the magnificent French shoreline turning green from the morning's orange hue, but most of them were up and about waiting for the ship to get to the port. At first, hardly anyone noticed. It sounded like just another hysterical tourist laughing at a joke or slipping on something. Even the trained security crew ignored it.

Salvatore Bollini, who was snooping around in the kitchen, trying to catch lazy staff, let out a deep sigh when he heard it. He had just gotten things back to order after the ransacking of his office and was trying to keep his head down after seeing who Benjamin had met at the Barcelona Cathedral. He didn't want to get involved with anything to do with the Sicilians. Especially if Don Luigi Valente was involved.

As another scream filled the air, Bollini slowly made his way to the door with a heaviness that only falls onto the shoulders of a man who believes he carries more responsibility than anyone else. *Who else, after all, was going to see who was screaming like that. He would catch them and teach them a lesson.*

He checked that his Taser was firmly embedded into its holster. He looked at himself in the round mirror that the chef had installed so that he could always see his cooks with one glance. Bollini made a quick pseudo-draw. *He was Lucky Luke at noon.* He blew the imaginary smoke off his finger and squinted his eyes.

Bollini doubted there could be any real danger. He pulled his tight jacket down at the bottom corners, straightened and walked out into the dining room. He intended to give the maître d' in charge a thorough grilling for allowing such a fiasco.

As he stepped through the swing doors, a third scream

rang out. It was from an elderly British lady who was standing against the railing next to the pork sausages.

"My Golly!" she yelled. "There is a rat! Humungous rats running around!" She screamed and pointed furiously between the tables. People parted like the Red Sea and jumped onto their chairs as a group of naughty boys ran up and down shouting and pointing. Their leader had his hand in his pocket and kept pushing the button on the electronic clicker Benjamin had given him.

The general panic picked up tempo and volume as more and more people starting shouting that there was a rat running around. Bollini almost choked as he poked his short neck under a table. 'Missy' smiled at him before turning and rushing away. Bollini yelling for his aide. His arms flapped like an origami bird as he screamed to those around him not to panic.

A group of young teenage girls then all screamed together and real panic set in amongst the guests. Someone knocked over a coffee pot and it exploded on the floor like a gunshot. Half the people didn't know what was it was all about but suspected the worst. The Tunisian incident was still very much on everyone's mind. Within a minute the entire dining room looked like an ant nest after it had been kicked over. People appeared from nowhere, shouting, running and jumping on chairs. An alarm started wailing in the background as Bollini kept yelling at the top of his voice. The alarm triggered a mass stampede from the dining room. Some guests started running to their evacuation points as they had been trained. Bollini ran around like a decapitated chicken. "Who put the alarm on?" he demanded to know. He eventually got into a security office next to the dining room.

"I have no idea what's going on?" his officer said. "We have nothing reported. No one has called. I sent Andrews to check. Maybe it was him when he heard you screaming."

"I wasn't screaming. It's rats!" Bollini howled. "What are you doing in here, you imbecile?"

"Sir? A call for you." The junior officer on duty pushed a phone into Bollini's hands.

"Si?" Bollini said, trying to act calm. He stood listening in silence for a minute. The officers around him could faintly hear the voice of Captain Pizarro yelling on the other end of the phone. Bollini turned white.

"Si," Bollini said again, putting the phone down at his side. He looked up at the men around him. His eyes glistened.

"Mama Mia!" he bawled. "What are you waiting for? Get everyone down here and find those rats. All hands on deck! Imbecile!"

He rushed at the junior officer, as though this was his fault. Then he stopped and slumped into a chair holding his head.

"Ratto! Ratto!" he kept wailing. "Why me? I hate the ratto!"

The other officers were stunned. It was not the situation that was worrying them but rather Bollini, their so-called senior officer. He seemed way out of his depth.

"Mama Mia," he cried, before pulling at his hair in despair.

The officers looked at each other in bewilderment. Eventually the next in command took over.

"Preliminary Procedures!" he calmly said. "Prepare for 'PP' while we figure what this is about. And someone, phone Marseilles, just in case!"

Outside in the dining room, the little boy with the snotty shirt, and his gang of friends sat laughing under one of the tables. It was the best thing that had happened to them on the cruise. "Let him loose again," one of them said. "I want to scare some more girls."

* * *

"WE'VE GOT SOME TIME," BENJAMIN SHOUTED TO VANDA, as they worked their way against the frenzied flow of guests, who had come out to see why the ship's alarm had sounded. He pulled her by the hand. "You lead," he said.

Vanda zigzagged effortlessly through the people. Benjamin knocked into every second person with the huge luggage trolley he had borrowed from the reception area. A lot of passengers were leaving the cruise in Marseilles and so lots of luggage was being ported from the bedrooms. No-one had noticed him taking the trolley.

They ducked into one the staff corridors and made for the service elevator at the end. There was virtually no crew around. They were all upstairs helping to calm guests and catch the rat. "Just pretend we work here," Benjamin said. "No-one will look at us twice." Vanda stopped at the elevator to catch her breath. "He might still be down there," she said.

"Who? Bollini?"

"No, the man I stabbed. I locked him in when I left."

"Great time to mention that little point," Benjamin said. "We can't go back now. Don't worry, we've got the bag with us." He patted the canvas duffel bag hanging from his shoulder. He could feel the sawed-off shotgun inside.

"I'll be ready for him," he said, "or anyone else for that matter."

Benjamin had taken on a new vigor since dawn. Vanda, on the other hand, was cautious. She had never liked Chatunga Lazarov from the moment she had first met him in Sicily. Now that she knew he was involved with the worst possible thugs, she was worried that they were being set up and used. And her finger still stung like a blue bottle.

"Actually," Benjamin continued, as the elevator door

opened. "I'm going to teach that animal a lesson after what he did to you."

"I can fight my own battles," Vanda replied. "Why do you think I'm tagging along and not up on deck with those paranoid crowds?"

As they stepped out into the downstairs service corridor, Vanda started to hyperventilate.

"It'll be OK," Benjamin said, assuring her. "We just need an hour or so. That fiasco about the rat will give it to us."

"I hope they don't hurt the poor thing," Vanda said. Benjamin never responded. He didn't expect to see Vanda's 'Missy' again.

"I hope Valente keeps his end of our plan and gets this stuff off the ship this afternoon," Vanda said.

"Chatunga assured me he would."

"I don't know who is worse, Ben? Your friend or his adoptive father?" Vanda said, rolling her eyes at the mention of Chatunga's name.

An eery silence filled the air as they pushed the trolley along. Benjamin felt a bit bad about the chaos he was responsible for up on deck. *It's innocent,* he reminded himself, hoping no one was getting hurt. *So much for his doing the right thing!* As the anticipation of seeing the rhino horn grew, he felt as though he was returning to his bad habits, like a dog. He could feel the disapproval of Astraea whirling around him as he followed Vanda into the deserted kitchen storage area.

"There," Vanda said. "Behind that locker!" The padlock was exactly as Vanda remembered leaving it. She trembled as she turned the key.

"Stand back," Benjamin instructed. He pulled the shotgun out of its bag and kicked the door open. He fumbled on the wall for the light switch, holding the gun firmly under his arm. The first thing he noticed was the sick smell. They both knew that stench. Vanda gagged.

They saw him, as they got to the bottom of the steel stair-case. Takis Evangelis lay on the old stained mattress. His eyes were closed and he looked at home amongst the garbage. There was no movement from him. His face was stained with blood and muck and his hands were over his hollow eye socket.

"What have I done?" Vanda exclaimed.

"That's quite a count you are accumulating,' Benjamin said, kicking Takis to see if he would wake up. He didn't move.

"Oh, dear!" Vanda said. Her answer was instinctive. She felt sick inside. She didn't want any of this. "He tried to cut off my finger. I was just fighting for my life. And you make jokes like I was on a rabbit shoot or something." She looked angrily across at Benjamin.

"I'm letting off some steam," he said. "You should too? What do you want me to say? Congratulations, you killed another one?" Vanda shot daggers at him and he moved the shotgun to his side, just in case.

"Whoah! Look at this!" Benjamin shouted, changing the topic as his eyes adjusted to the light. He opened one of the boxes. "No wonder the big boys wanted in."

His eyes had a wild look in them as he picked up one of the rhino horns and held it up in the light.

"I want to go," Vanda said. Her eyes narrowed and her voice was resolute. She didn't like the look in Benjamin's face one bit. It was corrupted, hollow and empty. He looked like an ex-junkie having heroin waved in front of him.

"I want no part of this anymore," she continued. "It's sick. You are sick!" She shouted. "These are endangered animals. You have no right!" Her fist hammered Benjamin's arm.

He snapped out of his trance and threw the horn back into the box, recomposing himself.

"I'm sorry," he said. "Instinct I guess? It's not my rhino

horn, this. I'm not the criminal here. I'm trying to get us both out of this mess in the cleanest possible way."

Vanda pulled back. She felt nauseous and confused.

"We're in this together Vanda. Remember? We have no other option." Benjamin's voice lowered and he moved to hold Vanda in his arms. "Please trust me," he begged.

Benjamin started packing boxes onto the steel staircase to carry up to the luggage trolley. As he filled the bottom steps, a voice boomed out behind him. "You're gonna wish you were never born!" The voice was thick and Greek and menacing. "Thought I was a goner, did you?"

Takis Evangelis was wide awake and in a rage. He looked like a zombie with dried blood dribbling down his cheeks. A one-eyed zombie! As he hurtled toward them, Vanda's first feeling was one of relief that she hadn't killed him. His chef's knife flashed in his hand.

"Come back for more, did you?" Takis snapped at Vanda. "I'll finish that finger of yours now and then take off the rest of your hand."

He lunged wildly at Vanda. The dark bloodied hole where his right eye once had been looked like a cave into his dark soul.

"Stand back, you wanker!" he yelled. Benjamin was incredulous. He reached slowly for the shotgun which was leaning on the wall. Takis never noticed and flashed his knife around like a madman. He swung wildly toward Vanda, aiming at her face, not caring where he might slice her.

Benjamin leaped forward and connected Takis square in the chest with the butt of the shotgun. Takis lifted clear off his feet and hit the wall behind him. He stuck there for a few moments like a swatted moth before crumpling into a heap on the ground. Benjamin couldn't control himself. He aimed the shotgun at Takis' foot and pulled the trigger. Vanda dropped to her knees sobbing and shaking as the shotgun dangled from Benjamin's lowered arm. Smoke filled the room.

The tendons on Takis' face pulled taught. He went rigid as though Riga Mortis was about to set in. He breathed deeply with a rasp. His eyes glazed as they focused on his left leg. It was a mangled mess. Then he passed out in the pain.

"I'm all in now," Benjamin said, putting the shotgun gently down beside the boxes. "As deep in as you are. Come on, we've got work to do. Help me load before he wakes up again."

"Let's tie this pig up first," Vanda suggested. "I'm not leaving him free again." She breathed out slowly as they tied Takis Evangelis up, avoiding his blood.

"Do you think he'll make it?"

"I don't care!"

Vanda put her foot on the heaving man at their feet. Takis was in bad shape and needed a hospital or else he would indeed be a goner before lunch. The blood was slowly pooling around his feet. It came out black and the room smelled like hell had opened up.

"It could be weeks before they find him. They use this room to hide stuff for a reason. No one knows it's here."

"Or just hours! His friends, Big George and the maître d' will be down here to check things at some stage. They'll find him in time. Besides he's not our problem."

"This is all our problem, Ben," Vanda said, as she hunched down in front of Takis checking to see if he was unconscious.

"Common, help me with this. We're running out of time! My rat ruse will only work for a short time. I can just imagine Senor Bollini right now." They both giggled.

"I'd rather be up there enjoying the spectacle than down here," Vanda replied, as she hauled a box over to Benjamin.

"They're not as heavy as they look," Benjamin said. Vanda didn't say another word. She wiped her cheek and got stuck in helping. To her, the boxes of rhino horn felt as heavy as moonshine as they lugged them up the stairs.

* * *

IT WAS OVER AN HOUR BEFORE COMPLETE CALM SETTLED back in the dining area of the ship, and it was just enough time for Benjamin and Vanda to move all the boxes up to their presidential suite. Most of the crew were scampering around Bollini, trying to catch 'Missy', who proved to be as elusive as sheet lightning. No-one had noticed anything unusual as two 'porters' pushed a trolley along the corridors. There were no staff milling around the entrance to the exclusive Yacht Club area and Benjamin had swiped effortlessly through. It had taken only two trips, not three as Benjamin had anticipated.

After the rat scare in the dining room, there was a general, but orderly concern amongst the guests and crew. A group of young boys, however, howled with laughter as they huddled over their new pet. They had eventually caught Missy but not before causing complete mayhem. By the time peace descended, Salvatore Bollini had collapsed into a hopeless heap outside the bridge. Captain Pizarro found him sitting with his head in his hands, muttering in his local Italian dialect. The Captain walked up to him and abruptly tore off the blue insignia on his lapels.

"Incompetent idiot!" the captain said. "Why did you call Marseilles, for heaven's sake!"

"It was the procedure," Bollini tried to explain. "In the book."

"For security emergencies, not rodent infestations!" Pizarro yelled. "Now I have to explain why a huge rat was running about in our dining area. This is not good!"

Pizarro pointed to the Marseilles dock front which was

now rapidly approaching. A few police vehicles and fire engines were parked on the waters edge with their lights flashing.

"Phone them and tell them there is no problem and no emergency," he instructed, besides himself with fury. The officers all knew that heads would roll. Bollini quickly got on the phone and the emergency vehicles withdrew as the ship berthed, their drivers cursing and gesticulating.

On board, Captain Pizarro did all that he could to calm the situation. Rodents on board were bad for business and might put him on the back page of every newspaper in Europe. After the Tunisian incident, any bad publicity he caused for the Mediterranean Shipping Company could mean early retirement for him.

"That imbecile Bollini!" Pizarro kept shouting. "I knew I shouldn't have promoted him."

In the chaos, Benjamin and Vanda had successfully done what they set out to do. The boxes of rhino horn had been safely moved up in their suite.

Vanda flopped down onto the big leather couch as soon as Benjamin locked the cabin door. She was exhausted. She thought that the boxes had weighed a ton.

"Thank goodness we had the luggage trolley to help us," Benjamin said.

"Did you hang up the do-not-disturb sign?" Vanda asked. Benjamin didn't answer her. He came over to where she was sitting.

"Vanda," he confidently said. "Tomorrow we get back to Genoa and we will walk off this ship in one piece, with our passports and this will be over. We'll be safe and away from this." He meant it, but she hardly believed him.

"How long are we now going to be holed up in here with this dreadful rhino horn before your good friend comes to collect it?" she asked. "The police could come through on a search at any minute. Did you see them outside? Lined up with their dogs and machine guns?"

"It looks like they are not boarding, and even if they did, they won't check the VIP rooms," Benjamin said. "They must have realized it was a false alarm by now. Chatunga promised that these horns will be out of here by lunchtime. What do you say we get freshened up and rest a bit? I'm exhausted and we've got a bit of time to play with."

"Are you sure they will quietly remove it while we're ashore?" Vanda asked.

Benjamin nodded.

She stood and stretched. Her back ached and her finger felt as though someone had put a blow torch to it. Her bandage was mangled and bloodied. "I'm showering first,' she said as she opened the door to her bathroom. "You can't use your bathroom with those boxes stuffed in there."

Benjamin took the shotgun out of the duffel bag. He stuck two new cartridges in the double barrel and snapped it shut.

"Just in case," he said, before falling back onto the couch and throwing up his legs. His eyes were heavy and he fell into a snooze as he waited for Vanda.

* * *

ASTRAEA OPENED THE DOOR AS SOON AS HE CLOSED HIS TIRED eyes. He knew straight away that he was in trouble with her. Dreams are meant to go away when you wake up. They are meant to fade away, visiting again only in some opaque form at another time. They are not meant to restart and carry on each time you fall asleep. Benjamin was not so lucky.

A cold shiver shot through his spine as though someone had emptied ice water down his shirt. Astraea had a radiance around her, a magnetic light that Benjamin had not fully noticed before. He was quickly drawn in. Fully connected, he basked in her glow. The ecstasy he felt was short-lived, however. Astraea was not bringing any grace with her. She was there for answers and Benjamin wouldn't be able to fool her. She lifted her hand and pointed directly at him. A ten-pound hammer drove a spike right through his heart.

"I thought we were getting somewhere?" she said.

Her hand morphed into the mangled vine that Benjamin had seen before, the tattoo extension that drew its life from the blue veins popping in her wrists. A live vine twisted across the room toward him, like a possessed serpent out to strangle him. It turned gently around his neck. Once, twice and then again. Then, like a python, who has its victim in its slithering grip, Astraea constricted. With each breath, she tightened.

Benjamin gasped for air, his feet dangling in space. A jolt of pain shot into his brain.

"Please!" he cried.

She held him in the position from across the room as though he were a horse being restrained. Then as his eyeballs rolled upwards, she released him. He dropped to the ground sweating and shaking.

"I thought you were trying to make right and fix it?" Astraea said.

"I am," Benjamin stammered.

"Let's see," Astraea replied. "Regret, check! Explaining what went wrong, check! Acknowledging responsibility for the dreadful mess of your life, check! Yes, you've done all that."

"Alright, so what's next?"

"Figure it out!" Astraea calmly said. "And do the right thing. Can you do that? Can you, Benjamin?"

Astraea relaxed her hold, as Benjamin nodded.

"Go shower," she said. "Vanda is finished."

And then she was gone, leaving only the faint smell of ivy lingering in his head.

* * *

After he had washed and changed, Benjamin peeked out of the cabin window. It was quiet outside. Salvatore Bollini had successfully convinced the local police that the events of the morning had all been a massive misunderstanding. The head of the Marseilles police had not been amused. He had promised to take the matter further. Pizarro had not been in the slightest worried.

"We'll send some complimentary tickets," he had said, to his pretty assistant, as he watched the angry policeman get back into his car. "That usually works."

Benjamin looked across the room at Vanda. She was sitting on the couch watching the news, silently hoping that a reporter would pop up with a breaking new story about the police busting open a smuggling ring in the Med and saving her from their evil clutches. She knew it was wishful thinking. She was in way deeper than she liked and her only chance of safety was with Benjamin's hair brained scheme. She turned and smiled unconvincingly back at him.

"What time are they coming again?" she asked.

"Lunchtime," Benjamin said. "We need to be out of here by then. They said it won't take them long to move this stuff off the ship."

"How are they going to do that? What about Fat George and Bollini?"

"That's Chatunga's problem. He's always been pretty inventive."

"Geez!" Vanda exclaimed. "Can you trust any of this, Ben? Chatunga Lazarov is pretty naive and stupid?"

Benjamin didn't answer. He looked out the window again.

"Hello, Benjamin? What are you looking for? You've been at that window all morning. Do you agree that we can't trust these people? Any of them?"

She hit the remote control and the TV screen collapsed into a white dot.

"Maybe," Benjamin said. His words were carefully chosen. He walked across to Vanda and sat down next to her. He took her hand in his and tried to kiss it. Vanda pulled away.

"Vanda, I think we have a future together," he said. "We could be good for each other."

"I have nothing Ben. I'm only here because I won a competition. A silly competition. And I want to go home."

"You haven't got nothing, Benjamin said. "You've got me!"

"I might need more!"

"We've got all that as well." Benjamin pointed to the boxes stacked in his bathroom. "Chat said he would cut us in."

Vanda shifted uncomfortably on the couch. There was an awkward moment as Benjamin composed himself. He brushed a drop of bulging moisture away from the corner of Vanda's eye.

She squeezed his hand back. Benjamin could see her jawline stretch, pulling tight over her resilient face. He hadn't seen that look in a long time in anyone.

"I guess I've also got this," she said, patting the sawn-off shotgun which was propped up next to them.

"I hope we don't need it," Benjamin said. "Let's get out of here. I want to be long gone when Chatunga arrives."

* * *

As THEY WALKED THROUGH THE CLEAN STREETS OF OLD Marseilles, Benjamin could not help but think about how his life might have been better off if he had not made a few bad decisions along the way. He thought of Africa, far away and yet so close. He had lost so many things along the way and he didn't now want to lose Vanda.

"Are there any things worse than being trapped?" he asked.

"Being ensnared by one's own crazy past is a cruel entrap-
ment," Vanda replied. "And some chasms are too vast
to cross."

Benjamin's past was painful and he forced his mind
to move on. Vanda slipped quietly into a rhythm beside
him and took his hand. She was warm and it felt nice.
She said little but read his thoughts. Benjamin liked it.
He liked her. She was kind and grounded but also had a
side to her that was unpredictable and volatile. It was
difficult to button her down. It was refreshing in an age
of wallpaper and veneer. She was authentic, the
real thing.

Benjamin wondered if atonement had a purpose? If it did,
then she could be it. He could picture them getting old
together. *If they could survive this!*

He snapped back to reality as a passer-buyer kicked a can.
It rattled across the road in front of them and hit his foot. He
instinctively kicked it back. The lad who had kicked it was
already walking away and hardly noticed.

A few blocks away from the harbor, they ducked into a
bistro to get some lunch. Chatunga had warned them to stay
away from the ship for at least two hours, but they planned to
take all afternoon. As they waited for their food to arrive, it
felt as though time was marching in slow motion. Vanda
checked her watch as the bells from a nearby church started
ringing. "Only one-thirty," she said. "We may as well make
ourselves comfortable."

Their table was on the far side of the restaurant.
Benjamin had chosen a spot where they could see the door
and the other patrons.

"An all-clear will be nice," he said.

"Yes, then we could then get on and enjoy the last day of
this so-called holiday in paradise," Vanda replied.

"We might have to come back for that," Benjamin smiled.

"I'm afraid this trip is irredeemable. If we could just extradite ourselves cleanly, it'll be a win."

"Benjamin?" Vanda asked as she flipped a white serviette over her lap. "Do you think we would be sitting here if none of this had happened. You know, if we had been two ordinary strangers who shared a drink in Genoa and then spent the week sun-tanning and enjoying the ship?"

"You mean no guns, blood, and gangsters?"

"No rhino horn either. What's it called in African again? Uphondo?"

"Zulu! Not African." Benjamin thought about it for a few seconds. "No," he continued. "You'd never have been attracted to me then. Rhino horn tends to have that effect you know. They say it's an aphrodisiac." They both smiled.

"It's true then."

"What?"

"That horrible situations pull people together. That fire forges love."

"They certainly make us see each other at our worst."

"And our best!"

"The brothers in arms stuff is real," Benjamin said. "I know from first-hand experience."

"You're hardly a brother!"

"You're hardly a sister either."

They sat there for an hour chatting. It was an hour where they forgot the rest of the day. They were immersed in each other, as though it was the last meal they would ever share together. Their last supper. The bread tasted good and the wine better. It was a red from Burgundy. They almost finished two bottles.

* * *

As they finished their lunch, Benjamin and Vanda

heard the noise. It was a dull thud followed by a slight shudder of the ground.

A few blocks away, down at the harbor, a lid from a dustbin sheared off its hinges and was flung right over the ship, never to be seen again. The poor people walking nearby felt it before they heard it. The shock wave hit them like a cricket bat. Time braked as pieces of glass and smoke missiles rushed into the sky. No one screamed. At least not at first. Smoke billowed dark and thick and dust filled the air. By the time someone yelled it was already starting to settle. Debris lay scattered across the quay. Someone cried for help. Then pandemonium broke loose and people scattered. Sirens and red lights appeared out of nowhere.

"I hope that is not what it sounds like, Ben."

Benjamin ran to the restaurant window, scanning the rooftops toward the docks. He couldn't see anything. The sky was clear where they were. A police siren started wailing in the distance.

"What has that idiot Chatunga now done?" Vanda demanded to know.

"How am I supposed to know?" Benjamin asked. "All they were meant to do was quietly get those crates out of our room."

"You didn't ask how?"

Benjamin chewed his lower lip and scratched the back of his head.

"I didn't expect this. Wait, it might not have anything to do with us or them." He spun around and motioned to the waiter for the bill.

"We need to get going," he said. "Hurry!"

He threw a pile of Euros onto the table and they briskly left. Vanda grabbed their half-drunk bottle of Burgundy as she scuttled past the table. She waved it in defiance to the waiter who was trying unsuccessfully to recover it.

"We might need this," she said, pushing the cork into its throat.

By the time they got to the road leading down to the harbor, scores of people were standing around in the street looking down toward the docks. A small plume of dark cloud was rising up into the sky. Benjamin and Vanda joined the crowd. They were too far away to see anything specific. Vanda took a swig of wine straight from the bottle and handed it to Benjamin.

"This holiday is a total disaster!"

There was a resignation in her voice as though she had finally given up trying. She took the bottle back from Benjamin who didn't say a word as she lifted it again to her lips. His eyes were transfixed on the smoke cloud.

The emergency services of Marseilles kicked into gear for the second time that day. Trucks, cars, and ambulances flooded the roads with howling banshees and blue lights. They looked like spokes of a wheel straining to squeeze into the chaos at the center.

Through the traffic jam, Benjamin noticed a panel van working its way out away from the harbor. He thought it strange, going against the stream of traffic. He watched it hooting and swerving, the driver waving the people in front of him away. Then it snagged free and accelerated up the road toward where he and Vanda were standing.

It stopped at a traffic light right in front of them, almost bumping Vanda over. Benjamin peered through the back window. The van was full of wooden boxes. The same type they'd hauled up to their room. The light turned green and as the van passed them, Benjamin noticed the driver. He had red hair and a skinny elbow hung from the open window. Big George Lazarov snarled at him. Their eyes briefly met and their heads locked together for a moment like two buffalos stamping the ground before a fight.

The van accelerated away. Benjamin turned and ran up the road towards some parked motorcycles. He shouted to Vanda to get a move along. She ran after him blindly. He chose the biggest bike he could find. A Kawasaki Ninja 1000. Its owner was nowhere to be seen. Benjamin took out a pocket knife and jiggled with a panel on the side of the bike until it fell off. He then pulled some wires out from the side, cut one and flashed some sparks. The bike roared into life as he swung his leg over it.

"Jump on," he shouted.

"Where did you learn to do that?" Vanda asked, as she tucked her feet in and wrapped her arm around his waist.

"Don't ask," he shouted back over the growling engine. "Hold on tight, we don't have helmets!"

He pulled the bike into the road and tucked covertly into the traffic flow about 20 cars behind the van that Big George was driving.

* * *

As the van turned toward the Avignon freeway, Benjamin wondered how long they should trail it for. *And why the hell was George Lazarov and his crew scarpering away?*

He breathed the humid air rising off the tarmac. The wind from the bike cooled it down, making it tepid as he sucked it down his throat. Vanda clung to him like a Vervet monkey on the back of its mother. Her face was resting on his shoulders. Her hands joined on his chest as though she were feeling for a heartbeat. It was there somewhere. Buried deep beneath primordial strata of fossils and dead bones.

Benjamin wondered if George Lazarov had somehow beaten his half-brother to their room and removed the crates of Rhino horn before they could. *Why else would they be speeding away in a large van?* And they'd been handed the perfect smokescreen to get away with it. Chaos on the dockside.

No! Impossible, he thought to himself. *No-one knew that they were up in the Presidential Suite. What if George spotted them moving the horn?*

The word 'atonement' rang in Benjamin's ears to the rhythm of the purring motorbike. He had to know what they were up to. He knew that if by some chance, George Lazarov had the horns in that van of his, their chances of ever going back to normal was slim. *The Italians would think he had double-crossed them and would be after him forever! And the Ng's? Who knows what they were still capable of? Vanda would be in big trouble as well. He had to know for sure if they had the rhino horns or not.*

Just before the on-ramp to the freeway, the van took a sharp turn to the right and pulled up under some trees. Benjamin carefully maneuvered the motorbike to a stop where he could see them but not attract any attention to himself.

"They're waiting for someone," Vanda said.

"No, see that building over there," Benjamin said, pointing. "It's a doctor's room. They need to get their friend stitched up. Must have found him down there with his missing eye."

"And foot!"

The side door of the van opened and three men emerged. Big George Lazarov blew cigarette smoke into the air as he looked around. A jacketless Panayotis Pappas helped prop up a hobbling Takis Evangelis.

Takis held a dirty cloth to his eye with one hand and hopped on his remaining good foot. His shirt was stained red. He was a bloodied mess.

"I can't believe he's still going," Benjamin said.

"Serves him damn right!"

"Told you so," Benjamin said, as the door of the van

slammed shut and the three men disappeared into the medical clinic.

"Come on. We've got a gap. We're taking that van!"

They rushed over. Vanda headed to the back door to confirm what was in the van but Benjamin grabbed her arm. "Climb in," he shouted. "They could be back any second."

The keys were in the ignition. Benjamin threw Pappas's discarded jacket aside and grabbed the wheel. He started it up and drove off as fast as he could.

By the time George Lazarov emerged from the clinic, Benjamin and Vanda were miles away. Pappas scratched his head, swearing. Big George exploded and turned to hit a bandaged Takis as hard as he could.

"This is all your fault!" he yelled.

Takis howled, not knowing what was more painful, his open eye socket, his crippled foot or his slapped cheek?

Panayotis Pappas threw his hands up into the air. "I've had enough of this nonsense!" he said. "Time to get out before those Sicilians get us."

* * *

BENJAMIN STEERED THE VAN THROUGH THE TRAFFIC. IT HAD a double cab in the front. The back section was sealed off and only accessible from the back door. It felt as though the whole of Marseilles was gridlocked on the roads.

"You think the rhino horn is in the back?" Vanda said.

"There are wooden boxes. It must be. We'll find out soon enough, as soon as I find a quiet spot to park," Benjamin answered.

"And what if it is? What are you going to do with it?"

Benjamin bit his lip as he thought. "Do you know how much it's worth?" he asked.

"I don't understand you,' Vanda snapped. "And I don't

like that look in your eye. Tell me, Ben, what's an innocent life worth? They were all innocent you know. Every one of those poor rhinos."

Inside Benjamin knew she was right. None of it was worth it! But old instincts were playing poker with his soul.

"Why don't we just keep driving? I know some people who'd love to take this off our hands. It could set us up for life. Both of us Vanda. Together."

"Together?" Vanda asked, as though he were mad.

Benjamin stared into the bumper of the blue Citroen in front of them. He hooted in frustration. Everyone on the road seemed to be honking and shouting. A finger shot skyward from the window of the Citroen. Sirens wailed in the distance down toward the docks.

"Dammit!" Benjamin yelled, hitting the steering wheel. "I can't do it! The cycle has to stop!"

"And you'll sleep well," Vanda said.

"I suppose then, I'll just hand it over to Chatunga as we said we would," he said. "Assuming it's back there."

"I told you not to trust him," Vanda replied.

"We'll be heroes in a funny sort of way."

"Who gives a crap what they think of us?" Vanda said, scratching around in the duffel bag next to her. Her hands coiled around the sawn-off shotgun as she pulled the bag up onto her lap. The barrel pointed squarely at Benjamin's hip.

"What are doing?"

"This is for your own good," she answered. "We're not giving the horn to anyone."

Benjamin turned to her, folding his arms over the steering wheel. He thought about what she had said and smiled.

"They'll end up blaming each other if it just disappears," he muttered to himself. "Put the gun away Vanda. I'm not the bad guy."

Vanda withdrew her hand from the bag but kept it on her

lap. She scanned the area. They were almost out of Marseilles, on a narrow road leading toward some small holding plots and farms.

"See that hill over there?" she said, pointing to a hillock about two miles away. It looks like a nice place to have a barbeque.

"Are you serious?" Benjamin asked.

"I love bonfires, don't you? We'll torch the whole thing with petrol." Vanda leaned against the window watching Benjamin closely.

"I don't think we should burn anything!" Benjamin exclaimed. "Give me a chance Vanda. I can get a huge price for it. It can set us up together. We could be on a yacht this time next week."

"Are you frigging kidding me!" Vanda replied. "A Yacht! You think I want to be on a yacht, after all that's happened this week on the MSE Grande? I'd rather be dropped down an oil well."

"I'll give some of it to charity."

"No, you won't!"

"All of it?"

"We're not keeping it, Ben. It's blood money! It will end us both up in prison! Besides, you're not going to argue with this, are you?" Vanda gave him a friendly nudge with the gun. "It's for your own good," she said.

"I've never burnt a fortune before," Benjamin eventually replied. "At least not literally. It will be the world's most expensive bonfire ever. You're crazy Vanda. Did anyone ever tell you, you're crazy?"

And I love it! he thought to himself. *And maybe I can still somehow save some rhino horn for myself?*

Benjamin pulled out of the traffic and turned the van down a street toward the hill. He never saw anyone following him as he zigzagged through the lanes on the outskirts of Marseilles.

"Are you OK?" he asked.

"No," Vanda replied. "I'm hacked off and had enough. Let's end this Benjamin. Let's take them down. Let's hurt them. Let's help those rhinos, even if they are dead."

Her face was red and drops of sweat were running down the side and her voice was filled with determination.

* * *

BENJAMIN SKIDDED THE VAN INTO A DEAD-END DIRT TRACK after the entrance to a park where the hill emerged from. A compost heap steamed to the left and an old tractor lay rusting next to it.

"It's more of a wild unkempt heath than a park," Benjamin said. Long grass and neglected flower beds indicated that it was hardly ever visited. He backed the van up next to an old corrugated lean-to, behind a building whose windows were smashed out. They were well out of anyone's way, hidden in the surrounding debris, with burnt out car wrecks littered around them.

Benjamin checked the rear-view mirror to see if anyone had followed them. The rectangular image that reflected back was clear. There was no sign of anyone.

"What's that behind your seat?" Vanda asked. "Take it out."

Benjamin fiddled behind his seat. There was a plastic Jerry can in the space. He pulled it out and shook it.

"Empty."

"There's a pipe attached," Vanda said. "We can siphon petrol from the tank." Benjamin held his hand up to his face as he opened the door. He squinted in the bright afternoon sun.

He handed Vanda the jerry can as he stuck the pipe down the hole on the side of the van. He put his lips to the pipe and sucked hard. A few drops of petrol hit his lips before he pulled away and plunged the bursting pipe into the throat of the can. He spat the petrol away.

"Just as well I don't smoke anymore," he said.

"I can't open the back," Vanda said. "It's locked. We need to know if the horn is here."

"Check inside the cab for a key," Benjamin mumbled, as he filled the jerry can with petrol.

"Nothing here but a jacket," Vanda replied. "'*Panayotis Pappas*' the label says. Our maître d' friend."

Benjamin went cold and dropped the half-full jerry can, spilling petrol into the ground. "What's in the pocket?" he asked, knowing what the answer was going to be.

"Why it's Missy's collar," Vanda exclaimed. "Ben, what did you do with her? Why is her collar in that man's pocket?"

"We're being tracked!" Benjamin shouted. "Turn it off!"

"Turn what off?"

"That collar. Give it here." Benjamin grabbed the tiny tartan collar from Vanda and smashed it under his feet in the dirt.

"You're making me nervous," Vanda said, as Benjamin anxiously scanned the surrounding bushes.

"I'll break the van door," Benjamin said. "We need to hurry!" He picked up a half brick that was lying on the ground and moved to the back of the van. "I'll smash the handle right off."

Before he could break the latch, a car skidded around the corner in a cloud of dust. Benjamin froze as Vanda leaped out of the way, sprawling in the bushes. Two people jumped out and ran toward Benjamin. He recognized them immediately. Tram and Lesley Ng were upon him before he could do anything.

"I wouldn't do that if I were you," Tram's familiar voice rang out. "Did you really think I wouldn't notice you conveniently running off? We lost you somehow in Barcelona, you back-stabbing bush jockey."

"You tracked us?" Benjamin stammered.

"We didn't. The rat did. It must be in the back there with the rhino horn. We've been tracking it since this morning. Thought you could steal it, did you?"

Tram held up a blinking app on his phone. He had a revolver in his other hand. Lesly Ng sauntered forward like a cat stalking a mouse. She took the brick from Benjamin and gently put it down on the grass. "Is that petrol I smell? Trying to hide your tracks are you, Mr. Rodd," she said.

"What do you care?" Benjamin asked, "You'll burn it anyway, being the honest government officials you say you are. Contraband remember? It's illegal and that means it gets burned."

"It would be such a waste to burn such a big fortune, don't you think?" Tram Ng said, positively beaming. "There are so many better ways it could be put to use, don't you agree?"

"You two-timing turncoat. You're going to steal it for yourself."

"The Vietnamese pension plans for secret service agents are woefully inadequate," Tram said. "Besides, I have a young lady to look after."

He smiled across to Lesley. She stood silently in her black bodysuit, haunting and elusive. Her face didn't even quiver beneath her oversized sunglasses.

"You're going to get screwed in more than one way," Benjamin said. "Do you think you can outsmart Valente? Or even Lazarov?"

"You'll not be there to see it, my old friend," Tram Ng casually said. "So, what do you care?"

"You're right! I've never cared for double-crossing petty thieves."

Lesley jumped forward and raised her hand to strike Benjamin. He was ready though. He dropped his center of gravity to avoid her blow and then tried to hit her back. She sidestepped and clubbed him on the side of his head with a steel spanner she was carrying.

Tram Ng laughed before jumping forward to help her. He pistol-whipped Benjamin to the ground. The last thing Benjamin saw before he hit the ground and blacked out was Vanda slipping away into some bushes on the side of the old building.

* * *

*A*STRAEA WAS HAUNTING.

"I should have guessed you'd be around," he said. "I'm in another mess, after all."

She swirled around him, like a mother comforting her wounded child.

"Am I out cold again?" he asked.

"You could say that," she answered. "Sleeping? Knocked out? What's the difference?"

Benjamin felt a sharp pain on his head and remembered falling into the dirt.

"Tram Ng! I knew I couldn't trust him."

"As it turned out, he was the one who couldn't trust you," Astraea said. "You double-crossed him!"

"I had to protect Vanda!"

"And yourself, no doubt?"

"I'm trying to do the right thing. You must know that, Astraea."

"I know," she said.

"The more I try and do it, the more I get sucked in. Sucked into this mess? My past? I can't shake it. Not even out here."

"No one said it would be easy." She reached out and warmly touched him on the shoulder.

He felt silly and his head ached. None of it made any sense. He had had dreams before, but this one was like a virus. Astraea! The beautiful enchanted women with the lovely nails and twisting creeping tattoos that just wouldn't go away. She was wise. Calming. So endearing and soulful. Benjamin was almost addicted to her and he liked it. She made him feel alive. She gave him hope.

"How do I finish this then?" he asked her. "What should I do?"

She smiled. "I knew you'd step over this line eventually. I'm proud of you, Benjamin."

She walked toward him and sat gently in the dirt beside him. She looked him in the face, her green eyes glistening. She started whispering, close to his face. "We're almost done here, Benjamin. I'm not going to haunt you forever."

A pinprick of pain hit his chest. He didn't want her to disappear out of his life.

"There's only one thing left now," she said. "One more thing you have to do."

"What?" he asked, looking up. "I don't understand?"

"Vanda knows. Follow her lead."

"I can't save the rhinos if that's what you mean. It's too big. There's too much money and there are a thousand butchers out there."

"It's not about the rhinos," Astraea sighed. "It never was about them. Try to save yourself! The rest will follow."

Benjamin nodded silently and let himself spiral up to consciousness.

* * *

THERE WAS SPINNING AND PAIN, FOLLOWED BY A BRIGHT light. Benjamin opened his eyes and squinted in the afternoon sun. Vanda crouched over him, gently slapping his face.

"Wake up!"

He blinked and let out a groan. Vanda propped him up against the van.

"You've been out for a while," she said. "Left me to my own devices, you did."

She patted the ground next to her. Benjamin looked over, noticing two empty shotgun cartridges lying in the dirt.

"What have you done?" he demanded to know, his bludgeoned senses finally waking up. Vanda wiped some dried blood off his cheek with a piece of cloth.

"There, there," she said softly, "it's going to be OK."

"Vanda!" Benjamin exclaimed. "Where are those lying Ng's?"

"That wasn't their real name. Did you know that?"

Benjamin nodded. "I suspected as much."

"I got his wallet. Here." Vanda shoved a brown wallet into Benjamin's face. It bulged with dollar bills and in the front slipper pouch was an ID card. Benjamin strained his eyes to read the fine print.

"It says Christopher Ganhuey."

He sat back thinking. The name was indeed familiar, from his past and his time in Vietnam.

"She wasn't his wife either," Vanda said.

"You're making me nervous. You mean she *isn't* his wife?"

"No, I mean she *wasn't!*"

"Vanda! What have you done?" Benjamin reached over and touched the metal barrel of the shotgun that was propped up on her hips. It was as hot as a boiled kettle.

"Where are they?"

"Exactly where they fell." Vanda nodded her head toward the inside of the van. "Inside there. It was them or me. It only took two shots and they didn't see it coming. I didn't miss!"

Benjamin struggled up to his feet, rubbing his head.

"It was easy the second time," she casually said.

"Oh, my word!" Benjamin stammered.

"And I've got some bad news, I'm afraid," Vanda said. "These boxes are all empty. There's no rhino horn in the van. Just some empty banana crates."

"Empty?"

"Actually, they're not so empty anymore."

Benjamin looked at her with his jaw open. He was trying to stitch the pieces together.

"Where were George Lazarov and his two mates going then?" he asked.

"Running away, maybe," Vanda said. "Abandoning ship? Or just helping to get his friend to a doctor?" She was completely calm, as though she had put the pieces together already.

"Think about it, Ben," she continued. "These Bulgarian smugglers have their plans messed up when we divert away from Tunisia. Up now against the ancient Sicilian mafia on their own turf. And also the Vietnamese cops. Legit or crooked, it doesn't matter. Lazarov must know he doesn't stand a chance. The risks are too high. I reckon they were probably scarpering out of here and leaving us to our fate."

"That means?" Benjamin couldn't finish his sentence.

"It means the horns are still on the ship. In our cabin," Vanda said.

"Unless Chatunga came through and got them out like he said he would," Benjamin said.

"But something exploded down there. It was no stealth extraction."

"We've got to go and find out."

"Wait. We have to finish cleaning this mess up first. There's no one around here and I'm pretty certain no one saw us come in here. Give me your lighter."

Benjamin threw her a matchbook he had in his pocket.

"I've already primed it," Vanda said. "Sucked out two more cans while you were snoozing."

Benjamin smiled. *He'd hardly been snoozing.*

Vanda struck a match and lit a piece of paper she had picked up off the ground. Stepping back, she threw it into the window of the van.

Ten seconds later the van was burning like a Swiss bonfire and by the time the bodies of the Ng's exploded into a thousand pieces, Benjamin and Vanda were on the road driving away in their car. Vanda wrapped a scarf around her face and Benjamin pulled his hat down.

They both stared dead ahead as the harsh reality of what Vanda had just done, sank in. Eventually, Benjamin broke the silence.

"There's nowhere to hide now!" he said. "I hope that rhino horn is gone out of our room or else they are going to pin this all on us."

"We going to be OK," Vanda replied.

* * *

THEY COULD SEE THE MSE GRANDE FROM A MILE AWAY. IT stood proudly in the harbor, the white hull shading the entire south-eastern dockyards of Marseilles. A few seagulls swooped down, attacking the sardine entrails that some fisherman were throwing into the water. Benjamin ditched the car down a side street, before they joined some other guests on foot, making their way back to the final night of their cruise.

Things had quietened down since the lunchtime excitement and the sky had almost cleared of smoke.

"It feels wrong," Benjamin said as they came out of the pedestrian tunnel that furrowed under the highway next to the docks. "We heard a bang. Saw the smoke. And all those fire-engines and ambulances. Now, nothing more than a few police cars?"

"Maybe it sounded worse than it was?" Vanda said.

"It's quiet around the Grande," Benjamin pointed out. "I wasn't expecting this. The police cars are all over on the other side of the docks. Whatever that explosion was, it looks like it came from there." He pointed past the enormous hull of their ship to the far side of the harbor.

"There's nothing happening here this on side of the harbor."

They both felt instant relief. They'd expected to find the ship swarming with port authorities and the dockside strewn with debris from an explosion."

Benjamin turned to a local man lingering next to the gate.

"Excuse me, sir," he asked. "What is going on over there?"

The man snapped some French and turned away puffing on his brown cigarette.

"Frog!" Benjamin muttered under his breath, before turning to the next person he saw. It happened to be Dr. Burlington, who had arrived back at the ship at the same time as them.

"Goodness gracious, you two," Burlington shouted at the top of his voice. "Where have you been?"

He had a pair of baggy pants on which his suspenders were not doing a good job of holding up or keeping his fatty rolls in place. He had gone up at least 2 sizes since they had left Genoa a week earlier.

"You've missed the action. Again! This morning, Boom!" He gesticulated with his arms, clapping his hands together as hard as he could. "I thought it was a navy cannon at first, a big..."

Vanda interrupted him mid-sentence. "What was it?" she asked.

Burlington's young girl appeared from nowhere and

slipped her thin arm into his fat elbow. She waved at them both. It was the first time they had seen her smile.

"I saw the man," she whispered.

She actually talks, Benjamin thought to himself. Her voice was soft and gentle. Benjamin wondered again how this brute of a man could possibly have won her over. It had intrigued him ever since he had first met them. They were indeed the oddest of couples.

"Hello Jessica," Vanda said.

"Boom!" Burlington interrupted, clapping his hands again.

Neither Benjamin nor Vanda flinched. Burlington seemed irritated that he couldn't get them focused on his boorish explanations. He raised his hands to clap again. Jessica calmly raised her hand. Burlington dropped his. He deferred silently to her as though she had him exactly where she wanted him, at the end of a rope that could be turned into a noose at any point.

"Where did it happen?" Vanda asked.

"On the other dock across the water," Burlington's girl said. It was a white truck with a tarp on it. I saw a man running away with the police chasing him. As they caught him, the truck exploded. Right next to the Gilberte."

"What's the Gilberte?" Benjamin and Vanda asked together.

"You know? The other ship that's been following us this week. It was a few hours behind us. That's how they do it. I don't think it's an MSE ship. Part of the Taurus fleet I think."

"This bomb? Explosion or whatever? It hit the wrong ship then?" Vanda asked.

Dr. Burlington looked at her as though she was mad. "What do you mean the wrong ship? We're lucky it was that one and not this one. It was the right ship. We at least get to leave Marseilles tonight. Those unlucky plebs had their cruise ended right here and now. I saw them offloading the luggage from the Gilberte. We at least, are unscathed."

Vanda turned to the Frenchman who had earlier dismissed Benjamin. "Do you know who it was?" she asked, in her best high school French. The man was instantly friendly.

"Some local spat with the mafia," he answered in perfect English, ignoring Benjamin. "Maltese or Italian? No Sicilian. They arrested a man. He was fighting like crazy before his van exploded. He could have blown himself up by the look of it, so he was lucky in a way. Cleaned it up really quickly, they did. Always do when it comes to the mob."

"Was anyone hurt?" Vanda asked.

"I don't think so, but that man is going away for a long time. They'll get him on terrorist charges having the audacity to try this in France."

Benjamin let out a slow breath. He could feel Vanda's hand slipping into his.

"We leave in an hour," she whispered. "We'll be out of this place soon."

Benjamin squeezed her hand.

"Let's get inside," he said. "We have one more night to live."

"That's the spirit, old chap," Burlington said, letting loose a broad grin. "We'll enjoy it together."

Vanda put her arm around Benjamin as they crossed the gangplank.

At the security checkpoint, there was no sign of Bollini or the captain. They had both hunkered down, not wanting to draw any more police attention to themselves. It made no difference anyway, because other than their consciences, Vanda or Benjamin had nothing incriminating on them. The old rusting sawn-off shotgun had partly melted on a pile of burning banana boxes, with its last two victims grimacing into eternity inside.

* * *

VANDA HEADED STRAIGHT FOR THE COUCH AS SOON AS THE door to their cabin slammed shut. The 'do not disturb' sign was still hanging on their door handle and no one had been in to service the cabin. She threw herself down in exhaustion. "I'm finished," she gasped. "Got any more of that emergency hooch handy?"

Benjamin headed straight for the bathroom. They had put the boxes of rhino horn in there and he needed to know if Chatunga had smuggled them out or not. The door banged into a box. Benjamin peered around the corner into the bathroom. It was piled high with the rhino horn boxes and it looked exactly as he had left it.

"No!" he shouted. "It's still here!"

He went to one of the boxes and opened it. He picked out the nearest object inside. The rhino horn was dirty and dark. It had been roughly hacked off. He rolled it over his hand with loathing. It was a big one. Worth a fortune!

Benjamin recoiled backward, dropping it onto the cold bathroom floor. It fell with a thud and lay there inert and dead. It felt like an evil magnet, sucking the life and vitality from everything around it. It looked like death. *It was death*!

Benjamin kicked it away but that didn't help how he felt. He walked back to the lounge and desperately caught Vanda's eye. She had kicked off her shoes and was stretched like a cat, out along the couch. Her blouse pulled tight against her body.

"Don't tell me," she said, "Your so-called loyal friend did nothing that he said he would?"

Benjamin nodded sheepishly.

"We're still here with this wretched rhino horn," Vanda sighed. "And they are out there." She pointed to the door. "A few of them are. I at least took care of the Ng threat."

She sounded callous and hard. Not the sweet country girl,

Benjamin had come to know. Benjamin opened his suitcase and pulled out two miniature bottles of gin. He had stolen them from his hotel in Genoa. He pulled the ice tray out of the fridge, knocking out a few cubes. He then carefully poured the gin over the ice into one of the crystal tumblers that lay on top of the fridge and added tonic water.

"Here," he said. "This will make you feel better." Vanda threw down the contents in one swig before Benjamin even had a chance to sip his.

"Thanks, I'll have another," she said, holding out her glass. "I'm right, aren't I? We're still stuck right in the middle of this crap, aren't we? Aren't we, Ben?" She then burst into tears.

Benjamin knew at that moment exactly what he needed to do. To save them, to get Vanda free and to fully atone for his role in the entire affair. He sat down next to her and put his arm around her shoulder. He handed her his drink and stared at the wall. He could feel the ship moving. They were leaving Marseilles and finally heading back to Genoa, where they could get their lives and passports back. He just had one thing to do first.

9

GENOA

Benjamin slept soundly for the first time since the cruise had started. He thought he heard a faint voice as he fell asleep, Astraea calling to him from afar, but she didn't come to him like the other nights. His head sunk into the pillow simultaneously to his mind sinking into the dark tunnel that pulled him in. Vanda lay next to him. Her eyes were wide open. She didn't blink as she watched flecks drifting across her dry eyes.

An hour before midnight, the bedside alarm rang at least five times before Benjamin stirred. Tightropes held him down. His body told him that he had been sleeping for only five minutes, but as his mind focused, he knew he'd been out for hours. Time for action! He reached over to wake Vanda. She was already up and in the bathroom. *Doesn't she ever sleep,* he thought?

He sat up on the edge of the bed, rubbing his eyes. They were sore and he didn't have to look in the mirror to know that they were bloodshot red.

"Are you getting up?" Vanda asked from the bathroom.

She sounded as though it was a fresh new morning and she had been resting for days. It was pitch dark outside.

"I'm not used to waking up at eleven pm,' Benjamin answered. "I'm normally going to bed at this time."

"I'm not used to being put in these predicaments." There was guilty accusation in her voice, as though she was a victim in the entire affair. *Which she was.*

"Neither am I," Benjamin lied, as he walked into his dressing room to throw on some jeans. Vanda didn't answer. As he pulled his last clean tee shirt over his head, he shivered in the cool air.

"What time do we arrive back in Genoa?" he asked.

"Mid-morning, some time," Vanda said. She had come back into the bedroom.

"I want to be first off the ship. Get far away from this," he replied.

"What are you going to do?" Vanda asked. "Are you going back to Africa?"

"I'm not sure. It depends on you, I guess. For now, I just want to make it through the night. Are you up for a safari?"

"So long as the rhinos are all alive," Vanda replied.

"You'll love my home."

"I can't wait," Vanda said softly. "This cruise has been a nightmare from the start."

"So much for it being a prize," Benjamin said.

"Yeah, hopefully that's still coming. I sure deserve it."

Benjamin backed into the bedroom tightening his belt. Vanda was dressed in black and her eyes sparkled in the dim light.

"Let's get going then," she said.

"You look beautiful," was all Benjamin could muster.

* * *

There was a chilly breeze on the balcony outside. Benjamin peered over the edge and could see white horses tumbling over the wake on the side of the ship. The gibbous moon reflected off the water and cut a crystal path out toward the eastern horizon.

"It's a straight drop down to the water from here," he said. Vanda held onto the rail as she looked down.

"I've never liked heights," she said before stepping back into the cabin. She disappeared for a second into the bathroom and emerged with an enormous black rhino horn. She took two steps out toward the railing and threw it with all her strength. It sailed into the night air. They didn't see or hear it, as it plunged into the waves below.

"I've got a great pitching arm," Vanda said, jokingly.

Benjamin chuckled, trying to see where the horn had landed. "I can see that," he said. "How deep do you reckon it is here?"

"I read somewhere that it's one of the deepest parts of the Med. The land sheers off and goes down about a kilometer."

"Excellent," Benjamin replied, rubbing his hands. "They'll be gone for good."

Vanda went back for another horn with a confident stride. Benjamin watched her with admiration. He thought he'd let her throw one more before he started helping.

"Do you know that you just donated a few hundred thousand quid to Davey Jones?" he joked.

Vanda called back from inside. "Yeah, but they were pretty evil quid, don't you think? Besides, I didn't donate them. How can you donate something that's not yours in the first place?"

Vanda re-emerged holding two prize specimens. "Here, your turn," she said, thrusting the smaller horn into Benjamin's hands.

As Benjamin rolled it over his fingers, it seemed to call to him. He could feel the pull. He had power and money and his old life back, right there, in his hand. *Should I, or shouldn't I?* He asked himself. He could feel the sweat dripping down. A vein popped in his temple as he shook. He closed his eyes and in his tormented mind, he saw Astraea flying straight toward him.

Do it now, she seemed to be shouting, *or you'll be lost forever.*

Benjamin opened his eyes and the world looked different. He closed his grip on the horn in his hand and braced himself to throw.

"One, two, three!" shouted Vanda.

They both flung their rhino horns as far as they could into the dark outside. The sea swallowed them up without even a burp.

"Oh, boy!" Benjamin exclaimed. "That felt good. Real good."

Vanda smiled at him. "Yes," she replied. "Kind of like penance."

They spent the next hour finishing what they had started. One rhino horn at a time. One piece of wood at a time. Each one fell into the inky night and sank down into the churning sea beneath the ship. At one o'clock in the morning, Vanda emerged for the hundredth time holding up two gleaming horns.

"This is the last of them," she triumphantly said. "Shall we?"

Benjamin took one of the horns from her and held it up in the light. It reflected his entire life with its rotten past. Vanda held back her arm to throw.

"Wait!" Benjamin shouted, taking her upraised arm. "Wait, Vanda. What have we done? This was worth hundreds of millions!"

"Fine time to reconsider Mr. Rodd," Vanda confidently said. "It's too late for regrets. Common! Stop hesitating for once."

She pulled her arm free and threw her last rhino horn out into the void.

"I'm done!" she insisted. She turned to go back inside. "Let's go eat. The restaurants are staying open extra late tonight. The last party till dawn on the MSE Grande. And I need a proper drink. Come on, Ben. We can still salvage our last night and have some fun."

Benjamin stayed out on the balcony. The final remaining rhino horn was still in his hand. He held it tightly as though it was some priceless family heirloom.

"I'm coming," he said. And then he secretly slipped the rhino horn into the inside of his jacket.

"Just getting a scarf."

* * *

THEY STEPPED INTO THE JAZZ LOUNGE JUST BEFORE TWO IN the morning. Vanda was giggling on Benjamin's arm and he couldn't stop telling her how wonderful and free he felt.

The place was packed with people trying to squeeze the most out of their last night on board the ship. Everyone seemed happy to be alive after the Marseilles incident and lucidly aware that in a few hours most of them would be returning to the mundane routine of their boring lives.

Vanda pointed to the far side of the room where Dr. Burlington and the O'Donnells were seated in a leather booth. They waved enthusiastically. Benjamin and Vanda made their way over through dancing couples and tired waiters. By the time they slipped into the leather couch, they both had a glass of champagne in their hands. Vanda threw hers back and beckoned a waiter to bring them another round. Benjamin sipped his glass scanning the room. He caught a glimpse of George Lazarov sitting alone at the bar counter. His shoulders were hunched and he was staring at his own red hair in the mirror opposite him.

Benjamin kept Lazarov in his peripheral vision as he caught up with the O'Donnells and resigned himself to Dr. Burlington's inevitable boorish banter. The doctor was initially quieter than usual. His young girlfriend was nowhere to be seen. Vanda asked where she was. Dr. Burlington made an excuse about her feeling ill, but no one believed him. Benjamin wondered which of the other young attractive men on board she had chosen to spend her last night with.

The subject quickly changed and Burlington brought up the explosion that had rocked the Marseilles harbor. Benjamin pretended to only have a mild interest but moved closer to hear what Burlington was saying.

"Some local gangsters," he said. "Almost blew themselves up by mistake, from the sounds of it!"

Burlington smiled with glee, as he frequently did when someone else's stupidity made him feel clever.

"Can you believe it? Smuggling drugs or something here in Marseilles? The TV news said as much."

"That doesn't explain an explosion," Benjamin said. "It doesn't explain anything."

"The TV said there's some turf war going on. The Eastern European mafia trying to take over everything. It must have been a botched hit, or something went wrong while they were dealing their drugs?"

Benjamin went cold. *Was it another hair-brained disaster involving Chatunga? Why would Chatunga have explosives in the first place? What was he planning on doing with it?*

"I've got a terrible feeling," he whispered to Vanda. "You

might have been right about my old friend." Vanda shook her head.

"How do they know all this?" Benjamin asked the table. "It only happened a few hours ago."

"They caught him. Jessica even saw it!" Burlington blurted. "He must have had ID on him or something. The idiot had a small bomb in his truck for some reason. A limpet. Lucky no-one was near when it went off, but you should have seen the dustbin. Boom! Jessica saw it all!"

The table went still. Burlington savored the moment. For once, he had everyone intently listening to him. "He was well known to the French police," he exaggerated. "A mafia hitman, perhaps?"

"They arrested him?" Benjamin asked.

"He's never coming out!" Burlington said, before reaching over for the plate of crisps in the middle of the table. He shoved some in his mouth and carried on talking with his mouth full of crumbs.

"What a trip?" he boasted. "First your mugging in Rome. Then that death the other night. Heaven knows what caused that? And now this, an exploding truck. As for that rat yesterday! Scared the lights out of me, that one did. What a trip!"

Benjamin grimaced and wiped away a crumb that had landed on his cheek. Burlington laughed before carrying on.

"Funny thing is though, the driver of the truck was lost. On the wrong pier, he was. The TV said he was let through the wrong security boom by mistake."

"Maybe he was heading our way?" Charlie O'Donnell said.

"Who cares?" Burlington said. "We're on the water now and miles away. They were there to pick up their drugs from somewhere and almost blew themselves up. Like Guy Fawkes, it was. Did you hear the bang!"

"Heading our way?" Vanda asked. She had been listening

in on the side and pulled Benjamin toward her. She whispered in his ear. "Your so-called friend was planning to blow us up!" she said. "Eliminating all the loose ends, I think they call it!"

"I can't believe it," Benjamin muttered. *Chatunga! It must have been him. It was just the type of botched up operation he would have master crafted. Or someone did this to him? Sabotaged the extraction plan, and set him up?*

"As I was saying, who cares how it happened?" Burlington said. "It just did. Pity the bomb never took out the mobster. If you live by the sword you should die by the sword!"

Benjamin shoved the bowl of chips into the doctor's chest. "No one ever deserves to die," he said, before getting up and heading toward the bar counter.

As he walked away, Benjamin could hear Burlington asking Vanda why he was so grumpy. He missed her answer.

George Lazarov was still at the bar working his way through a bottle of Jack Daniels. The bottle lay on the counter next to him in a puddle of liquid.

Benjamin sat down on an empty stool next to George Lazarov before he even knew he was there.

"Hello George," Benjamin said. Lazarov turned slowly.

"Aha," he said, "I was wondering when you'd show up."

"Chatunga was your brother!" Benjamin snapped.

"Half-brother," Lazarov casually corrected. "My bastard half-brother.'

"You did this to him?"

"Wrong. He did it to himself," George replied. "He always was the stupid one in the family. No wonder my father disowned him. He'd have gotten us all killed by now."

Both of them sat staring into the mirror in front of them.

"I've got what you asked for," Benjamin said.

"It's a bit late for that, don't you think? What do I care now for one little sweet when the packet is gone?"

"You threatened us both if we never got your missing horn back to you!"

"Yes, but Luigi Valente, and my bastard brother, they've stolen everything now. After you told him where it was."

"I don't care about your squabbles with Luigi Valente,' Benjamin said. "I don't want it. I'm keeping my end of our agreement and you'd better keep your end."

He reached into a small bag he had brought from the room with him and pulled out the last rhino horn.

"Here!"

Benjamin slammed the horn onto the counter in front of Lazarov. It nicked Lazarov's shot glass and his spilled whiskey started running toward the edge of the counter.

"Are you mad?" George exclaimed as he grabbed the horn and pulled it onto his lap out of sight.

"What else?" he demanded to know.

"What do you mean, what else?" Benjamin replied. "That's all we have. It's all we ever had. One bloodied rhino horn. Dropped upon us by your own goon. One misplaced Uphondo horn. And a ruined cruise."

"I know you were working with your old Zimbabwean friend."

"He's gone now!"

"Then where is the rest of it?"

"How should I know?" Benjamin shouted. "Why don't you ask your own double-crossing friend, Tram Ng? You know? The chap you handed me over to back in Vietnam! We only had the one horn. That one on your lap."

Lazarov stared at Benjamin. Neither of them flinched. *Poker at its best. Texas Hold'em!*

"The Ng's have disappeared," Lazarov eventually said. "Their van... no, my van was found burnt out just outside Marseilles earlier in the evening. Two bodies inside. Cremated, I believe. At first, I thought it was you and Missus

Slade, but clearly, I was wrong. The police want to question me in the morning. Know anything about that little fire?"

"I can't help you," Benjamin said, turning to leave. "I don't know how they did it but they did. The Vietnamese usually get the rhino horn in the end. Don't they?"

Lazarov grabbed him by the arm. His grip was firm and resolute.

"*Mr. El Dilletante*, if you are playing with me, you will regret it!"

Benjamin stepped in close to his adversary's face. "I'll be waiting for you, Mr. Big George Lazarov!" he said.

Lazarov nervously looked around the room to see who might have heard Benjamin. He had protected his discreet pedigree for twenty years. He was not about to allow Benjamin to blow his cover. He wanted to stay incognito in every pub, bar, and port from Lisbon to Beirut. He had the Lazarov empire to protect.

He kept quiet as Benjamin continued.

"The Vietnamese police. Or the Italians. They might know what happened to your stuff, but I don't."

They were both sweating. Benjamin leaned in even closer and whispered defiantly into George's ear. "We had a deal, you and me," he said. "I bring you back your rhino horn and you let us walk away. Remember?"

"What about my friend Takis? What about what you did to him? He might not even make it," Lazarov said.

"He deserved what he got and I'd ditch him if I was you," Benjamin said. "Even Vanda kicked his ass."

Lazarov sat back sullen in his chair. "If you ever turn up in my business again, you're dead!"

"Goodbye, Mr. Lazarov."

Benjamin turned and walked back to his friends. Vanda was chatting to Kevin O'Donnell. She moved up for Benjamin as he got there.

"You look pale," she said.

"I always struggle when I play poker," he whispered.

* * *

THEY GOT TO BED AS THE SUN WAS RISING. THE EARLY hours of the morning had been spent dancing, drinking and shouting things into each other's ears, that neither of them could hear because the music was too loud. They didn't sleep. It was hard to think that they were just a few hours away from walking off the ship in one piece. They both knew that their old lives were gone and that it would never be the same again. Benjamin kept talking about atonement. Vanda kept going on about how she would be buying her own shotgun back in Plaquemines. The early morning light slowly painted the distant shore of Italy.

"What about Valente?" Vanda asked as she lay in Benjamin's arms.

"I assume he'll be keeping his head down," Benjamin said. "It was never his rhino horn anyway. He was trying to steal it from Lazarov. I predict that he'll slink away with his tail between his legs, wishing he'd never gotten into bed with Chatunga."

"What if they link Chatunga to you?" Vanda asked.

Benjamin smiled wryly. "They'll be chasing a ghost," he said. "I'll be long gone. Back home in Africa. I can change my name. Maybe there's some good I can do, to save a few rhinos instead of killing them. Maybe you can join me?"

"Maybe I will," Vanda replied. Benjamin's heart raced.

"Big George thinks Luigi Valente or the Vietnamese got the rhino horn. He hasn't got a clue about the truth."

"Well, the truth is all well hidden now, isn't it?"

"Under a kilometer of water."

"I was thinking more about it being safely hidden away in our clean consciences. That's where it counts."

"You're right," Benjamin said.

"Just tell me one thing, Ben," Vanda asked. "Your little poker game with Big George? What if it backfired on you?"

Benjamin stroked her hair. "The Sicilians ended up blaming the Bulgarians, who suspect the Asians, who in turn think it was the Sicilians. It was a nice downward spiral to nowhere. I tried not to think of it backfiring."

"You're a busker, Ben. I knew it the minute I saw you."

"It worked somehow."

"I hope that no one blames us for the Ng's," Benjamin said. "Nothing worse than getting bust on a bluff."

The ship's horn blew. It was the last wake up call for the guests on board. Genoa was calling the MSE Grande home and the ship slowly started to stir.

"What say you we try and be the first ones off?" Benjamin asked.

"You read my mind," Vanda replied. "I can't wait!" They both rolled off the bed and started packing.

"Don't forget my brooch!" Vanda shouted. "The one you 'borrowed' from me when we first met. I'd like it back please."

Benjamin put his hand in his pocket and felt for the pearl brooch with its diamond circles. He caressed its contours and shouted back.

"I'm afraid that got lost back in Marseilles. When they hit me on the head."

Vanda was not happy.

"I'll buy you another one!" he shouted. "When you come and visit me in Africa."

An hour later, they had picked up their passports, signed their documentation and were waiting with their bags at an exit door. Their freedom lay a few steps down.

"Senor Rodd?" a voice suddenly boomed out.

They both nervously swung around together. Salvatore Bollini was standing behind them wearing a plain white dress uniform. Captain Pizarro had demoted him to the lowest rank possible and put his assistant in charge of security.

"You were not going to slip away so easily were you?" Bollini asked.

Benjamin's heart sank. The last thing he had anticipated was another encounter with Bollini.

"Without saying goodbye?" Bollini continued. He finished his sentence extra slowly before breaking into a broad smile and holding out his hand. Benjamin took it and shook it hesitantly, without saying a word. As they tugged each in a feigned duel of the wrists, Bollini pulled Benjamin forward and whispered into his ear.

"Mr. Rodd," he said. "If Don Luigi Valente ever needs someone here on the MSE Grande, tell him I am his man. OK?"

Benjamin said nothing. He nodded, scarcely believing how stupid Bollini was. He asked no questions and no explanation was given. He had never known whether it was Bollini who was trailing him in Barcelona, but his suspicions were now confirmed. Bollini was thoroughly corruptible, just like everyone else.

* * *

AS BENJAMIN STEPPED BACK ONTO THE GENOA DOCKSIDE, he heard Astraea for the last time. Her voice sounded like it had a week earlier when at the exact same spot he had walked aboard.

"Benjamin Rodd," she whispered. "I'm proud of you!"

Her voice was a gentle kiss fading away. And then she disappeared for the last time.

He turned to Vanda.
"Did you hear that?"
She was gone too.

HE PUT HIS HAND IN HIS POCKET FINGERING THE PEARL
and diamond brooch. Shrugging, he headed toward the bus
station. He needed to get home. He had an appointment with
Dr. Miller at nine o'clock on Monday morning.

ABOUT THE AUTHOR

Zane Schumacher is an emerging freelance writer and poet who believes that little things can make a big difference. This is Zane's first book.

zane@crakatoa.co.za